I0642842

DARKNESS
AT FIRST LIGHT

CARLISLE CRIME CASES #3
A CHRISTOPHER SNOW & ERIN MCCOY MYSTERY

J. M. WEST

MILFORD
HOUSE

an imprint of Sunbury Press, Inc.
Mechanicsburg, PA USA

MILFORD HOUSE

an imprint of Sunbury Press, Inc.
Mechanicsburg, PA USA

NOTE: This is a work of fiction. Names, characters, places and incidents are the product of the author's imagination or are used fictitiously, and any resemblance to actual persons, living or dead, business establishments, events or locales is entirely coincidental.

Copyright © 2015, 2018 by J. M. West.
Cover copyright © 2015, 2018 by Sunbury Press, Inc.

Sunbury Press supports copyright. Copyright fuels creativity, encourages diverse voices, promotes free speech, and creates a vibrant culture. Thank you for buying an authorized edition of this book and for complying with copyright laws. Except for the quotation of short passages for the purpose of criticism and review, no part of this publication may be reproduced, scanned, or distributed in any form without permission. You are supporting writers and allowing Sunbury Press to continue to publish books for every reader. For information contact Sunbury Press, Inc., Subsidiary Rights Dept., PO Box 548, Boiling Springs, PA 17007 USA or legal@sunburypress.com.

For information about special discounts for bulk purchases, please contact Sunbury Press Orders Dept. at (855) 338-8359 or orders@sunburypress.com.

To request one of our authors for speaking engagements or book signings, please contact Sunbury Press Publicity Dept. at publicity@sunburypress.com.

ISBN: 978-1-62006-648-5 (Trade Paperback)

Library of Congress Control Number: 2015954538

FIRST MILFORD HOUSE PRESS EDITION: May 2018

Product of the United States of America
0 1 1 2 3 5 8 13 21 34 55

Set in Bookman Old Style
Designed by Lawrence Knorr
Cover by Lawrence Knorr
Edited by Celeste Helman

Continue the Enlightenment!

Dedicated to:

Law enforcement officers and service
personnel who strive to keep citizens safe and
the soldiers who fight to keep us free

From *Paradise Lost*

. . . [H]e views
The Dismal situation waste and wild:
A dungeon horrible, on all sides round,
As one great furnace flamed, yet from those flames
No light, but rather darkness visible:
Served only to discover sights of woe,
Regions of sorrow, doleful shades, where peace
And rest can never dwell, hope never comes
That comes to all: but torture without end
Still urges, and a fiery deluge, fed
With ever-burning sulfur unconsumed:
Such place Eternal Justice had prepared
For those rebellious, here there prison ordained
In utter darkness. . . .

—*John Milton*

1

Death casts a pall of absolute darkness—solid and devoid of sense or sensation, a psyche or any other living trait, a shock nearly beyond human comprehension—and certainly far from the realm of daily conversation—unless it's somebody else's. But the abandoned shell tells much, as Dr. Haili Chen, Cumberland County coroner and Fire Marshal Lane Rusk hovered, waiting for a scrim of light to illume the stark scene before them. Rusk's assistant, Russell Garrett, lumbered among crowded markers carrying a tripod and camera, kicking clumps of dirty snow from his path.

Approaching sirens howled in the distance.

A female corpse dressed in eighteenth-century garb, skirt and legs partially burned, was lashed to the cannon in front of Molly Pitcher's monument in the Old Carlisle Cemetery enclosed by a limestone wall at the corner of South Bedford and East South Street. In the east, a dove grey ribbon of light exposed a disturbing scene.

The previous night's downpour had swept the victim's cap to the ground, freeing limp, mouse-brown curls that hugged the cannon. Eyes—wide pools matching the gray sky—gazed into the void, her face a mask of surprise and terror. Fine crow's feet, a mole beside her left eyebrow and a wide mouth pulled in a death grimace. A stout, stumpy handle protruded from her chest. Beneath the barrel, her legs and hands were lashed together.

Rusk circled the corpse, examining the scene with a perplexed frown, heavy eyebrows drawn; his mustache quivered as he nosed the charred shreds of burned cloth, bodily fluids and decaying flesh. He scraped a sample from the leg and cut a scrap of the skirt to test. The woman had a decent build, as the wet, coarse homespun clung to her body; she wore no underwear.

"Where's Detective Snow?" he inquired of Dr. Chen to break the dreadful silence where winter ruled, despite the calendar marking March. A silent cloak of white fog hovered where sounds echoed eerily. Chills shimmied through Rusk's open coat; he shivered and zipped it.

"On his way." She consulted her watch, set her leather bag on a nearby stone marker, with an apology to the deceased. She unsnapped it and extracted her thermometer from the inside flap where each sterile instrument was tucked into its own pocket.

"TOD?" He tried again, assuming she'd estimate.

"Hard to say without a liver temp."

"Rain and sleet a factor," Rusk commented as he caught the tripod that Garrett had carelessly set on crumbling concrete. "Steady. Take your time," he directed. He'd hired the kid fresh out of college a few months ago when a semi shot across the median and totaled Detective Snow's Jeep Wrangler, a horrific scene that had stopped traffic Thanksgiving night for hours while police and firemen squelched the fire. Rusk had read about the couple's incredulous leap for their lives and their son's birth on the slopes of I 81 in the paper the next day.

"The fire's a problem," the coroner said.

"Ah, you can smell the accelerant." Gasoline.

"Could have been a lightning strike had he refrained."

"He?" He disagreed but kept his opinions to himself. He knelt to tip a soil sample into a sterile container, capped and labeled it.

Chen waved Rusk's pronoun query aside. "Figure of speech."

Snow tromped up to the trio, slipped on a patch of ice but righted himself by grabbing the monument's pedestal. He nodded at Dr. Chen but stared openmouthed at

Rusk's hair. "Bad hair day?" The strands cresting each wave on the man's head had a slight orange cast.

"Tried highlighting with hydrogen peroxide while on vacation."

"They have kits in drug stores for that," Snow quipped.

"Are we waiting on Christmas?" Dr. Chen stomped her boots to keep the circulation flowing. Prongs of cold stabbed through her calves despite wool leggings and socks under her traditional black slacks.

"Mac's got the camera," he said absently as he perused the body; it looked like a grotesque Halloween display. "An Amber Alert's on the morning news, so we'll be getting calls. Though we currently have no details. Who called this in?"

"Your wife's back on the job?" Dr Chen voiced her surprise as she gestured across the street. "A group of kids from the apartment complex flagged down the Three Musketeers." CPD had nicknamed the new hires—Gabriel Summers, Shannon Mahoney and Chase Rivers.

"Today." Detective Erin McCoy—Mac to the squad— had been on maternity leave. Snow stepped closer to examine the murder weapon, smiling inwardly at the coroner's allusion to the new bikers.

Materializing from the fog, a sleep-deprived, top-heavy Mac appeared, Shadow at her heel, nodded without speaking, pointed and clicked her Powershot. She rose over the corpse, snapped several from various angles, zooming in for close-ups of the embedded weapon, blood congealed at its base. Captured more droplets on the desiccated grass. The air stung with a sharp rusty tang. Mac stepped back for full-length body shots, laying a ruler by the drowned cap and blue hair ribbon. Charred clogs lay beneath the cannon, one tipped sideways. She covered the immediate vicinity quickly, sensing the coroner's impatience. Turning and photographing the surrounding graves, her eyes simultaneously swept the area for physical evidence. Finally, she shot Molly

Pitcher's, or Mary Ludwig Hays McCauley's, towering monument, statue and the plaques that summarized her valor at the Battle of Monmouth.

Shadow nosed the frozen ground, sniffed the corpse, sneezing at the acrid odor, rounded the cannon and McCauley's pedestal—scouting. The K-9 officer strayed, her nose leading her from grave to grave, whether from curiosity or seeking, she alone knew.

Ignoring the dog, Dr. Chen waited for Snow's nod, gloved up and then took the body's temp, palpitated the hair for wounds, found a bump over the left ear and worked down, examining the exposed face, throat, and torso closely, then the extremities, moving her hands along the body. She avoided the burned legs until Rusk and Garrett had completed their prelims and photos. "We'll wait until we get her into the lab for the postmortem, but with active rigor, I'd say this homicide occurred within the last twelve to fifteen hours. And no, detectives, I cannot pinpoint COD or TOD accurately until I get her on the table. Need any more time?" she asked Snow, who shook his head. She waved at Hemmer—idling the meat wagon—to collect the body and picked her way gingerly across the slippery surfaces to her Taurus.

"Strange," Snow commented, scratching his weak wrist from habit. The cast had been removed, so it felt exposed —even covered by his shirt and parka. His eyes raked the macabre scene again. "Looks almost like a prank, like the kids toppling cemetery stones except . . ."

Mac paused beside him, their elbows touching, adding, "It's not Halloween. It's staged like a sacrifice. It's hard to believe that stubby weapon penetrated the lungs or heart."

"Doesn't mean the knife is short. How can you tell?" asked Rusk, his hazel eyes settling on Mac's auburn curls twisted back and clamped hastily at the nape of her neck; stragglers framed a face with prominent jade eyes and a wide mouth. He smoothed his mustache with his thumb and forefinger, dropping his hand when he realized the nervous gesture.

"Well, I'm not a doctor, but the handle doesn't look like any weapon I've ever seen," she remarked. "It looks antique, blackened by age and cook fires, like a re-enactor's tool or utensil." She measured the handle. "Four inches. End looks hacked off."

"No point in speculating. Let's get photos printed and mounted when we get to HQ. Any ID? Purse lying around?" Snow scanned the vicinity but saw nothing of note. "Let's widen the perimeter, search for evidence. The killer may have dropped something in his haste to leave." He called Carlisle Police Headquarters and requested that Detectives Zachary Fields and Reese Savage join them. "And Sonja, please check the missing persons database or any news releases about a missing woman dressed as Molly Pitcher, likely reenactors. See if there are events scheduled in the vicinity."

"Didn't realize there were Revolutionary War reenactors," Rusk boxed up his shiny red tool kit, which matched his candy-apple truck, having collected what he needed. Dusting snow and grit from his pants, he stood slowly, joints cracking. He wore a saddle leather jacket over a heavy tweed sweater and jeans.

"Yeah, there are. Someone set her on fire to destroy evidence and perhaps her identity, but the rain put it out," Mac surmised. "Covering it up suggests some degree of guilt, but the killer's not going to turn himself in or call the media." Their breath puffed out in foggy moons as they spoke. In the dim sepia half-light, oblique sunlight filtered fitfully through gunmetal clouds. "They were sloppy, unprofessional: the double knots were hurriedly tied, and they left evidence."

"Mac, check your phone for any Revolutionary War encampments around here. I think Pennsylvania's Fifth Regiment is headquartered in Bucks County, but I haven't heard of any sequestered here. Find out if there are others. When exactly was the Battle of Monmouth?"

She glanced at her husband with unabashed admiration. "You remember the battle where Mary Hays manned her husband's cannon when he fell, injured? I'm impressed."

"Dad's an American History Prof, remember? Besides, she's a folk hero; everyone's heard of Molly Pitcher," Snow said.

"Hmm. The body and statue are dressed alike. The killer's sending us a message," observed Mac while searching her iPhone. Scanning the text, she read, "'Born in New Jersey and reared in Philadelphia, Mary Ludwig moved to Carlisle to work for a Dr. and Mrs. Irvine. Met, married Hays here.' To answer your question, 'the battle occurred on June 28, 1778, near Freehold, New Jersey.'

"Question is, did our victim live here? And we're assuming she portrayed Molly Pitcher, but we don't know that. Her garb could also be circa Civil War. Gettysburg reenactors meet early to train new members, conduct meetings, and take minutes—like any other organization. So we need to check motels, too. And the Army Heritage Center has an Annual Reenactor's Day to recruit new members."

"Civil War reenactors rehearsing four months early?" Snow sounded dubious. He scanned for Shadow, spied her at the Baker marker several feet away, snuffling in the dead grass and pawing the snow. "Find out the date of the AHC event, then."

"Still, it's Colonial clothing much like common folk would wear.

OK. Scotch that." She called Dr. Chen's office, left a message requesting a call if she found any sutlers' labels in the victim's clothing. Staring at one website, she exclaimed, "Wow! The clothes are really expensive: a hundred dollars for a gathered skirt like she's wearing, seventy-five for a scarf and fifty for the cap! Hers look homemade. And she should also have a wool cape. I wonder where it is?"

"You're assuming that she and her persona share the same socioeconomic group; our victim may have been comfortably middle class." Frigid air passed through Snow's Dockers, so he shifted his weight, then dodged behind a headstone. "Did you get the shots of this blood trickle? She bled out here." He kneeled as he spoke to peruse the drops, so he missed her jaundiced glance. Not even a rookie would overlook a blood drop pattern. But against the cannon, it was hard to see.

"Her hands were chafed. Maybe she shared her husband's hobby. I can't imagine living without amenities like running water in a warm house with modern appliances. In July, Gettysburg reenactors wear wool; the campfires are smoky, the tents airless." Mac pocketed her cell and resumed searching to return circulation to her limbs. Inside leather gloves, her numb fingers refused to bend, so she laid the camera on a nearby headstone. Stepping over gravesites, she checked on Shadow: the dog found a wadded frozen cloth—likely a handkerchief. "Good dog." Mac rewarded her, dropping the frozen ball into a paper bag.

The graves were jammed together without an apparent pattern—some too worn to read the inscriptions. She noted names and dates; a number were contemporaneous with Hays McCauley. While they combed over the markers and monuments, a car door slammed nearby, echoing off the stone fence. Fields and Savage emerged, each carrying two cardboard cups of steaming coffee. Mac's eyes lit up. "You brought us coffee!" She nodded her thanks at her colleagues. Zach's watch cap was pulled over his sandy crew; Savage was hatless, his obsidian curls frosty, ears ripe plums. Both wore their CPD issued parkas.

Stumbling over a stone, Zach handed her a cup. "Oops. Not just ordinary coffee for our prodigal couple—a mocha cappuccino for you." He smiled, bowing slightly as he handed the lidded cardboard cup to Mac. "McCoy, it's really hot, so don't burn—"

"And a caramel for you." Savage handed Snow the other cup.

"Thanks." Snow sipped to test the temperature and then drank the hearty caloric latte. He pulled earmuffs from his pocket and handed them to Reese. "Your ears look frostbitten. Let's cover every inch of this cemetery, and then the neighboring streets. Knock on doors; ask if anyone saw a woman dressed in Colonial garb—or anyone, male or female—in this vicinity yesterday between five and midnight. Our victim had no ID on her. Check the parked cars, too."

The warm brew flooded Mac's mouth and throat with welcomed heat, speeding to her stomach—the caffeine jolting her awake, the whipped cream tempering the heat. She was still nursing Ian. Chris's mother, Erica, had the baby and would feed him milk Mac had stored in the freezer. She'd learned that lesson when the Marcellus Shale killer tried to kidnap her from HQ. At home the baby had fussed and cried, and a harried mother-in-law handed over a famished baby when Erin finally arrived home. Shuddering from the memory, she turned away to complete the grid. Two hours later, she'd unearthed three old-fashioned hairpins, a sodden matchbook from The Rustic Tavern and a torn piece of navy wool flannel caught on the wrought-iron gate. Her husband was bagging a pipe stem as she approached carrying evidence bags.

Savage's boots clopped down the outside perimeter of the cemetery. Shaking his head when he reached the wrought-iron gate—no witnesses. "No one recalled any shouts or loud noises. One old guy asked, 'Who'd be out in last night's downpour?'" He handed Mac a baggie containing the stump of a beeswax candle and cigarette butts. "Where's the boss?" he asked. His eyes were dark as raisins, brows like boomerangs, eyelids squinted to keep out the vicious wind. Water swirling down the street pooled over soggy leaves, clogging the drain. Cupping his hands, he lit a cigarette and leaned against the wall.

"Did you know each cigarette you smoke takes seven minutes off your life?" Mac ignored his question but couldn't resist asking her own, since Savage had supposedly quit when he'd had a heart attack last summer. "You do the math."

"Yeah, so I'll miss the shitty years." He shrugged.

"What an attitude." Snow rounded the corner shaking his head at his former partner. "Let's head back to HQ, analyze what we have. Reese, would you track down the bikers, get their statements; they were first on the scene. Where's Fields?"

"The boy scout?" Savage shrugged. "Probably helping the senior citizens."

Across the street, Fields checked the empty road, and then darted across to the others. "I have something! A couple dressed in Colonial costume grabbed a sub at the South Mountain Deli." He nodded toward the tiny concrete-block building and raised an oil lantern in his gloved hand. "The owner said he thought they were married the way they were arguing. They fumbled around for enough change to pay for the sub and two drinks. She called him Sam. They left this on the floor in front of the counter. It has prints! He didn't find it until he closed."

"Good work, detective," Snow smiled. Though often too talkative and clumsy, CPD's newest homicide detective showed promise because he tracked clues tirelessly. Earnest and trusting, his interviews contained the most arcane and irrelevant information because he allowed people their tangents. But now and then, he'd glean a gem of a clue. "Get a description?"

"Better: I got their surveillance tape!" he crowed brightly, brandishing a disc case in his other hand.

"Good work!" Snow nodded. "Meet you at HQ." Savage had already turned his Bronco's ignition over, peeled

away from the curb and whipped a hard left the second
Fields had shut the passenger door.

The glowering skies spit icy sparks; sleet needled
them. Snow motioned for Mac to follow him as curdled
gray clouds massed overhead threatening more precip.
Her index finger in the air, she stopped to answer her cell,
listening while approaching the Explorer. Halted abruptly,
hand up, palm out. "Yes, sir, I can take that call."

Chris waited, one brassy brown eyebrow quirked,
waiting.

"Chief March wants Shadow and me to take the Amber
Alert case."

"Why?" he asked, his hand on the door. "He has a
lead?"

"A Carlisle woman called in to say her granddaughter's
missing. She's nearly hysterical. Chief said she needs a
woman's touch, and it's a good opportunity for Shadow to
prove her mettle. Shadow, come!" Mac opened Silver's
passenger door; the dog leaped in—always ready to ride.
She threw Chris a kiss.

"Call me then," he said, frowning. "It's your first day
back, so pace yourself."

"I will, after I've talked with the grandmother. Maybe
the kid skipped school to hang out at the mall with
friends. Though you'd think the girl would've called if she
could. Anyway, if she's been kidnapped, I'll have to focus
on this case, so . . ." she ruminated aloud.

"We can work out the logistics later when we know
more. Love you." Snow folded himself into his Explorer,
headed toward HQ.

McCoy's Honda swerved right out of Cemetery Lane,
through town toward Holly, then left down Lindsay Lane,
the caller's residence. She hopped out, snapped the leash
onto Shadow's harness ring and hurried up the walk, a
comma leading to a red brick and clapboard Cape Cod. In
the quiet, established neighborhood, generous lots
separated a dozen houses along the right side of the rural

lane. A wire fence marched down the opposite side—
beyond that, an empty lot was dotted with maple, locust,
birch and straggly pines. Crystal-coated tree limbs,
arborvitae and low-slung yews hugged the house. Erin
entered the frozen, bewitched Narnia, the wonderland
crusted with snow like divinity. Dormant grass crunched
underfoot like shredded wheat.

2

The doorbell pealed. Mac wiped off the dog's paws with a hand towel she kept in her car. Inside, footsteps approached. The red oak door opened two inches, caught on the chain. The woman's red-rimmed eyes noted Mac's shield, closed the door to release the safety. A pause, then the door reopened, the woman waving her inside, eyes glancing nervously at the dog. "Nasty day. Thanks for coming. I'm coming unglued not knowing what's happened to my granddaughter. I'm June Browning."

Browning shuffled to a wing chair, gesturing for Mac to take the sofa—which faced the bay window across the room. Instead, she took the armchair beside Mrs. Browning, the light at her back.

"I'm Detective Erin McCoy, and this is K-9 Officer Shadow. Sit, girl. Lie down." Mac had a treat ready as Shadow complied; Mac kept her leashed. Dug a recorder and spiral notepad from her saddlebag purse. "Shadow is trained in search techniques to aid the CPD in crimes of this sort."

"Crimes? Is missing a crime? I filed a missing persons report on Emma." Browning blinked, eyes registering confusion, eying the digital recorder as if it were a coiled snake. Her fingers fidgeted in her lap.

"Sorry. I just came from a crime scene. I meant *cases* like this. The recorder helps me remember crucial information. When did you report your granddaughter missing?" Erin jotted notes.

"Last night." She twisted the hanky in her hands. The lavender knit slacks and matching sweater were echoed subtly in her eye shadow, her nails manicured a pearly opal. "Will you start searching?"

"Depends on the circumstances. In any event, I need information if we are to locate her. How long has Emma been missing? Do you have custody?"

"Thirty hours. See I thought she was at Gwen's—a friend's—party. Custody? Not really. Emma visits summers and just stayed last June. Her parents travel quite a bit. Ash, my grandson, enjoys their nomadic life. But Emma's rebelling. At fifteen, she needs peers, structure, and a delineated routine, so I enrolled her in Carlisle High in September. She's taking AP classes in math, science, humanities, and English. Very bright and intuitive, she usually tells me where she's going. And her mother was driving up last Friday to see her. They live in Lancaster, but Emma made plans to spend the night at Gwen's, told me to tell her mother she was busy."

"So what happened between them?" Mac asked, her fingers flexing along Shadow's neck.

"Emma was tired of her parents' lifestyle. Her father teaches history at the community college; my daughter Margie is a seamstress. She can make anything: drapes, though curtains are more the fashion these days. She makes all their clothes, even coats—well, except Jack and Ash's slacks.

"Anyway, they travel from April to August, and their hobbies keep them busy. Like any teen, Emma likes to shop, buy clothes like ripped jeans, tank tops and those gauzy blouses. She wanted a phone; so I bought her a cell —to keep me informed of her whereabouts, take her to a doctor's appointment or whatever. Excuse me." She jumped up suddenly as if she'd been goosed and scurried from the room.

Shadow looked to Mac; sensing the dog's restlessness, she slipped a chewy from her purse. Shadow latched onto the dream bone and gnawed away. Browning returned, handing Mac a 5 x 7" school photo. "Will this help—put it on the news or the alert?"

The girl's long teak hair, falling in loose waves, framed a thin oval, delicate face with a sprig of freckles across her nose. Her head tilted slightly. Lined with kohl and lashes with mascara—her blue eyes gazed past the photographer. A quirk of her bow lips lent her an enigmatic—a distant, almost aloof demeanor. The pale blue sweater against a dark heather blue backdrop complemented her eyes.

"She looks older—I'd have guessed late teens or even twenty," Mac noted. "She projects maturity in that Mona Lisa smile. Well, the makeup and the serious expression make her seem older too."

Browning sighed deeply. "Yes, I agree. And you look young, too. Who would guess you're a detective? She takes advantage of her maturity."

"Meaning?" Mac asked. "She's dating?"

"Oh, yes. Her boyfriend is Wyatt Weber. They're both active in athletics and extracurricular activities—he plays basketball and baseball.

She plays field hockey and swims. He works at Target, she at Pet Smart. Emma loves animals, especially dogs and horses."

"And what do you do, Mrs. Browning?"

"Please call me June. I'm retired. Well, I work Wednesdays and Thursdays at the Bookery—you know the used bookstore next to Bosler Memorial Library? Anyhow, I've called Gwen and Wyatt's mothers, but they haven't seen her since Friday. And someone called from the pet store saying Emma didn't show up for her shift. That's when I knew. Hasn't missed a day since she got the job last summer."

"Do you know the manager there?" Mac checked the recorder but had her pen ready.

Browning shook her head. The woman's variegated strands of permed hair reminded Mac of hickory bark. "No, but I'm sure if you go . . ."

"Yes, I'll ask. Anything else you can tell me?"

Browning hesitated, as she turned her head toward the window.

"Emma's different. Likes her privacy, so a couple of times, she forgot to call me. The first time, she and Wyatt went to Hershey Park, lost track of the time. The second, she stayed in the library until closing and then went to Wendy's with her study group. Very sheepish when she came home. We had words then; she promised it wouldn't happen again. But if she's lost in a book or daydreaming, the hours just 'unspool'—her words. I'm frantic. I tried calling her mother, but her phone goes to voicemail. I left at least ten messages. Can't reach her father either. So I called the Carlisle Police to report her missing." The woman seemed on the verge of crying again; her chin dimpled, trembling. Blinked hard and shivered. "Oh, sorry. Would you like coffee or something?" she asked listlessly as they both stood. Shadow sprang up, ready to go. Browning stepped back.

"No thanks. I just finished one. I'd like to see Emma's room."

"Why? Oh, so your dog can sniff." She motioned them to follow.

"Yes. The more I learn about her tastes and habits, the better informed I'll be about the choices she makes." They mounted the steps to the first room on the right facing the spacious back yard. Sparsely but tastefully decorated, a vibrant blue and green quilt and shams with decorative pillows covered the bed; above it, photos, notes, tickets and other mementos were pinned to a bulletin board. Priscilla curtains adorned the dormer window. A single maple chest stood to the right, capped with a domed gold and black treasure box. Under the window, a closed laptop sat on an antique desk beside a stack of texts. A paperback mystery topped the stack. The cord snaked down to a printer under the desk on a wide wooden stool.

Powder blue wall–to-wall carpet underfoot. A full-length mirror hid on the back of the door.

Browning hovered tentatively in the doorway, eyes tracking Shadow's movements. Mac studied the bulletin board. "Could I take—"

"Yes, certainly. Anything you need." Browning answered absently, waving her hand. "Shall I check her hamper for something she wore . . ." She sidled along the wall, inching toward the closet.

"Definitely, preferably with her sweat in the fabric. I'll return Emma's things when we find her. Can you identify the people in this picture?" Mac stuck the pins back into the board, leaving the blue ribbon with "Freestyle" stamped in gold lettering.

McCoy accepted the red hoodie that Browning proffered.

"Sure. That's Gwen to Emma's right and Wyatt to her left. The boy beside Gwen is her boyfriend, Kevin." Gwen's chestnut hair with golden highlights was clipped back off her forehead; the rest fell to her shoulders. The guys wore camera smiles; only Gwen's seemed genuine. Emma's parted lips looked as if she were speaking. Both tall, Wyatt lean, Kevin bulkier though chest and arms, each had one arm slung along the girls' shoulders. Wyatt's black curly hair tipped into commas; one eye squinted against the sun's glare, the visible one blue. The other's sandy hair was gelled into peaks; hazel eyes in a square, scruffy face. All were casually dressed in tees and jeans. "They were at the high school decorating for homecoming last fall."

"So are the couples still together?" Mac examined the tickets—one to the Camp Hill theater and another to a concert.

"Gwen and Kevin are. Emma and Wyatt—not so much. She's content to entertain herself. Her studies, job and swim team come first. But they have classes together and study together now and then. They're not going steady, if that's what you're asking. Emma is quiet—still adjusting to public school and is more cautious than the others."

"She's not a partier, then?"

"Oh, no. Well, Gwen's sleepover was a birthday party, but I don't know what else they did. They don't provide details, and I refuse to give her the third degree about her activities or even ask about her family issues, even though her mother is my daughter. I try to stay out of their conflicts. I've enough to do minding my own business. So, can you find her?"

Shadow had scooted partially under the bed and emerged shaking a house slipper like it was a rat, her head whipping back and forth. "Shadow, drop it! She has a thing for slippers." Pocketing the photos, Mac leashed her dog, pried the slipper free, rolling it into the hoodie. "All of this will really help. Does she have her phone with her?"

"Oh, I don't rightly know." Browning scanned the surfaces while wringing her hands. "She must, I don't see it; it's usually attached to her ear."

"If you could give me hers, yours and her parents' phone numbers, that'd be another good way to track her. I'll send the photo to the media and get started as soon as I return to Headquarters." Mac would also send officers to interview every known pedophile living in the area. She checked her watch on their way downstairs. Browning disappeared but returned promptly with their phone numbers on a card.

"Would you please call me when you learn something?" she asked.

Mac nodded. "If Emma contacts you, or anyone else calls about her, let me know."

"Yes, of course. Thanks for coming so quickly. Did she run away?"

"You could better answer that than I can. Was she unhappy?"

"Not exactly—nor happy either. She's Tuesday's child, full of woe. It's such a gulf to cross, going from home-

schooled to a regimented public school. She likes her
college classes, though. I worry that she's hurrying
through the fun years, you know?"

Mac stopped and thought. "I suppose. Teen years are
trying. I'll send a tech to tap your phone." Mac handed
her a card, collected her recorder from the stand between
the wing chairs and bid Browning goodbye. She thumbed
her husband's cell; Chris picked up. "I need to swing by
the house so I can feed Ian." She handed Shadow into
Silver, hopped in the driver's seat.

"Wait up—I'll be there in a few minutes."

While waiting, she updated her notes, snapped
Emma's photo with her iPhone and then emailed it to
Sonja. "If we get Emma Hawthorne's photo to the media
quickly and set up a hotline, we should get tips rolling in
by the time I'm back from lunch. And send Huddleston
over to 122 Lindsay to trace and monitor calls from her
grandmother's landline. Once the photo's out, call area
hospitals to eliminate that angle." Next she called Elena
Michaels, a WHTM weekend anchor and reporter, left a
tip on her voicemail on the probable ID of the Amber Alert
missing teen.

Chris pulled alongside, lowered his window. "Hey, good
lookin', how about hooking up with me?" Then pulled in
front of the Accord.

She climbed into his passenger's seat. "Hey, bourbon
eyes. Lock those lips right here." He did, with gusto.

"Think you can make our Jane Doe's postmortem at
two?" He gave her half of his sandwich. They usually
packed lunch, but her first day back from a twelve-week
maternity leave had been a hectic scramble. They'd
collided at the Kuerig, fumbling K-cups. Shadow had
threaded between them, pawing for breakfast while Ian
fussed until his grandmother arrived to watch him.

"Hmm. This is delicious." Mac gobbled down the hot
Italian hoagie.

"The deli toasted it. That's your Coke. I finished mine."

"Oh, I shouldn't, double caffeine today," but Mac grabbed it, pulled on the straw. "Can't promise I'll be back by then. Have to interview this kid's classmates, teachers and coaches to get out in front of this missing persons case." She showed him the girl's school photo.

"Cute girl. Think it's an abduction?" he asked.

"I do. She's Emma Hawthorne, June Browning's granddaughter. She's fifteen, responsible enough to call if she were delayed or went someplace of her own accord."

"That girl's fifteen?" He took the photo for a closer perusal. "Could've fooled me."

"Afraid so. Too young to drive, so I have plenty of questions to ask her boyfriend." She showed him the photo of the four teens together. "And her best friend and her boyfriend. I need to get rolling on this."

"Try to make the autopsy, OK? Meet you at home."

Mac followed him home, stopping at the Lisburn-Boiling Springs Road intersection, passing through, one-handing the steering wheel left into their driveway.

He tapped the garage door opener, bounded into the bungalow to greet his mother and hug his son before the kid glommed onto his mother. "I think he's grown since I've seen him this morning," taking Ian into his arms and kissing him. "How are you both faring? Long day?" he asked Erica.

"He's fine. Just changed his diaper, put some ointment on that rash around his waist. Maybe he's allergic to plastic. I could order a diaper service. . . ." She stopped, greeted Erin, "How's your first day back?"

"Hectic. Shadow and I have the Amber Alert case, Chris a homicide. Come to mama, baby." Ian stretched his arms out. Mac took him to the rocker in the living room to nurse, leaving Chris and his mother in the kitchen discussing diapers. "Can someone keep an eye on Shadow, bring her in please?" She collapsed and let her four-month old bring her back to Earth from that adrenalin-charged state, the hallmark of a new case.

He smelled powder fresh, his hair still damp from his bath. "Did Grandma bathe you, baby?" She propped a pillow under her arm to help bear his weight, rocking gently while he nursed.

"Bye, babe—Gotta get back to the station," Chris smiled from the doorway. "If you can't make the PM, that's OK; Savage can, but we have a four o'clock briefing on both cases." He leaned down to plant kisses on his wife and son.

The microwave beeped, Erica heating a mug of soup. The fridge door opened and closed; the kitchen stool scraped back. "Shall I make you a cup of soup or sandwich?"

"Oh, no thanks. We shared a sub on the way home." Erin closed her eyes for a few minutes to plan her afternoon.

"What about dessert?" Erica, looking chipper in a red sweater and jeans, sipped soup from a mug.

Mac's eyes popped open. "Did you make something?"

"Baked custard. Whipped cream?"

"Oh, plain. I had cream in my coffee this morning."

"Nonsense." The fridge opened and closed, followed by a shushing sound. "You're feeding two, remember?" She laid the cup and spoon on the stand beside the rocker. Ian turned his head toward his grandmother, stretching out his hand. "Come, let Nana burp you so your momma can refuel.

"How's your first day back? Tiring?" Erica asked while she paced and patted.

"Just the opposite, really. Running on caffeine and adrenalin. I'll probably crash tonight, though. I have interviews this afternoon. Thanks for the custard!" After Ian had finished, she slipped out the mudroom door.

3

Classes were changing at Carlisle High, students milling the halls. Lockers clacked shut as teens hailed friends who were part of their clique. Mac searched for the main office while Shadow parted the waves. Eyes cut from her to the dog; bodies tensed, sensing 'cop,' probably for the wrong reason. She flashed her shield, curtly requesting that the principal locate Gwen Davis, her boyfriend Kevin—"Don't know his last name. And Wyatt Weber. I need to speak to each—separately. Stagger them twenty minutes apart, and please park me in an empty room."

"If this is police business, they must have a parent with them if you intend to interrogate them. What's this about?" he asked.

"Only if they're underage. I'm investigating the Amber Alert—Emma Hawthorne is missing. They or their parents should have no objections in providing information that could lead to Emma's whereabouts. You may sit in on the questioning in loco parentis. Did you know one of your students was missing?"

He blinked myopically behind horn-rimmed glasses. "Why, no. Let me check." Ducking into his office, he scooped up the absentee sheet and skimmed it. Mac followed him into a generic space, his desk beside a window that faced the front of the building. Shadow sniffed the airless space, the desk, snuffled papers. The principal gave the dog an irritated glance, as he shuffled loose sheets together, placing them on the top metal in-box. "She's absent, yes. That would be her first since she entered CHS."

"She hadn't missed a day?" Mac queried. "That should tell you something."

"I saw the Amber Alert on the news, but no one mentioned a name."

"CPD just learned her identify from her grandmother. Now we'll broadcast her photo nationwide. Can you tell me anything about her?"

"No, she's rather reticent. But I'll have my secretary print you her schedule." Sidestepping her question, he buzzed the outer office. "You can talk to her teachers. Ah, Betty, would you copy Emma Hawthorne's schedule for—" He gestured at Mac.

"Detective Erin McCoy and K-9 Officer Shadow," Mac offered.

"Detective McCoy while I pull Wyatt Weber and Gwen Davies from their classes. They all hang out together." He handed Mac the absentee sheet. "Kevin Lowe is also absent."

He escorted her to a small conference room across the hall. She let Shadow scout out the surroundings while digging her recorder and notepad out of her bag, depositing them on the table. Pulled out a chair but remained standing. "Perhaps I should've used my backpack—would've fit right in. Nah, Shadow's a dead giveaway, aren't you girl." The brass knob turned, latch clicked. In walked a six-three student wearing his numbered basketball jersey over a black tee and jeans. Haircut like former star Christian Lightner's, he carried texts and a lab manual at his hip and laid them on the table to extend his hand. "Wyatt Weber. How can I help?"

She took his warm hand in hers. "Detective Erin McCoy." She nodded toward the seat and took the end one herself, thumbed on the recorder and identified the participants, date, and case number. "Did you know Emma Hawthorne was missing?"

He shook his head. "Not until just now. The principal told me she's the Amber Alert. I thought that was just for children." He tipped his chair back.

"At fifteen, she's considered one."

Eyes wide, he let the chair thud back down on four legs. "FIFTEEN? She can't be; she's a junior taking AP and college classes."

"Nevertheless, she's a minor. How long have you known her?" McCoy asked.

"Damn. I had no idea she was so young. I've known her since last June. When school started, she helped me with Chem and Calc so I could maintain my sports eligibility. She's a whiz but made me promise to keep it a secret."

"Why? And you dated?"

"Hmm. You went to high school, right? Well, we hang out, mostly with Kevin and Gwen. He's on the basketball team, too, and Gwen's a cheerleader. Em's in the band. And we're in English together too."

"Were you intimate?" Mac asked calmly, noting the flush creeping up his neck and his knee bouncing.

"I, uh. That's personal." He hesitated, deciding.

"As the boyfriend, you're a person of interest," Mac informed him.

"No, we haven't hooked up, if that's what you mean." He fidgeted nervously, suddenly interested in his texts—whether from embarrassment or lying, hard to tell.

"A good thing. Sex with a minor would be statutory rape with or without her consent." Mac locked eyes on his, waiting to see where they strayed.

"Holy shit! Sorry! Whew, thanks for telling me. She's totally off limits from now on!" He maintained eye contact, tracking Shadow in his peripheral vision, rolling his shoulders, but his hands remained steady.

"How old are you?" Mac asked.

"Turned eighteen last week." The dog sniffed his jersey, then jeans. He didn't slide away but watched her.

Mac smiled. "Funny, Shadow turned one on the Ides of March."

"An ill omen: 'The graves stood tenantless, and the sheeted dead did squeak and gibber in the Roman streets.' Honest, we're not a couple. She's sociable to a point but enjoys solitude too. Studies and reads a lot. What's the dog doing?"

Mac smiled at his allusion to *Hamlet*. "An ill omen *for* Caesar. She probably smells what you had for lunch or likes you. That's good because if she'd sniffed drugs, she would have sat and barked once. Then I would've arrested you. Shadow, come, sit." Mac handed her a treat. "Where did you guys hang out?" She laid the photo in front of him.

"Oh, that. We were decorating for Homecoming. I took her to the dance, which she does divinely. Think she's had lessons. We went to Hershey Park last fall and again to see the Christmas lights."

"That's it?" Mac let doubt color her voice.

"Well, we saw 'Wall-E' and 'The Dark Knight' with Gwen and Kevin. Emma and I ate at the Carlisle Diner and went to dinner a few times. Let me think: Juliana's, The Rustic Tavern, and Wendy's often. Do you want a list?"

"That would be helpful—for last week. What else can you tell me about her habits? Are you in her study group?"

"Hardly. No, study groups are for her college-level courses. She spends a lot of time at Bosler Library; her grandmother volunteers there. I needed tutoring. You know she's gifted and talented, right? Her paintings in the Art room, essays and poetry are entered in the Gold Key Competition. She had 1560 out of 1600 on her SAT's. But she's moody, too. Some call her aloof; that's because she's new here. She was home-schooled through eighth grade." He stopped to take a breath and shrugged. "Acclimation's tough at this level."

"When did you last see her?" Mac continued.

"Last Friday in Senior English, at lunch and at her locker before the last period. No, I'm lying. Kev and I stopped at Gwen's that evening before the slumber party for about a half hour."

"Were you part of that slumber party?"

He smiled crookedly. "No. It was a chick thing."

"Did you talk to her any of those times?"

"Said hello, wished her good luck at her swim meet. She wished me the same for my basketball game. Friday night she seemed preoccupied."

"Did you win your game?"

He nodded but chewed his lip, so he knew something more.

"Did you see or hear anyone else speak to her? Was anyone watching her furtively?"

He shook his head. "I didn't notice. Classes had dismissed early for a pep rally in the gym that afternoon." His attention was slipping.

"Did you walk her to the rally?" Mac feared that he'd slip away without revealing what he knew.

Again the head shake, his curls trembling with the emphasis. "She had a call. The halls tend to be noisy, so she plugged her other ear to hear and ducked into the girls' restroom. But she was frowning."

"Did she say anything?" Mac waited.

"Must've been talking to her mom," he said, hunching one shoulder.

"Why do you infer that?"

"She said, 'I'm not coming home.'"

"How do you know she wasn't talking to her grandmother?"

"She never uses that tone of voice with Mrs. Browning. That's all I remember." He consulted his cell. "I have a test in a few minutes. May I go?"

She nodded, handed him a card. "If she calls or you can think of anything else . . . One more thing: Did anyone dislike or threaten her? Anyone bully her at school or online?"

"No! She avoided conflict and most people." He unfolded his length from the chair, relieved to be finished, his hand on the knob.

"Thank you for your cooperation." She stood and stretched, donned her parka, pocketed her recorder, and shouldered her purse. Walked around the grounds to relieve her dog. The damp March wind pierced her slacks, pinched her face and bit her fingers. She returned to the girl's lav to check the stalls for names, numbers or any graffiti and voided her own bladder. No luck there. Back in the small conference room, she checked her voicemail messages. First Sonja, saying the hotline was buzzing. The second from Chris, saying Savage was accompanying him to the Jane Doe's PM.

The conference door stood ajar. A girl in a red sweater dotted with white snowflakes over jeans sat in the chair Weber had vacated, trolling through her smart phone. Her manicured nails were oyster shells. She jumped and turned guiltily, seeing Mac and Shadow. Tucked the phone in her backpack at her feet. Folded her hands together. Mac stalked into the room, took her time removing her CPD parka and arranged her things on the table. Ms. Davies waited calmly.

"Thought you were a cheerleader," Mac said, indicating her lack of uniform.

"Football." The teen smiled.

The shepherd sniffed the air around Gwen. Mac said, "Shadow, come. Sit. Lie down." She held out a bone. Shadow flopped down with an attitude, her demeanor saying, "What again?" But she complied. Mac gave her the hambone. "Stay."

She gleaned a bit more from this interview. Gwen chatted willingly about the teens' activities, answering the detective's questions in detail.

She reiterated some of Wyatt's recollections. "Emma came to my party, handed me a gift, dropped it on an end table and excused herself from the sleepover. I wasn't surprised. I invited the cheerleading squad, and they're polite to her but not friendly. I asked if she needed a lift, I'd run her home, but she said no; she'd take the CAT." Her shrug signaled what-could-I-do? "Anyway, I called her Saturday morning. Her cell went to voicemail, and I haven't heard from her since." The blonde highlights in the photo had faded; her chestnut hair had been layered in a more becoming style that framed her face. Her eyes seemed concerned but not disturbed at her friend's absence.

"She gave you no indication that she was planning to run?" Mac asked.

Davies eyes widened, her mascara-laden lashes exclamation marks. "Did she run away? She seemed content here. But for home-schooled kids, public school's a big adjustment." She shook her head emphatically. "No, Emma loves her grandmother and likes Carlisle even though she's not effusive about us . . . or anything except art."

"Anyone threatening or bullying her? No spats or fights?"

"Emma? She barely speaks. I've never seen her argue with anyone, well, except her mother, but who doesn't do that?"

"Any teachers or coaches make her uncomfortable with unwanted advances or sexual innuendoes?" Mac kept plying the waters.

"No, nothing of that sort." Gwen chewed her lower lip.

"Who were her favorite teachers? Would she have confided in anyone here if she were afraid of someone?"

"What makes you think she was afraid of anyone here?" Davies wondered.

"Well, if she didn't run away and no one's heard from her, someone kidnapped her. Her grandmother reported her missing this morning, and we've put out an Amber Alert on her. You haven't seen the news?"

Gwen Davies shook her head slowly. "We only watch it during homeroom, and that's mostly commercials. I was busy with homework."

"Where should I go next to find out about Emma?" Mac asked.

"Did you talk to her parents? They live in Lancaster." Seeing Mac's headshake, she ploughed on. "You mean at CHS? Her favorite subject's Art; she likes Ms. Deloria, the art teacher and Mr. Roberts, her swim coach. And beyond that, I don't know, except she'd confide in Wyatt for sure."

"Can you add anything about Emma that I haven't asked?" Mac said. A knock on the door interrupted. Zach Fields stuck his head in; Mac raised her forefinger and pointed to the recorder. Shadow leaped up in greeting, but her handler gave her a 'stay' signal, so the dog huffed, flopped back down. Fields nodded and ducked out.

"Wow, is that your partner? Isn't he hot?" Ms. Davies remarked.

"Oh, what can I add? She's brainy and artistic. Her favorite color is blue, favorite flavor is raspberry, and she likes French toast. She's moody, prefers her dad. Feels like an outsider here. Reads a lot." The teen shrugged. "And wears mostly monochromatic clothes with colorful scarves like Isadora Duncan."

Mac handed her a card. "Call me if she contacts you or you think of or hear anything else that might help us find her." The teen nodded, hopped up, shying away from Shadow, pulled out her cell, thumbs keying and scurried out as Fields entered.

"You rang?" He grinned.

Mac summarized what she'd learned thus far on the Hawthorne case, instructed him to find and interview the swim coach, handing him Emma's schedule. "And then talk to each teacher—even if you have to interrupt their classes. I'm off to the Art Room. Do you have a recorder?"

"Yes ma'am." He showed her his pocket recorder, notepad and pen. "I came prepared. OK, Coach Roberts, let's see what you know." He darted down the empty, familiar hallway. Then Mac remembered Fields had graduated from CHS.

After receiving directions, Mac hiked down to Ms. Deloria's domain, where she was teaching a lesson in acrylics, strolling from one easel to another while eleven students scrutinized a still life display of a ceramic vase containing a trio of oversized artificial three-leaf clovers, a St. Patrick's Day top hat beside it. One stool sat empty, easel covered.

Mac stood in the doorway, showed her shield, and then stepped inside the classroom with her dog at her knee to peruse the walls decorated with student artwork. She stopped at a grouping signed EH. The middle was a 16" square canvas with a red background behind interweaving branches—dark swaths of black and brown —with one bloodshot blue eye in the middle staring straight at the viewer. The painting to the left depicted a gnarly tree, its twin branches ending with a woman's head on the left, a wolf's visage on the right. A snake hugged the trunk. Embedded in the trunk's base, a fetus slept, head down. The third was a stained glass abstract of a deconstructed Tiffany lamp, imitating Picasso's blue period. Glancing casually at the others as the young teacher in a long navy jumper and red turtleneck made her way to her, gesturing Mac into her adjacent office—a supply closet with a desk.

She smiled. "You're here about Emma Hawthorne. You're studying her paintings," she observed. Her eyes cut to her class. "How can I help you?" So Mac put the same questions to Ms. Deloria that she'd asked the teens.

As they concluded the interview, the art teacher handed Mac Emma's sketchpad. "As you can see, her work is insightful and more sophisticated—and disturbing—than most students her age. Yet despite the subject matter, her work is arresting. I'm not a psychologist, but something is bothering Emma, but instead of talking about it, she paints and sketches. Perhaps something in here might give you a clue as to what happened to her. Please keep it confidential and return it to me. She would not thank me for sharing it with you."

Mac thanked her and left the class after she snapped the paintings with her iPhone. She started as it rang while she captured the last one. "Detective McCoy."

"Mac, it's me," Snow related. "Impound just called; they have a 2000 Camry there. The purse inside and the DMV tags say it belongs to a Marjorie Hawthorne. Care to meet me there?"

"Damn, no wonder Mrs. Browning couldn't reach her daughter! I'm on my way. Thanks. Bye." She tapped Zach's cell, asked him to stay at the high school until he'd finished interviewing Emma's teachers. "And check in with the guidance counselor and photograph her locker, bag the contents." She listened to his response. "Yes, all of it. And get it to the lab. I'm heading to Impound."

"What's there?" he asked. She could hear water sloshing in the background.

"They found the vic's car." Mac leashed Shadow, turned in her visitor's badge at the office and hustled out the front doors. Shadow dropped her rear and tinkled before they headed to CPD Impound lot and garage. In route, her mind shuffled through the information she'd collected, mulling over the possibilities. "Whatever happened, if Emma had been with her mother, the murderer likely took her."

Shadow's eyes stared out the passenger window at the streets of Carlisle.

4

At the site, Mac drove through the gate of the chain-link fence, parked beside her husband's Explorer. She and Shadow shuffled through the slush and entered the garage where a Savannah-colored Camry had center stage —all four doors open, trunk and hood up—crime scene techs crawling over it while Snow watched. A patchwork purse lay on the counter with its innards dumped on plain brown paper. First, Mac photographed the items around the vehicle, including one flat tire, a wool blanket, tote containing yarn looped over needles with a woolen scarf half-completed, worn, dirty boots, and a cauldron with antique cooking utensils. She gloved up and carefully separated each item, snapped the camera, while she looked for an antique knife or the mate to the murder weapon.

The guys gazed at her K-9 Officer but said nothing as Mac kept the dog beside her. Besides nosing at the boxes, tires, car mats and tools, Shadow did not disturb anything.

The purse divulged more: a driver's license bearing a dated but recognizable photo of the deceased, a cotton handkerchief, comb and brush, a worn black wallet containing a wholesale club card and a photo of Emma like the one Mrs. Browning had given her. A second photo depicted a dark-haired boy around the age of ten leaning against a horse stall. The horse pecked playfully at the boy's tousled hair. Mac turned it over and read 'Asher and Butterscotch.' The wallet also held fifty in cash, a library card but no credit cards. "So, she wasn't robbed." In the zippered fold, several receipts had been paper-clipped to a card—Amish Country Store with an Intercourse address. Mac slipped the card out, dropped it into a glassine, labeled and dated it.

"Got all the photos you need?" Snow's breath at her ear startled her; she reared up sharply, but he drew back in time to avoid a collision. "Shit, Mac, watch it. Where's your mind?"

"On my work, of course. You should know better than to sneak up behind me," she whispered defensively but smiled. "No harm done."

He nodded and kissed her forehead, then stepped away. "I wasn't sneaking. Just observing you work."

"Knock it off, you two; we need to dismantle this car. Are you done?" asked Impound manager Ryan McKenna.

"No, sir, I'm not." Mac returned to her work, shooting as much as she could of the Camry's exterior and interior while the men in their paper coveralls took a break. Two stepped outside to light up. "Find any prints, Captain?" She asked McKenna.

"Oh, at least a dozen; you'll get copies, but it'll take time to run this many through AFIS."

"Anything else we should know about?" Snow asked, notepad in hand as he circled the vehicle. He took a mud sample from the front fender, kneeled to pry dirt and grit out of the tire with his Swiss army knife and studied the perforated flat tire. Used his mini mag to check the wheel wells.

McKenna handed him a book—a ledger. "This was under the driver's seat."

Snow paged through it, scanning. "OK, so Regiment Six Continental Revolutionary War Reenactors—a list of names and duties with a schedule of reenactments—none in this area." He slid it into an evidence bag. "We need to contact these people right away."

"Must've been here to see her daughter," Mac said. "Mrs. Browning said Emma refused to see her mother but failed to mention her daughter's line of work. You'd think—"

"Well, somebody knew. So the gravesite's a symbol." Snow bagged, labeled the ledger. "I won't seal it; we need to interview those listed. Think we're gonna need a box. How soon can you give us a run down on the punctured tire?"

McKenna examined the tire closely. "Hard to see, but it was punctured by a nail or something similar."

"Hell, I can see that. So, not damaged intentionally?" Snow jotted the info down.

"Then why ask? How can I know that?" McKenna asked, scratching his head with hands blackened by grease and grime. He caught Mac's look and grabbed an old rag from the counter and wiped his hands ineffectually.

"You just added your prints to the scene," Snow commented.

"And you saw me do it." The man's irregular features broke into planes; he smiled as his eyes flicked defiantly. "It's a little difficult to—" Anticipating Snow's next order, he pulled latex gloves from his jeans. "Assuming we finish in the next hour," consulting his watch, "we can tear it down, shoot an email to you tomorrow."

"Good enough. Mac, I need to get back to HQ for the afternoon briefing, but I'll excuse you ladies if you have to pursue your Amber Alert case." He scratched Shadow's ruff while he spoke.

She nodded, preoccupied with returning to the high school to touch base with Zach. "You notifying next of kin?"

"Is Mrs. Browning stable enough for this blow? Well, never mind. It must be done." He frowned, "I always dread this task."

"Want me to go along?" Mac offered.

Snow brightened. "I do. Let's do that first. Then I'll have Lancaster police track down the husband, find out where he's been." He loaded a carton with the evidence bags and stashed them in the Explorer's cargo bay, dusting his hands. Pulling Mac into an embrace, he bussed her lips. "Going with me?"

"Let's drive separately. I need to backtrack to the high school, see if Fields finished the interviews. And then I'll scoot home to feed Ian and Shadow." She checked the iPhone. "To give your mom a break. We can't expect her to babysit him all day every day."

"Why not? Let's wait until she complains. Or you could just call Fields. Tell him to come to the briefing to update us on the Amber Alert case, now that they're connected."

Mac nodded in agreement as she ushered Shadow into the passenger's seat of the Accord. Snow idled the Explorer, letting Mac lead him to the Browning domicile. Together, they followed the walk to the door and rapped. It flew open as if Browning had anticipated their arrival. She'd brightened at first, but at the serious set of their faces, her smile faded.

"What's happened?" she asked, the anxiety written in knitted brows and worried eyes.

"I'm afraid we have bad news," Mac began.

"Emma's not dead!" She wailed, threw her hand up to cover her mouth in an attempt to recall the words, as if they could wound or portend ill omens.

"No. It's your daughter, Marjorie. We've found her. Can we sit down?

"Is there someone you could call? A friend, relative or neighbor?" Snow said, gesturing to the sofa, but June took the wing chair. The detectives settled on the sofa. His eyes darted to the mantle dotted with glass figurines.

"No, my son's abroad. My husband left twenty years ago. Just tell me. Does she have Emma? Did Margie take her back to Lancaster on one of those reenactment things? Or did they have a car accident?"

"Why didn't you tell me about the reenactors earlier?" asked Mac—the main issue on her mind.

"I didn't want to get into it, but that's why Emma left home. She grew weary of her parents living in the eighteenth century. Oh, as a child she didn't mind dressing up in Colonial garb, eating at campfires and watching from the sidelines. Margie and Jack just eat up that 'living history.' Parading around like Revolutionary War folk toting muskets and long rifles. Staging battles. Then Emma participated too—played the fife, marching along to Yankee Doodle or some such." The woman shook her head sadly. "Now her younger brother's a drummer and flag bearer. He loves it, but Emma's burnt out. That's why she came to live with me." Browning looked from one detective to the other, noticing the digital recorder. "Why, is that important?"

"Yes. We found Marjorie Hawthorne on the cannon in front of Molly Pitcher's statue," Detective Snow said.

Again, the woman's hands flew to her face. "She plays Mary Ludwig; Jack portrays William Hays! They reenact the Battle of Monmouth, the one they claim turned the revolution around." Then it dawned on her what the detective said. Browning crumpled against her chair, her head in her hands.

The woman stared out the front window, watching the sun descend as tears tracked her cheeks. "Poor Margie; she's—was—only forty. What happened?" Her voice projected weariness of crenulated years rather than curiosity. "Did she suffer? Does Jack know? He had to meet Franklin and Washington in York. Or was it von Steuben? Something about historical archives and munitions or supplies. They have a reenactment in April —Washington's army tailing the British to New York. I'm sorry." Finally, she turned red-rimmed eyes toward them. "I guess it doesn't matter now. But what about Emma?"

"Has anyone called about a ransom? Did our IT civilian swing by to put a trace on your phone? Could she have run away?" Mac asked.

"No calls. I would've called you. Yes, a man named Jay." She pointed to a corner of the living room where a receiver sat silent in its cradle. "He did the one in the kitchen." Browning led the way to an antique secretary. All the compartments held neat stacks of envelopes, bills, a roll of stamps, pens, and notepad by the phone next to a stack of *Taste of Home* magazines. A bulletin board mounted above the desk held names, business cards and post-it notes. Dead center sat a sepia-toned photo of the family attired in Colonial dress, faces flushed. None was smiling but staring straight into the camera—shocked back in time.

"May I borrow this photo?" Mac pulled the pin away and took the photo while her husband photographed the bulletin board with his cell.

"If it will help find Emma. That was taken two years ago; Emma was thirteen, Asher nine. They've both grown since." Browning's shoulders sagged; her mouth quivered. Tears pooled and fell. "God, what a mess!

"What should I do? Do you need me to come to the mor—" She choked on the word. "We really need to find Jack. He'll take care of things." The woman sank onto a kitchen chair, a lone placemat at the round pine table, a sugar bowl and salt and pepper holding center court. The kitchen, a bit dated, was nonetheless spotless, the almond appliances marching along the south wall, the knotty pine cabinets polished to an orange shine.

"We found her abandoned vehicle with her purse inside. Photo ID. We're very sorry for your loss," Snow said.

Mac noticed the teakettle on the stove, found tea bags in the third Pfalzgraft canister. A clear squat jar held a handful of tollhouse cookies. "Shall I make you a cup of tea? Or coffee? Call anyone to stay with you?"

"Hot tea on a cold day. That would be lovely." The woman sighed, the lines in her haggard face settled. "No, my neighbor—bless her heart—would be a distraction. Nice as a sunny day but a non-stop talker. Besides, the young man with the Lennon glasses said he'd be back soon."

Mac dunked a chamomile bag into the piping hot water, added a cookie to the saucer and placed it before Mrs. Browning. "We can find our way out if you're sure you're all right, but call if you need—"

"Yes, yes. Please, find Emma." The grandmother waved them out as she automatically reached for the sugar bowl.

They escaped the pall interior to be slapped by the March wind, its bite refreshing, a cleansing of the grief—and Mac sensed—guilt weighing upon the woman inside who had lost a daughter and granddaughter the same weekend. "God, sometimes this job's depressing."

"Part of the territory," Snow said, kissed his wife's temple. "You handled that well. Thanks for helping. See you later."

When Mac climbed into Silver, Shadow threw her a withering glance and jumped into the front seat. She rubbed the dog. "Oh, come on! You've got a fur coat. I've only been gone fifteen minutes."

As she turned left onto Holly Pike, sirens squealed; her pager hummed and cell vibrated. A Black and White sped toward Carlisle. Pager read Dispatch. She called in. "Dispatch. Your partner's calling for backup. Ninety-nine Hillside Drive."

"Ten-four. Over." Mac mounted her bubble, wheeled around, and tramped on the accelerator, behind her husband's SUV. By the time they arrived on the scene, Fields was zip-tying Kevin Lowe's hands behind his back. Flat on the ground—face planted on the sidewalk. Lowe's six-two, two-twenty frame sprawled out as Fields sat on the teen's behind. One of the new cycle squad members—Chase Rivers—removed his helmet to inspect his Yamaha's dented front fender.

"—And while I was talking to his mother, Lowe rabbited out the back, across the lawn and over the fence hauling a backpack. At the top of the fence I stopped and zinged him with the slingshot you gave me. He ran into the street, rubbing his neck and nearly lost his manhood straddling River's bike," Fields relayed.

The three laughed, while Lowe's toes drummed the pavement; he was an angry hornet—humming because he couldn't speak. His backpack had spilled several dime bags of marijuana, a small postal scale and a wad of bills.

Mac called HQ; Shadow bounded out of the vehicle, barking at all the excitement. "Why'd he run?"

"Hmm . . . suing for pleas bru-tal—ity," mumbled the prisoner. "Keep dog leashed."

Fields tapped the back of Lowe's head. "Shut up, mule; that was just to get your attention."

"OK, enough," Snow ordered. "Let's get 'm up, take him to the station." Fields stood; both men looped hands under Lowe's armpits and pulled him to his knees.

"Why'd you run, son?" asked Snow.

"I'm not your son." The side of his face was scraped raw.

"What's Homicide's beef with a teenager?" Chase finally spoke.

Snow stopped and stood to his full height and smiled tightly. "Thanks for your help, but we'll take it from here."

The cycle cop stopped, thought about it and then shrugged at the dismissal. Without another word, he climbed aboard his cycle and left.

"I need to interview Lowe," Mac said. "Maybe he saw Emma Hawthorne before she disappeared." Her husband shot her a look, eyebrows raised. "But I can talk to him once he's in the box. Please hold him for me." She consulted her watch. "I have to run home first. Shadow, come."

Fields said, "You're under arrest for three counts of felony possession of a controlled substance, intent to deliver, fleeing the scene and resisting arrest. You have the right to remain silent—"

"Yeah, I know my rights. I want a lawyer and a plea deal," Lowe said.

"Well, listen to the enlightened," Fields commented.

"What makes you think you can broker a deal?" asked Snow.

"Didn't you hear the lady? I have information regarding Emma Hawthorne and her mother." His eyes roved over Mac like she was a slab of prime rib and licked his lips.

"I'll be at HQ in one hour. I'll talk to you then." Mac waved as she let Shadow in, dropped into the driver's seat and drove away from the curb. The men wrangled the teen into the Explorer.

After nursing and cooing over the baby during her lunch hour, she gave the dog water, let her out and then gated her in the mudroom.

By the time she'd returned to the station, the men were still in the box with Kevin. She watched from the one-way. She could lever with the drug violations if he had valuable information. "I'll offer him a choice—trial or rehab after he dishes. If he's just blowing smoke, then. . . ."

Snow sauntered out of the box and shut the door. "I can hear you out here thinking. We're getting nowhere. He's mum until his lawyer gets here. Want a crack at him? I need to get a few sodas."

"Sure do. If he has something concrete I can use—a lead to Emma, then I'll deal with him." Flicking on video, she stormed into the windowless room that smelled of sweat, frustration, and fear. She settled beside Fields. "Now, Kevin, here's what I'm prepared to do. Give me something useful, and I'll deal. I won't dance, kiss your ass or take prisoners. Start talking or I walk because I have to find Emma."

The fair-haired boy of summer considered her words, silently contemplating, weighing his options. "You just want to know about Emma right? Nothing I say will leave this room? Don't want to rat on her."

Mac nodded affirmatively. "That's right."

Kevin nodded. "All right. See, Wyatt and I were hanging out at Gwen's place. Last Friday she was having a sleepover. We grabbed some burgers and Cokes and ate dinner in their rec room before the other chicks arrived. Emma was in a bad mood, pacing like a caged animal. Gwen was nervous; she couldn't greet her guests, talk to us and console Emma. Wyatt tried, got nowhere. So he left for his game. He also works weekends as an usher at Allenberry Playhouse."

"But you stayed?"

His boyish face flushed but he nodded sheepishly. "Around back the Davies have a sunroom—well, a covered terrace they enclosed. So I circled around the house and snuck into—"

"Why? To eavesdrop?" Mac interrupted sharply.

He nodded meekly. "I had nothing else planned, lost my eligibility to play. Anyhow, it's right off the family room. So I cracked the window to listen. Just wanted to find out what was bugging Emma. People think she's aloof, but she's just shy, communicates in other ways." He stopped.

"We're listening," Fields chimed in. "So far we haven't heard any leads."

Kevin threw Fields a resentful glance and said to Mac. "Can he leave?"

"Sure. Fields, go get coffee. You'll get your turn." Mac bumped his shoulder and nodded toward the door. When the door clicked closed, Mac said, "Go on."

"Emma said she had to go before he got back."

"Wyatt? Why? Was she angry with him?" Mac asked.

"She didn't mean him; she knows his schedule. Gwen begged her to stay. When the doorbell pealed, Emma jumped like a scalded cat. Dropped a gift box on an end table. Gwen answered the door; Emma let herself out through the sunroom."

"And ran into you."

"Yes. I tried to act surprised, like I was waiting for Gwen, but she shrugged it off. I lit up and offered her a toke, and she took one. I offered to take her home; then her cell buzzed as we climbed into my car. It was her mom. They argued about her coming home but agreed to meet at the Old Graveyard."

"Where Molly Pitcher's buried on South Bedford and East South Street?"

"Yes. I dropped her off and drove home."

"Didn't stay to eavesdrop or offer her a ride home?" Mac asked.

He shook his head and chewed on a hangnail, then spit it out, waiting for her reaction. "I drove around the block."

"That's it? Did you see her mother at the cemetery?"

"Yeah. She was leaning her arms on the stone fence."

"Was she alone? You left two women alone? What time was it?"

"Her mother said she'd take her to her mother's. Her Toyota was parked behind the fence on Cemetery Lane. Still light out."

"How did Marjorie Hawthorne seem?" Mac asked. When he frowned, she suggested, "Angry, concerned, worried?"

"No. Frustrated, pissed. She wanted Emma's help with upcoming events. I didn't hang around."

"Where'd you go after that?"

"Went to see a movie."

"What movie?" Mac pressed.

"*The Curious Case of Benjamin Button.* Brad Pitt's awesome."

"Did you like the movie? Did you keep the ticket stub?"

"No, but I can tell you what it's about. See this baby was born old—"

Mac threw up her palm to halt the plot summary. "I haven't seen it yet. Anything else you can tell me that I haven't asked?" She pulled a card from her purse.

"No. Don't tell Gwen or Mrs. Davies, OK? They'd get mad."

"What about Mr. Davies? What does he do?"

"He's an anesthesiologist at Carlisle Regional Medical Center. Doc's not home much." His voice sounded indifferent.

"Mrs. Davies—she works?"

"She a part-time visiting nurse. She's OK but too sweet and gushy, know what I mean?"

"OK. We'll talk to all the parents." She stood, rapped on the door, signaling Snow and Fields to enter. "Call me if you can think of anything else." She laid her card on the table.

"You're interviewing my parents?" He slammed his fists down.

"All of those involved. Standard procedure." She stood, looking down at him, hand on the door. "Thanks for your help. We'll see how it goes."

Snow and Fields waited. "Your turn. Thanks for letting me talk to him," she said sweetly, knowing she'd broken the ice and given them the entry they needed. Lowe had admitted seeing and talking to Emma and her mother, so he may have been the last person to see Marjorie Hawthorne alive.

A third person entered with the detectives. The suit, his lawyer—Robert Orndorf, one she hadn't met, so she observed for about ten minutes until they began questioning Lowe. Mac drove home to relieve her in-laws; she suspected they had fixed dinner at the bungalow.

Her mother-in-law hugged her. "Oh, Erin, we're so glad you're home. Hope you don't mind, but I put some rice cereal in Ian's bottle. He was so hungry and tuckered out. He's asleep now." Erica Snow looked drained, so Erin hadn't the heart to tell her that she preferred to nurse him exclusively until he had teeth.

She paused. "No that's fine." She dropped her purse on the coffee table, removed her pistol, and lifted her shoulder holster off. Tiptoed into their bedroom to peek at her sleeping infant, rubbing her thumb across his curled fingers. Back in the kitchen, she noticed two places had been set at the island. Her father-in-law rose to greet her, as did mouth-watering scents percolating from the Crockpot.

"Good evening. Is Chris on his way?" he asked eagerly.

Erin shook her head. "No. He's interviewing a teenage drug dealer. I suspect it'll take awhile. Thanks for making dinner, but I can wait on myself. You two do too much as it is. I'm thinking about advertising for a nanny. You can't put in ten-hour days like we do."

"Nonsense. He's our grandson. We're happy to mind him. It's just that as we age, we don't have the energy we once did." Dr. Snow, retired Professor Emeritus of History, Shippensburg University, returned to his seat where a cup of coffee sat on the woven placemat.

Erica dished up a serving of coq au vin swimming in gravy replete with mushrooms, carrots, celery, and Yukon gold potatoes. Green beans on the side with a warm dinner roll. "Your dad called. We're happy to babysit, but we'll abide with your and Chris's decision. We really adore him; he's such a doll most of the time and goes right to sleep! We had to rock ours—all three of them—for hours. They rarely napped—very active. Well, let's be on our way, dear, so you can relax."

Her husband rose slowly, smiling ruefully as he drained his coffee and set the cup in the sink. "The old folks must go to bed soon."

Erin saw them to the door, thanking them for their help. Finishing her meal, she stacked her dishes, rinsed, slotted them into the dishwasher and then called the Davies and Webers, making appointments for the next afternoon. Then she remembered.

5

"**The sketchbook!**" She dashed to her car, Shadow following, whining to go out. Mac retrieved Emma's book from under the driver's seat. She hopped up and down while the dog piddled. Bitter cold chased them back inside. She collapsed on the recliner to study the sketches while waiting for Chris to come home. Shadow grabbed her Kong from her bed and settled beside the recliner to finish the frozen treat. "That's supposed to be for bedtime, girl," but she let her have it.

Emma's sketches were puzzling. Granted, Erin knew little about art except that she liked van Gogh's "Starry Night" and Monet's "Water Lilies." Of course, Da Vinci and Michelangelo were geniuses, David's statue being her favorite. She smiled, reminded of her husband's build.

Emma's first sketch depicted an earlier version of the painting in the CHS art room: a tree sponged onto the page growing an African woman and a wolf's head, a snake coiled at its base, and a fetus curled below. Another, obviously Medusa scowling, had smoking muskets for hair. The third depicted a smoky campsite, grey spirals climbing. Flames engulfed ghostly faces—of her parents? Another was an earlier sketch of her beaver prison—the one eye in this sketch dropping a crystal teardrop. "OMG, I just got that!"

She called Dr. Drummer's HQ landline and left a message, asking if he'd peruse these sketches and offer his insights at tomorrow's briefing. "The sketchbook contains dark themes of purgatory, confinement, hostility, and perhaps sexual abuse. I'd appreciate your

44

input. If you're busy tomorrow, give me a ring, and I'll make an appointment. Thanks."

Shadow yelped and bounded to the front door before the deadbolt slid back. Chris pushed in, patted the dog and stripped to his tee, laying pistol and holster on the end table—watching the wagging tail—and then moved his things to the island. Lathering face and hands in the mudroom, he disappeared into the bedroom and finally returned to the living room to gather Erin in his arms and deliver a lingering kiss. "Boy, you taste good, but I need food. What smells divine?"

"Coq au vin—your mother's. It's delicious." Erin zapped the roll and green beans in the microwave as he dished himself a hearty helping of the stew. Poured a glass of tea from a pitcher in the fridge.

"Too tired to talk shop?" he asked, as he forked food in.

"Update me. What did I miss at the briefing?" she asked.

"While waiting for Fields . . ." Snow raised his eyebrows at her.

"Oh, sorry, I forgot to remind him, but he should know to attend briefings," she said.

"He arrived late. Anyway, we posted your photos on the boards. Summarized the evidence, including what we found on and in the car. McKenna was right—many prints. Jay's running them through AFSIS. He sent an officer to monitor Browning's calls. The murder weapon is a three-pronged antique fork used for cooking in a fireplace or over open fires.

"Chen emailed you the prelim, but the Vic was probably unconscious when fatally wounded. Her vagina contained a fresh semen sample. The LT informed the Captain of the Sixth Continental Regiment we'd be on site Wednesday to question them. Lancaster police ran Hawthorne to ground; he'll be here tomorrow morning. The Chief apprised him of his wife's murder and daughter's disappearance. He's distraught, but there's no way to sugarcoat it."

A howl interrupted him. Checking his watch, frowning, he jumped up and ran to the bedroom, reappearing a few minutes later with a fighting mad Ian, arms and legs thrashing, seeking a full breast. Erin hurriedly washed off and lowered herself onto the rocker. Once the infant had latched on, she nodded at Chris to continue.

"Why's he off his schedule?" he asked, checking his watch.

"Erica mixed rice cereal in his last bottle."

"Oh, huh." Pausing to recall his place, he continued. "Hawthorne's bringing dental X-rays and Emma's fingerprints with him. Said they had both kids printed. He's leaving his son with his sister. He'll meet us at ten a.m. after our briefing."

"What did Fields add? He didn't have my interviews with the teens and the Art teacher. She gave me Emma's sketchbook, which I've asked Dr. Drummer to examine and share his insights tomorrow."

Chris nodded. "Let's not mention teens just yet." He shuddered. "I hope I wasn't as obnoxious as Lowe when I was one. Zach reported the swim coach had only good things to say about Emma. Ditto with the math, science and English teachers. And Zach had shots of the girl's locker and brought her stuff in as per your instructions. They're locked in your office for now. We'll listen to the interviews tomorrow."

"Emma's locker?"

"Right. Emma's locker contained one surprise. You know how the kids decorate their lockers with memorabilia, photos, mirrors, whatnot?"

Erin nodded.

"Besides the usual books, a gym bag and clothes, swimsuit and a towel, she'd painted black bars on the inside of the door."

"Like a prison," Erin commented.

"Exactly. You're not surprised."

She pointed her chin at the sketchbook lying on the ottoman. "Her sketches are emblematic of isolation, containment, anger—maybe even rage and possible sexual abuse."

The detective picked it up and thumbed through the charcoal and pen and ink book. "She feels threatened but hasn't told anyone at school. Has her grandmother seen these?" Chris wondered.

"Oh, no. The art teacher specifically told me to keep them confidential. Sharing them would be a violation of trust. Two of the sketches—the eye caught in that beaver dam and the woman/wolf tree—are in acrylic in the art room. They're entered in the Gold Key art contest. Are we looking for a pedophile and a murderer, or are they one and the same?"

He shrugged, scooped up the baby, put him against his shoulder, pacing and patting the infant's back. When Ian belched, Chris handed him back to his mother for part two. "Could be, or these could be separate incidents."

Erin shook her head. "No, Lowe's interview places him at the cemetery: he dropped Emma off after they left Gwen's slumber party. He claimed they were both fine, though arguing. Apparently, her mother wanted her to return home. Emma declined. Did you hold him?"

"Damn right. Arrested and detained. He'll be arraigned tomorrow. Savage will cover the court proceedings. You and I are talking to the father, and I brought the security tape from South Street Deli for you to watch. It's in the vehicle. I'll be right back." When he returned, he put the DVD into the player, powered it up, and they watched the grainy footage. Marjorie Hawthorne was facing the camera. The man, a few inches taller, had his back to the camera. Both were wearing period clothing, the oil lantern on the floor in front of the deli case. The man's hair was thinning at the crown; his fair hair held suggestions of waves—little wiggles. It was styled like the bust of Caesar's commonly displayed in museums.

"What do you make of it?" Chris asked.

"They're certainly arguing—the way her head's wagging animatedly. Can't tell much about him; he's older."

"Hmm. It's late, let's go to bed. Hawthorne will be barreling into HQ in the morning. And I want a little snuggle time myself."

* * *

Next morning, Chief had barely finished the briefing when a stranger entered the station carrying a brown folder. Dressed causally in jeans and a sweater under a fleece jacket, his stooped manner indicating anxiety, grief —anguish, a man barely holding himself together. "I'm here to see Detective Christopher Snow," he told Sonja Hamilton.

"Do you have an appointment?" she asked. The man nodded—his mouth a slash in his drawn face.

"Your name, please?" She stood, half swiveled toward the offices.

"Jack Hawthorne." He straightened to six feet as if girding himself for battle, clutched his folder tighter. Long, bituminous hair tied back, blue eyes—attractive in a Celtic rough-hewn way, he followed Hamilton stiffly down the hall and into the detective's office. The detective was waiting with a young auburn-haired woman Hawthorne assumed to be staff until his eyes dropped to the shield on her belt. Both frowned and stared when Sonja announced his name.

"I'm sorry. Did you say *Jack* Hawthorne?" Snow asked, taken aback by the stranger—not the man in the video.

"Please have a seat, sir." Mac indicated the one vacant. "Would you like coffee, tea or water?" Sonja waited in the doorway.

"Coffee would be welcomed. A spot of cream, no sugar. Thanks." He sat, still clutching the folder in his lap.

"Married to Marjorie Hawthorne, father of Emma and Asher?" Detective Snow queried.

He nodded. "I'm here to see my wife and find out about my daughter. And see my mother-in-law about funeral arrangements. Margie drove up here Friday to bring our daughter home. And now. . . ." His voice trailed off. "Now I don't have either one."

Snow reviewed the necessary facts of his wife's demise, omitting the more gruesome details, and Mac shared the essentials about Emma's disappearance. They questioned him closely, asking him about his own movements last Friday.

"I went to York to meet with Franklin and Washington, or the men who portray them. We were hauling Revolutionary War muskets, munitions and supplies to our encampment. We ate at a fifties' diner around eight, and Ash and I returned to Lancaster late to order provisions."

"June tells me your wife played Molly Pitcher," Mac added.

Hawthorne nodded solemnly. "She wanted to train Emma for that role eventually because my wife's been reenacting for eighteen years. Margie was perfect; she knew every detail about the Battle of Monmouth. Washington trailed the retreating 9,000 British Regulars' rear guard, escorting 1500 wagons carrying the Tories and provisions stolen from Philly. We reenact that engagement. But Emma has a mind of her own; she wants to study art. Margie's strict and refused to give in to what she called 'the girl's whims.'"

"Do you know if Margie met anyone else while she was in Carlisle?"

He shrugged. "Not really. This is her hometown, so she could have. I imagine she spoke to her mother."

Mac shook her head. "No. According to my source, Emma met her mother at the Old Carlisle Cemetery near Molly Pitcher's grave. Do you know the one?"

His eyes focused fully on Mac. "What are you suggesting?"

Mac blinked. "We're just seeking information. Did they get along?"

"They fought like cats, but Margie's much stronger from hard physical work. And I know you have questions." The man finally laid his burden on Snow's desk, his handprint clearly visible. "Here are the records you need. I'd like to see Margie. Can we talk about your ideas for locating Emma on the way? I can make a plea on TV." Blue eyes filled but he shook his head, gritted his teeth. "I'll do anything to help. She's my only daughter; she's only fifteen." On the last word, he laid his head on his arm, overcome.

Snow gave him a moment and then stood. "Of course. This way."

Mac rose, telling Snow, "I have appointments with her friends' parents, so I have to meet with Fields to divide and conquer, as it were." She smiled wanly. "Please excuse me." She offered her hand; Hawthorne shook it, nodding. "We're so sorry for your loss. CPD will do our best to locate Emma and find the person who killed your wife." She stopped abruptly, clamped her lips on 'in time' and nodded as the men left for the morgue.

She found Fields in the break room, talking on his cell. He concluded his conversation, rose to greet her. "I'm waiting on an assignment. I interviewed Emma's teachers and swim coach, but the trouble didn't come from that quarter."

"I need to swing by the house to get Shadow. I'll take the Davies if you see the Webers. I imagine Lowe's parents attended his arraignment at the courthouse. You might want to start there, catch them before they leave;

they'll be in a sour mood, but Emma can't wait. Try to pin him on specifics."

Zach nodded and then shook his head. "Savage is there. He can talk to the Lowes. I'll call him. We should stick together; you know, the regs?"

McCoy hesitated, nodded. "Thanks, good idea. All right, let's go." She related the conversation with the father on the way, ran into the mudroom, let Shadow out—waving hello and goodbye to Erica at once, mouthing quietly, "I'm at work." Grabbed the dog's vest. After tending to business, Shadow hopped in the back of their new white K-9 SUV.

"Traveling in style," Zach's eyes ran over the panels and seats.

"Oh, yes, and Shadow has her own safety harness behind that grill."

"And you want to intimidate," he guessed.

"I want their attention and cooperation. It's possible one of them knows something that could crack our case, and I need Shadow's nose to help. I have Emma's gym bag in the back."

Together they approached the Davies' residence, a cedar-shake Craftsman-style dwelling, walked past double ivory columns onto a covered porch. Rang the bell. When the door opened, Mac and Fields had to adjust their sight downwards, as the middle-aged man who opened the door sat in a motorized wheelchair. Mac checked the door again. "We're looking for Dr. Davies, Gwen's father." Shadow barked sharply, which drew all eyes to her.

"You've found him. What? Surprised? Most people react the same way; luckily, those who need anesthesia are already at my level." He chuckled good-naturedly, ignoring the dog but taking her measure in his peripheral vision. "I assure you, nothing's wrong with my mind. Do come in and shut the door behind you. My wife's on a call. If she gets her patient's BP stabilized, she'll be back by the time you're done with me. If not . . ." His shoulders lifted as he led them past a wooden butler holding coats into a spacious family room off the formal foyer.

The family room boasted dark cherry Colonial furniture, with a pub-style sofa, an army of brass tacks marching along the edges. A Persian burgundy and navy area rug hugged the hardwood floor. An entertainment center probably hid behind floor-to-ceiling doors at south end. A stone fireplace with gas logs covered the west wall. To the left the kitchen gleamed with inactivity. Through a bank of the sunroom's windows, a covered pool lay dormant for the season. "Thank you for seeing us. We're here to inquire about Emma Hawthorne. From talking with the teens, she was here often. When did you last see her?"

"She hasn't visited regularly since she started working at the pet store. Yes, Gwen's friends are always coming and going. My daughter's such a social butterfly. Last Friday Emma came to Gwen's birthday party but didn't stay long, Gwen said. I wasn't here. The weekend before, the foursome went to the movies, I think. Mrs. Browning dropped her off here; the boys picked them up in Wyatt's car. Her disappearance on the heels of her mother's death is very distressing."

"How do you know about Mrs. Hawthorne? Her ID was just confirmed this morning," Mac said.

"It's all over the morning news. Every local station is carrying it. They have video of the family at a Battle of Monmouth reenactment. You know her mother played Molly Pitcher?" he asked, as if it were common knowledge. Perhaps among the locals it was. "Does your dog need to go out?" Shadow kept shifting, tugging at her leash.

"No, sir, she doesn't. Shadow, sit. Lie down." She complied, grumbling. "This is Shadow, my K-9 officer, certified in search and rescue. She probably smells Emma. If I let her off the leash, I bet she'd aim straight for your daughter's room. What would she find?" Mac's tone let him know who was in charge of the interview.

His hands tightened on his chair, and he drew up stiffly. "Let her."

Mac pulled Emma's gym tee out and let the dog whiff. "Shadow, seek." The dog wheeled around and scampered across the foyer into the bedroom adjacent to the front porch. Mac followed at a more sedate pace, while Zach stayed with the doctor, asking him about 'the foursome.' Sure enough, Shadow zeroed in on the eggplant floor lounger in the corner, sat and barked. Of course, Emma's scent lingered. More casually appointed than the family room, the bedroom was tastefully furnished in pink and deep purple throw pillows against ruffled European shams. Mac rewarded her for the find and returned to the family room where the dog loped to the end table, sat and woofed again. That confirmed Lowe's account of Friday night's events.

Dr. Davies smiled smugly, as if that little demonstration proved anything, which Mac found distasteful and small-minded. "Find anything of value?" he asked.

"You knew we wouldn't, since we know Emma was here recently," Mac asserted.

"Of course. I think I mentioned that," Davies reiterated.

"Do you know of anyone who disliked, threatened or bullied the girl, online or in person? Anyone show an unnatural interest in her?" Detective Fields returned to formal questions. They continued in that vein until Mrs. Davis blew in the door via the laundry room, hurried across the kitchen, shedding her coat and purse on the way. Her husband introduced the detectives.

"Please sit down, detectives. Hello, dear." She paused behind the wheelchair, her hand resting protectively on his shoulder. Then she strode forward to shake hands. Hers were cold. "May I get you something to drink or eat?"

She gestured to the sideboard harboring liquor bottles and then in the direction of the kitchen.

"A mocha would be lovely," Mac said.

"I'll take coffee with a bit of cream and sugar, please." Zach smiled like an earnest scout, sitting down on the sofa.

"Nothing for me, darling. I have to go to work," the doctor said.

Mac joined her partner on the sumptuous leather sofa and concluded the questions they had for Gwen's father. When Mrs. Davies reentered, Davies excused himself.

"Thanks. Lovely home," Mac commented as the lady of the house lowered a tray with oversized cups and Lorna Dunes to the table. Mac reached for the frothy one and sipped, the rich marriage of coffee and chocolate warm and soothing.

"Thank you; we built it about fifteen years ago when the girls were little. Now then, I'm Susan. What can I tell you? We're so sorry to hear about poor Margie's death and Emma's disappearance. Jack must be shattered. Marjorie and I grew up together, you know. We were best friends until high-school graduation. But as family and work occupied us, we drifted apart. Then she moved away after she married and began reenacting.

"And that's a little weird, if you ask me. Living like it's the 1770's; that's going a little too far, expecting your kids to follow a life of privation—no electricity, their only concession running water in their house." At Mac's frown, Susan clarified. "Emma told us. And the girls' friendship has helped Emma adjust to CHS, plus she's studious, which is good for Gwen." She smiled too brightly, eyes on the recorder, perhaps overcompensating for her husband's brusque behavior.

Susan Davies was more forthcoming with details as she informed them of the girls' habits and haunts. She seemed naturally chatty and unrehearsed—the opposite of her husband. "I knew something was bothering Emma lately. She's acted preoccupied, more reticent than usual. She and her mother argued about her participating in reenactments. Moving in with Mrs. Browning was a suitable compromise, but Marjorie usually gets her own way, and there's hell to pay if someone crosses her.

"Last Friday, Emma was here for a while but left suddenly with Kevin, who'd been lounging in the sunroom. We recently enclosed it and added electricity." McCoy or Fields had only to ask, and Davies's words ran like a leaky faucet.

"You were aware that Lowe was in the sunroom?" asked Fields.

"Of course. He must've been waiting to see Gwen, but we were busy with preparations and answering the door."

Upon leaving the dwelling, Fields asked Mac, "Think we should have a look around? Something was off with the doc, who seemed anxious or nervous about our presence, like he has something to hide but was pretending not to."

"Other than the smugness? I agree he doesn't ring true, but we can't go further without a search warrant. What reason would you list for probable cause?" Mac's phone rang as she loaded Shadow into the vehicle. Her husband. "Yes sir? What's up?"

"You two better head back to the station. You've got to see this feed Huddleston found."

"He found Emma?" Mac asked excitedly, hoping for a lead.

"In a manner of speaking. I have a call on my landline." Snow disconnected.

"Love you, too. Come on Fields, back to the salt mines. Apparently, Huddleston found a clue."

6

Mac allowed Shadow a quick trip around the station, gave her water and settled the dog in her office while pouring herself coffee, leaving the door cracked just in case. In Conference One, the detectives, LT Stuart and Chief March were huddled behind Huddleston's computer. As Fields and Mac entered, the others slid aside to make room for them, taking seats at the table. March picked up the phone and quietly dialed the FBI's BSU.

On the computer screen, Emma Hawthorne sat on a daybed, clad in a baby doll nightgown holding a teddy bear in the crook of her arm, a large lollipop in her other hand. Face bare of makeup, looking younger than fifteen, she seemed uncertain, biting her lip. Her teak hair braided in pigtails, she pouted for the camera. Minced forward barefoot, shook her head no, backed up, and leaned against the bed. Then she folded the covers back and laid her props down. Slowly unbuttoning her gown, she turned her back to the camera, let it drop. Turning to face the camera, her skimpy underwear hid little. Then the feed blacked out.

"Son of a bitch. We were looking at this from the wrong angle. Her abduction isn't necessarily about her mother's case; it's about pedophilia. This is pay-per-view."

"Thought we'd talked to all the pedophiles in this area," Zach Fields tugged at his chin. "Ya know, she looks legal to me."

"She's a child. How many guys did you interview?" asked LT Stuart.

"About fifty in the area from Mt. Holly to Camp Hill," Savage said. "Looks like we need to cast the net wider."

He groaned wearily. "But the ones I talked to didn't give off guilty vibes. The indignant ones let us look around their domiciles. Others showed us their meds or appointment books with their shrinks. But none had the sophisticated PC hardware lying around to pull this off." He gestured to the computer.

"Can you tell where the feed originates?" asked Snow, pacing. "I'll have to tell the dad. Has to be related to her mother's murder. They were last seen together, so whoever killed the mother probably took the daughter."

"Yes, but how do the Revolutionary War reenactors tie in?" Mac wondered.

Huddleston, hunched over the keyboard, fingers flying, tried to track the site's origin. "It's being routed through a dozen sites, including New York and Amsterdam. It'll take time to untangle these threads."

"Could be any one of them. Didn't Browning and Susan Davies say Emma and her brother participated in the reenactments until last summer?" Zach flipped through his notes.

"The younger brother still does," Mac answered. "OK, then, we're now looking at some unknown pervert who likes pubescent girls and may be involved in child porn as well."

"No luck with the parents?" asked the Chief.

"We just spoke with Gwen's parents, Susan and Dr. Davies. Odd duck, but I'll wager that whoever is on that security cam is the perp! Because when Jack Hawthorne walked into Snow's office this morning, he shocked us sideways—not the guy in the video. Not to mention his name's Jack, not Sam."

"Let's look at that footage again; better yet, get it on the air." Chief said. "If he's local, maybe someone can ID him." He turned to Fields. "Did the deli owner know them?"

Fields shook his head. "He called them strangers."

"All right, everyone sit down, summarize what we've learned thus far, starting with Mac and going around the table. The FBI is on its way. Let's line up our ducks before they get here."

Snow groaned inwardly but would be the first to admit the CPD needed more manpower. "Let's hope Perez comes instead of Howard."

"I don't give a damn if Howard brings his entire unit. We want this girl returned to her grandmother to finish the school year. This shit's not going down on my watch." March dialed Dispatch. "Call in the cycle crew. This could be tied to local drug use because that Lowe kid is also swimming in this stew."

"Sir? We just dispatched them to the Lowe residence on a domestic disturbance." Paula Flood sounded nervous.

"Great! What next? Call Mahoney in anyway. Rivers and Summers can handle that call. Who's next on rotation?"

"Sir, Greg Castle, but he's monitoring the electronic surveillance at the Browning residence."

"OK. Mac, you and I will conduct a press conference in fifteen. Huddleston, did you capture that feed?" The IT civilian nodded, still working on tracking the routing. "Print a still; we're going to inform the public. Snow, you'll notify the father ASAP? See if he can drive up here again. If so, I'll postpone the press conference until four. Lieutenant, let's pull Castle in cause this perv isn't going to ask for a ransom. Put Castle with Summers and Rivers to post flyers, check with their informants, follow-up with the deli owner and get a photo of the couple—we need to blow up the head shot and disseminate photos and bring in the guy in the deli—"

"That's not her husband, sir," Snow reminded. "Not a couple."

"She was having an affair?" Chief threw up his hands in frustration, then pushed away from the table, and paced between Margie's board and Emma's. "McCoy, ask Sonja to send someone from PR over to work with you on a press release, then notify the papers and post online. Not in our backyard!" He ran his hand over his bristles; the more he paced, the angrier he became. Then he stopped and huffed a couple of breaths. "What am I missing?"

"I asked Dr. Drummer to evaluate Emma's sketchbook and left it in his office. That may open other avenues. Perhaps being abused, she's angry, uncertain and afraid. An adult in her world has betrayed her. If we can interpret her drawings, maybe we'll find some answers. But her teacher said it's confidential, so we have to keep it in house," Mac said.

Snow joined in. "We're heading to the Valley Forge encampment of the Sixth Regiment's Continentals' site tomorrow. Howard's unit can accompany us to assist with interviews. Everyone is a potential suspect because Emma's been around these reenactors for years. They've watched her grow up, and I think one of them has her. Mac, can you photograph every man there? We'll leave at eight a.m. I need McCoy, Savage and Fields. Mahoney and Storm can come, ask questions too."

"SHISSE!" yelled Huddleston, scrubbing his hands over his face. "I can't trace it; he routed it through a dozen different places. Does Emma have her cell with her? Maybe we can track that."

"You can try, but the kidnapper probably trashed it. Still, get a subpoena for her phone—We have her number?" Chief March asked.

Mac nodded. "And try it. Can't hurt."

Stuart shook his head. "Our best approach is this all-out media blitz. Let's see what shakes loose. Keep our noses to the ground; add the FBI resources—and yes, Dr. Drummer. Can Agent Howard give us a profile on our killer and the vic?"

"Susan Davies, Margie's childhood friend and Gwen's mother, said the mother usually got her way—was strict with her daughter. Emma rebels, but Kevin Lowe drives her to meet her mother at the Old Carlisle Cemetery. They clash. Mother winds up dead," McCoy summarized.

"All right, give Howard that interview, put your heads together with Dr. D—all you psych people, including McCoy, do the profile. We'll keep Huddleston working on tracking this video."

"Any hotline calls on the Amber Alert?" LT Stuart asked the group. Silence. "Well, that probably means no ransom request, and nobody's seen her on the streets. We can eliminate the runaway theory."

Into the pause that sank the conversation, Dr. Drummer materialized as though summoned, lightly tapping on the door then slid quietly through the doorway. "Are you expecting me?" He looked around at the faces—mildly surprised, guilty-looking detectives caught in the middle of something. The Chief waved him in.

"Mac left the Amber Alert teen's sketchbook in my office, and I've been studying it. You're right, this girl has violence in her past, feels trapped and is seeking escape but seems sad that no one's interested in her plight or able to rescue her from the abuse—or neglect. Did you scan the entire book?" He queried Mac, who shook her head no. "In the back, she sketched people. Here's a woman, who looks like your homicide victim and a man with black hair. A third is her boyfriend, I presume." He turned the sketch around for them to see. Mac nodded. "Here's an excellent sketch of our new fire marshal. Does Lane Rusk know Emma?" No one answered, so he continued. "In this one," turning the portrait around again, "the mother's scowling looks accusatory, as her brows are downward slashes and her forehead's creased." He flipped the page. "This could be her father or—"

"That's her dad!" Mac exclaimed, noting the likeness of Jack Hawthorne, his burly brows relieved by the vivid blue eyes, the cheek dimples, trim mustache and squared chin. "The girl used pastels for Rusk and her father, her mother, a charcoal sketch; she sees her mother in terms of black and white." She pushed the teen's photo across the table. "Emma's black hair and blues eyes favor her dad."

"How does this help us?" asked Savage, the perennial doubter.

"This is her only communication with us at the moment," responded the psychologist. "Her abduction substantiates her fear; whoever kidnapped her has been stalking her for some time. She's been in Carlisle about nine months, and most teens are notoriously careless—either thinking they're invincible—immune to crime or too preoccupied with their electronic toys to notice someone's attention until it's too late."

"No offense, doc, but that's a lot of speculation," Savage said, groping for his vibrating cell phone and ducking out quietly.

"OK. Now that we know this, do your observations alter our plans?" Stuart asked, his palm pilot in hand.

"Wait," Dr. Drummer said. "There are more sketches. Perhaps Emma's kidnapper or her mother's killer is in here." He held up another—a profile of a teen with hair gelled into dark commas, leaning against a tree, his wrist resting on his bent knee. Drummer showed the group.

"That's another of her boyfriend, Wyatt," Zach said. "And the next one's Kevin Lowe. Hah! It looks like his mug shot. Wasn't he arraigned this morning?"

"Yes," Savage responded, as he returned to the room, pocketing his cell. "Lowe was charged with three counts of felony possession, one attempt to deliver a controlled substance to a minor, possession of drug paraphernalia, fleeing the scene of a crime and resisting arrest. Bail was set, and he'll be bound over for trial.

"That was Elena. She's on her way over to work on the Amber Alert piece. According to her, Jack Hawthorne's in route. I directed her to the PR office." Savage returned to his seat.

The Chief nodded. "Thanks. McCoy, with me. The rest, to your tasks. See if Agent Howard can meet us in Philly. Snow, take McCoy, Savage, and Fields tomorrow. And Mahoney, as she has more experience than Storm. Doc, feel free to sit in on this media report, but answer questions briefly; skip any in-depth analysis. Let's not speculate on camera. Press conference no later than five, I want it on the six o'clock news. Huddleston, if you get anything else on that computer, call me."

The detectives divvied up the assignments. Snow called his team together to hash over the questions for the reenactors. "I'll talk to Hawthorne, but we need to question the reenactors who play Washington, Generals Sir Henry Lee and William Howe, and Captain John Andre. And wasn't Anthony Wayne in that mix? They're the principals in the Monmouth Battle. They were likely present in every reenactment going back—maybe a decade. And the young Hawthorne brother, Asher, may tell us something."

"So we'll all need recorders, or I can take the camcorder if you want to line them up," Zach offered.

"Good idea! Yes, take it. That'll save time and manpower. More efficient and we'll have a permanent record in case these men go to trial." Snow said. "Of course, Agent Howard will have his own men, queries and agenda, since the kidnapping falls under his purview. But the homicide is ours. We'll try to work with the feds, or we'll work around them, whatever we have to do.

"Savage, call Rivers, see if he'll keep an eye on the Lowe kid; his parents bailed him out. We want to know his whereabouts. I don't want him skipping out. He knows much more than he told Mac, and now we can lean on him."

7

The next morning, Snow left the parking lot driving the K-9 SUV, McCoy riding shotgun, Savage and Fields in the back and Shadow in the cargo bay. Shannon Mahoney chose to ride her bike. On a tight schedule, they made good time driving east via the turnpike. On her cell, McCoy relayed CPD's questions to Agent Isola Perez, Howard's liaison. "We have a double mission at Valley Forge: investigating Marjorie Hawthorne's homicide and her daughter Emma's kidnapping." She explained Huddleston's capture of the live feed of Emma on a roaming pay-per-view porn site. "We couldn't key on the source because the perp routed it through New York, London and Amsterdam, but we believe they're still stateside, as the airlines haven't alerted us to any ticket issued to Emma Hawthorne."

She listened to Perez, jotting her own shorthand—no vowels—in her spiral notebook while Fields checked his equipment, batteries, back-up, and cameras again. Savage kept his own counsel, often staring morosely out of the window.

McCoy said, "Shadow and I will search for Emma's trail at the reenactors' campsite on the chance she's at that site, so if you and Agent Howard—"

"Then we'll be tailing you," Perez responded. "At this juncture, the Hawthorne homicide remains in CPD jurisdiction. We'll target the kidnapping investigation. Entering congested traffic, so we'll meet you at the site." She disconnected.

"Perez says you're on your own with the Hawthorne homicide." She sighed as Chris glanced her way. "They'll be tailing Shadow and me."

"Thank you!" Snow looked up as if his prayers had been granted.

Upon arrival, the feds set up the perimeter while Mac let Shadow out, leashed her, gave her water and waited while the dog watered the field. Though their breaths ghosted before them, the air whispered of spring, the bitter March wind dying down. The ground beneath them had begun to thaw.

Detective Snow and Agent Howard reconnoitered for about ten minutes, while McCoy tugged sweats from Emma's gym bag for the dog to sniff. "Shadow, search." The dog nosed the ground immediately, leading Mac straight to the crude huts the Continentals erected to pass that long, harsh winter of 1778 with few provisions and inadequate clothes to protect them despite Washington's pleas to Congress. Around the site, people clustered in front of their tents, squatting near breakfast sizzling in iron skillets over camp stoves.

Snow and the other detectives approached the men—and a few women—hovering around their heat source. He hunkered down, quietly explaining CPD's presence and mission. As soon as a site was readied, Fields, camera ready, started shooting interviews.

The dog pulled up short, sat but failed to give her usual sign of discovery. Jack Hawthorne nearly stepped on her front paws when he emerged clothed in homespun, surprised. He blinked and shook his head, reaching up to graze his chin with his thumb, then sat on a campstool. The two men who emerged behind him were shorter, the older with thinning hair, sandy mutton-chop sideburns and spectacles resting on his nose. His eyes, nose and mouth were bunched together. The rounded paunch suggested Epicurean indulgence. The third man had nearly colorless brows; short, stiff blond hair comingled with silver; a boxy body, and erect posture. Hawthorne introduced the first as Franklin, the second as von Steuben. Both bowed slightly, right foot forward and said, "At your service, ma'am."

"This is K-9 Officer Shadow; I'm Detective Erin McCoy, Carlisle Police Department, Homicide. I'll need your real names and ID. We're investigating Marjorie Hawthorne's homicide and Emma's kidnapping."

"Did you get a call?" Hawthorne asked, while von Steuben lit the fire and filled a speckled percolator with water, measured coffee into the basket and set it on the stove.

Mac shook her head. "We believe she left the cemetery with her kidnapper. And thanks for the appeal to the public. If someone sees your daughter, he or she will call our hotline." To the strangers she said, "Now, tell us where you were last Friday night between six pm and midnight, your roles here, who knows Emma and who among you showed uncommon interest in the child."

"I'm Franklin Ferris. We met Jack in York to drive the muskets, munitions and supplies to Philly. The rest of the Sixth Regiment met at the Hampton Inn, planning our summer itinerary and the logistics of the Battle of Monmouth. We are also mourning the loss of our esteemed comrade, Molly Pitcher."

Hawthorne dropped his head in his hands and stared at the ground, clearly grieving. He shook himself, cleared his throat and stood abruptly. "Sorry, excuse me. I need a breather," leaving the others to provide information. Shadow lunged at him, but McCoy signaled a "sit and stay" command while she thumbed on the recorder.

Since they'd interviewed him yesterday at the station before the press conference, she let Hawthorne go. Von Steuben resumed his stool after laying strips of bacon in an iron skillet. From an ice chest, he pulled out a carton of eggs and a mound of dark bread. "I'm Stefan Shultz," he said with a faint accent. "We all know Emma. She helped her mother carry water to cool the cannons, fill the canteens, and mend clothes. Often she schooled the younger children, and lent a helping hand. She's been around camp for ten years, a cute little kid but quiet and jittery—as though she expected someone to yell at her. And we did, from time to time.

"We'll miss Margie because she knew exactly what to do on the march. She and Jack are experts on the Battle of Monmouth, but she's a strict parent—apt to smack her children for a transgression, ask questions later. Kept them busy with chores. Emma chafed against such restraints, while Asher is still excited to participate in our living history." He turned the bacon over, one piece at a time, with a three-tined fork similar to the murder weapon. Shortly, he laid the bacon aside, drained the grease from the pan into an empty coffee can and then broke several eggs into the skillet.

"About three years ago, someone gave the girl a sketchbook, and she discovered a talent for drawing. She'd perch on a fence post or tree stump and sketch for hours. When not drawing, she read books." Ferris added. "After that, she openly balked at the labor this lifestyle requires," his hand gesturing around the camp. "Margie brooked no opposition; they argued openly. When Emma threatened to run away, her parents allowed her to live with her grandmother and go to public school." He shrugged in resignation. "Emma told me she wanted to live in this century. She wanted to watch TV, have a cell phone and wear clothes she could buy at the mall."

"Notice anyone spending too much time or showing too much interest in her?" McCoy asked.

"Now that's a strange question. When not working, acting or studying, the children run around together. There are seven regulars: Emma and Ash, Washington's Foster and Libby Winters, my daughter Heidi, and Sir Clinton's two boys. More appear during summer; their parents are extras. Apologies, ma'am, but we call one

another by our Revolutionary names. You'll meet them."
He pointed out the commander, his long hair pulled back
and clubbed at his nape. The tallest in the tight circle of
men near the first tent, he was conferring with a slight,
strikingly dressed man in maroon breeches, silk
stockings, shirt, vest and coat.

"Are you familiar at all with reenactments?" asked
Shultz.

McCoy nodded. "I'm from Gettysburg, so I grew up
watching Civil War skirmishes. I remember the stifling
heat, the smell of smoky fires—scents of sausage, baked
beans and wet wool."

Ferris nodded. "And, unlike the Colonials, we have
modern conveniences. Still, in camp we experience
privations but can all return to modernity—such as it is—
when we complete our stint in August. The Hawthornes'
home *is* a cabin. They live and breathe reenacting, like it's
. . ."

"An obsession?" McCoy suggested.

"No, more like a calling—call it nostalgia for a simpler
time or total immersion in history," he said. "I was going
to say they live this era year around. Emma's not the first
child to rebel or pull away, nor the last I'll be bound.
Frankly, I'm surprised she didn't run away before this.
She and her mother were usually at odds."

"And Jack Hawthorne?" Mac asked.

"Hays is the peacemaker—a quiet man himself, he
acted as referee often, which Margie resented. A willful
woman herself, she liked to think she knew everything
and was always right, bless her soul. And had a sharp
tongue to boot." The sun winked off Ferris's wire-rimmed
spectacles. "But there's one who sometimes singled
Emma out for special treatment—a candy bar, a toy or
small knick-knack."

"Who is he?" Mac shoved a treat at the restive Shadow,
who had sat long enough.

"He's no longer with us. He was diagnosed with MS about five or six years ago. Portrayed Nathanial Greene, the Quartermaster General. Wait, what was his real name?" Shultz turned to the other man as he dished out breakfast into shallow wooden bowels. He offered Mac one, which she took.

"Thank you." She broke off a piece for Shadow, then broke the yolk with the bread and chewed.

"Dawes? No," Ferris contradicted himself. "Hawthorne plays William Dawes, too. You know, the ride?"

She nodded, quoting verses learned in school. "Listen my children and you shall hear/the midnight ride of Paul Revere.'"

"Dennis? Danby? Something like that. Oh, a memory's a terrible thing to lose. Someone will remember." Ferris rubbed his temples.

"Did Hawthorne know about Samuel Gray and his wife's affair?"

"Don't think he noticed. Talk about someone being buried in his work," Shultz said. He pointed toward the drive where a wagon had pulled up. Hawthorne unhitched the two drays and led them to a corral behind the semi-circle of tents. As the day warmed to a balmy forty-nine degrees, the regiment hummed with industry. About twenty men assembled in the common area between the huts and tents. "Excuse, me, ma'am." He stood and bowed slightly. "That's my cue."

He swiped his mouth with the back of hand, snapped to attention, and marched before the men. "All right, you rawboned recruits, step lively. First we'll march in step before we carry weapons. We'll hammer the lot of you into Continentals in three weeks, or my name's not von Steuben! At my count: left, right. Had a good home and left, right!" He pivoted on his heels, his boots squishing along the slushy ground. His 'recruits' tramped along behind.

Who knew? Mac thumbed off the recorder.

The eighteenth century Prussian officer Frederick von Steuben volunteered his considerable expertise to the American Revolutionary War effort; he whipped the regular Continental enlistees who had only known the smithy, the plough, the saw and mill—into shape. He led by example, providing discipline and organization by tracking and maintaining weapons, munitions and supplies—which had a tendency to walk away when the soldier's term expired. Unlike the duplicitous General Charles Lee, Washington and Franklin liked von Steuben —no small item in the political milieu of the divided Congress and the colonial stew. The British governors had lost control; the rebels grew restive and resentful of taxes and the British occupation, but Tories wanted England's protection. Outside the cities, they saw the frontier as lawless outposts abundant with immigrants and marauding Indians.

The armies included the well-trained British regulars and Hessian mercenaries. The opposing American Colonials, state militias and the Scots didn't blindly obey commands or recognize authority unless or until they were provided with good reasons for their orders. They relied on common sense, a trait von Steuben admired.

Mac followed Shadow, who was tailing Hawthorne. *Stands to reason,* she thought, *his scents would be mingled with his daughter's.* The dog hightailed it to the last tent and entered, sat and 'woofed.'

"What is it, girl?" She gave her a treat, observing the meager furnishings. A feather pillow and wool blanket covered the parallel single cots. Along the back two more cots had been placed end to end. Two upended crates served as end tables, each topped with a kerosene lamp; a chest at the foot served as storage. Along a post suspended from the upright poles, clothes air-dried. A collection of tools, a set of keys, and reading glasses crowded the top shelf of one crate; toy soldiers, a bag of marbles and a lacrosse stick were jumbled on the bottom.

To the left, a tin on the top shelf—a sewing kit—next to a basket of knitting with feminine toiletries on the bottom. Propped against the back were a small box of pastels and a sketchbook. "Good dog!"

"What are you doing in here?" Jack Hawthorne stood at the entrance, lifting the flap back, letting in and light and fresh air.

"Sorry for intruding, but Shadow found Emma's art supplies. I need to take them with me." She pulled on gloves and bagged the evidence.

The man's lips thinned and mustache bristled, but he said nothing.

"Someone said a man who left the Sixth Reenactors Regiment about six years ago was fond of Emma, singled her out for special attention and gifts. Do you know his name?"

Hawthorne shook his head, distracted by conversation outside, looking back over his shoulder. Mahoney and Savage were strolling past the tent toward the corral and smithy, their convivial banter carrying on the air, as did the honeysuckle scent she wore. Reese wore jeans and a sports jacket over a crew. Ponytail swinging, Shannon's black leather jacket, pants and swagger reminded Mac of Catwoman.

"Here," he leaned over the chest at the foot of his wife's cot and threw up the lid. "Might as well take it all." Neatly folded, side by side were garments, including knitted shawls and bonnets, one set smaller than the other.

"I'll return everything." Mac sifted through, looking for books or something a fifteen year old might treasure. At the bottom, she found school texts and a science workbook. "Are these Emma's?" Apparently, she'd taken her valuables to her grandmother's. "I don't think I'll need the clothes, but we have a psychologist studying her sketches. I'll take the books, too."

Hawthorne scratched his head, making eye contact. "For what?"

"Anything that might communicate her state of mind. Based on her school art, she seemed angry and afraid. Something in the sketches might give us the information that will lead us to her. Thanks for cooperating. I know how hard this must be for you.

"Can you tell me when your wife's funeral will be?" From his stormy expression, she put up her palm to forestall an argument. "The kidnapper or killer may show up." He nodded and gave her the information. As they exited, Agent Perez entered the tent.

Shadow bee-lined for Chris, who was still conversing with 'General Washington,' sniffing the man's boots and pant legs. Her husband turned toward her. "General, this is my wife, Detective Erin McCoy and K-9 Officer Shadow. They're investigating Emma Hawthorne's disappearance, along with the FBI." As both hands were occupied, she nodded, smiled and said, "Pleased to meet you, General. May I ask your real name?"

"Clark Winters." He smiled down and asked, "Would you consider being Molly Pitcher for the next three months? We are sorely in need of our popular heroine. You look roughly the right age."

She considered the offer. "Well, thank you, but my full-time job, infant son and husband are more than enough." She glanced at Chris, whose wry smile said plenty, but he didn't comment.

Winters laughed. "How can I be of service?" He bowed slightly. "Though time and tide wait for none, I can spare a few minutes. Would you like to sit in my tent? It's misting out here." He separated the flaps for her. She and Shadow followed.

Snow declined. "I need to check on my personnel. Thanks for your time. Meet you at the vehicle when you're through, Mac."

Winters leaned over a cooler, offered her a coke, which she accepted. She popped the tab and sipped. "When did you last see Emma Hawthorne? Did anyone in your regiment show an interest in her? She's been missing since her mother was murdered Friday night, so we're seeking some connection." Shadow shifted as if to explore the tent, but Mac tugged the leash, commanding her to sit.

"Your dog seems bored. I'm sorry, but Mistress Hawthorne did not accompany her parents to the camp this year, and Molly—pardon, Margie—told me her daughter was living with her grandmother and attending high school in Carlisle.

"It's a travesty that citizens are not free to walk abroad at night," Winters added, shaking his head. "We shall miss our Molly Pitcher. Brave and outspoken, she was a crowd favorite, especially when delivering that line about the cannon ball passing between her legs any higher—are you familiar with the anecdote?"

Mac nodded. "Do you enact that event? Someone shoots cannon balls between her legs?" she asked incredulously.

"Well, we don't use the ordinance the Brits used in 1778 but, yes, a redcoat ruins one of her skirts during every battle reenactment; few are aware of its significance. The Continentals and militia fought the British regulars to a draw that day and may have defeated them if General Lee had followed Washington's orders. Instead, he retreated; his men scattered. Then Clinton's soldiers stole away in the night."

"Yes, sir. I grew up in Gettysburg, so history lives in our blood."

Mac had a few more questions, which Winters answered but offered no new insights. Neither could he remember the man who left years ago.

"Reenactors come and go, but there was one the kids called the Pied Piper who grew up with Margie. Did you ask Jack?"

She nodded, thanked him for his time and left, jotting down that tidbit. She tried Hawthorne one more time, approaching his tent. He looked up from cleaning his musket; eyes leveled on hers but said nothing.

"We are truly sorry for the loss of your wife. If you could answer a few questions about. . . ."

"I doubt you'd understand, but I'm angry, worried and grieving. I'm furious about Gray and Margie but unable to do anything about it. It's like history. People can't accept the unvarnished truth; it's too complex. The colonists looked to the Crown for protection and security; the rebels had to *sell* the idea of a revolution to them. Jefferson's 'pursuit of happiness' was truly a revolutionary notion.

"Hadn't the Old Testament God punished rebellion? Created a hell for betrayal, banished Lucifer for eternity? Molding herself into an eighteenth-century heroine, Margie unwittingly created hell in our home life. Always strife. For me, suspicion lurked in shadows like whores, pointing fingers. I buried myself in my work. Hell, the big picture is impossible, so I focus on the moment.

"Margie threw her energies into Molly Pitcher and worked laboriously for our family and the Regiment. But the wider the chasm grew between her and Emma, the greater the distance between my wife and me. I cannot answer questions about your homicide or Emma's kidnapping. Rage just ties my tongue. I'm sorry. Would you please leave?"

She nodded, snapped back the flap. "We'll meet again."

The detectives and FBI agents spent the afternoon gathering dirt and plant samples, clothing scraps, litter, and papers. They put tracking devices on the wagons and photographed the scene. Surprised that all went well—no dust-ups—Mac collected her equipment, called Shadow and loaded them in the SUV. While waiting, she marveled at this historical oasis in such close proximity to the city of Brotherly Love, remembering that the original Ben Franklin's home, and many others, had been plundered by Brit John Andre before the exodus to New York.

Would Franklin have been surprised by the hustle, the drone of traffic, honking horns, the street vendors, cramped environs and city odors? Probably not, as he'd organized the first street sweeper for the city, initiated the first lending library, invented spectacles and the Franklin stove, and wrote *Poor Richard's Almanac.* He also printed newspapers long before entering politics. It was also his idea to communicate news among the colonies by horse express.

They discussed what they'd learned, with Savage more voluble than he'd been on the trip down, mentioning Mahoney numerous times. He held up a glassine containing a thin three-pronged fork, the tines blackened with age and use. "The blacksmith gave me this." It looked similar to the murder weapon, though the handle was longer.

Mac turned in her front seat. "Did he say to whom it belonged?"

Savage laughed. "To whom? You sound like a school marm." He shook his head. "Typical cooking utensils at the ordinaries of the day where travelers stopped for meals. 'People bring their things with them; others leave theirs behind,' he said."

"Find anything that might lead us to a killer?" she asked Chris.

"Won't really know until we get the lab to analyze what we have, but no letters or clear markers, no admitted confessions, arguments or threats to Marjorie or Emma, if that's what you mean."

"No, I wasn't expecting a miracle to drop into our laps, but the video of Emma concerns me. A pedophile is one thing—and dangerous enough, but if the killer has her. . . . Oh, I did learn one important fact."

"Yeah, what?" asked Savage, speaking directly to her for the first time during the drive home. Chris glanced at his wife from the driver's seat, eyebrows raised quizzically.

"That the kids called the man who left the Pied Piper; he supposedly grew up with Margie Browning, so he may still live in Carlisle! So I intend to ask June Browning about her daughter's childhood friends and whether she kept in contact with any of them." Mac rooted through her backpack for her phone, thumbing the number. Shadow was snoring in the back, worn out from traipsing all over the campsite—sniffing, seeking, working her nose and paws all day.

"Hello, June? This is Detective Erin McCoy. I'd like to stop by tomorrow morning to talk with you about Marjorie's childhood companions." The woman responded warmly about elementary class pictures. "Oh, yes, that could be helpful. Shall we say, around eleven o'clock? What? No, I won't bring my K-9 officer. Thanks. See you tomorrow then."

"What, she doesn't adore your sniffing hound? Can't understand why; it's not like she stinks when she's wet," Savage sarcastically remarked. "Speaking of dogs, can we pick up the pace? I need to drop off some kids at the pool."

8

LT Stuart, Chief March and CPD Homicide Squad Christopher Snow, Erin McCoy, Reese Savage and Zachary Fields joined Officer Shannon Mahoney, Coroner Haili Chen, Fire Marshall Lane Rusk and FBI agents Lionel Howard and Isola Perez for the latest briefing on the murder and kidnapping. On the white board behind them, the Lieutenant was bulleting the major facts amassed thus far on the Marjorie Hawthorne homicide on one board, the details of Emma's kidnapping on the other.

First, Dr. Chen summarized her findings. "The victim sustained the contusion from blunt force trauma on the left side of the cranium, resulting in a hairline fracture and brain swelling that possibly rendered her unconscious. A three-tined fork pierced the chest, puncturing the right ventricle of the heart; arterial stray would have stained the killer's clothes." She detailed other pertinent information: the Colonial garb, the condition of her bound wrists, ankles and legs.

She added, "Intercourse preceded the homicide because I found no evidence of force. Whoever deposited the semen did close to the TOD. Sexual activity could have accelerated her heart rate and exacerbated the blood flow and—"

"Hastened her death," concluded LT Stuart.

"What a way to go," Rusk remarked.

Dr. Chen lips thinned at Rusk's remark.

The squad poured over crime photos, the macabre scene displayed in vivid theatrical detail in the vein of Poe or Hitchcock, including ghostly fog that snaked along the tombstones. The bronze statue of Molly Pitcher holding a cannon ramrod towered over all.

Rusk reported the accelerant was gasoline, ignition a common cigarette lighter, the condition of the skin, and extent of tissue damage to the woman's leg (referring everyone to Chen's autopsy report), the ash contents—both human skin and cotton cloth—and finally, the effects of that evening's downpour. "So no surprises—the fire indicates premeditation. Whoever set the fire had not accounted for Mother Nature's intervention."

CPD IT guru Jay Huddleston entered the room with Dr. Drummer.

Each detective in turn added his findings to the record until Marjorie's board was updated before turning to Emma's. McCoy and Fields summarized the school interviews. "I have an interview scheduled with June Browning about the Pied Piper who left the regiment. He may be the kidnapper," Mac said.

Then Jay Huddleston explained his futile efforts in locating the source of the live feed of the teen's coached striptease. "The original site is buried in the ether."

Quietly, admin Sonja Hamilton wheeled in the TV/DVD to show the FBI agents the feed they captured. Agent Howard, buttoned down and dapper in a dark navy suit and tie, leaned forward. "How long has Emma Hawthorne been missing? Any calls on the hotline, tips from the Amber Alert or the tap on Browning's phone?"

"Eighty-four hours." Mac informed him. "No, nothing helpful."

"Agent Perez will accompany you to the Browning interview; I'll stay to review your records, reports and analyze the DVD. I'll need to talk with Huddleston and get a copy of this." Sonja handed him a copy of the autopsy, the detectives' reports and Emma's video.

"CPD sent close-up stills from the online feed this morn—" Mac said when the sudden clamor of ringing cell phones and beeping pagers startled those assembled.

Savage paled as he pushed back and hurried from the room. Dr. Drummer, who had yet to apprise the team of his observations, quietly followed the vet. As Rusk was leaving, he threw back, "There's a fire at the hotel downtown."

Snow snapped his pager off. "Possible homicide at the Colonial. I'll take Fields." His eyes glanced at Mac; his slight shrug signaled he'd rather have her. The Chief nodded as two more deserted the aborted briefing. The rest waited for Chief March to dismiss or reassign them.

March scrubbed his hands over his face, took a minute to process the information, collect his thoughts. "Right. You know your assignments. Report back here at five for an update. Carry on, Sonja. Lieutenant, if you'll send the media the police report."

Agent Howard turned toward the TV; using the remote, he started the DVD—a notepad and pen in hand, Huddleston at his elbow.

* * *

McCoy pulled into the Browning drive while Perez reviewed the first interview. Inside, Mrs. Browning sat a tray with coffee and muffins on the coffee table in front of the sofa. "Thanks. Mrs. Browning, this is FBI Agent Isola Perez." June's eyes rounded knowingly as she poured, and then perched on the edge of a wing chair.

"How do you do, ma'am," Perez said, taking the couch.

McCoy nodded. "Coffee sounds great. Thanks. Yesterday, we interviewed reenactors. Although most spoke of Marjorie and Emma, they claimed they haven't seen your granddaughter this season." She added cream to the coffee but let it sit. Mrs. Browning nodded again, waiting, her hands twisting a tissue. "Someone said a man paid Emma a lot of attention; he was a childhood friend of your daughter's. Can you tell us about her boy friends?" She paused to separate the syllables.

Browning frowned, thinking. "Goodness. So much was going on then—my husband left, then the divorce—and I was working, trying to hold us all together. How to recapture the magic? It's a lightning bug that flits across the memory, occasionally illuminating those treasured moments—" She stopped and swallowed. "But reality intervenes. You said boys. I remember one who came to her birthday party in third grade, Clayton Roberts—not at all bothered by the gaggle of girls. Marjorie called him her 'playground playmate.' By fifth grade, a boy teased her in science class during a project making the solar system. Dennis? But you mean boys she dated?"

"We'll interview them as well," Isola said while Mac was sipping the strong, nearly scalding brew.

"Her on-and-off steady during high school was Rory Brown until the family moved away. His dad was military. She mooned awhile but wasn't one to mope for long. Then she met Jack—a Messiah college student, a lifeguard at the local pool. They dated until Marjorie finished college and married. Emma was born eight months later." She smiled ruefully and shrugged. "Of course, she had other dates, but the kids usually palled around in groups.

"Oh, Byron Davies lived down the street then. How could I forget? Guess because they moved as well. He and my son Todd, Margie, and Susan rode bikes, went fishing and canoeing at the Children's Lake in Boiling Springs and skated at the rink on the Holly Pike with their church youth group. He was two years older, but . . . Margie always insisted they were just friends. When she and Susan played together, Byron and my son would hang out."

Mac's instinct sent barbs across her bow. "Susan—Dr. Davies' wife? Is Byron related to Gwen's father?"

"Why, yes, Susan married Don. Byron was his older brother."

"Was?" Perez leaned forward, listening intently.

"Yes, Byron died in a boating accident on the Susquehanna—washed overboard during a freak thunderstorm. The family was inconsolable; he was only sixteen. Thank God Margie wasn't with him then. I put my foot down on that invitation. Fourteen's too young to be out on that river without adult supervision."

"You were working?" Mac asked. "Was he alone on the boat?"

"Oh, yes, the library's open all year, you know. No, his brother Don survived. He'd been wearing his life jacket and clung to the capsized rowboat."

Perez poured a second cup, and then motioned to the others, who declined more. She sat the carafe down and picked up a muffin. "Was your daughter also close to the surviving brother?"

Browning deposited her mug on the tray and returned to her seat, shaking her head. "Oh, no. Don was different. Always studying or off by himself collecting bugs and butterflies, doing experiments or something solitary. Also, he was sick a lot when they lived here. I only saw him a few times, walking home alone from the bus stop." She shook her head at the memory. "But smart! He became a doctor. You know the Ugly Duckling tale? Donald had a big head, prominent eyes, thick glasses, and a croaking voice. The kids called him Frog, teased him mercilessly. But he grew up handsome, his body catching up to his head, and married Susan."

"Do any of the others still live in the area?" asked Perez; she crossed her legs, the cloth of her pantsuit swishing in the pause.

"Besides the Davies, I don't really know. After graduation, Margie lost contact with old friends, especially once she and Jack married and got involved with reenactments."

"Can you tell us anything else? Any sibling rivalry between the Davies boys? Or between your son and daughter?" asked Mac, with an uptick in adrenaline. "Any memorable conflicts?"

"Oh well," Browning flicked her wrist dismissively. "You know kids, the usual scraps and scrapes. My kids sometimes argued over which video game to play or about taking turns on the trampoline. But they all got along for the most part." She looked at one woman, then the other expectantly. "How will any of this help find Emma?"

"We don't know yet," Perez answered. "But the more we learn, the more stones we can uncover. We need to examine every possible connection, interview everyone who knew her."

"You still haven't received any ransom calls?" asked McCoy.

Browning said. "No. Is that a bad sign?"

"It just means whoever has her doesn't want money." Mac kept silent about the video feed, though it bothered her. "Thanks—" Her cell vibrated. She excused herself and returned to the foyer, leaving Perez to conclude the interview. "Detective McCoy."

"Mac," Sonja said. "Mrs. Davies just called. She found Emma's purse, wants you to pick it up."

Mac thanked her and returned to the muted blues and greens of Browning's living room. "Sorry, we have to go. Please call if anyone contacts you or you think of anything else."

Browning nodded at a stack of photo albums on the end table, a cloth tote folded on top. "Do you want to borrow the pictures? I thought we could look at them, and I'd identify the kids . . ." Her voice trailed as her face fell, bereft of company.

"Yes, ma'am. I'll stay. I'd especially like to see the Davies boys." Perez smiled warmly at the woman. "Detective McCoy can pick me up after she's finished with her errand."

"Of course." Mac nodded and left, checked her watch. "I should return in about an hour. Then I'll drop you at the station because I go home for lunch."

"How is your baby boy?" Browning asked. At the quizzical look on Mac's face, she explained. "I saw the article about his birth along I-81 in *The Sentinel* last year. How lucky you all survived that terrible crash. Why, the truck driver burned alive—"

Mac face flushed, remember the scene vividly. "Oh, the baby's fine, thanks. He's nearly four months old. If you'll excuse me, I can find my way out." Mac left for three-thirty Belvedere.

9

Mac scanned the property as she pulled to the curb. "Should've gone home for Shadow," she murmured, shouldering her backpack while mincing carefully along the sidewalk and up the front walk to the door.

Susan answered immediately. "Come in, please. Gwen found Emma's purse in her closet. Our housekeeper must have put it there, thinking it was my daughter's." They trekked down the hall to the family room and Davies indicated a seat on the pub sofa.

"Good morning, Mrs. Davies," Mac began, remained standing. "Thank you for calling. Is Gwen in school?" The woman nodded. "May I speak with the housekeeper?"

Susan blinked and paced, then collapsed on the ottoman when Mac gestured her to sit. "She's not here. Do you have to talk with her? She's timid, and her English is limited."

"May I call you Susan? If she found it, I need to speak to her. What's her name? I also need a phone number and address."

"Yes, of course. Address? I don't recall, but I have her phone number. Shall I ask her to come over? I don't know her schedule; she cleans several houses. Excuse me a minute." Susan hurried to her immaculate, cold, stainless kitchen and jotted a phone number on a post-it note. "No, I just assumed, since Gwen denied knowing it was there."

"Is the purse still in Gwen's closet?" Mac extracted a large evidence bag and latex gloves from her backpack, ignoring the question.

"Yes. We didn't want to touch it—fingerprints." Davies turned, crossed the foyer and entered her daughter's room, opened the walk-in closet and pointed to the top shelf. "The Hunter green corduroy one." Mac stood on the stepstool provided and lifted the teardrop purse with a flap and barrel closure from the line-up. It had straps that could separate and be worn on the back. Patted the shelf to see if anything had dropped out but felt nothing. Giving the closet a cursory once-over, she saw nothing suspicious. She stepped down, carried the purse out of the shadows, and dropped it into the clear evidence bag.

"Aren't you going to look in it?" Davies asked.

"No, the lab techs will examine it—if you're sure it's Emma's?"

"I'm positive. She had it last Friday. I remember seeing it on the floor by the end table in the family room. I'm surprised she didn't take it with her." Davies eyed the purse warily, obviously anxious at its presence.

"Maybe she forgot it. Did she leave in a hurry?" Mac asked.

"I didn't see her. The other guests were arriving, and I had to keep an eye on the quesadilla cheese dip and chili, chill the soda in a tub of ice."

"Were Wyatt and Kevin here as well?"

"They were here—oh, yes, Wyatt left earlier. Kevin was hiding in the sunroom. Did Emma leave with him?" Davies studied Mac, trying to read her expression.

"I cannot discuss an on-going investigation. Tell me, you and Marjorie Hawthorne were friends." She pulled out her notepad and took a seat. "Do you remember Clayton Roberts or a Dennis? You didn't mention Byron Davies or that your husband's family was the Browning's neighbors."

It was Davies's turn to be discombobulated. Red flushed her neck; her eyes flashed. "You didn't ask. What of it? What does what happened twenty years ago have to do with Margie's death or Emma's disappearance?"

"That's what I'm trying to find out, ma'am. Our childhoods create the adults we become. Good day. I'll see myself out." Mac's boots clacked against the foyer tile. She turned to catch the woman clutching the sides of the ottoman, staring into space. The door clicked shut. Mac pulled the note and cell from her pocket and thumbed the number. After ringing four times, a voice instructed her to call back later or leave a number. She did, then, sliding into her car to drive home, she called Sonja and gave her the number to trace. "It's Susan Davies's housekeeper's number. I have a hunch, and I need her address. Thanks."

She hadn't sealed the evidence bag. Donning latex, she flipped the purse open and checked the girl's wallet. A CHS student ID stared back at her. She glanced through the contents, searching vainly for a cell, then closed the purse, dropped it back into the evidence bag.

At home, Erin rushed through the mudroom door— Shadow jumping excitedly. "Down girl." She nudged the dog gently in the chest with her knee. "You know not to jump on people," but ruffled her fur playfully, then washed and practically grabbed her son from her mother-in-law's arms.

"Oh, goodness, you're leaking. I'll take Shadow out." Erica grasped the leash, snapped it quickly to the dog's harness. Shadow bounded out.

Erin cuddled Ian. "Hello, pumpkin. I know you're hungry." He grabbed for a breast and latched on before she could sit down. "You Snow men," she laughed at her pun, "are all alike!" She settled him into the nook of her arm as she nestled onto the rocker. "Ah, that's better." As the baby nursed, Erin could feel the pressure easing, her body calming.

Shadow led Erica back in; the dog trotted to the living room and sniffed Ian's toes while he nursed. Now and then, the baby kicked, the dog retreated, and then she'd advance and sniff again. Her mother-in-law assembled sandwiches in the kitchen, brought Erin's out, setting it on the plant stand by the rocker. They'd removed the

English ivy when Shadow arrived because she shredded the leaves, stripping them from the stems. "Coffee? Is Chris coming home for lunch?"

"No thanks. I'm good for now. Thanks for the sandwich." She shook her head. "The Chief sent Chris to a suspected homicide at the Colonial Hotel. The Fire Marshall left our briefing because a fire broke out there as well. He'll be lucky to get home by midnight." She burped and switched Ian. "All right, time for dessert, pumpkin." When he smiled up at her, his cheeks dimpled, coaxing a warm smile from his momma.

"Oh, look, he's smiling. Gosh, he's just adorable—just the best mix of you both." Erica chewed a bite of turkey and cheddar on whole wheat. "Boy, what a run of bad luck that place seems to be having. First, someone let it run down, and then derelicts booked rooms and drugs invaded. If someone asked me, I'd turn it into a drug rehabilitation center and provide people with help and counseling."

"There are organizations available like you describe. Some people, like Savage, refuse to seek help. Time and again, he's evaded seeing our psychologist—knowing he needs help combating depression and his sense of alienation. Plus, he should quit smoking. I wish he'd talk to someone besides my dad. And it isn't enough to talk; Reese needs to substitute—oops! Sorry, baby, mama wasn't paying attention." Ian had tried to pull away and spit up enough to dampen his romper.

"Erin, here, let me change him." Erica gathered him up and propped him on her shoulder; he belched ingloriously and both women laughed.

Munching thoughtfully on her sandwich, Mac's mind roved over the information about Emma's kidnapping while mentally reviewing the contents of the teen's purse. "No cell phone, so either she has it with her, or the kidnapper trashed it."

She slid hers from her pocket, speed dialed HQ, asked for Huddleston. At the beep, Mac said, "Would you trace Emma's cell phone number? It's in Emma's folder—on my desk. If it's still operational, we can locate the phone, get a lock on the girl that way. Thanks." Disconnected. "And I've had enough coffee for one day." She levered up, deposited her plate in the dishwasher. Slid a can of ginger ale from the fridge, popped the lid and sipped while mulling over approaches.

And if Anita Esteban were legal and denied shelving the purse, "Maybe I can get a subpoena for the Davies's house. Someone's hiding information or harboring secrets. I aim to pry those secrets out." Again, she dialed Esteban's phone number.

The woman answered. "Ola? Hello?"

"Is this Anita Esteban?" asked Mac.

"Si. Yes. Habla usted Espaniol?" she asked.

"Si, lo hablo un poquito," Mac smiled. She probably sounded like a first grader. "Me llmo Detective Erin McCoy. I'm looking into Emma Hawthorne's disappearance. I'd like to ask you a few questions about the Davies. It won't take more than ten minutes—diez minutos. Con permiso to stop by your place before I return to work, por favor." A long pause stretched. Mac let the silence work as Erica cooed at Ian, while she dressed him in his Eagles sweats.

Finally the woman sighed. "I'm at Elmwood Park Apartments, number cinco-cuarenta—five-forty. I'm on lunch, have another cleaning at one."

"I'm at lunch too; I'll be there in ten minutes." Disconnected. "Erica, I have an appointment . . ." They nearly collided at the doorway. "Oops. Excuse me."

Erica had Ian parked on her hip and held his play mat in the other hand; Erin smooched and tickled him gently. "I'll be back when I can. Let us know when he tires you out; we can find a part-time sitter." She slipped into her parka, shoved her Glock into her shoulder holster and shut Shadow behind the gate in the mudroom. "No, baby, can't come. You may frighten the lady. Bed!" She fished out a rawhide roll to keep the dog occupied, scurried out the door and sped to the apartments near the MJ Mall. "Please don't change your mind," she whispered.

Anita shied away from the door and gestured Mac inside. Though old and dated, the walls had a fresh coat of pale yellow; new multi-colored striped curtains graced the windows; the apartment held spare, second-hand furniture, Formica kitchen counters, but all was clean, tidy and dust free. She gestured for Mac to sit across from a tortilla wrap and chips on a Fiesta plate. "Coffee or tea?"

"No, ma'am, gracias. I just finished lunch."

Anita took her seat but waited patiently for Mac to speak.

"Please, finish your lunch. I need to ask you if you put Emma Hawthorne's purse—verde bolsa—in Gwen's closet."

The woman's eyes widened. "No. I no see her at all. I saw she missing, poor child. My Cecelia—" She nodded toward a photo in a magnetic frame on the fridge—"is thirteen. I so sorry."

"What day do you clean for the Davies?"

"Every Monday—cuatro—four hour. I help with parties some too."

"Would you recognize Emma's purse if you saw it?"

"No say. American girls have many, no? I like Emma; she often at the Davies'." She took another bite of her chicken tortilla, sat it on the plate and chewed thoughtfully.

"Do the family members come and go when you're there working?"

Mac asked.

Anita held up a forefinger and swallowed, took a drink of water. "I work from ocho—eight to eleven a.m. House is empty, quiet. Very nice. I like." She smiled slowly. "Gwen in school, Mr. and Mrs. at work. Once a month I see Mrs. Davies. She pay me."

"Gracias por tu tiempo." Mac laid a card on the wood table, eliciting a smile from Esteban. "Your English is better than my Spanish. Please call me if you think of anything that would help us find Emma. I can find my way out."

Anita nodded. "Mrs. Davies and the doctor very fond of Emma, treat her like they treat Gwen. Emma at the house often." She smiled again and escorted Mac to the door anyway. "Adios."

Mac called HQ. "Ten-nineteen. Ten-four." She smiled as she cornered onto Noble Boulevard, headed back to work. Her phone dinged. A TM from Huddleston: *copy that. Located site. One hundred yards from 330 Blvdre.* Mac dialed Sonja for Judge Acorn's number. "I need a subpoena for 330 Belvedere, the Dr. Donald Davies residence for possible kidnapping and other charges." She explained the cell ping. Skidding on a patch of ice in the parking lot, she slowed, parked, slid out, hurried into HQ, stopping by Sonja's desk. "When the judge faxes that search warrant, would you buzz the conference room?" Fields was hovering in front of the TV. She blurted out, "We're getting a warrant to search the premises of the Davies's domicile because Huddleston traced Emma's cell phone—Where is everyone?"

Fields pointed to the newscast: "Fire exploded windows at the hotel and damaged the roof and second floor at the point of origin." The reporter pointed to the area down the street, which had been cordoned off with yellow tape, roads blocked with police cars and fire trucks. "Traffic's backed up. It's too dangerous for us to approach, but Assistant Fire Chief Russell Garrett is with me to assess the damage. Can you tell us what's happening? Is the fire under control?" The reporter asked.

Smeared with soot and grime, Garrett looked shocked. "Good news: most escaped safely. Bad news: one male victim unresponsive, but we don't have an ID. It's too early to say what caused the fire, but it's an old building, so perhaps the electrical system's faulty. The man who called it in saw sparks fly from that second-story window." He pointed to a man, arms crossed, watching the conflagration from across the street—roaring water slamming against the hotel, while ash, sprays of mist, soot and debris like bits of cloth snowed from the window as firemen pitched charred furniture out.

"Is Chief Rusk available for comment?" asked the reporter.

Garrett shook his head, thumbed back toward the action. "He won't leave until the last ember's out."

"The police presence thus far has not been explained, so we'll give you a complete report on the six o'clock news. This is Nelson Daley, ABC News, back to you." Daley backed away from the camera, as the cameraman panned the scene to record the carnage.

10

LT Stuart and Detective Snow hustled through the ER entrance, flashing their shields, following the gurney and the EMT's. A Physician's Assistant and triage nurses nodded grimly but brushed by the cops to attend to the unconscious victim wearing an oxygen mask.

The PA said, "What do we have here?"

"An unresponsive male with second-degree burns and suspected DO with paraphernalia found at the fire scene. Smoke inhalation, a weak, thready pulse, wrist and ankle bruising." The EMT handed a nurse the needles in a clear plastic container.

"We'll need those: evidence," Snow said tersely.

The PA's lapel pin read Nina Patel. She opened the male's eyelids, motioning for the EMT's to slide the gurney into an examining room. They hoisted the teen onto the bed and backed out, laying a clipboard at the foot, his feet extending well beyond. Patel perused the chart, lowered a shelf from the wall, exposing a laptop, brown fingers flying over the keyboard. "In due time, Detective."

A female in a white lab coat entered carrying a tray of glass tubes, swabbed a prominent vein on Lowe's hand, stuck it and took three small vials of blood and exited wordlessly.

Stuart and Snow stood in the doorway right outside room thirteen.

"We need the results of those blood tests." Snow indicated the tubes of blood.

"Have a subpoena?" Patel asked. "I need an ID."

"No, he's already under arrest, been arraigned and is currently out on bail. Whatever's in his system, we need to know."

Stuart added, "Just put down John Doe for now and move him to a secure location before whoever did this learns that he's still alive."

"I need a positive identity—a medical history. Has he been at CRMC before?" Patel repeated. A nurse breezed into the room with surgical scissors, cutting away the burned, acrid clothing and started an IV, replaced the oxygen mask with a sterile one attached to a computer monitor, and tethered the patient, as numbers blinked on the screen, the machines beeping. Lowe's burned skin looked like a cheese pizza.

Snow told the nurse, "Please bag the clothes for me." To Patel,

"He's Kevin Lowe, a senior at CHS. Lives on Hillside Drive." Fingers flew; finally, his records popped onto the screen.

"He was here for an appendectomy in 2003. Allergic to penicillin." Speaking to herself, she studied the screen and shook her head. "We need to contact his parents for permission to treat."

Stuart thrust a cell into Patel's hand. "Safe frequency." She nodded, called the number listed in Lowe's records, spoke explicitly, calmly and succinctly in a clipped British accent. Answered a few questions, then with a 'goodbye,' shut the clamshell and returned it to the Lieutenant.

"Why do you suspect that somebody else did this to him?" Patel indicated the injection site on the left arm.

"We can't discuss an on-going investigation—nor do we have the time to go into it, but the boy's life is in danger. We need him alive and awake to question him. He may be our only connection to a murder and kidnapping. We'd like you to go out and tell the media that the patient succumbed to his injuries. Tell the parents the truth, if you must, but we may have to move the entire family to a safe haven until we catch the killer."

Patel worked efficiently over the patient, palpitating his organs. She eeled through the two sentinels and called for a burn unit, an MRI, EKG and other tests. Hospital personnel streamed around them, assisting other ER patients squirreled away in separate rooms. Coughs and moans seeped out—and a woman's agitated voice adamantly refusing to stay overnight while a RN tried to reason with her. A huge u-shaped counter ate the middle space. White-coated people stared into monitors, the lights ghosting their faces. Others bustled, intent on their tasks.

Voices broke through the doors to the ER rooms. "We're the Lowes; our son's back here." Mr. Lowe said uncertainly—a burly middle-aged man with straight brown hair parted on the left, wearing casual khaki Dockers and a black pullover. His bottle-blonde wife, clad in leopard-print sweater and black leggings, loaded with rings and bangles, nodded worriedly, her eyes shifting from the detectives to PA Patel.

"Yes, please come with me. You can stay with him, but he's unconscious and until he is stabilized—" Patel ushered the Lowes into the room, explaining Kevin's condition and treatment in lay terms. Snow and Stuart took positions outside the door—within earshot.

"He'll be all right, won't he?" Mrs. Lowe's voice rose.

The detectives waited until the Lowes questions were answered, their anxiety alleviated momentarily. The father eased out of the room and introduced himself to the detectives. "I recognize you from the arraignment," he said to Snow.

"I'm Lieutenant Les Stuart." The LT extended his hand and shook Lowe's.

"How about we go to the lobby and talk?" Snow directed the man through the door and back near the vending machines—away from the others watching the overhead-mounted TV. He explained finding Kevin in the burning motel room and the CPD's request to report his death. "Otherwise, whoever did this will come back to finish the job."

"To the hospital? Surely he wouldn't dare. Are you suggesting that someone tried to kill him?" The man sat back against the vinyl and stared, his grey eyes glaring. "Who in the hell would do that? And why?" His voice rose in incredulity.

"Well, is your son a suicidal pyromaniac?" asked Snow bluntly, but then eased off a bit. "Didn't you notice his wrist and ankle bruising?"

Lowe nodded and then shrugged. "Kevin lost his Division One college scholarship when he was arrested. Who knows? He may wind up in jail, but . . ." His voice dwindled as his wife joined them in the lobby.

"Whatever you think, Kevin didn't do this." She collapsed onto a cushion next to her husband, suddenly looking her age. Her husband relayed to her what the detectives wanted to do.

"Announce he's dead? But that's not true!" she exclaimed.

"No, we've asked Patel to announce that the burn victim succumbed to his injuries. We won't mention his name or the drugs." He held his palm up to stop Mrs. Lowe's protests. "I know the symptoms, ma'am; your son has them all, and he was arrested for marijuana possession, use and intent to sell, but I suspect someone else injected him to shut him up. He didn't have marks on his arm when we arrested him."

"Oh, because of Emma's disappearance?" she asked.

"Or her mother's murder," LT Stuart added.

Both parents nodded, accepting the statements. "Okay."

"And we'll move him to a more secure facility," Snow added.

"Prison?" Mr. Lowe asked. "What kind of health care—"

"FBI safe house with armed guards 24/7 until these cases are closed. By the way, where can we reach you?"

"I manage a car dealership over on the Pike." Lowe plucked a card from his shirt pocket and handed it to Snow. "Our home number's on the back. Oh, and Dottie owns a boutique on Pomfret Street."

Mrs. Lowe rummaged in her oversized alligator bag for a business card and handed one over. "Please take good care of him. He's our only child." She sniffed as she stood. "I'm going back to his room until he wakes up."

Her husband nodded. "You know, this is partially our fault."

"Why do you say that?" asked Stuart.

Mrs. Lowe answered. "We spoiled him, giving him everything he wanted. Here we thought he was bound for college and a decent life. Now look at him." She approached the glass and gestured to be buzzed back into the ER.

"She's right," Lowe added. "I've always worked long hours, and even when Dottie's home, she's working. Basically, Kevin's been on his own since he was thirteen. He had friends; they all palled around together. Joined the Y. Went to summer camps. But this is the first real trouble he's been in. Can you tell us where he'll be?" he asked forlornly, scrubbing his hands over his face as if climbing out of a nightmare.

"No, but we'll keep you informed of his progress. He may have witnessed Emma's kidnapping or her mother's homicide. Or both," Stuart said kindly, giving Lowe his CPD and cell numbers. "Call me anytime but answer no questions—from reporters or anyone else, in person or on the phone. Keep quiet and he stays alive. Talk and we can't guarantee his safety."

The big man's shoulders slumped dejectedly, but he nodded. They all rose and shook hands solemnly, sealing the pact.

11

With Fields in the K-9 SUV's passenger's seat, Mac
sped to Lisburn, wheeled down the drive to the bungalow,
darted inside and emerged with Shadow in tow. Climbing
back in, she snapped on the rotating lights, retraced her
path, turned left onto Belvedere, and screeched to the
curb at three-thirty. Fields shouldered out, subpoena in
hand and rang the doorbell. Three motorcycles thundered
around the corner but stopped a block from the house.
Mahoney, Rivers and Summers dismounted and swung
around back, the last cop carrying bolt cutters in case
they met resistance or padlocks.

Susan Davies answered, the ready smile disappearing
quickly. "What's the meaning of this intrusion?"

"Step aside, ma'am," Fields said, putting the subpoena
in her hand. "We're searching your house and the
grounds." He stalked towards the back of the house.
"Where're your husband and Gwen?" He stopped in the
arch to the family room.

"Gwen's in school. My husband went to Baltimore for a
medical conference."

Mac and Shadow strode through the open door. "Have
a phone number where he's staying?"

"No, I—uh, didn't even ask. My schedule's hectic
enough." She hurried after them. "What are you looking
for? Maybe I can help."

"Emma Hawthorne. Her cell phone is on the premises.
What kind of car was he driving? Do you know the
plates?"

"A Beamer. EGN 0330. I think 'eggnog' and our
address. Well, I gave you Emma's purse. Let me check

Gwen's closet. Maybe it fell out." She tried to brush past Mac, who blocked her forward motion. "No, ma'am. Have a seat in the family room. We'll talk when we're done." She buzzed Mahoney. "Will you stay with Mrs. Davies and search the family room?" Shannon entered through the covered terrace.

"Fields is upstairs, Rivers can cover the rest of the downstairs." Mac trod through the house and terrace, aiming straight for the pool house. The window curtains were drawn. Kicking herself mentally for bypassing it earlier, Mac circled the covered pool, weapon down at her side.

The door was padlocked, but Summers snapped the lock in two and stepped aside. "I'll take the back yard." He nodded at the expansive, fenced-in half-acre lot. Ivy snaked up and over the stockade fencing. Weeping willow branches bowed over, tendrils obscuring any view from the street or the neighbors.

Mac opened the gym bag and let the dog sniff Emma's shirt again, then unleashed her. "Seek, Shadow." The dog surged through and nosed the summer furniture, the stacked flowery cushions, the changing and powder rooms, an empty wicker hamper and slatted wooden bench. She looped to Mac's side quietly, pushing her hand, a signal to move on. "Damn, I thought this was it!" Eyes roved, seeing no proof that Emma had been here recently. "So let's join Gabe, girl. Seek!" She shoved the shirt near the dog's nose. Shadow bounded off, nose to the ground. Mac hared after the dog, aimed like an arrow at a gazebo near the middle of the lot, holstering her Glock.

They came up empty: no Emma, but Shadow unearthed the cell, hidden or discarded under a clump of sodden leaves. Then they found the gate—so egress had been through it. Even though ivy trailed over it, the gate swung outward silently on oiled hinges to a narrow, unpaved lane.

"So Emma came this way, perhaps dropping the cell." She opened the back—no battery.

"Or someone else tried to make it look like she did. Wasn't that Lowe kid with her when she left here last Friday?" Summers scratched his scruffy jaw, his sandy brows drawn in a 'v.' "Why would they come this way unless a car was parked here?" He trod through the gap and hunched down to study the sidewalk and lane while he snapped on gloves. On the fence of the next property, a blue hair ribbon was caught in the boxwood hedge. He tugged gently, dropped it into the glassine. "If I'm not mistaken, this was around Emma's head in her school picture."

"Someone buried her phone after removing the battery." She dropped it into an evidence bag. "I was sure the pool house would give us something." Grabbing her cell, she called HQ. "Would you put an APB out on Dr. Donald Davies' BMW, PA plates EGN 0330. He's supposed to be at a medical conference in Baltimore. See if any cameras en route captured his vehicle. Thanks." Thumbed end.

Mac asked Summers, "Would you call Huddleston, see if he's pinpointed that computer feed? Fields and I can finish here." The dog was scratching in the dirt along the back fence wall. "Shadow, come." Mac smacked her leg and tugged a treat from her pocket. "That's somebody's else's property." They walked along the lane, examining the structure for a rear gate but found none.

The others approached from the Davies' house.

"Emma's not upstairs," Fields reported. "I even checked the attic." He dusted the cobwebs from his jeans. Raked fingers through his crewcut.

Mahoney shook her head also. "The woman's calling her lawyer."

Mac shrugged indifferently; her attention was divided between finding Emma and watching Shadow—still snuffling along the fence, afraid the dog might start digging. "Thanks for helping. We found her phone and a hair ribbon. Shannon, would you go back, ask about other properties the Davies own? I can't shake the feeling that she's close."

"So you think the Davies have her?" asked Mahoney, retying her caramel hair snugly in a low ponytail.

"I'm willing to entertain other theories, but it's my best guess. Kevin Lowe doesn't have her," Mac answered.

"And he's in no shape to tell us where she is. The fire company pulled him from the burning motel," Rivers remarked. Of the three, he really looked like a cyclist—scuffed black boots, ripped biker jeans, a chain snaking from his back to front pocket, black tee and leather jacket. He had razor cut two-toned hair, pulled into a stubby tail. His creased face bore several mean scars, and a barbwire tat circled his wrist. His eyes gleamed like blue-green marbles. "He took Emma to the Molly Pitcher gravesite, knowing what awaited her. Then Fields arrested him for possession and intent to sell. He's no boy scout."

"Then we'll interview his parents, find out his background. Perhaps he's the kidnapper, maybe even the killer. Panicked and hid the girl to keep her from talking. Now he's seriously injured or worse and can't communicate. Still, he's a lead," Fields surmised.

"Except who tried to eliminate him? We might overlap with the homicide investigation. Fields, with me. We need to canvass the neighborhood, find out about the Davies' comings and goings," Mac said.

Rivers opened the side gate; Shadow tore down the sidewalk, shouldered aside the worn gate of an unassuming grey Cape Cod with white trim, black shutters and doors. The house looked like a throwback to another era—rundown yet resolute, the yard neglected. Blinds hid the windows. Scrambling to the front door, Shadow scratched and barked, her tan and black ruff rising. No one answered; the dog trotted around back, nose to the ground.

Mac phoned Mahoney. "Shadow's got a scent. Come cover the front of the house behind the Davies'." Sprinting around back, they found Shadow sitting on the covered patio beside the door, its paint peeling despite the storm door. Dead leaves littered the backyard. A brown spider was spinning a web in the corner formed by the patio roof and the siding. Mac shuddered and pointed. "Could that be a brown recluse? Reminds me of *Charlotte's Web*." She shook herself out of reverie, while trying the doorknob and giving Shadow a dog biscuit. "Good Girl. It's locked. Chase, can you—"

"On it." His cell materialized. He thumbed speed dial. "K-9 officer is signaling a find. Search tax records on a property on unmarked lane off of Belvedere ASAP directly behind 330 Belvedere. Judge Acorn or Lewis." He listened, and then pulled out his Glock. "Chief said probable cause. Stand back." From his jacket, Rivers pulled a square of contact paper and covered the lower pane. Tapped the pane with his pistol's handle; broken glass adhered to the paper, coming away in one piece. He reached in, unlocked the door. Still it didn't budge. "Must be a floor bolt." Quickly, he crawled through the opening.

Mac held Shadow back. "Sit."

"Let her go, do her job," Summers said. "We'll be right behind."

Mac released her. In one bound, the shepherd leaped, sailing through the opening. Rivers threw the floor bolt, swung open the door for the others. The men followed Shadow, who cleared the first floor without finding anyone. Upstairs, Shadow's nails skittered across hardwood floors.

The environs smelled musty. Standing in the mudroom, with the kitchen/dining room to the left, narrow hallway, living room straight ahead, Mac tried the door tucked under the stairs. Behind it, scratching. Locked? She leaned hard, trying to force it open. Suddenly, it gave way; she tumbled down open wood steps into pitch black, landing hard on her tailbone, dislodging her weapon. The pistol clattered to the basement floor. Pain knifed up her spine. The door slammed shut and locked. Leaning sideways, she reached for her taser, but someone kicked her hand, her fingers stinging from the contact. Taser flew out. She pulled in her injured hand, crabbed beneath the stairs. She grabbed the man's ankle—pulled hard, causing him to stumble. Barking and muffled voices echoed overhead. On hands and knees, the man moaned. A thump, another, and a third strike connected. The man's body thudded to the concrete. Something clicked: then silence. Another person was gasping for breath.

The basement door heaved open from its hinges. Shadow, the first officer down, stepped around the still body to lick Mac's injured hand. Footsteps thundered down, Maglites and pistols held at ready. Before them stood Emma Hawthorne, blood splattered across her baby doll nightie and bare legs, a golf wedge on the floor beside her. Hair in pigtails, eyes smudged with dark circles and her mouth a wide 'O.' An unearthly patch of light projected from the next room through the open door, a computer emitting white noise. A furnace or hot water heater hummed in the far corner.

To the right, a washer, dryer and laundry tub squatted under one tiny window, its light extinguished; someone had concreted the window well. To the left, an assortment of plastic containers and cardboard boxes were stacked against that wall. That window admitted threads of twilight through a grill. Straight ahead, a door to a paneled room stood ajar. Emma dashed to the laundry tub, but Fields followed to explain quietly that he needed to document her condition. She nodded mutely, bent over and vomited.

12

"**That filthy old** man smells nasty. Get him off of me."
She swiped at the blood and matter. Eyes welling with
unshed tears, she looked down at her sheer nightie—fair
skin flushing pink and crossed her arms over her breasts.
Emma scurried back to the laundry tub, wet a dingy
washcloth and wiped away the blood.

The late Dr. Donald Davies lay face down, the back of
his head and neck a bloody mass, hair matted like a
scarecrow's. He faced the steps, eyes wide with surprised
shock. Summers rounded the stairs and reached a hand
to Mac, frozen crab-like beneath. Rivers picked up Mac's
weapon, handed it to her.

"Holster this. Are you hurt?" His hazel eyes read her
face; he dialed 911. "Officer down. Emma Hawthorne
located. We need two ambulances at domicile behind 330
Belvedere. Lane unnamed." To Emma and Mac, he said,
"Stay put. You're both going to Carlisle Regional."

Meanwhile, Summers called the coroner to collect the
corpse. "DOA." His eyes scanned the dingy basement.
"Let's get some light bulbs down here!" Emma whimpered
wounded objections but submitted once light burst from
an incandescent. Behind the door, a desk held a laptop
with a webcam attached aimed at the daybed. To the
right, a three-foot concrete wall enclosed a shower—a
curtain drawn three-quarters the way around. Over the
drain stood a portable commode.

With activity buzzing around the crime scene, Mac
clawed her iPhone out of her cargo pocket left-handed
and notified HQ of their ten-twenty. Mahoney retraced her
steps to ask Mrs. Davies about the neighbor's domicile.

Mac eased to her knees to assist the others before the ambulance trespassed on their crime scene.

"Stay put, McCoy!" Summers growled. Front paw on Erin's thigh, Shadow licked her handler's head wound.

* * *

The ER hummed with determined activity. Clenching her teeth against the pain of the IV poke, Mac suffered the indignity of having her clothes cut off and bagged for evidence, her broken pinky splint and taped. The doctor stitched above her eyebrow. X-rays showed a hairline fracture in her coccyx. She'd swallowed a pill and succumbed while listening to a female PA explain the rape kit process to Emma as her grandmother cooed to her gently.

Upon arrival, Snow insisted on seeing his wife. He watched her breathe while Patel noted her injuries. Two wet spots dotted the flimsy hospital gown but warmed blankets covered her from the waist down. Her husband pulled one up to her shoulders, mindful of the attached wires and monitors. "What's the coccyx?" His mind roved over basic biology. "The tailbone? What can you do for that?"

"Exactly. Nothing. Time and TLC will heal it." She handed Snow a script for Oxycontin. "Use these sparingly since she's nursing."

"Concussion?" asked Chris.

"No, her pupils reacted well but she'll have one hell of a headache. I've noted her injuries. Physically, she'll heal in a few weeks. I'd recommend warm sitz baths and limited activity while the fracture knits. Or apply heat for fifteen minutes, then cold. She can probably resume normal activities in two weeks if she's careful."

One corner of Chris's mouth quirked up despite his concern. "Mac and careful are strangers. Our job requires risks, but I'll try to slow her down for awhile." He folded the prescription slip and tucked it into his pocket. "When can I take her home?"

"We can release her once the doctor sees her, but she needs to be awake for that." Patel consulted her watch. "Two-three hours."

Snow nodded and stepped over to the next cubicle where Emma Hawthorne was propped up in the raised bed, her teak hair loose about her shoulders, staring into a new smart phone. He nodded at June Browning, whose worried frown and slight shrug telegraphed her unease.

"How are you feeling?" Snow asked the teenager. Her eyes, cold blue as the winter sky, made contact, but she said nothing. He heard her nonetheless—*How do you think, idiot?* "Do you want to talk to Dr. Drummer, the CPD psychologist? He'd like to talk to you. I would, too. Can you tell us what happened?" Silence. "You need anything? I'll get you a chocolate—no, raspberry—shake. How about a sandwich? You must be hungry."

Emma studied the detective for a full minute, perusing his brassy light brown hair, wide forehead and deep amber eyes as if she would draw his face. The silence expanded. Reaching for the can of ginger ale on the tray table beside the bed, she said, "Thank Detective McCoy. I'll talk to her." She nodded toward the next room, then returned her attention to her new toy, her index finger trolling.

"Let me know if you want that milkshake." He nodded, gestured for Browning to step out of the room with him. Outside, he guided the grandmother down the hall and spoke quietly. "Can you tell me anything?"

Browning cleared her throat. "Emma said Dr. Davies was a 'pernicious pedophile who preyed on pubescent girls.'" She gestured air quotation marks. "The PA said she had excessive bruising, that he violated her . . ." Her voice broke; veined hands covered her face. Snow waited until she regained her composure. "But we won't know more until the rape kit comes back from the lab. Her wrists and ankles are chafed from restraints. They clipped her fingernails. I don't know what they might find. She's lost five pounds, but surely the bastard fed her. She said he unscrewed the bulbs and hid them when he left. Screwed them back in when he had the webcam on her." She shrugged helplessly.

"I love Emma, but I'm not equipped to deal with this trauma. Should I send her for counseling? Return her to school or keep her home? Draw her out or wait until she volunteers information? She's always been quiet, but this . . ." She gestured toward Emma. "And she never got along with her mother; Margie could be harsh. She spanked the child, said that Emma was unruly, temperamental and high-strung—always in motion. Said she had ADHD, but I don't know if that's accurate. Oh, Jack's on his way. He's taking a few days off to be with her." She finger-combed her hair and shook her head.

"CPD needs to interview her for the record. She killed a man. I'll know more after I've talked with Mac, my detectives and the CSU. In the meantime, you can talk to Dr. Drummer." He handed her the shrink's business card —"He'll give you coping strategies. Emma might exhibit signs of PTSD—post-traumatic—"

"Yes sir, I know what that is. She's already afraid of the dark and doesn't really want to be left alone, so . . ." Browning stepped purposely forward. "Thanks." She pocketed the card, squared her shoulders and pushed open the door. "We'll contact you when she's ready."

Snow let her and the topic go for the moment. He stepped into the reception area to call Fields and the Musketeers for updates. Requested the lab to rush Emma's tests. Informed the Chief of his immediate plans to take his wife home when she woke. Punched CPD admin Sonja Hamilton's number to email him the reports ASAP.

"Oh, Agent Howard's arrived, sir. He wants to speak with you. He's waiting in your office." Sonja said. "Shall I send him to CRMC?"

Snow sighed. "Yes, but I'm taking Mac home when she's conscious."

"Shall I give him a copy of the files on Marjorie Hawthorne's case?"

"No, just Emma's. We're going to need his manpower to crack what may be a porn and drug ring. Might as well take advantage of FBI resources."

"Yes, sir. I'll send him over. Is Mac all right? I heard she was injured."

"Physically, she'll heal in a few weeks—luckily no life-threatening injuries. She's on medical leave until the doctor clears her." Snow ended the call. To himself, "This time, though I'd like to seal her in a pumpkin shell: the risk the woman takes! Doesn't always have to be the first through the door!" Anger simmered but he capped it temporarily. Taking a couple deep breaths, he marshaled his thoughts and facts before he met with Special Agent Lionel Howard.

13

Agent Howard and Isola Perez breezed through the double ER doors, scanned the lobby and arrowed straight back to Snow sitting near the vending machines. Howard, dressed in expensive sartorial splendor, took the orange seat beside the end table and lamp. Perez sauntered over to scan the machines, fed it some bills; it spit out two bottles of water. "Can I get you something to drink, Detective?" she asked.

"How about coffee?" he nodded at the complimentary beverage station with a Keurig, a rack of various coffee pods and condiments. "Any bold; one cream and sugar, please." Perez handed her boss a bottle, set hers on the table and padded to the coffee table, returning with a cardboard cup, complete with a protective sleeve and plastic lid.

"Thanks." Snow nodded and sipped. "Damn, that's hot!"

Once his agent was settled, Howard pushed back in his chair, crossed his right ankle over his left knee. "After notifying CASMIRC of the Amber Alert, we sent operatives out with the girl's photo to all fifty known pedophiles in the tri-county area." Howard said.

Perez acknowledged, "Unfortunately, the Child Abduction Serial Murder Investigative Resource Center kicked out no known killers in this area. Our source tells us CPD apprehended the kidnapper. Both Detective McCoy and Emma Hawthorne are hospitalized. The report mentions your homicide case, noting Kevin Lowe dropped Emma off at the Old Cemetery on Bedford and South. Correct so far?"

Snow answered, "What source? Yes. Our cases overlap."

"Well, bring us up to speed." Howard shook his head, unwilling to divulge the source and flicked a navy thread off of his suit while Perez thumbed on a digital recorder and laid in on the end table.

"Both Mac and Emma sustained injuries. When Mac wakes up, I'm taking her home. The teenager's awake but will only talk to Mac. You can try," Snow said to Perez, "but she refused to talk to me. Her grandmother said her granddaughter was 'violated.' My men and the crime scene techs aver that the teen killed Dr. Davies with a golf club after Mac tripped him up. We don't know why, well yes we do, but *why* after the fact. I'll send you the postmortem when it's completed.

"When Lowe regains consciousness, we need to interview him. He was out on bail—drug charges—when someone tried to make an attempted homicide look like an accident or DO. The arsonist may be the same perp who torched Margie Hawthorne, but drug and porno rings are involved. We found payments on the doctor's phone bills corresponding to his computer porn site. Once our IT guy traces the numbers, we'll have the patrons but not necessarily the ringleaders. Lowe may be a mule, user, seller—or all three." He paused to check his phone. "His court date is April 7, but his defense can probably get a continuance with special circumstances."

"What does Mac say?" asked Howard. "She's an eye witness."

"She hasn't said anything yet." Palm out to stop any speculation, Snow said, "And won't until tomorrow, so you'll need to stay, email or call. She's experienced enough traumas for one day. We both need to go home for a few hours." He downed the remainder of his coffee, tossed the cup in the trash.

"I'd like to talk to the girl," Perez pushed off the chair and stood.

"Good luck. The girl's furious, pugnacious and anxious. Startles easily—shows signs of PTSD. She'll need a shrink for some time." Snow responded. "I tried to bribe her with a milkshake—no dice."

Dressed casually in tan slacks and a chocolate brown sweater, Perez nodded and stepped authoritatively up to the receptionist area, then disappeared through the doors. Doors sighed open again; a nurse's aide appeared and said, "Your wife's awake but groggy. We'll bring her out in a wheelchair in a few minutes, if you wish to pull your vehicle to the entrance." She turned and padded quietly back.

Agent Howard pocketed the recorder. "Between you, me and the lightshade, I think you're right, but that girl will stand trial for murder. My agents are relocating Lowe as we speak. I'll call you if or when he wakes. I need to depose Detective McCoy, but it can wait until morning. Assuming she won't report to work, I'll stop by your place at ten a.m.? Meanwhile I can go to the CPD for the reports."

"That's fine. See you then." Snow shook Howard's proffered hand and exited the building to get the Explorer, consulting his watch as he walked. "Nine o'clock! Damn! We can't go on like this!"

* * *

At home, Mac eased onto a pillow to nurse Ian, his little face puffy from crying, hiccupping while nursing. "I'm sorry, baby; I had no idea I'd be gone so long. You had milk. What's a matter? Miss Mommy and Daddy? We've really screwed up your schedule. We'll try better." She rocked gently as not to jar her tailbone, which smarted with every sudden move. Periodically, she sipped soup that Erica had left in the Crockpot. Erin suspected Chris was perturbed and planning the best way to broach the topic while he loaded the dishwasher and tidied up.

On her knees, Erin bathed her auburn-haired boy, strapped in his bath seat in their bathtub filled with the three inches of warm water. He patted the bubbles, cooed then grabbed and bit the rubber ducky, dropping it to grasp another with singular concentration as it floated past.

"Here, need help?" She handed him a plastic octopus—which he threw down, reaching for the seahorse instead. "Oh, independent, are we? I'd like a picture of that scowl, little man. It reminds me of someone else I know." She rinsed his hair and his glowing, glistening body while he grunted in displeasure. "Up we go!" Wincing at her coccyx's twinge, Erin laid him on his hooded towel, wrapped him in it and patted him dry. "Time for pj's, little bug." She wrestled on his sleeper. "Now, you're clean and dry!" He disappeared, giggling, as Chris whisked him up and away to spend some time with him, despite the late hour.

Erin readied for bed, cleansing her face, sliding into knit pj's and eased onto her side. Water and Oxycontin sat on the bed stand, which she gulped down to dull the pain in her butt. Running water provided a soothing backdrop, so she fell asleep before Chris came to bed.

Next morning, pain woke her. Habit dragged her into the shower; she wrestled shampoo through her stubborn curls. Danelle, her best friend, had partially straightened, lightened and trimmed her unruly locks when Ian was born. Gingerly, she patted a towel over her sore body, stepped out of the shower to face her husband, naked, arms extended to the doorframe like the Vitruvius man.

She stepped across to meet him, swimming in those big, bourbon eyes. He knew her well. Her fingers feathered along his torso.

"What are you doing?" he asked while she continued her ministrations. Her hands roved over the taut skin.

"Getting a reaction." She smiled.

He eased his knee between her legs, put one of her hands against each doorframe, covered them with his and bent to kiss her gently, tenderly. "Push against the frame. I'm going to part the red sea with my staff," and proceeded to show her.

"Just don't touch my bu—" she started. He shut her up with a kiss and continued his work, driving her insensate with wave upon wave of pleasure until the last thrust jolted her coccyx; pain needled. She gasped and tried to back away but he held her hands a minute more.

"Wow, and here I was expecting something else," she said as she eased quietly into the bedroom to dress. He caressed her affectionately and headed for the kitchen, since he'd already dressed. For breakfast, he fixed egg-white omelets with cheese and toast lathered with fruit spread. Chris doctored their coffees, topped them with a spot of whipped cream and sat across from her.

"All right. I'll bite. Why do you have to be the first through the door? Why take those risks when Ian depends on you for his very sustenance? Every case winds up with you injured and hospitalized." Stormy eyes accused her.

"Rivers and Shadow were first in!" She tossed her fork on the table. "Summers, too! Of all people, you should know risk is part of our job. The basement door was locked; I tried to force it. I suspected Emma's life was in danger because I heard her whimpering. And I was armed."

"So you took a header down the stairs. Where was everyone else?" he demanded.

"Clearing the house." Her cell pinged—a TM. Chris pushed it out of her reach. "Hot dogging can get you killed, Erin. As your immediate supervisor, I'd sideline you but can't because Emma will talk only to you. We need her to tell us what happened. She's the key to the entire case, but I won't let you endanger your life to solve it!"

"You're being unreasonable. Would you talk to Savage or Fields—or any man on the force—like this?" she gritted her teeth. "No, you'd commend him for a job well done." Her chin jutted out defiantly.

"For what, letting the victim kill her assailant? And I'm not married to the guys on the force!" Too late, he realized he was shouting. Startled, Ian wailed from the other room, and Shadow growled a warning.

"You sexist pig! See what yelling accomplishes? That's dirty pool, pulling rank now!" Mac rose, but Chris strode across the room.

"You do this on every case. I'll change him," he offered.

Seething at the double standard, Mac breathed deeply as she picked up her coffee, grabbed a throw pillow on the way to the rocker, threw it on the seat and eased down, unbuttoning her cardigan to nurse the baby. Chris laid Ian gently into the crook of her left arm.

"Need another pillow?" he asked curtly, as he folded the pack and playpen to take up to his parents' house.

"No thank you." She refused to look up.

Chris packed his lunch, picked up his cell and called the Chief. "Mac won't be in today. She was injured yesterday in the line of duty."

"I saw the news. How is she?" Chief March asked, concerned.

"She has stitches in her head, a broken pinky and a pain in the ass. The ER PA assistant recommended a week's medical leave, two before she returns to duty." He listened to March's laughter while Erin shot him her middle finger.

"Tell her to take it easy for a few, but she'll need to talk with Emma Hawthorne soon. Briefing at nine. You can head the press conference at ten. I have someone on the other line." He disconnected.

"Good day, dear. Have to go to work and handle the press. I'll get the Musketeers to brief me on yesterday's adventures. By the way, Howard and Perez are coming to depose you at ten." He peered out the door. "I'll call Mother and tell her to pick up Ian then." He breezed out the door whistling a happy tune from *The King and I* as though venting had restored his equilibrium.

14

Mac emailed her report of the police incident to HQ.
Precisely at ten, Agents Howard and Perez rang the
doorbell. Howard, ever debonair, bowed slightly, brought
her proffered hand to his lips and kissed her knuckles.
His left arm swung into view; he offered her a snack
basket, a container of daffodils nestled in the center.

"Why, Agent Howard, how kind! Thank you very
much." Erin noted the box of Krispy Kremes, organic
granola bars, teething biscuits and two dog biscuits in
cello, among other things. Draped over the flowers, a wire
snaked to a dainty silver daisy pin—a lapel camera. While
Perez set up the tripod, Mac eased over, collected her
iPhone while getting three mugs of coffee. TM message—
need intrvw. EM. Plse call.

"How is the little lad?" he asked. "Teething, I assume?"

Mac smiled at his astuteness for a bachelor. "Yes, he
has four coming through." Once the preliminaries were
concluded, Mac settled and the video started; she
answered their questions, describing yesterday's incident
succinctly but volunteered nothing additional.

"What happened after you fell down the steps?"
Howard asked.

"Davies kicked my taser out of my hand, broke my
little finger. I tucked my head and rolled sideways,
scrambling under the open stairwell and tugged his
ankle. He tripped, fell down the last three steps and
landed on his knees; they cracked. He moaned."

"Then what did you see?" Howard prompted.

"Nothing. It was pitch dark. I heard three thumps."

"Three thumps?"

"A blunt object contacting with the body."

"How did you know he was a man?" asked Perez.

"I could smell Polo—and sweat and something else. Plus he was taller than I, wearing men's loafers. It was Dr. Donald Davies."

"What was the something else?"

"Semen."

"How did you identify Davies?"

"Visually, once we had lights at the scene. We were looking for him and had just exited his domicile." She felt her phone vibrate. Howard nodded at her to take it while Perez switched off the camera and warmed their coffees. TM from Mahoney: *2nd domicile Davies' mother's. To Sarah Todd to interview her.* Mac sipped the coffee and frowned at its bitterness—no chocolate creamer. Set the mug aside, nodded for them to continue.

"Why did you enter the second dwelling?" Howard apparently watched the news or had inside information.

An FBI agent embedded in CPD? Mac wondered. "We found Emma Hawthorne's cell, battery removed, then Summers untangled Emma's hair ribbon from the hedge at the house behind the Davies' domicile."

"You knew the ribbon was the teenager's how?" he asked.

"Guessed. She wore one like it in her school photo. Summers bagged it as evidence. My guess—the teen was leaving us a trail."

"I presumed you knocked first and identified yourselves?"

"Yes, sir. We did, several times. No one answered," Mac answered.

"When you tumbled down the basement stairs, why were you alone?" Perez again.

"K-9 officer Shadow, Summers and Rivers were clearing the upstairs."

"Why did you fall?" Howard sounded as if he really wanted to know.

"The door was locked, so I heaved into it a second time; it flew open. Davies was standing behind the door, top step."

"Why didn't you use your weapon?" Perez inquired.

"I knew Emma was being held there but couldn't see, didn't want to shoot wild in the dark."

"So she killed her kidnapper?"

"I didn't see that. It was dark, as I said." Mac could envision this being played out in a courtroom.

"Was there anyone else in the basement?

"Not that I could see, sir."

He smiled at her formality, letting Perez conclude with the subsequent details. They thanked her for her time and cooperation.

"Thanks again for the gift basket," Mac said.

"My pleasure. To aid in your recuperation. Wear the flower pin on your next assignment. FYI, we have the witness Lowe under guard in an undisclosed location. I'm meeting with Snow next to track this pedophile ring. I've pulled in DEA as well. As soon as you've interviewed the Hawthorne girl, send me your report. I'll assume the kidnapping case is closed." He bowed slightly and left Perez to attend to the equipment. Within minutes, the black Escalante rolled out of sight.

After she called her mother-in-law to bring Ian home for his next feeding, Mac called the hospital, learned Emma had been discharged. She called Snow. "How did the briefing go?"

"Emma Hawthorne has been arrested and arraigned for the murder of the anesthesiologist, bail set. She's been released to her grandmother's care under house arrest until the trial. She's on the docket for April seventh, while Lowe's trial has been postponed," he informed her, matching her formal tone.

"No jury in America will convict her," Mac said.

"Maybe we can work out a plea deal. How are you feeling?"

"Other than my tailbone aching fire, fine."

"Want me to bring lunch home and watch Ian?"

"No thanks, I'll fix something. You work your case."

"Will you be able to talk with Emma soon?" he asked. "I'm at a standstill on her mother's homicide."

"Did you try to match the semen?" Mac wanted to know.

"Not yet. I've asked Chen to test Davies's. Thankfully, Kevin Lowe's tucked away for the time being; it's unlikely we can get a sample from him at this time."

"He's in this deep, withheld vital information when arrested. Has Huddleston pulled any more off of the doctor's computer?" Mac asked.

"Yeah, he's traced the numbers—one to the state police commissioner, several others to the state house, and the reenactor who plays John Andre. The Lancaster number's out of order. He's still working on it."

"I'll go to Browning's house this afternoon," Mac offered.

"Don't push yourself if you don't feel well enough. Officially, you took a sick day. It can wait until tomorrow. Tell you what; I'll bring supper home around six. What are you in the mood for?" He tried appeasement. She heard his office door open and a muffled voice.

"Surprise me. I'll let you go." She wasn't going to argue about his mixed messages. Instead, she called Elena Michaels. Their conversation was brief. "Please go through proper channels. We'll set something up informally when I know more."

"But you were there—an eyewitness; it's your collar. You nailed the bastard," the reporter insisted. "I want to give you the credit."

"Elena, I wish I could, but I need to work an angle right now."

"Come on, I've already talked to Fields, Summers and Rivers."

"Then you have the story. I need to go."

"I know the Hawthorne girl will only talk to you," Michaels said.

"Where do you get your information? You have an inside snitch?"

"Nah, I just know where to hang out for juice. OK, I'll ask your boss. Then I'll call you back tomorrow. How are your injuries?"

"I'll survive. Thanks for asking. See you soon. It's time for Ian's lunch." She snapped the cell shut and let Erica in, kissed her cheek and smooched her son. "Hey, baby, what did you do this morning?"

"Oh, we played. He's trying to crawl. He can scrunch up onto his hands and knees but hasn't coordinated the forward motion yet. Once he gets in gear, watch out. He'll be moving."

Erin parked herself gingerly in the rocker; Ian latched on while Erica warmed chili she'd brought and made grilled cheese sandwiches. They chatted about the baby, their husbands and Easter.

"I'm planning a leg of lamb with mint jelly. How's that?"

"Hmm?" Erin jostled Ian on her lap until he laughed and then blew gentle raspberries against his palm. "I've never tasted it, but go ahead."

"What? Why?" She rounded the island, poked her head into the living room, her hair bobbing toward her chin.

"I try not to eat anything with a cute face." She wrinkled her nose. "Sounds childish, I know, but don't change your plans on my account."

"What does your family fix on Easter Sunday?" Erica asked.

"Usually ham or turkey, maybe even a casserole. We're not so traditional for Easter as we are for Thanksgiving and Christmas."

"I'll take him, OK? Lunch is ready." Erica put Ian in his park and playpen with a few toys, patting his back.

"Work on crawling, baby." She laughed and straightened, returning to her lunch as the doorbell rang.

Erin hadn't sat down. "I'll get it." Glancing out the window, she saw a handsome chiseled face, hazel eyes, a sturdy neck—long dark hair clubbed back, and buckskin-clad shoulders. She threw open the door. "Stepfather . . . Jason! Please come in. I'm so glad to see you!"

From behind his back he produced a stuffed bear holding a bouquet of mixed carnations and rosebuds with baby's breath. One arm hugged her to him. He leaned over and kissed Erin's forehead. Looked up at Erica's pale stricken face, her hand to her throat. Jason smiled, eyes concerned, palm up, and said, "I come in peace!"

"Erica, this is my stepfather, Jason Lightfoot. Stepfather, my mother-in-law, Erica Snow." Erica smiled sheepishly at her initial reaction at seeing a Native American in the flesh and extended her hand in welcome. "And thank you for the bear bearing flowers. Is he for Ian?" Erin added.

He shook his head. "No, his gift is still in the truck. I wasn't sure if he'd be up. I'll get it soon."

Mac threaded her arm through his and drew him toward the table. "Sit down, have lunch with us and tell us what brings you to Carlisle."

"You do, daughter. A newspaper reporter said you'd been 'sidelined by injuries incurred in the line of duty.'" He crouched down, lifted Ian into his arms. "Remember me, Little Fox?" Ian smiled, revealing two upper and lower teeth. "Look at those teeth!" He tossed him gently in the air and took the end chair, bouncing him on one knee, one hand steadying the baby's head. "I'd love a bowl of chili, but please don't go to any extra trouble." He aimed his comment at Erica and turned to Erin. "Tell me about it."

So Erin gave him a laundered, condensed version of the previous day's events because her mother-in-law was present. He nodded, listening while turning Ian to face the table. The baby smacked his palms and licked his lips. Erin ripped off the cello, handed Ian a teething biscuit from the snack basket. The baby grasped it with both hands and gnawed while Erica served Jason soup and crackers as they discussed Erin's ordeal.

"You need to carry a knife as a last resort." He handed her a four-inch knife with a bone handle sheathed in leather. The grip had four indentations; it fit her hand exactly. "It was your mother's. She strapped it to her thigh. Wear it where you can grab it quickly. Surprise your assailant. Slash hard and fast. Next time, you'll be prepared. Practice. If you need my help, just ask." In his peripheral vision, he watched Erica back away.

"I will. Thanks." Erin hefted it, sliding it into the sheath, easing it out. Tying it to her thigh wouldn't work because she wore slacks. "Think I'll tie it around my calf: it'd be hidden in my boot as long as it's cold out."

"Practice until handling it is second nature. Once it's in your hand, use it. Don't hesitate. Here, let me show you. Here, buddy, down you go." He laid Ian in his pen. He stepped away from the table and demonstrated. "Once in hand, thrust up, underhanded. Don't waste time switching positions, either. I know you can't try now; you're sore. Keep it handy and practice whenever you can. If someone disarms you, you have a backup."

"Oh, thanks! How thoughtful! I'll practice," she promised. She hefted it, sheathed it, and pulled it out again. Slashed an imaginary foe.

"Keep working with it. You'll get the hang of it soon enough. Keep it on your person at all times. I'll get Little Fox his stuffed animal and be on my way."

15

After putting Ian down for his nap with his new stuffed raccoon, Erin walked Shadow, leaving the bungalow to Christopher Snow senior, who'd magically changed places with his wife. "Erica had errands to run."

"Really?" Erin asked her father-in-law. "Here I thought my stepfather shocked her."

"Really," he'd assured her, his blue eyes twinkling ironically.

Erin drove to the Browning place once more. She found Emma ensconced in her bed in blue lounging knits, a laptop on her knees, which she closed upon seeing Mac and laid it on the bed beside her.

Emma looked ethereal—had she sprouted wings, Mac wouldn't have blinked. Her hair had been razor cut to chin level; it kicked out at the ends, a more sophisticated look. Though not beautiful, that pale skin, teak hair and savvy lean look lent a maturity that belied her fifteen years. Her winter sky eyes drank in everything. Her bruises had faded some, the doctor's blood washed away, but the pout of discontent remained.

"Good afternoon, how are you feeling?" Mac asked. "You look really different with that neat haircut."

Emma regarded her obliquely. "Better than you, I expect." She half-shrugged while indicating the white ladder-back chair in the corner between her bed and the dormer window. "I feel used. What's the point, really? Abused, kidnapped and now under arrest for coming to your aid." She stuck out her leg so Mac could see her house arrest anklet.

Mac let the comment slide, took the throw pillow and eased down gingerly, taking out her recorder, mentally noting that the teen had said 'abused' first. "Now I'm here to listen, if you want to talk."

"Why should I? Your husband arrested me and marched me out of the ER. What's the matter—sore ass?"

"You could say that. Honestly? He didn't tell me that." Mac's eyebrows shot up. "Did the media catch it?"

"No, it was too damn early. What's the dif? I can't go to school, so Nana enrolled me in Cyber School." Emma circled her forefinger in the air, a 'big wup' signal.

"Well, you could've had teachers come from CHS to tutor you. Or send assignments back and forth online."

"And carry gossip back. No thanks." She crossed her arms petulantly, chin quivering.

"Seems Cyber School may be the best option for a student as bright as you—gives you more time for your art and in-depth studies. Study for classes, finish your on-line college courses and put a portfolio together of mixed media pieces for college entrance interviews."

"Oh, sure. I'll jump right on that: abuse, rape, porn traffic and murder make good art subjects," Emma tossed back.

"Hurt engenders creativity better than happiness. Some of the best literature comes from heartache; the author E.L. Doctorow claimed literature 'spreads the suffering.' Your paintings on the wall in the Art room prove that—two of them depict darkness. The third symbolizes life. You have a fine, mature talent," Mac asserted. "That's the second time you mentioned abuse. Were you abused as a child?"

A long minute stretched out. And then another, followed by the girl's sigh. Mac could almost hear Emma weighing arguments in her mind. She let the silence stretch. Finally, the teen sat up, crossed her legs beneath her. "How do I know I can trust you?"

Mac returned the shrug. "You mean because I'm a detective?" At the teen's nod, Mac continued. "I'm a woman, too, so I will be more sensitive to your predicament because I was raped in college and kept silent until I married because I was afraid of society's censure—blame the victim. Anyway, at this point, I'm you're only hope."

Emma nodded. "Well thank you, Princess Leia. Yes, my mother abused me as a child, claimed I was difficult, so I learned how to run and hide until Dad came home. She's old school—'spare the rod, spoil the child'—so she peeled hickory switches to whip me with. See these white scars?" She hiked up her pant leg. Indeed, fine white lines crisscrossed the back of her legs. "She'd say, 'These are my hugs and kisses.' I could never figure out what I did to piss her off. I'd sigh, and she'd smack the back of my head. Ask for anything—cookie or apple—not an iPhone or pad, she'd take a broom and sweep me out the door, even in the rain."

"Your father never intervened?"

"Well, he worked days, often had classes, seminars or graded student essays at night. My brother was born about the time the abuse started, and I get what postpartum blues are now, but at three? And she was smart enough to leave me alone when Dad was around, but I blame him some." She fiddled with her ankle restraint.

"Were you difficult?" Mac wanted to hear more.

"Don't you see why? Marjorie was a sadist. If I talked back, she sent me to bed without supper. She used yardsticks, spoons and a book once to discipline me. So, yes, I ran away. Joining the reenactors only made her worse—gave her an excuse for corporeal punishment. They took me to a doctor when I was five; he claimed I had ADHD, prescribed Ritalin. I'd run to the bathroom, spit it out. When school started at re-enactment sites and others took turns teaching, things got better for a while.

Dad taught American History. It came alive in his words—and actions—because he dressed the parts, showed us muskets—even brought a cannonball for us to see." She stopped to contemplate her blue toenails and picked at a hangnail, lost in reverie.

"Go on," Mac prompted.

"I like learning but hate stupidity. I got in fights, knocked a kid's tooth out once and threatened another with a knife. . . . What? I didn't actually use it on him. I shot a squirrel with my .22—things any boy might do without reprimand. Anyway, with other people around, Marjorie had to be more careful, more cunning. She'd snap the clothesline at my neck when we hung laundry outside. Threw a hornets' nest at me once—though that may have been an accident. Had me tend bees without wearing netting."

"Did you tell your grandmother?" Mac probed, seeking any adult who might have the child's best interests at heart.

"Nah. What's the point? She lives here; we live in Lancaster, spent months in Philly rehearsing—travelling as far as New Jersey for reenactments. 'Oh, look! A family affair,' people would comment. And 'What cute little kids,' all decked out in our drab Dickensian homespun. Not that I minded playacting at the time: whatever kept Marjorie away from me. At twelve, I started spending Augusts with Nana during her vacations. She took me to the library with her. So many books—so much to read. Plus, I participated in a college study. Researchers told Nana I had too much of some chemical in my brain that stimulated the 'flight or fight' syndrome, not enough serotonin."

"What did she do?"

"Do? Nothing drastic, just took me to swimming, art and karate lessons. We went to Massey's for frozen custard, the Hershey Park Zoo, Baltimore Aquarium, movie matinees, the bowling alley and skating rink. Down to the Yellow Breeches to go tubing. Taught me to knit. So the withdrawn, finicky, reckless and moody Emma transformed into a well-behaved child during August. It didn't occur to me until last year to ask to live with Nana, but Marjorie tried to ruin that too."

"By driving here to argue for you to return to the fold?"

"Not at first. Nana bought me a cell phone when I was twelve, so I could call her when I needed a ride from the pool, mall—or wherever. But I couldn't take it home because there's nothing modern in our house except running water. The washer and dryer are hidden in a closet behind knotty pine doors. Mother cooked on a Franklin or in the fireplace, so the food's 'authentic'," making air quotes. "We knit, crochet and sew by hand. Oh, yes, that's Marjorie's forte—she's—was—a seamstress."

"So I've heard." Mac noted Emma's quizzical glance. "We interviewed reenactors last week, and several mentioned your mother's valuable contribution to the regiment as Molly Pitcher, her talent for sewing."

"Yeah, well, that's her choice, her legacy, not mine. She told me to major in Early American History and eventually 'become' Molly Pitcher. I want to go to art school or college. You think I still have a chance?" She sat up and smiled as June Browning appeared in her doorway with a tray of chocolate milk and cookies—and a mug of coffee. Her nana smiled, tiptoed quietly back out of the room and eased the door shut.

Emma handed Mac the mug and picked up the glass and a cookie. "Have one." She offered Mac a chocolate chip cookie.

"Thanks. May I have a bit of your milk?" Mac asked.

Emma tipped some in, smiling at the request. "Nana's special: she doesn't crowd or interrogate me but actually listens when I talk!"

"You were asking me about college. Concentrate on working toward that goal. I think any jury will empathize with you. Now, can you tell me anything about the night you were kidnapped?"

"Kevin drove me to the Old Carlisle Cemetery around dusk. I told him to go when I saw my mother's car. I thought she'd take me to Nana's. But we argued; she slapped my face, and for the first time in my life, I slapped back. She purpled with rage and came after me with a fork. All of a sudden, Kevin and Dr. Davies appeared, told her to back off or they'd call the police. She started in on them. They tied her up. Doc told Kevin to go, and he took me to this creepy abandoned home." She stopped to finish her cookie and milk. "I don't know where Gray got to."

"Davies just showed up to rescue you? Just happened to have rope?" Mac's voice tinged with incredulity. "I thought he was wheelchair bound."

"You and a lot of others. He has MS, which is why he had to drop out of reenacting but he can walk."

"He was with your parents' regiment?"

Emma flipped her fingers. "Other way around. Davies was the regiment's doctor. He administered medicinal supplies, stitched people up, that sort of thing. Played the quartermaster. Maybe he carried rope in his trunk. Who knows? I thought he was creepy, always singling me out for lollipops, magic markers, journals and sketchpads. Told my mother art would be a good outlet for me."

"Again, didn't your dad notice this preferential treatment?" Mac asked, shifting uneasily on her pillow, her tailbone aching. She wanted a break but dared not interrupt this interview.

"Not at first because the Doc brought other kids goodies, too."

"Were Mrs. Davies and the girls a part of this group?" asked Mac.

Emma shook her head. "No. When I met Gwen I asked about that. Her mother's a nurse with two girls involved in swimming, tennis lessons at the country club, and ballet—the kinds of things doctors' kids do. Wouldn't take them out of school. Her sister's in college now."

"What happened while you were incarcerated in that basement?" Mac let the slippery details of the homicide at the cemetery slide for a bit.

"Entombed you mean? Asshole took the light bulbs with him, cuffed me to the bed when he wasn't there. Oh, you mean when he *was* there? You want to hear all the sordid little details?"

Mac did not answer, just tilted her head, listening and observing intently, letting her silence suggest consent.

But Emma's demeanor changed, her face becoming a mask of indifference, her body stiffening. "I don't want to talk about it. I want a lawyer. I know about the Fifth Amendment." Her lips clammed shut.

Mac shut off the recorder and stood up, actually relieved to be finished, satisfied with the information she'd gleaned. "I understand. Just realize that every sordid detail will emerge during a trial. The media will scatter it across the nation because this case begs attention: kidnapping, murder, arson, and the victim killing the villain.

"Well, thanks for your time and cooperation. And the cookie. I'll certainly share your cooperation with my superiors." She treaded softly toward the door, waiting for a cue to stop or Emma to change her mind.

"And the tape. I suppose it's not confidential," Emma said.

"No, Emma, it's CPD property, but I won't share it with everyone."

"Just the police?" the girl asked.

"Well, the Assistant District Attorney and any psychologist the prosecutor and defense engage for the trial will request it as part of discovery—unless you're willing to plea bargain."

Emma's headshake sent Mac out the door. After stopping to confer with Mrs. Browning and thank her for the treats, she left. Since this was officially a 'sick day,' she went home to soak her sore butt.

16

By the time Snow returned home, Mac had soaked her
bum, iced and changed the bandage on her broken pinky
and typed her report on Emma's interview. On the carpet,
Ian commando-crawled a few inches toward the toys and
rattles anchoring the corners of a large throw. She tapped
send, emailed her report. Shut down the computer.

"Hey, are we eating tonight?" Chris's voice tunneled up
the stairwell like a megaphone, as he bounded up to the
bonus room.

Mac kneeled, scooped Ian into her arms, debating
whether to lift him while he struggled mightily, grunting.
"Phew, Stinky!" she said.

"I'll get him," Chris picked him up, parked him on his
hip, the wet diaper leaking onto his shirttail. He lifted
Mac up with his other arm. He tried to refrain, but a
smile sneaked out. "Still sore? Did the doctor tell you how
long—"

"Two weeks," she answered tersely. "Ah, your shirt's
wet."

His eyes roved over her desk where her recorder sat.
"May I listen to your interview?"

"Yes, but I thought you were hungry."

"Did you eat supper?" Chris asked.

"No, I hadn't noticed the time." She took the stairs
gingerly—one step at a time—to avoid jarring.

"I said I'd bring it home, remember? How did you get
Ian up here?"

"Your dad."

"My dad?"

"He came down after Jason Lightfoot startled Erica—and then she was too embarrassed to stay after she yelped at seeing a Native American in the flesh." She flashed a genuine smile. "And he held up one palm and said, 'I come in peace!'"

Chris nodded, changed Ian's diaper while Erin rummaged in the fridge for something to eat. Then she smelled potpie simmering on the back burner. *Bless you; you brought dinner.* A plastic container of salad sat on the island. Suddenly feeling the tightness in her breasts reminded her; she washed and waited in the rocker until Chris delivered Ian.

"Do you want hot rolls?" Chris asked from the kitchen.

"No thanks, not with the potatoes and potpie noodles."

Once the table was set, Chris joined Erin in the living room. "How did the interview go?"

Erin smiled. "She changed her mind at first, didn't want to talk because you 'perp walked' her out of the ER. But we talked over an hour. She had plenty to say about her mother that might be instructive."

"Tell me."

"She called her mother a sadist; if half of her story is true, Marjorie should have been arrested for child abuse. But more to the point, she described her version of her mother's homicide."

"You don't believe her?"

Erin gave Ian to Chris to burp so she could readjust her position and the nursing bra, shift her weight. "It's not what she said, but what she left unsaid. Anyway, at that point, she asked for a lawyer."

Chris's eyebrow lifted. "Really?" He passed the baby back to her.

"Cited the Fifth. Had she not been kidnapped. . . . Never mind. Just listen to the interview, see what you think. How was your day? You look frazzled. Though, come to think of it, the first thing you do when you get home is undress." She smiled.

"For your benefit, love. Now, let's eat. Did Jason bring the raccoon?" He parked Ian in his seat and sat him at the table. Ian kicked and grunted until Chris handed him a cracker. Ladled the potpie into shallow bowls.

"Uh huh. Isn't it dear?" Erin divided the salad, poured raspberry vinaigrette over hers. "Thanks for bringing dinner. Yum, it smells homemade." Scooping up a spoonful, gently blowing the steam, she swallowed. "Wonderful but very hot." She tempered the heat with a mouthful of cold salad. "Rough day?" Weariness was etched in his eyes.

"Jack Hawthorne barged into my office unannounced and demanded to know why I was 'railroading' his daughter to prison, ruining her life. Claimed she was only defending herself, though he wasn't there. Still, the mild-mannered, bespectacled Professor exploded. I couldn't get a word in. Finally, Stuart steered him out of my office and took him to the break room to mollify him with coffee and donuts. Out front, a press conference ensued about Emma's condition, her arrest, and your condition. I pulled Summers and Mahoney out to help.

"Then Hawthorne stormed out and lectured the media for sensationalizing the story—mind you—while simultaneously pleading for his daughter's privacy until the issue is settled. Seemed totally unaware of the irony. I imagine it made the six o'clock news."

Mac shrugged. "How did you expect him to react? Shake your hand?"

He threw her a quelling glance—a flicker of defiance in those deep amber eyes. "I'm doing my job. Anyway, he wasn't finished. He demanded to know why she hadn't been released into his custody, so that took another hour to explain. I'll be glad to be done with the Hawthornes." He served himself another bowl and raised his eyebrows toward her.

"No thanks. I'm full. Bring anything home for dessert?" Erin asked.

In answer, he opened the fridge and pulled out two round fat apple dumplings shiny with a cinnamon glaze. He tore off the cello and zapped them in the microwave, squirting a generous dollop of whipped cream on top.

"Your mother's?" she asked. She pushed herself up to make coffee.

"None of hers left. These are from Fiddler's—at the Mayapple Golf Course. They're pretty good. And I'm sorry about arguing this morning. You worry me—taking off on your own. I just want you safe, don't you see that?" He sat beside her.

"Yummy." She set the mugs down and spooned in the apple goodness.

17

Next morning, he whispered, "Go back to sleep" when
Erin's eye opened to check the clock. "I'm taking the
entire squad to arrest the phone porn peepers—say that
ten times without tripping over your tongue—on Dr.
Davies's computer."

"Witty alliteration!" she rejoined. "So early, too."

"You're staying home?" Grinning, he stepped into
brown slacks, stretched on the sweater he'd worn the
night Erin 'claimed' him, grabbed socks from his bureau
and boots from his closet.

"The Musketeers, Shadow and I closed the case." She
shut her eyes, pulling her cold right hand under the
covers. "I'll get up when Ian wakes."

Chris bent over to kiss her. "Wish me luck."

"Good luck. Wear your vest." After snagging a sport
coat, he dashed out and halted at the gate. "OK, girl, I'll
let you out while I make a to-go mug." The dog darted out
and scrambled in quickly from the cold and sat in front of
her dishes. "Coming right up." He added a scoop of dog
food and ran water from the laundry tub tap. "Here ya go,
girl." He ruffled her coat, hustled to the kitchen to chug
caffeine and left via the mudroom.

Erin hauled out when the baby started fussing,
frustrated that his milk wasn't forthcoming. "You smell
like a latrine, baby." He'd leaked through double diapers,
plastic pants, and sleeper onto the sheets, soaked
through to the mattress pad. "Ah, Daddy didn't change
you this morning." Wetting a cloth in warm water dabbed
with baby wash, she swiftly stripped, washed and
changed him. By the time he was wearing clean, dry

clothes, he was wailing. With him in her arms, she eased into the chair. The second Ian found his milk source, he sucked greedily. "Don't choke yourself, baby." She stroked his cheek after tucking a bib under his chin. She leaned back and shut her eyes, using the time to ease into the waking world's demands.

"Music of the Night" unfurled from her iPhone; she let it go to voicemail. Next the landline pealed. Ignored it. Burped Ian, settled him on the other side. She glanced at the red digital numerals: eight thirty. When he finished, she parked the baby on her hip; Erin stripped the crib and threw it all into the wash. By the time she put him in the playpen, the phone trilled again.

"Hello." Popped up the top of the coffeemaker, dropped in a K-cup, waited for the blue blinking light. On autopilot, she pushed the button.

"Oh, Erin, you're up. I called to say I can't keep Ian this week because I have to go help Dreena; Kyle fell from a rock-climbing wall and broke his wrists, hit his head. He's in Boston General." Erica said, breathless from packing. She paused, took a breath. "Jeff called. I need to taxi Kayla around. Sorry this is such short notice, but Christopher's taking me to Amtrak in Middletown in an hour. I'm packing. Should I call Chris? Or your dad? A friend to help you?"

"Sorry to hear about Kyle's accident. Please don't worry. It's fine. No need to call anyone. I'm off sick today. I'll manage. Just go. Enjoy the time with Kayla."

"Oh, dear, I knew you'd understand. Sorry to abandon you. I'll call in a few days when I know more. Bye." The phone clicked.

On voicemail, CPD secretary Paula Flood's reported: "Public disturbance at the Browning residence on Lindsay Rd. Savage and Officer Castle requesting your assistance." Mac blinked, downed her coffee, scrubbed her face, dressed, hauled Ian up, and stuffed him in his coat and mittens. Shouldered her holster and pistol, pocketed her taser. Grabbed Shadow's leash. Dashed to the car. Secured baby and dog. Speed dialed her Dad on the way. "I need you to come to Lindsay Road—third house on the right, off Holly Pike across from Marsh Drive, a car lot on the opposite corner. I've been called to the scene." Clipped her badge to her belt.

"Be there in half an hour," Ethan responded. "I'll find you." No questions asked—that brought tears to Erin's eyes. She checked the rear view mirror: Ian's wide blue eyes mesmerized by the activity. A convoy of media vans topped with satellite saucers lined the curb: ABC, CBS, NBC, CNN and Fox. At the Browning drive, Mac honked to part the reporters and curiosity seekers. Savage and Castle were motioning people back, cordoning off the yard. She put Ian's carrier on her back, pulling his hood up, slowly lifting and turning him. Let Shadow out, who growled menacingly at the congregation. Grumbled murmurs met her ears. Speaking to no one, she popped her trunk and grabbed her mini bullhorn. Elbows out, she plowed through, people giving way.

Out of her peripheral vision, she caught Elena Michaels, her voice calling Mac. She recognized Jane Lennon from Channel Eight and Nelson Somebody. Someone commented about the baby. On the front porch, facing the restless crowd, bullhorn up, Mac said, "Listen up, everyone. You're trespassing! Please move off of the private property to the sidewalk or street." Castle seemed comfortable with crowd control, but Savage was pale, sweating despite the cold. "Call for backup," she said in an aside.

Reporters shouted questions, but the police ignored them. Officer Castle called Dispatch for all available units. "They won't leave until you feed them something," he said quietly. Shadow patrolled the eight feet in front of them, her eyes scanning the crowd.

"You are disturbing the peace. If you persist, we shall have to arrest you. BACK UP!" She yelled. One of the reporters handed her a microphone, and then they complied with her demand. Ian kicked her ribs, fisted her hair but otherwise remained quiet.

"Will you answer our questions?" the CNN reporter asked—his breath puffed clouds in the frosty air. "We want to know how Emma Hawthorne feels after her ordeal."

"Angry," Mac answered. She let Shadow pace. Her presence and a throaty hum subdued the crowd.

"Will she come out and talk to reporters? Tell us what happened?"

"No, she's a minor."

"Will her grandmother talk to us?"

"I don't know." She turned to Savage, asking him to call—handing him her iPhone. In as stage whisper, "Under Browning." Then louder to the media. "We'll check."

"Why isn't the teen in her father's care? Was he denied custody?"

"She's currently living in Carlisle. CPD has no jurisdiction in Lancaster."

"Did you find a connection between her abduction and her mother's homicide?" Elena Michaels ventured.

Mac's eyes roved to hers. "We're pursuing that avenue but cannot comment on an on-going investigation."

"You apprehended the kidnapper. Can you ID him?" Someone called from the group.

"Dr. Donald Davies."

"Did you kill the doctor?" Another inquired.

"No." Mac steeled herself to refuse the next question.

"Can you tell us if Emma was harmed?" another voice emerged near the Fox truck.

"Yes."

"Can you give us specifics?"

"Not at this time."

"Did you sustain any injuries?" Again, Michaels probed.

"You can see for yourself. I have stitches, a broken finger," she held it up to the cameras, "And a cracked coccyx." That brought chuckles. She felt Savage lift Ian from his carrier and carry him inside when the door opened and June Browning emerged in a red corduroy coat, knit cap, and mittens. Mac handed her the mic. Several B&W's wheeled down the street. Doors slammed. Officers climbed out of vehicles.

"Please, no more questions. My granddaughter has been traumatized and needs time to heal. She's alive. For that we are thankful. Thank you for your concerns, but please respect our privacy. We will share our experience when we're ready. I also want to publicly acknowledge the valiant efforts of the Carlisle Police, especially Detective McCoy and the others. Now, excuse me." She returned the mic to Mac and retreated behind her front door.

"Detective McCoy, what happened to Kevin Lowe? Was he a part of this crime?"

"No comment."

"Is it true that Detective Snow is pursuing others in this case? Is the FBI involved?"

"Detective Snow's working a homicide; the FBI is assisting CPD. That's all. No more questions. Please honor Mrs. Browning's wishes and find news elsewhere. CPD will hold a press conference once we have more information. Thank you. Goodbye." She turned to collect Ian. "Shadow, sit. Stay. Guard." She said loudly enough for all to hear. Savage and Castle stood sentinel at either side of the door.

A twitch of the curtain caused Mac to glance up at the second-story window overlooking the drive. She caught a glimpse of Emma's black hair—a taller, darker shadow behind her, a hand on her shoulder. Wyatt or her dad?

As the media trucks lumbered away, a Chevy Bronco chugged to the curb; a bear of a man unfolded his six-three, 240 pounds from the driver's seat. He had a weathered face, sandy hair, wore casual khakis and a down vest over a Chamois shirt. He smiled when he saw his daughter, sauntered up and plucked Ian from his carrier, nodding to Castle and fist-bumped Savage. "Hey, man, how's it going?"

"It's going, sir, now that the dust has settled," Savage replied.

"Hey, lad, what're you doing out in this cold?" He bussed the baby's cheeks and Erin's. "Do you want to trade cars? I'll take the wee bairn home if you have to go to work." He held out his keys. "Later, Reese. Let's have dinner around six. Meet me at the bungalow."

Savage smiled for the first time. "Pleasure, sir."

"Thanks for coming, Dad." They traded keys. "Would you take Shadow, too? Shadow, up, in!" Secured her beside Ian's seat. "I need to call in, stop by to update the Chief. There's a bottle in the fridge, but I'll try to be home by four to feed him. He should nap. Oh, and his bedding's in the washer, clean sheets under the changing table. I'll explain when I get home."

Ethan buckled Ian in his car seat, opened the Accord's driver's door. "Got it covered sweetheart. You take your time. Will Chris be home in time to go out to dinner?"

"No, he took the rest of the squad to Philly to round people up, but you and Savage go ahead. I'll expect you have things to discuss he wouldn't want me to hear. Love you." She kissed his cheek, climbed into her dad's vehicle, adjusted the seat and mirrors and drove to HQ.

"In my office, McCoy," the Chief barked as she pushed through the front doors. "Didn't know you were appointed the CPD spokesperson. Did you clear that press event with PR?" He motioned her to sit in the visitor's chair as he swung around and settled in his own desk chair, chewing on a licorice stick.

"No, sir. Not my monkeys, not my circus. Dispatch sent me, so I did what I had to do to contain the scene and avoid a media stampede. I kept my answers short. Maybe they won't run it." Mac lowered her purse to the floor, easing into the chair gingerly. The dull ache near the tailbone quickened. "I didn't say anything that they can't verify elsewhere."

"Oh, they'll run it all right. And it just so happened you took your infant son along?"

"No choice, sir. My mother-in-law had an emergency, Snow's in Philly and my Dad had to drive from Gettysburg to get him."

"Get a backup sitter or a nanny. This is a volatile case. Any crazies in the group targeting you could have easily picked you or the baby off."

"Targeting me? They were at the Browning domicile to talk to Emma or her grandmother."

"And Marjorie Hawthorne's killer is still at large." He laced his fingers together, resting his chin on the bridge, elbows on his desk. "Go into every scene expecting trouble, and you won't be surprised or caught in the crosshairs. And sick day means just that. Next time, tell Dispatch to call the next officer in the rotation. How did your interview go with the girl?"

"I sent in my report." She saw his dark eyes flicker impatiently. "Well enough, sir, but she's angry that she's under house arrest, claims she killed her kidnapper to defend herself and come to my aid."

"She's lucky she's not in jail. Is that how the situation went down?"

"No, sir. I tripped him, would've restrained him because he was injured. I taped Emma's interview, plan to give it to Dr. Drummer for evaluation. I imagine defense will retain their own shrink as well."

"Did Emma Hawthorne at any time ask for a lawyer?"

"Yes, sir. That's when I terminated the interview."

"OK. I have a hunch she'll want a trial instead of plea bargain. Did you broach justifiable manslaughter with mitigating circumstances?"

"No, sir. Her trial date's set; I think she wants exoneration. Secretly, I think she enjoys the attention," Mac said.

"The jury and media will give it to her. Now go home while I try to get Snow on the horn to see if he'll be interrogating prisoners here later." He picked up the receiver. "Ring Detective Snow, Paula."

Mac scooted out before he lectured her again about not wearing her vest. At home, Ethan had put Ian in his crib for a nap, had hot coffee waiting and chocolate nut croissants plated. "Sit down, lass, and tell me about your Amber Alert case. I heard on the news that she's home with her grandmother. The police report listed her arrest in *The Sentinel.* So is it closed now?"

Erin savored the warm pastry: dark chocolate and almonds treating her taste buds, chased with hot mocha. "You know quite a bit, dad. Today the media camped on her grandmother's lawn to get the scoop. Dispatch called me to the scene because I'm the primary. Long story short, there will be a sensational trial because Emma thinks she can beat the rap. I can't say much more, so no, the case is not closed. Chris is mopping up—arresting the men who paid to see the kidnapper's videos. So two pluses: Emma's alive, and the porn ring's stopped." The caffeine kicked in. "But the Chief told me to get a backup babysitter." She frowned at that. "Erica had to go to Jeff's to help with Kayla while Kyle's in the hospital." She described her nephew's accident.

"Say no more. You've found him." He smiled nearly ear to ear.

"You're working." Erin protested.

"Well, I took the rest of the week off. Jake's a partner now and offered to buy the place. I told you he wants to expand. He's young, ambitious and industrious, so he can handle whatever comes up. I've been waiting for an excuse to get to know my grandson, so I can watch him this week for sure." His guileless blue eyes danced.

"You don't need an excuse to see Ian, Dad. But thanks. If you're sure." She patted his meaty hand splayed on the island. "That's great."

"'Course I'm sure. Who knows? Maybe I'll retire and your mother-in-law might lose her day job." He reached up to tug one of her curls. "Ian reminds me a bit of Liam at that age: both raring to go, to get into life. Good, happy little lads. I'm thrilled to be a part of his life, to watch him grow. Now you go ice your tush; I'll clean up the kitchen." He stood, stacked the dessert plates and set them in the sink. Then he eased Erin up from the chair.

She grabbed an ice pack and did exactly that, taking her cell along to call June Browning to see how she and Emma were faring. Then called the florist's to send a snack basket to Boston General for Kyle Snow. Followed with a warm sitz bath, she finally eased into knit pajamas, returned to the kitchen. Her dad had a pot of beef vegetable soup simmering in the Crockpot.

"Poor baby, you look battle-scarred, stitched and broken." Her eyes narrowed, ready to argue. "No, I'm not going to lecture you, but I'm not leaving you alone until Chris comes home."

"I'm fine, Dad. My Glock is locked and loaded, if I need it. You and Savage go out, have a good time." She sniffed the delectable aromas steaming from the pot. "This smells wonderful. Thanks. You've made enough for an army!"

"Yes, I invited Savage over. If you won't go out, we'll go upstairs and play pool or cards or just talk quietly. I'm concerned about him, looked like he was on the verge of a breakdown today. He needs a hobby, activity, something to focus his mind on here, now. It's hard to fight PTSD alone, Erin. Is he seeing the CPD shrink?"

Erin nodded. "It's a requirement of his continued employment. He's assigned desk and assist duties and can't return to the field or carry a weapon—until who knows when? I understand psychology, but I'm no expert. He hides his demons well, but he seems isolated, alienated and numb. He has that haunted, bruised look about his eyes. Because work's become a familiar routine, his episodes have lessened. But today's aberration made him hyper alert—the reason Dispatch called me.

"But if you don't mind, I'll eat now, then feed Ian and go to bed. Do you mind entertaining Savage alone? I know he would prefer it."

"Sure, you need your rest. But there's something you're not telling me. He seems fond of you, but you're no fan of his. I sense animosity or a strain between you two, which has to be awkward at work. Why?"

"Let's just say I find him forward, unpredictable, rude and crude. I feel he's competing with me for Chris's attention. And he resents me for marrying his best bud. At Ian's birth, he touched. . . . Oh, never mind, I'd really rather not talk about it."

"OK, but he's worth salvaging. I wish you'd try friendliness, for your husband's sake." Ethan ladled out a healthy portion of soup, sat it at Erin's place at the island while she climbed carefully onto the cushion. He slid garlic bread from the oven, poured iced tea for them both. "Unless you'd rather have coffee?" he asked.

She smiled. "Tea's fine. This is wonderful. Thanks, Dad. How was Ian?"

"Asleep when we reached the house, so I tucked him in bed and rummaged in the fridge and freezer for something to fix. What time do you expect Chris home? Shall we let dinner simmer?" Father and daughter spooned down the hearty soup and munched on bread.

"I really don't know, haven't heard from him all day." She said and sighed heavily. "Could be anywhere from nine to midnight. But I'm working from home tomorrow, so you needn't drive up. But Thursday, I have an appointment with the ADA, Emma and her lawyer at nine."

"Then I'll be here at eight-thirty. I'll put the rest in the fridge then. How about dessert?"

"You fixed dessert too?" she asked.

"Rocky road brownies—your favorite as a kid. Reese is bringing ice cream and hot fudge topping." Ethan reached around, pulling her up gently, kissing her forehead. She hugged him.

"Any word on your nephew's condition?" Ethan asked.

"No, but I assume Erica will be gone for a couple of weeks." Plodding toward the bedroom to check on the baby, she shook her head at dessert. "Tempting, dad, but I'll save that for breakfast. I'm full." At the doorway she turned. "And thanks for helping with Ian today and making dinner. Won't Janelle expect you home?"

"My pleasure. Nah, she has a double shift at the ER."

Since Ian was still sleeping, she crept softly into the shower to ready for bed after his eight p.m. feeding. The warm, pulsing water kneaded tension from her shoulders, but her head, broken pinky and cracked tailbone ached. After Ian had filled his little belly, she returned him to his cradle to rock his way to dreams while she took an Oxycontin.

18

Looking world-weary, Chris tossed the local newspapers onto the kitchen island; his day was plastered across the front page: CPD & FBI NET SIXTEEEN IN PORN RING! The slug above read: **Three Senators and a Police Commissioner Part of Dragnet!** The two-column lead:

> FBI and CPD fanned out at eight a.m. yesterday morning in the Tri-county area, arresting sixteen men in connection with the alleged porno ring led by suspected kidnapper Dr. Donald Davies of Carlisle. CPD Homicide Detectives rescued the Amber Alert victim, Emma Hawthorne, missing for a week. The teen remains under house arrest until her trial for her kidnapper's homicide.
>
> Senior Detective Christopher Snow and FBI Special Agent Lionel Howard, BSU, and their teams netted state Senators Alvin Arnold, Tony Dinato and Harold Pinto. They also arrested Police Commissioner Kermit Knight, plus other prominent citizens. The one still at large, according to an anonymous source, is reputedly a PA Supreme Court Justice.

While eating oats topped with dried apples and walnuts with cinnamon toast, Chris cocked his head to listen for Ian or Erin. He scanned the rest of the article but rushed to shave and shower after gulping down the bold French Roast.

Clean, dressed and propped awake with caffeine, he lifted his son and crooned to him while lofting him several times to hear the baby giggle and see his dimples. Drool dripped onto Chris's face; he wiped it away with the back of his hand and settled him in his playpen while Erin dressed casually.

"Are you going in today?" he asked, letting the dog out the French doors, then the sliding sunroom door. Still March, still freezing, so she skittered back in quickly and headed for the mudroom, gobbled her food in forty seconds then returned to plop in front of the crackling logs, mesmerized by the flickering flames.

"No. I'm staying home unless you need me. What time did you get in last night? Were Dad and Savage still here?" Erin popped a mudslide k-cup in the Keurig. Shadow wandered back to the kitchen, watching Ian attempting to crawl across his playpen while blowing saliva bubbles.

Chris made a second cup. "Uh-huh. Around ten. They were outside watching Shadow lope around the yard. I inhaled a bowl of soup, thanked them for lending a hand, said goodnight and came to bed. We probably should look into a back-up sitter. How you feeling, babe? Your color's a little better this morning, but your stitches look angry."

"Oh, it's lavender or willow days for me. I took an Oxi. Yesterday was a zoo—I was dispatched to an impromptu media blitz at the Browning domicile then had to justify my actions to the Chief." She cut a square of brownie, nuked it, topped it with vanilla ice cream and hot fudge, and then sat down to indulge. Her eyes roved the newspaper headlines. "I can read about your day."

"Lavender or willow days?" Chris raised his eyebrows and rubbed his knuckles across his chin to smother a grin but said nothing about his wife's breakfast. He scraped the rest of the oats into a plastic container for the next day. Tucked his pistol in the paddle holster at the small of his back. Crossed over to his wife, turned her head toward his and kissed her lips.

"Sleepy and weepy."

"Take it easy today, then. I'll call you between interrogations and arraignments."

"Sixteen? I'll be lucky to see you next week."

"After we're done, Howard's taking the lot to federal court. He can have all the paperwork, thank you. I need to get back to Philly and find Marjorie Hawthorne's murderer and John Andre. Bye, Ian. Be good for mommy. See you tonight."

Slowly, Erin rinsed and loaded the breakfast dishes. Next she bundled the baby into his stroller and walked Shadow. Even though the last week of March was blustery and chilly, the flowering pear and lilacs sprouted greenery, and brave daffodils and hyacinths speared the air. Shadow lugged on the leash in an effort to reach the pipe, her first training apparatus. "No, girl, not with the baby. Heel!" Then the dog turned to gnaw on the stroller wheels. By the time they returned to the bungalow, she was exhausted. "Shadow, bed. Stay." Closed the gate to the mudroom. Put Ian in his pen, pulled it to the gate so baby and dog could keep each other company and started the laundry.

The landline rang. On the fourth ring, she snatched it from the base in the kitchen before it went to voicemail. "Hello. Snows' residence."

"Erin, how are you doing? Christopher just phoned about your injuries. You should've called. Do you need me to come home?" Erica asked with concern. "Are you in pain?"

"No, stay with Dreena. My tailbone aches, but I hardly notice the broken finger. Dad's watching Ian this week, but since I was called out on my sick day yesterday, I'm taking it today. But thanks for calling. How's Kyle? Is he home yet?"

"Oh, yes. He's mending, taking advantage of his days off school. We're reading *The Lion, the Witch and the Wardrobe.* Maybe he can return to school Monday. Excuse me a sec." She turned her head away and asked, "What? Oh, Kyle thanks you for the snacks. Now that he's home, Dreena picks Kayla up from school and runs her to ballet, swimming lessons and youth choir. How's Ian?"

"Fine. He's playing with the dog at the moment. But we went for a walk, and he's ready for a nap. Thanks again for calling." Erin feathered her fingers through her son's waves. He was grabbing at Shadow's fur, though little fingers couldn't quite reach. "Say hello to Nana, Ian." He made some strange gurgling sounds while Shadow whined for attention.

"Well, I'll let you go. If you're sure you're OK . . ."

"Yes, I'll mend, and Dad's coming tomorrow. Chris watches Ian when he gets home, too. Don't worry, we're good." She assured her mother-in-law.

"Well, bye. Hugs and kisses," Erica said.

"Say 'Hi' to everyone. Goodbye." Mac ended the call, set the receiver in its cradle and then laid Ian in his. She'd bathe him after his noon feeding. "But its tough juggling all the balls." She sighed and returned to her chores. Checked her email, deleted spam and answered the rest. One from Sonja popped into her in-box about another disturbance at the Browning residence: *FYI: Dispatch sent Mahoney to arrest Gwen Davies for trespassing, disturbing the peace and making terroristic threats. Media's at scene—will be on news. She's in lock-up. Should Dr. Drummer see her? It's your call, as primary.*

So Mac's fingers typed, giving permission, *with video on.*

The action unfolded on the noon news, Gwen screaming, "Let me in! You killed my dad and my boyfriend. You've ruined by life! And I befriended you, you crazy little freak. I'll throttle you! Make you a pariah at school. No one will ever speak to you again!" She hammered the door until Mahoney and Summers arrived. Parked their cycles. Removed their helmets. Shannon's hair anchored down, Gabe's fashionably mussed. Still new to the force, their arrival turned heads. The two tried to calm Davies. She resisted, turning on them, arms pin wheeling wildly. "Why isn't that juvenile in jail? She killed my dad! Arrest her!" So they restrained, arrested and removed Davies from the scene with "No comment" to the press. No one came to the front door, so the media dispersed.

Mac stayed home. Davies could cool her heels; overnight in lock-up might alter her attitude, though she felt for the grieving teen.

Her cell sang. "Detective McCoy." She folded laundry as she listened.

"June Browning. Do you know when this media scrutiny and attacks on my granddaughter will stop? I just filed a restraining order against Gwen Davies. I'm thinking of sending Emma home to her Dad. He wants her removed from this 'poisoned milieu.'"

"No can do. She has to remain at her current address until her trial, since she insists on one. If she plea-bargains, perhaps we could get the courts to adjudicate quickly, but a judge would likely remand her to a juvenile detention center. She did kill someone, Mrs. Browning."

"She was saving your life!" Browning countered. "Emma's a victim. Who knows what that monster did to her and perhaps to others? She's certainly not talking. The media camp at our door daily. Now Gwen's venom is splashed all over the TV. What do you suggest?

"On top of that, I had a pipe freeze last night—had to send Emma to the crawl space to insulate it! I'm at my wit's end," June lamented.

"And I share your concern. We just have to wait for the trial. You're doing the sensible thing by ignoring the media. Whatever you do, don't lose your temper or that too will be broadcast. Keep Emma out of sight. A photographer might've caught her at the window last week. Unfortunately, she's become a celebrity. She has to lay low, and your comings and goings must be discrete. Use the back door, go early or late; try not to leave Emma alone for long. Certainly, her family can visit." The silence spooled across the airwaves, but Mac let it lengthen while she washed another load and then tiptoed to the bedroom to check on Ian. She didn't mention seeing Wyatt.

Finally, Browning sighed. "All right. Thanks for listening. Will you talk to Emma? She needs some reassurance."

"Sure, put her on." Mac let Shadow out, walking out with her.

"Hello?" A small, timid voice whispered. "What am I supposed to do for the next two weeks?"

"Hi, Emma. I'd suggest you keep busy with homework, paint, sketch, and read. I'll repeat, start an art portfolio for college. We can talk this through, but ADA Lawson would need to be part of that, to discuss your options. A trial will be sensational because people are interested in your plight, which will keep you in the limelight."

"You mean voyeuristic; they're not interested in me personally."

"I can't deny that. You know, another opinion would be helpful. Call CPD psychologist Dr. Drummer; talk to him. The court will order a psych evaluation anyway. He's very nice, a good listener and will explain what to expect in court. And you may speak to your attorney any time." Mac avoided subjective commentary of her own, withholding the fact that criminal behavior has consequences, even for crime victims. "It helps to stay busy. Go online and look at colleges you're interested in. It's too early to apply, but you can write sample essays, study the forms and get a handle on the process. Complete your online college course and high school graduation requirements. But stay off of social media sites. Don't give anyone ammunition which can be used against you. Try to stay positive. Your trial starts in two weeks and should last another two. Your family may visit, but Wyatt shouldn't. By May first, this will all be over."

"But I can't live here anymore." Emma stated. "You heard what Gwen said."

"Yes, well, she's hurting too. Her father's funeral is Friday. Kevin's memorial is next week." Mac didn't mention Emma's mother's funeral was also slated for

Friday, since the teen couldn't leave her grandmother's house. *Surely Mrs. Browning would attend her daughter's funeral. Would she leave her granddaughter alone?*

"OK. I'll try. Thanks. I don't want to talk to men," Emma insisted.

"The court will take that under advisement. Would you rather have a female defense counselor? The court appointed Robert Orndorf, but you can retain another with whom you'll feel more comfortable."

"Yes, well. May I talk to a female psychologist?"

"Your attorney can suggest one, but ADA Lawson has asked Dr. Drummer to evaluate you for the prosecution. Call Denise Wilhelm, a criminal lawyer; she's in the yellow pages. If she has a full caseload, she'll recommend someone else. We have a plethora of lawyers in this area."

"OK. Thank you." The teenager ended the call.

Erin found cod in the freezer, transferred it to the fridge. She could wrap it in parchment with lemon, butter and herbs, so laid the paper on the counter. For lunch, she wrapped a slice of ham around provolone, ate while nursing the baby. Her cell rang, but she let it go to voicemail. "Waa! Waa!" He burped but refused to continue, so she walked him up and down the hall. Shadow came, sniffing his booties—concerned. Erin checked Ian's clothes and diaper, finding nothing amiss. He grabbed at her hair while she tried to redress him, kicking and fussing. "Fine! Let's go out." Bundled him up, trundled him into his stroller, leashed Shadow and hiked the trail through the woods. By the time they'd returned home, Ian was willing to finish lunch, which she augmented with stained bananas.

The dog pushed against her knee, wanting attention. "Really, after that long walk? You want to work, don't you, girl? But I can't leave Ian alone. So there you are. We'll train if Chris gets back before dark." To appease her, Erin gave her a dream bone. Checked her phone messages.

"Tick, tock, the mouse went up the steeple clock/The clock struck twelve; the mouse ran down/Looking in the churchyard town. /Hickory, dickory dock." Mac checked —blocked number, the voice disguised. Called Huddleston, asked for a trace on it, "but it's probably a burner." She frowned. *Mouse? Churchyard?* She mulled over the warning until a knock at the front door diverted her attention.

"Just wondering how you're doing and if you need any help." Chris's father stepped in. "I saw you walking Ian and the dog. I can watch one of them, if you like. Or both if you need some time alone." Dressed in jeans and a pullover, he looked relaxed. Shadow bounded in to greet and sniff. The Professor bent to ruffle her fur.

"Well, both together can be a handful. Thanks for the offer. Ian's finally asleep, but I can take Shadow through her obstacle course if you don't mind hanging out in case he wakes up. Would you like coffee or tea?

"I can fix it myself, but thanks." He powered up the Keurig.

"When's Erica coming home? She called yesterday to say Kyle is improving." Mac bundled up again.

"But he's probably falling behind in school work. She's coming home Monday, since Kyle's pediatrician cleared him for school. He was lucky; I hope he's done rock climbing for awhile—or his parents make him wear a harness and a helmet in the future." He held both palms up and followed her to the back door. "Kauffman came by, said to give you this. I put the other half in the hunter's blind and a surprise in a new place." He handed her a handkerchief that contained half a joint, shreds of marijuana spilling out. "Said he'll email you about K-9 training and remind you about Shadow's shots," digging a folded piece of paper from his pocket, he laid it on the island.

"Kyle will catch up, and it's nearly impossible to protect kids from accidents all the time. I certainly had my share growing up. Hey, just let me run the dog through her course a couple of times." She checked her watch.

"Take your time. I'm retired. If you allow me to use your laptop, I'll go online to look for new recipes. And shop for a new driver." He winked and made a swinging gesture. "I'll keep my ears alert for Ian." He sat on a stool in front of her closed MacBook.

"Be my guest. And thanks again." She bussed his cheek, pocketed her cell, and shoved out the back door with the contraband tucked in her pocket. Shadow nosed it and bounded toward the obstacle. For half an hour, Shadow crawled through the pipe, ran, threaded her way over the rock pile, scampered up the slide, slid down and leaped to the hunter's blind, stopped abruptly and sat. "Woof!"

"Good dog!" She tossed her a treat; the dog leaped forward and continued her course. In the scarecrow's straw nest, she found a hambone, lugging it out. Shadow looked at her handler, questioning and pawing it. Erin laughed. "Sure, you can have the bone," so the dog mouthed it, trotted jauntily back to the start line and flopped down to gnaw industriously.

"Hope it's not too salty. But let's go in. Home, Shadow." They both aimed for the back door as the light waned; dusk hovered ghostlike, and shadows stretched among the trees. Hitting a cold spot in the yard, Mac shivered, and hairs rose along Shadow's spine. Both heads swiveled side to side, expecting someone or something to spring, but they pushed through the back door safely.

She thanked her father-in-law for the breather. "And lord, you put the fish in parchment. I can smell it baking. You're so helpful; you'll spoil us. I'm so lucky the men in my life can cook!"

"And why not? You're family." Christopher Senior hugged her. "I was tempted to wake Ian, but I know he's on a schedule, so I refrained."

"Wait! I hear him fussing. Let me change him, and you can hold him until I wash up and get ready to feed him."

"Oh, let me change him. I'll have him ready in two shakes."

"He might've messed himself," Erin warned.

"Like I haven't wiped little asses before—even your husband's!"

He laughed heartily at the memory. "Why, once, he was plugged up for a couple of days, but when he finally let loose—"

Erin laughed and backed away, waving her hands. "Too much information!" She went to the mudroom to freshen up, tossed a load of laundry in the washer. By the time she settled in the rocker, Christopher Senior brought the baby out—powder fresh. "Just wet and hungry, I'll bet. You'll be OK? I'll be off then. Twenty more minutes on the timer."

"Thanks for watching Ian. It really helped. Won't you stay for supper?"

"No thanks. I have chili to reheat. But I found a recipe. Tomorrow I'm making Baked Pastitsio—a lighter version with ground turkey and a chicken broth roux instead of a béchamel sauce for the pasta layer. I'll bring you some so you won't have to cook. What time should I come down tomorrow?"

"Nine o'clock. Chris and I have a funeral to attend. Thanks again."

He nodded once, and then slid out the door quickly.

19

Friday postponed dawn; overcast skies threatened precipitation. The Snows dressed in black suits, Mac's silver daisy cam pinned to her lapel. Leaving Shadow and Ian with Chris's dad, they stopped by Lindsay to pick up June Browning, noting the cycle in the driveway.

"Officer Mahoney is staying with Emma, against my granddaughter's wishes." The woman wore a black pantsuit over a charcoal crewneck sweater and carried a patent leather purse. Taking the Turnpike to Lancaster, the couple updated Browning on the previous day's events.

"How's Emma doing?" asked Snow.

"Well enough, considering she feels trapped."

"Is she working on her studies and art?" Mac asked.

Browning's lips tipped up slightly. "She started an acrylic but won't let me see it until it's done. Cyber School in the mornings and painting during the afternoons. She studies but without any enthusiasm—has a hard time concentrating." Her grandmother shrugged.

"Has she talked to a psychologist?" Snow asked.

"Well, her attorney called Vicky Alwine, whose office is out near the hospital. They're emailing. The court must approve, and Mrs. Alwine has to agree to come to the house. I called Jack, and he'll pay her fee, so . . ." Her head turned toward the Explorer's window; rain peppered the car. "Why does it always rain on funeral days? And do you always go to the victims' funerals?"

The detectives nodded. "We follow every avenue we can to find criminals. Killers often appear at funerals; they want to observe and absorb the grief." Mac refrained from adding—'by gloating.' "Your daughter's killer may be among the crowd."

"But he'll recognize you as Carlisle police," Browning claimed.

"So we'll be unobtrusive—cover our shields." Mac handed Browning the sepia photo of the family that she'd taken from the bulletin board.

"The perp may even be disguised." Snow said. "But we always learn something that moves the case along. We'll stay in the background if you're worried."

"No, that's fine. My only worry now is Emma. Though I'll mourn for Margie, it's too late to worry about her. Such a strong-willed child, she was always so self-confident but rigid in her beliefs—she alone knew best. Never once did she seek my advice—about anything. Yet she gave everybody hers." She sighed, air expelling from her thin lips.

They arrived at the funeral home just as the music died, leaving their umbrellas in the vestibule. June Browning signed the resister, picked up a memorial bulletin and walked down the aisle alone, gazed at her daughter for the last time, slipping the family photo into the casket. She sat next to her son-in-law who nodded in greeting. Asher reached across his Dad to grasp his grandmother's hand briefly. Reenactors, including Winters, Ferris, Shultz, and others occupied a dozen chairs. Susan Davies and the Lowes had motored from Carlisle, and perhaps area friends and neighbors attended. Snow's eyes roved, searching for the man from the security cam, Samuel Gray, aka John Andre.

Different speakers extolled Margie's service as Molly Pitcher, her dedication to family and the regiment. Ferris, who portrayed Ben Franklin, said, "We shall miss her energy, enthusiasm, devotion and commitment to the cause. She wore many hats—reenactor, educator, seamstress, cook, and the Sixth Regiment's secretary. She was taken from us too soon, and I fear she cannot be replaced. We offer our profound condolences to her family for their loss." He took his seat as Hawthorne stood and turned to face the mourners to say a few words. Then a tall man with gray hair and a waxy face took the podium; the funeral director reviewed the exit process and rules for the funeral cortege, directing the family to pull their vehicle directly behind the hearse. June accompanied Jack and Asher.

At the burial site, people crowded under the canopy. A reverend stepped in front and read the Biblical passage about Christ being the way, the truth and the light. "He who believeth in me . . . shall never die." The spray of lilies and ozone split the air; raindrops dotted flowers and the shiny bronze casket, which was finally lowered into the ground. "'Know thy birth, for dust thou art, and shalt to dust return,'" intoned the minister.

Under her umbrella, Mac shivered, stepped aside to let mourners toss earth or flowers into the grave. She managed to capture several unfamiliar faces with her pin camera, including one who looked Amish by his dress and beard. She faced front as the undertaker spoke. "Jack and Asher invite you all to their house for the wake."

The service completed, individuals stopped to speak to the family and then dispersed to their vehicles. June approached Mac and Snow. "Will you come to the house to eat?"

"You'll need a ride home?" Snow asked.

Browning nodded. "I don't want to leave Emma for long. But we can manage one more hour, can't we? I'll ride with Jack."

"Of course," Snow acknowledged. They followed the convoy to an austere rustic cabin west of Lancaster surrounded by Amish farmland, barns, and covered buggies. The rain abated, leaving everything soggy. Inside the log house, women placed an array of piping hot and cold dishes on the plank table, the desserts on the kitchen counter next to the coffee urn. People lined up and loaded plates with chicken, potatoes, macaroni and cheese, salad, deviled eggs and other items. Some perched on seats; others mingled, speaking quietly to friends and neighbors.

Jack walked up to the detectives. "Please help yourselves; you'll be less conspicuous with plates in your hands." He smiled thinly. His twelve-year old son appeared at Hawthorne's elbow. "This is Asher."

"I'm Christopher Snow, and this is my wife, Erin McCoy. We're so sorry for your loss and wish Emma could be here with you."

The boy shrugged, his plate wobbling. "That's OK. I understand. Pleased to meet you. Call me Ash."

"We hear you're a reenactor, Ash. Do you enjoy it?" Mac asked.

His eyes lit. "I do. History is my favorite subject, especially the Revolutionary War, well, the Battle of Monmouth. We practice and practice. I'm the drummer boy and flag bearer." He stood taller.

"And when do you study?" asked Chris, moving along with the boy. Ash picked up a glass of tea while the detective selected modest portions of various dishes. As the containers emptied, women replaced them with others. Mac chose tossed salad, chicken and dumplings, one deviled egg and a scoop of mac and cheese.

"I study all the time. I'm reading about Paul Revere. Who's the poet who wrote about the midnight ride?"

"Longfellow," Mac supplied.

"Well, the poem's certainly *long*." Ash smiled. "We have school at camp, too. I study English, math, geography, history, music and science."

"Does Ferris, I mean Mr. Franklin, teach science?" Mac asked.

"Yes. How did you know?" The boy nodded. "Ah, you know history too. Dad teaches history."

"We know our nation's history." Snow smiled. "And proud of it."

"Excuse me." Asher seemed so earnest, those inquisitive hazel eyes, dark hair neatly combed, his shoulder blades bony wings protruding from his navy shirt. He wandered away to sit with the other children.

"I'm glad he didn't mention Molly Pitcher," Mac whispered.

"Are you catching this?" Snow nodded discreetly toward the room.

"Yes." She leaned against the farmer's stone sink to eat while guests filed past them, already selecting dessert. She contemplated the devil's food cake covered with fudge ganache.

"Then I'll mingle." Her husband merged into the crowd. Mac tossed her empty paper plate away and picked up the cake slice.

June walked up to her and nodded, her eyes scanning the desserts.

"See anything suspicious?" she whispered. In a normal tone, she remarked, "Salad and chocolate cake—now that's a combination."

"Not yet. Let us know when you're ready to go." Mac felt out of place; then she felt a twinge in her abdomen. *Oh, no not again! Nah, just nerves.* While the assemblage —a well-disciplined group—was polite, they also guarded their tongues. She threaded through the crowd to talk to the man called Lafayette. As she approached, he withdrew his fob and consulted a round, antique watch. His dirty blond hair, tied at his nape, narrow face with a patrician nose, protruding eyes and wide mouth marked him unique, not handsome. His impeccable charcoal suit, grey dress shirt and vest seemed tailored to fit.

"Almost one." Lafayette bowed slightly and said, "At your service, ma'am" with a distinct accent.

"Detective Erin McCoy. May I ask your real name?"

"Je me souviens de vous. Jean du Bourbon." He stepped back in an alcove that Mac would equate with a mudroom; wooden pegs held several wool shirts and jackets with boots parked underneath a low bench. The back door led to a spacious yard with furrowed fields beyond.

"Get out. Really? The house of Bourbon!" Mac exclaimed.

"Really. Royalty has little cache these days, which is why I prefer the eighteenth century. Can you imaging coming to America then? The dangers and excitement? A nation to build and discover! Continentals, Scots, the Brits, Hessians and . . . secrets and spies. "

"Why did you come to America? How did you become Lafayette?"

"First, to attend college. Second, to volunteer my services. For a while, I was a translator at the UN, but I find reenacting far more engaging and entertaining. I met Jack and the others at Valley Forge, so I volunteered my services. They accepted because I fit the part. Voila!"

"How long have you been with the reenactors?"

"How long have you been beautiful? Seven years."

Mac blushed unexpectedly but ignored the question. "What can you tell me about Margie's death? Did you know Dr. Donald Davies?"

"Our Molly Pitcher? Ja lis les journals. Well, she and Davies knew each other. Davies portrayed General Charles Lee, the man who failed to follow Washington's orders to attack the rear guard of British Regulars. He doctored injuries, too. No love lost between those two men, then or now. Yes, he left—because of an illness, I believe. Darren Goodman portrays him now." He indicated a fortyish and stylish gentleman with long sooty hair streaked with silver combed straight back and clubbed with a velvet ribbon. He wore a frocked coat from another century. "And I'd enjoy our conversation more another time; now is inappropriate for this discussion.

Please come to our new encampment or call. I must bid you au revoir." He shoved a business card at her, bowed curtly and slipped through the back door.

"Hmm, he didn't even bid his host goodbye or thank him for his hospitality. Wonder why he scurried away so quickly?" Mac mumbled.

"Talking to yourself again?" Her husband whispered behind her. "As long as you don't answer yourself."

"But I do enjoy entire conversations with myself—my corpus-colloseum at work. It's how I process information."

He shook his head, frowning at the term. "Your what?"

"It means both hemispheres of my brain communicate with one another in ways that men's do not. Ah, so the answer is that Lafayette acts as though he has something to hide. He wouldn't answer my questions."

Chris laughed, his eyes crinkling and head shaking. "Try another time and place, darlin'. Let's collect our guest and go home."

20

April mewed in quietly, leaves peeking from trees, perennials pushing through the soil, rain dripping imperceptibly from the eaves. Trench coats, boots and umbrellas became de rigueur, as dampness permeated stone, pavements and roadways. Overhead, gray clouds enclosed people under a dome; sprinkles misted courtroom windows where the defendant sat with her attorney, Denise Wilhelm. Emma fluffed her hair damp so the ends kicked out. She wore a pale blue sweater, a delicate silver chain with a faceted sapphire, a sedate navy skirt, and ballerina flats.

On the other side of the room the DA had the prosecutor's seat with ADA Chase Lawson waiting until the jury was seated.

Outside the courtroom, reporters from the three local networks, CNN and Fox bustled about, making last-minute observations to their viewers before filing into the courtroom. The clerk opened the doors; security took positions; the reporters poured in, jockeying for seats. Mac waited in an antechamber, watching the flurry of activity on the closed-circuit TV monitor. Her palms perspiring at being called first, she shifted uncomfortably, her tailbone aching, then rose and paced.

"All rise!" Judge Acorn entered, nimbly mounting the massive judge's bench that dwarfed her. Her black robe fit her trim figure well, except for billowing sleeves flapping like wings. Standing a moment reading a note, she laid it down, looked around the gallery—her dark eyes preying momentarily on the reporters. The gavel sounded the call to order.

"Counselors, approach the bench." The judge covered the mic and whispered to DA Collins, ADA Lawson and Wilhelm. They nodded solemnly and returned to their respective tables.

Collins opened with a conciliatory tone, acknowledging Ms. Hawthorne's terrible ordeal at the hands of her kidnapper. "The sordid details have been bandied about by the media, and I'm not here to question the defendant's motives. As a parent, I'm outraged that a fifteen-year old would be treated with such callous disregard. Ordinarily, we wouldn't reveal a minor's name, but the Amber Alert broadcast her identity. And I salute the intrepid detectives who worked around the clock to return her safely to her family.

"However, Ms. Hawthorne retaliated and killed her attacker."

"*Alleged* until proven otherwise," Wilhelm remarked.

Collins frowned at being interrupted during his opening argument; his dark crew bristled but regaining equanimity, he corrected himself. "Allegedly killed her kidnapper. She claims self-defense. While I do not condone what Dr. Davies did, I am in this court to prove that Ms. Hawthorne's life was not in jeopardy at the time the detectives beat down the basement door of the abandoned house. Indeed, CPD Homicide Detective Erin McCoy's statement describes in graphic detail her and others' steps in subduing the kidnapper and containing the scene." He approached and gestured to the jury. "And it is for you, the jury, to attend closely to the evidence and then decide guilt or innocence. Thank you." He nodded to Wilhelm as he seated himself.

Defense counselor stood, skirted the table, and faced the jury, making eye contact with each. "It's my job to prove that my client had been traumatized for a week by a doctor whose Hippocratic oath compelled him 'to do no harm.' Dr. Davies died as a consequence of his own crimes. Emma Hawthorne, a bright and talented fifteen-year old high school student new to the Carlisle area *is* the victim. She was kidnapped, violated and forced to strip in front of a camera to titillate porn subscribers. Try to imagine her situation: cuffed and incarcerated in utter darkness for a week, wondering whether the kidnapper's next appearance might bring more abuse, violence or worse. She feared for her life.

"As a result, she suffers from PTSD and, in her mind, felt the threat continuous and imminent. She defended herself until CPD detectives came to her aid while others arrested the child porn purveyors. I will prove, beyond any reasonable doubt, that because of her inventiveness and assertiveness, she is alive today. Any verdict besides 'not guilty' would be a travesty in the face of these facts. Thank you."

The prosecution began by calling Detective Erin McCoy.

DA Collins introduced and identified McCoy to the jury. He walked her through the preliminaries, asking questions about her K-9 Officer Shadow, her duties, and commented on her last collar—the Freeway Road Rage Killer during last Valentine's Day freak snow squall and her assist with the Abby Benedict arrest. "The first earned a conviction; the second, an acquittal," he informed the jury. Next, he asked Mac how she was acquainted with Emma Hawthorne.

"Her grandmother called CPD to report her missing and gave me her school photo to disseminate on our Amber Alert system."

"So her identity was broadcast across the various media outlets?"

"Yes, sir, and on electronic highway screens."

"So the public was already familiar with her name and likeness, correct?"

"Yes." Mac thought one 'sir' sufficient.

He continued in that vein, steadily laying the groundwork for finding her at the doctor's mother's domicile.

"She was held in a locked basement when you found her. How did you find her?" Mac explained how CPD tracked her cell phone, finding the trail of items leading to the abandoned house.

"Were you alone when you found her?" He turned to face her after pacing to the jury and back.

"No. My K-9 Officer was clearing the building with Officers Fields, Rivers and Summers."

"Why didn't you let her?" asked the DA.

"Objection to this line of questioning," Wilhelm said from her seat. "Counselor is baiting his own witness. And what's the relevance?"

"Sustained." Judge Acorn made a move-along motion.

"All right. Where were the K-9 and other officers who accompanied you?" Collins rephrased the question.

"Upstairs." Mac would volunteer no further information.

"Was the upstairs of the domicile vacant?" he asked.

"Yes."

"Do you know why?"

"The owner resides in a nursing home."

"Why did you go through the basement door?" the DA asked.

"I head whimpering—a sound like an injured animal might make."

His next question about her header down the steps provided smiles and a few chuckles around the courtroom as she described how the locked door suddenly flew open. Step by step, he had her describe the doctor's attack and her response, his tripping and falling to his knees, moaning in pain.

"What happened then?"

"I'm not sure," Mac admitted.

"Why?"

"The basement was in total darkness," she replied. "So I couldn't see."

"What did you hear?" He tapped a pencil against his open palm, waiting impatiently for what should have been routine.

"Dr. Davies's labored breathing and moaning. Then three thumps. Then the other officers thundered down the stairs." Mac wasn't going to make his job easier.

"Was anyone else in the basement?" he asked.

"Yes. Emma Hawthorne."

A gasp escaped from the gallery. Pens scratched on papers, and fingers tapped furiously on electronic devices.

"Did anyone turn the lights on?" Collins queried.

"No. There were no bulbs in the fixtures," Mac stated.

"Detective McCoy, how did you know you'd found your Amber Alert victim?" His dark hair quivered, furry eyebrows crawled up and eyes flashed, but the tone of his voice revealed nothing.

"My partners had Maglites."

"What's your assessment of the teenager in question?"

"I'm not a doctor, but—" Mac began.

"No, but you're a Homicide detective with nine years of experience in law enforcement. I'll repeat the question—"

"She was in shock, sir."

"Did she admit killing Dr. Donald Davies?"

"Objection!" Wilhelm leaped to her feet. Beside her, Emma, though pale, wore no expression other than that of an attentive listener in court for the first time, drinking in every intonation and gesture.

Judge Acorn put up her hand like a stop sign. "I'll allow it if you amend the question, Counselor." Defense counselor sat down.

"Did Emma Hawthorne admit hitting the doctor over the head?"

"No, she did not," Mac answered emphatically. Her tailbone stung, sitting in the hard chair, so she shifted her weight. *Why didn't I bring a cushion?*

"Before the other officers arrived, was there anyone else in the basement besides you, Ms. Hawthorne and Dr. Davies?"

"Not that I could see."

"Thank you, Detective. You may step down," Collins said dismissively.

"Not so fast." Wilhelm came to her feet again. "I'd like to cross." The judge nodded.

"Let's go back to your statement. You said my client was in shock. Can you describe her physically when your first saw her?"

"Yes. She was wearing a sheer baby-doll nightie; her hair was braided in pigtails, and she was barefoot. She had restraint bruises around wrists and ankles. She was pale and her skin clammy; her eyes were wide with shock with pupils fully dilated. They looked bruised from lack of sleep."

Wilhelm pressed a button and Emma's photo from the video popped up on a white board a clerk had rolled into place. "Like this?"

"Exactly."

"Can you explain why she was so attired?" asked Wilhelm.

"Dr. Davies had a web cam mounted on a laptop; he headed a porn ring, charging pedophiles to view images of Emma."

That was news, as CPD had not released the identities of all the men rounded up the day before. The courtroom buzzed. Down came the gavel; the judge demanded order in the courtroom. Several reporters, including Curt Dash of Channel Twenty-One, scooted out of the courtroom to track that story.

"So when you said Emma was in shock, you meant that literally?"

"I did," Mac said.

"Have you seen that look before?"

"In soldiers with PTSD." She nodded knowingly.

"Objection!" Collins stood. "Detective McCoy is not a medical doctor or psychologist—"

"Overruled. You introduced this line of questioning," Judge Acorn reminded him. "Continue," she said to Wilhelm and leaned forward.

"Are you saying Emma Hawthorne was exhibiting symptoms of Post Traumatic Stress?"

"Yes ma'am."

"Can you describe them?"

"She was hyper-alert, perspiring despite the chilliness of the partially finished basement. The shock and isolation seemed to numb her senses. In the ER, her movements were jerky. She lapsed into silence, refused to cooperate, then grew depressed when we discussed her predicament later."

"Did she say anything to you at that time?"

"That she was trying to protect me."

"Were you injured in the scuffle?" Wilhelm actually seemed concerned.

Mac held up her right hand. "Broken finger, seven stitches where my head hit the stair, and a cracked coccyx." Someone snickered.

"Thank you, Detective McCoy. That will be all." Wilhelm smiled, knowing full well that the prosecutor's witness had just aided the defense.

ADA Lawson stood. "The Prosecution calls ER Physician's Assistant Nina Patel to the stand."

Mac did not stay. Elena cornered her in the lobby. "Do you have a few minutes to comment on these proceedings?" Her cameraman stood a short distance away. Mac nodded, and Elena turned, canting her head to indicate a more private venue. "OK, please follow me." She descended the stairs, entered a conference room, pointing to an empty, cushioned chair. Michaels threaded a mic under Mac's sweater, snapped it to the ribbed crewneck as the cameraman did a silent countdown while Elena took the seat across the table. "Elena Michaels reporting from the Carlisle courthouse where Homicide Detective Erin McCoy just testified to rescuing fifteen-year-old Emma Hawthorne from her kidnapper's lair. Mac, can you describe the crime scene where you discovered Ms. Hawthorne?"

"Five officers and K-9 Shadow were involved. The basement was dark, but once my colleagues appeared, some light enabled us to see Dr. Davies and Ms. Hawthorne."

"No one turned on the lights?" She asked.

"The kidnapper had removed the bulbs from the sockets."

"And once the lights were restored, what could you see?"

Mac described the rear of the basement, the daybed, shower stall, computer and web cam but omitted the sordid details—items like the tools and toys the CSU collected as evidence. Carefully, she visualized what had been published in the police reports, kept her answers brief.

Michaels walked her through that day, asking about Shadow sailing through the window. Certain that the few minutes had expired, Mac felt light-headed in the stuffy room and signaled time out, hands below the camera's eye. A sneeze was building, and she buried her face in her elbow just in time; a second followed shortly.

"Cut! We'll edit that out. Give me one more minute to thank you and send it back to the studio." The countdown again, followed by the signature signoff. "Would you be willing to do a longer piece featuring Shadow? Maybe reenact the scene?" Michaels queried.

"Perhaps in a few days if my schedule permits. You know, Corey Kauffman, the K-9 Instructor, trained Shadow and me for months until I could take her home. Why don't you do a feature on him?" Mac suggested.

"I could, but I'd want Shadow in the clip," Michaels related.

"OK. I'm technically on medical leave. Let me check my schedule, and I'll call when I return to work. We can meet at the K-9 Center, as we're required to train sixteen hours per month. You can tape an 'attack,' and we can demonstrate what Shadow does."

"Yes, I like that idea. Let's shoot for next week if that's feasible. Thanks for the interview. It'll be on the six o'clock news. Let's go," she directed her cameraman. He followed, her words trailing behind. "See if we can get the ER PA or the psychologist to give us a few."

Mac's phone played three bars from "The Music of the Night" before she answered. "Trip along, busy bee. The mouse wanders and watches thee. The clock strikes three. Hickory, dickory, dee." Click, call ended.

"Is that supposed to mean anything to me?" she asked her phone. *Someone warning me away from the case?* "If so, it's a little late and you skipped two." *Or warning me of something yet to come?* She sat for a moment, contemplating possible connections of the nursery rhyme to Emma's case, which she'd soon learn was wider and darker than she could imagine.

She returned to the waiting room adjacent to the courtroom to see if Dr. Drummer was testifying yet. The trial trailed along, the prosecutor calling several teens and teachers to provide a context for her behavior. All reported an industrious, shy, new student attempting to adjust to CHS. "Kudos to Collins—providing a balanced view." *Luckily, Gwen was tied up,* Mac smiled. *In more ways than one.*

Next, Dr. Drummer testified as to Emma's likely frame of mind during her kidnapping and confinement. He pushed his Lennon glasses up the bridge of his nose, awaiting the next question.

"Detective McCoy said that Emma Hawthorne displayed PTSD symptoms when the detectives rescued her. Do you share that opinion?" DA Collins asked.

"Let me qualify that I didn't see her until a week or so later, but I found no evidence of the severe, sustained reactions that the Detective described, but the time lapse could be a factor," Dr. Drummer admitted.

"How would you describe Ms. Hawthorne's behavior?"

"At first sullen and uncooperative, which I attribute to her current attitude toward men." A split screen—one on the witness, the other on the defendant—appeared on TV. Emma's head came up sharply; she frowned, her first visible reaction to any testimony thus far. "Understandable under the circumstances."

"Continue." DA Collins said.

"Overall, she's justifiably angry, and her behavior toward her kidnapper appears a normal, healthy reaction to her horrific ordeal. Her emotions run the gamut from anxiety to anger, from querulous to depressed."

"So you're disagreeing with the lead detective in this case?"

"With all due respect, sir, you're putting words in my mouth. I'm saying after two weeks, Ms. Hawthorne's range of emotions falls within the norm for people who've had similar experiences. Panic attacks, frustration, rage, depression and rebellion against the attacker are typical."

"But that describes most teens' behavior at times. Did you hear the ER Physician's Assistant report that Ms. Hawthorne was not physically raped?"

"Objection! Calls for a conclusion from hearsay. This witness is not a medical doctor," Wilhelm observed.

"Overruled. The witness may answer the question."

"Yes," Dr. Drummer said.

"And therefore?" asked Collins.

"The lack of semen does not change the trauma the teen experienced or emotions she'll feel about her ordeal."

"Can you tell us anything else that might have motivated the bright, young teen to club Dr. Davies? Did she claim self-defense?" Collins probed.

"She was trying to protect Detective McCoy. She's convinced that the doctor was going to kill McCoy and then turn on her."

"Anything in her past that might give us a clue to her demeanor?"

"Objection. Is the DA on a fishing expedition?" asked defense counselor. "Does Dr. Drummer know anything about her past?"

"Sustained. Narrow the question."

Switching up, Collins asked, "Have you seen Ms. Hawthorne's artwork?"

"Yes, some of it." Dr. Drummer eased back in the witness chair.

Mac held her breath because she'd told Drummer that the teen's sketchbook was confidential.

"Can you come to any conclusion about the depiction of anger directed toward men in her art?" the DA asked.

Drummer smiled slightly, his blue eyes guileless. "I have no expertise in art interpretation whatsoever."

"Answer the question, please," Collins insisted.

"I'll take a stab at it. The three displayed in the art room at CHS show typical teenage angst, anger, and rebellion against authority. The one with the eye in the branches"—When the painting materialized on the board in vivid color, the witness paused—"depicts isolation and alienation, which I attribute to her being a new student at CHS." The witness's eyes stayed on the DA, the defendant's on the painting.

"So she has no deep-seated animosity that would explain murder?"

"Objection! Prejudicial!" Wilhelm leaped to her feet.

"Sustained. Patience, defense, you'll get your turn," The judge admonished.

Mac shook her head, stood, grabbed the strap of her purse and headed out the back door, covering her auburn curls as she left. Drawing on oversized sunglasses and her trench coat, she escaped unscathed, rounded the building and hurried to her Honda. She climbed into the driver's seat, fired the ignition and hastened home. Time to relieve her babysitter.

21

By the time his wife was pulling into their drive, Detective Christopher Snow had wrestled John Andre— rather the man who portrayed the British major in the Battle of Monmouth—into his Explorer. The Sixth Regiment mutinied.

"See, here, Detective, where are you taking Andre?" asked Ferris (Ben Franklin).

"Nowhere. I *am taking* Samuel Gray to HQ to arraign and process him for buying, possessing, viewing and disseminating childhood porn across the Internet. And for corruption of minors and leaving a crime scene."

"Sure you got the right man?" asked Darren Goodman, or General Charles Lee, who retreated rather than attack the British Rear Guard escorting the wagons and Tories from Philadelphia to New York—a direct insubordination of General Washington's orders.

"Is this aggression necessary?" asked Lafayette, aka Jean du Bourbon.

"What proof do you have?" asked Washington (Clark Winters).

Ferris wisely stood aside, peering through his rectangular spectacles, smoking his pipe. "Do ask your wife to reconsider standing in as Molly Pitcher for our rehearsal next week."

Though the second week in April, the ground was still boggy at Valley Forge, so the men decided to decamp, load their wagons and travel further east to higher ground. These weekend warriors had to contend with the loss of Margie Hawthorne, who had mastered Molly Pitcher's work ethic and devotion—one bright heroic spot in an otherwise lackluster battle that could at best be described as a draw. Her widower, Jack—who portrayed Will Hays and William Dawes, looked drawn and depressed.

"Poor man, no wonder, he canna sleep: wife murdered and his fifteen-year old daughter kidnapped and on trial for killing her attacker? Can you believe it? And Asher wanders around, a lost 'un for sure," Shultz (von Steuben) said in an aside to Winters. "It's demoralizing. People lose their moral compass when misfortunes dog them and wander in a fog of darkness. Civility disintegrates."

Washington nodded, watching the police and FBI confiscate Andre's rucksack and other belongings, but he had a reenactment to organize with nearly fifty new recruits. Finally, he backed away. "Let's not interfere with the police."

"You won't find any girlie photos on my computer," Gray insisted. His hands and legs shackled, he tossed his head to throw unkempt hair out of his eyes. The man had retained the boyish round cheeks from his childhood—now flushed crimson—but was probably pushing forty. His hooded eyes harbored some secret—a power withheld.

Snow waved the subpoena in the air as he claimed the driver's seat, Agent Howard sliding in the passenger's seat with his men following in the Escalade. "We're searching all electronics here and in your townhouse. We'll find Emma Hawthorne on your phone, perhaps?" They pulled away while those left behind broke camp.

"It would behoove you to admit your illegal activities. You and the others will be tried in federal court in D.C., old boy," Howard added.

"You are under arrest. You have the right to remain silent . . ." Snow intoned as he drove west toward Carlisle. Muddied from boots to thighs, he was famished and weary—fourteen hours flushing out the culprits. "That's all of them. I need a shower when I get home; I feel filthy."

"How about stopping for food?" suggested the FBI agent.

Snow shook his head. "Erin's injured and struggling with Ian, interviewing Emma, and testifying at the girl's trial. My mother's out of town, so I'm hoping our dads helped but don't know for sure. She needs me at home. Next time."

In response, Howard took out his cell, ordered his men to stop at a Carlisle eatery for food and take it to the CPD. "I'll take a grilled chicken salad, but get a variety—enough for eight—and burgers with fries for you carnivores. Make that two salads."

Snow did the head count and said, "Mac likes the BBQ chicken salad. I'll take fish and chips. Thanks."

"You heard that? Deliver the BBQ salad to their Lisburn Road address. Yes, meet us at CPD HQ. It'll probably take an hour to process this perp, but he's coming with us afterward."

"I'll expect my Pennsylvania long rifle and my musket back. The rifle is forty inches long, has a triangular maple stock, long, shallow trigger guard, brass fittings, and 35 caliber octagonal barrel. It's valuable, made in Lancaster County in the late 1700's. Ask Hays, I mean Hawthorne."

"You'll like Carlisle," Snow said. "During the Revolution, 'it was a frontier town with five houses, became the county seat and, by the 1760's, a busy hub in Cumberland County in 1750.' Matter of fact, Mary Ludwig Hays lived there before she was married and afterward with her husband before he joined the Continentals. Then she followed him into battle. Now, who followed Marjorie Hawthorne to Carlisle? She was seen with a man named Sam. Why were you with her?"

"Hmm." Gray clamped his lips together.

"So you don't care to share your participation in this sordid little child porn ring? Or tie up the loose ends? Or admit you witnessed a murder? Or did you participate? Margie Hawthorne was last seen with you; we have it on a surveillance tape. So unless you want to be booked as an accessory to murder, you'll talk. It's now or never. Once the feds take you . . ." Snow looked in his rear view mirror, but the prisoner remained silent for the rest of the journey, staring out the window at the visible darkness, listening to the tires hum, his eyes darting back and forth. *Trapped!*

Back at the station, Snow and Howard let Samuel Gray stew while they ate and then interrogated him for three hours. During the questioning, Snow received a call from Huddleston. "Excuse me. I have to take this." He stepped out of the box. "Any news for me? I need something to lean on Gray."

"Oh, yeah. Several things. We found Emma's video on his iPad, which was locked in a safe. Gray is also Susan Davies's brother, so there are two connections for you. And a sitting Pennsylvania Supreme Court judge. Book 'im, Dano. And I'm done for the night." Huddleston disconnected.

Snow looked at his watch: 10:00 pm. "Oh, shit!" He stormed into the box, circled around and slapped the back of Gray's head with his open palm. "We found the evidence on your iPad. Now I'm getting your DNA, and locking you up until your arraignment. Besides receiving and sending kiddie porn, participating in Emma's abduction, I'm charging you with accessory to kidnapping and murder if your DNA matches the semen in Margie Hawthorne's body. I'll recommend compulsory registration as a sex offender, evaluation and treatment— like chemical castration. Agent Howard, this one stays."

"That's not how it was!" Gray sat up, his lanky frame rigid with anger, indignation or blustery bluffing. He chaffed at his restraints, eyes glazed as if waking to a nightmare, his body rocking back and forth in a chair bolted to the floor.

Agent Howard stood, dusted lint from his vest, adjusted his Windsor knot, and bowed slightly to Snow.

"Kudos. Good work, Detective. I leave the *gentleman* to you." Pivoted on his heel and marched out, his two agents who'd been monitoring through the one-way following.

"Hey! Don't leave! I demand a lawyer. You can't railroad me: I didn't kill Margie," Gray insisted. "It's not what it looks like!"

Snow, too, stood up, called the front desk. "Which detective is next up in rotation? Fields? Is he on duty?" A pause while the night duty receptionist answered. "Send him and another officer in to book and jail this piece of trash named Samuel Gray. I'm going home for the night. I'll interrogate him in the morning." He stared into carbon eyes boring into his. "You can call your lawyer in the morning. And you can kiss your damn valuable rifle and tech toys goodbye. They're now property of the CPD." He exited the box—knowing a night spent behind bars might loosen the man's tongue. "He's up to his eyeballs in this shit! We'll get to the bottom of this sordid affair yet.

"And I hope Erin's sound asleep," Snow added to himself.

At home, he let his wife sleep. After stripping off his sweaty shirt, muddy slacks and washing up, he slipped into sweats and took Ian's midnight feeding. A bottle sat ready in the fridge. While it warmed, he lifted his squirming son, grabbed a dry sleeper and diapers, and crept into the living room. He laid him on the carpet and changed his diaper, crooning quietly. Bottle warmed, he settled in the rocker and let the sweet baby lull him into a better frame of mind. Ian burped, Chris returned him to his crib asleep. Chris showered, then quietly slipped into his side of the bed and snuggled up to his roan beauty— her auburn curls splayed across her pillow. Leaning over to whiff the honey and lemon scents of her hair, he sighed as he watched her eyes rove in REM. The stitches—jagged z's across her hairline; at the middle, cinnamon freckles ran to the left side. Long, rusty lashes brushed her pale cheeks.

He frowned at the risks she took, trying to prove she's tough enough to belong on the Homicide Squad. Chris shut his eyes, wanting to touch her, gather her body to his and smother her with kisses, but he nodded off, contemplating the sorry state of his case.

22

Mac heard birdsong; her eyes fluttered open; the clock read six. Startled, she glanced over at sleeping Ian, which meant that Chris took the last feeding. Casually she rolled against her husband, her fingertips stroking his hip, his abdomen, his thigh and . . . His eyes snapped open. He pulled her gently to him, buried his face in her hair, her neck; kissed her lips, throat, her engorged breasts, working south. Her hand latched onto him, stopping his downward trajectory. So he readjusted, maneuvered into her—holding his weight off, then lowering enough to touch and rock, nibbling her lips with his: connecting, greeting, communicating and transcending. Fifteen minutes passed before they surfaced.

Erin sighed, pulled his body onto hers; he rolled to his side—mindful of her injured tailbone and held her against him until Ian stirred. He lay on his back as she stretched her arms.

"Not yet," he whispered. "Just one more minute."

"I've got him. I'm leaking anyway," Erin admitted.

Chris licked his lips. "I noticed."

Erin inched away quietly, changed the baby, his solemn lake blue eyes wide in dawn's first light, mapping her face. Beside her, Chris scooped Ian up. "Why don't you slip back in the bed where it's warm?" Then he waltzed the baby into his mother's arms. "I'll get a fire going, chase the chill out of the living room."

"You found John Andre?" she asked as the baby suckled.

"Oh, yeah, only he's Samuel Gray. I'm betting this bird will sing, but it's a long story. I'll update you while we eat.

I'm glad you went to bed 'cause I didn't get in until eleven. You slept well?"

"Well enough." She smiled and then turned her attention to Ian. "I have news, too, about Emma's trial. But you go first."

"Finally, we caught a break with a big fish who has much to lose. Found out he's Susan Davies' brother, the one in the South Deli security footage. Left him cooling in jail. He knows something."

"He admitted having an affair with Margie Hawthorne?" She followed him to the chilly living room, easing onto the rocker, patting the baby's back until he burped.

"Not yet, but he will. He also lawyered up, but Huddleston found Emma's video on the guy's iPad when they searched his house. Oh, Howard sat in on the questioning—"

"Yes, Isola brought me a BBQ chicken salad, courtesy of the FBI. Said you ordered it. Thanks!" She kissed him as he leaned over to cover her feet. "While we ate, I updated her on Emma's trial."

"Wait a sec." He stacked logs atop the kindling, lit it, dusted his hands, closed the screen and stood, watching as the logs caught; flames licked the air. "How did your testimony go?" Chris dropped to the ottoman.

"OK. Though I think DA Collins overstepped when he had Dr. Drummer on the stand. Asked him if he knew the lab reported that Emma wasn't 'actually raped' when Chen or the ER Physician's Assistant should have fielded that one."

"Meaning the doc didn't use his penis but objects instead? Does that make her ordeal any less traumatic?" In the kitchen, he pulled out a skillet, plunking it on the stove. Grabbed eggs and Canadian bacon from the fridge. "Egg muffins OK?" he asked.

"Fine with me. I'll have mine open-faced light. Did you get any sleep?" She switched the baby to the right side.

"Yes, some. Are you going to court today?"

"No. I think Dr. Chen, Lane Rusk, Mahoney and Summers are testifying today, though Wilhelm will call me too. I have a feeling this case is an exercise in jurisprudence. The jury won't convict the teen based upon anything the DA has said or done thus far. He damaged his credibility with that spurious remark; it bought Emma empathy. Watch the media pounce on that."

Erin laid Ian in his park 'n' playpen with some toys in the opposite corner. "Watch his commando crawl." Sure enough, the baby rose up on his elbows, inching along until his fingers reached the musical cell phone. He patted the buttons to hear the chimes.

"A little bobble head." Chris dropped muffin halves into the toaster oven, broke eggs into the skillet, and peeled slices of cheddar from the pack. Flipped the eggs, topped them with cheese. Out came the muffins. He set them on the island; Erin poured OJ. "So you're staying home?"

"No, today's a training day for Shadow. Going to K-9 Instruction."

"Who's keeping Ian?" Chris bit into his muffin. "Hmm. Homemade is better." Laid the sandwich on his plate to brew a mug of coffee.

Erin broke the yolk to moisten the muffin and then forked a bite into her mouth. "Dad. We'll be training from ten to three. When I get home, Dad'll spend some time with Savage. When your mom gets back, I think she'll sit Monday, Wednesday and Friday, and Dad, Tuesday and Thursday."

"Did he sell the Ragged Edge?" Chris fixed his wife a mocha.

"Sort of. He works there part-time, managing the original. Jake's opened two others. But I also have a backup in case of another emergency—the D.A.R.E.

officer on maternity leave? Lee Jeffers. Her baby's due in three weeks. She volunteered."

"She can manage two babies? What's her husband do?"

"In an emergency, yes. Don't think we've met her husband. But I hope I won't need to call her. And Sonja offered, too."

"Good enough. Gotta hustle." He took his coffee with him to shave and shower.

Erin glanced to see if the baby was occupied, let Shadow out and jogged around front to get the paper, gauging the weather: sunny but cool. The banner headline blurted: "DA Claims Teen not 'Actually' Raped!" The entire front page covered the trial, including snippets from hers and Dr. Drummer's testimonies. Shadow nosed her hand. "Done girl? Want breakfast?" Back inside, she dished out dog food, poured water, left the gate open to check on Ian. He had moved on to the drum that Jason Lightfoot had made him. Tidied the kitchen while the baby seemed content.

Chris came out of the bathroom in boxers, scooped the baby up and tossed him gently into the air. "Let's get a bath in the laundry tub, kiddo."

Erin trotted off to the bathroom to shower and dress, slipping into jeans and a sweater. Tied the knife to her calf with sheath's leather straps. Tugged on old boots. The doorbell chimed. Scurried to the door to let her dad in. He lifted her into a bear hug, setting her down gently, her towel turban slipping to her shoulder. Shadow pushed by her to greet Ethan. He ruffled her fur. "Where's my grandson?" He followed the sounds of splashing.

Behind him, Savage stepped inside as well. "Well, aren't we bright and chipper this morning. Do something with your hair; you're dripping."

"Kiss my ass." Erin hied off to the bathroom.

"Make it bare."

She just kept walking. Savage at eight a.m. was a little much to endure. "Get your mind out of the gutter," she threw over her shoulder.

"Your ass is a gutter?" he laughed at his own humor, aiming for the Kuerig to make a cup of joe.

Ethan, cuddling Ian in a towel, turned into the master bedroom to dress 'the bairn' while Chris dressed. Snow emerged, shrugging into his sport coat. "Let's motor, Savage. Did you drive?"

Reese shook his head. "I'm coming with you. I have an appointment with the shrink."

"Well, that's progress. Did Ethan pick you up?"

"If you say so. Yeah, he came through Holly, stopped so. . . . I put the house up for sale."

"Really. Why? Too big for one?"

"That and I've finished remodeling it. Need to make a clean break with the past. Elena's helping me stage it."

"So much for a break with the past. She gets half?"

"Yes, but I found a two-bedroom raised ranch on Lisburn, just off of Middlesex . . ." Their conversation drifted out the door as they left. "Needs a little updating . . ."

Inside, Ethan rocked Ian as Erin harnessed Shadow. "Training Day, girl." She started to pack lunch, but her Dad stopped her.

"I brought soup, sandwiches and cookies. Out in the car in a cooler."

"Here, Dad. The baby's asleep. I'll just tuck him in while you get your cooler."

The landline rang while Erin was in the bedroom. When Ethan entered toting a Styrofoam cooler, he caught the last of the message: "When the clock strikes nine, you're running out of time. Hickory, dickory, dock."

Erin stood statue still a foot from the phone. Ethan lowered his burden to the island. "What's that all about, Erin?"

So she collapsed onto the nearest stool and shared the three nursery-rhyme messages with him, one captured in a glassine, dated and labeled, the second on her iPhone's voicemail, plus the one they just heard. "But I have no clue what they mean or how they relate either to the homicide, the kidnapping or the trial. Besides the nursery rhyme, the sender's hacking phrases from 'The Midnight Ride of Paul Revere.'"

"Have you told Chris?" Her dad's tone was stern. "Someone connected to the reenactors or the Hawthorne homicide case?"

"Not yet. Not sure, could be either, I guess."

"What're you waiting on? These threats should be in Evidence and under investigation. You're pushing somebody's buttons. They're warning you off."

"But I don't want to broadcast it because whoever is doing this wants attention. Ignoring the messages seems the best option at this point until I figure out the source," she explained.

"'Forewarned is forearmed.'" Her father quoted.

Erin sighed. "I suppose. I'll tell Chris today, OK?"

"It won't solve the problem, but I'll feel better if he knows."

"He may take me off the case." Erin hunched her shoulders.

"What case? You found the Amber Alert teen. That was your case: job's done. Homicide case is Chris's."

"I thought so too. It's a little late to send me warnings if my job's done. But maybe I've stumbled onto something that I don't realize I know. I've been trying to replay the last two weeks in my head but can't think of anything specific tied to the reenactors." She shrugged into her shoulder harness, stuck her pistol in the holster, layered a red fleece over and led Shadow out the door. "Be back for lunch. Don't tell Chris, OK? I'll tell him. Promise?"

Ethan nodded as he loaded the food into the fridge and settled down to enjoy a cup of coffee and read the news.

23

At noon, Mac and Shadow left K-9 training with a word to Kauffman about Elena Michael's planned profile.

Corey rubbed his nose. "Well, she can shoot what we're doing, but she'll will have to wait until after three to talk to me."

"Good enough. Thanks." Off she sped to HQ, dropping by the interrogation box to see if Chris were still questioning Gray. She flipped on audio. The defendant and his lawyer Orndorf were facing the one-way. Gray was sweating, his unwashed hair matted to his skull, his wrists and ankles restrained. In an aloof, condescending tone, the lawyer interrupted Chris on a self-incriminating question.

Snow pounded the table with his fist. Savage sat beside him.

"Damn it, man. We have the evidence, and I'm losing patience. You want to swing for this alone when we know others are involved? If convicted, you're looking at life—"

"Look, I'm a lawyer. I know my rights. OK! OK! May I have a drink of water? I'm dying in here." He turned to his lawyer.

"When you say something useful," Savage answered.

"All right! I was having an affair with Margie. I've known her since college. We hook up several times a year when we could both get away. We're discreet. But I didn't kill her or kidnap her kid. I may be foolish, but I don't have a death wish. Jack would kill me."

"No great loss, I imagine. If you'd commit adultery and watch kiddie porn, you'd probably cross other lines as well," observed Savage.

"We met at the Colonial Hotel downtown and got sandwiches at the Southside Deli. When I left Margie at the Old Carlisle Cemetery; she was waiting on Emma to join her. She wanted to photograph Molly Pitcher's gravesite and statue. And if you were astute enough to notice, I did not open that email from Davies."

"How did you leave? Her car had a flat," Savage said.

"No—it did? We drove separately. I had court the next day."

"What a damn hypocritical pervert! Sleeping with the mother, peeping at the daughter? I should castrate you myself!" Snow thundered. "Won't even mention the juvie kickbacks! What a piece of work."

Gray paled. "I'm telling you the truth. She was alive when I left."

"Did you wait until after her conversation with her daughter, circle back, maybe thinking you'd land a twofer?" Snow sneered. "You're disgusting. Savage, take over, I need some fresh air."

The moment he saw Erin, he smiled. "I thought I sensed you observing. How am I doing?"

She leaned in to kiss him; freshly shaved, he smelled of sandalwood. "Laying it on pretty thick, aren't you?"

"He won't talk otherwise. I want the whole story."

Mac snorted. "Not likely. Come home for lunch? Dad brought soup and sandwiches. And chocolate-chip cookies!"

Chris pulled her against him and kissed her back. "Think I'll take you up on that. An hour of good, wholesome food sounds great, but then I need to finish this. Gray's arraignment's tomorrow; I need to know what to charge him with. Meet you at home. Guess I'll get the perv some water."

"See you in a few. Shadow's in the car." Mac, famished after their workout, slid out the side door and drove home. Her Dad had seafood chowder simmering and the sandwiches plated with a side of slaw. "Should I add a plate for Chris?" he asked his daughter.

She nodded as her husband cruised through the mudroom door. After eating half of a turkey special from the Ragged Edge, she nursed Ian while Chris and her dad talked about the break in the weather, Savage and the porn ring.

"Think you corralled them all? I was reading about Emma's trial but saw nothing about a porn ring. Poor lass: imagine the shock! And it could be dangerous for whoever knows them." Ethan observed, emptying a cello of oyster crackers into the chowder.

"You will tonight or tomorrow. The media have it now," Erin said from the rocker. "They have a new angle with legs that'll radiate across south-central PA, maybe even the nation, for weeks."

"Hey, I'll take the critter out, give you two some privacy. Be back in ten," Ethan said, telegraphing a message to his daughter. "Let's go, girl." The dog never turned down an offer to romp out of doors.

"Oh, that was abrupt. What can we do in ten minutes? You have something to tell me?" Chris found a Coke in the fridge. He joined his wife, taking his usual place on the oversized ottoman, pulling her feet into his lap, massaging them.

"How do you know I have—oh, that's wonderful! Yes, I'll admit Dad railroaded me into telling you." Erin told him the story of the nursery-rhyme threats.

"Why didn't you tell me sooner?" Chris's hand tightened on her calf.

"What's to tell? I'm still trying to puzzle it out. When I had something concrete, I would've told you. I don't want to burden you with—"

"Let's not do this again. I'm your husband and direct supervisor. Burden me. The threats are crimes; they should be placed in evidence and investigated. They put you directly in someone's sights. I don't like that—or being kept in the dark." He stopped, held up his palms. "OK, you're telling me now. I want all the messages. I'll take them back to HQ and put Savage and Huddleston on them, then send them to the lab. Maybe others can make the connections."

"But don't you see? This guy wants attention. I don't want the media to catch wind because it's a distraction."

"We'll keep it in house for now. But we need taps on the phones to trace any more calls." He pocketed the written one in the glassine. "Come to papa, little man." He lifted Ian to his shoulder, paced and patted until a burp erupted, then cradled his son in his arms and sang softly to him. "Smile, I want to see those dimples. Atta boy! You and your momma are my panacea and talisman. Bless you, both. Love you." To Erin, he continued, "We'll get to the heart of this threat together. Now I've got to run. Back to momma, you go! Whee!" Swinging, Chris lowered him to Erin's lap, thanking Ethan for lunch as he left.

"I have to return to training, Dad. I'll be back by four. Goodbye, baby. Be good for Papaw. Here, trade you." She handed him Ian and took Shadow, repeating the morning's ritual—donning the holster, Glock and jacket, grabbed the leash and a packet of treats and returned to K-9 training.

Shadow "attacked" Kauffman—unrecognizable in a padded outfit to weather the dog's teeth and claws. Then she cut her time on the obstacle course by six seconds— alerting her handler to three finds: a bloody rag, a dime bag of hash and a burned, charred cloth from Margie Hawthorne's skirt. Michaels and her cameraman had free rein—staying well out of the way, getting their questions answered after the session.

"Thought you said next week?" Mac asked, gulping water after jogging the course with her dog. Perspiration beaded her forehead.

"And let you stew about it all week? Trust me, this is better because you all acted spontaneously. Thanks, really, for the suggestion," she said as Mac and Shadow walked them to the gate. "Viewers can see how Shadow helped with Emma's rescue—a good follow-up."

"Don't overplay my role. CPD rescued the teen. Matter of fact, did you talk to Fields, Mahoney or Summers yet?"

"I tried. Fields said pretty much what you did; the others had no comment, referred me to the CPD PR spokesman. Don't worry; I'll include them. Now I'm off to interview Gwen Davies and her mother. Get their side of the story. It has legs, too. It's traumatic, losing a husband and father that way." Wide-eyed with excited busyness, she and her cameraman climbed into the ABC van and sped off.

"Glad that's over." Kauffman wiped his sweating brow with the back of his sweatshirt's sleeve. "OK, new defense strategy. Let's train Shadow to escape a locked vehicle. I'll open the gate, you drive your vehicle in, and we'll work on lock, unlock."

"Wouldn't it be easier to leave the trunk unlatched or windows open?" she asked.

"Who said life should be easy? Will you have time to do those things during a police chase? And who leaves the windows down in this weather? Move it. But we'll show Shadow that way out, too."

After an exhausting hour, Mac and Shadow motored home. "Good girl. You did well. Let's go."

24

At the HQ briefing, the Homicide squad met to summarize the Hawthorne cases. Mac highlighted the court case and testimonies to date. "I assume the Musketeers are testifying now," she checked her watch. "The jury will probably find the homicide justified, given the circumstances—unless the DA has an ace up his sleeve."

"Which could very well be the Lowe kid," Savage commented.

"Is he well enough to testify?" asked the Chief.

"Don't the feds have him?" asked LT Stuart, making a note to call.

"Yes, as far as I know," added Snow. "But I want to discuss the nursery-rhyme threats Mac received. Someone has sent her three so far; they seem linked to the reenactors because . . . Mac go ahead."

"The sender's hacking phrases from 'The Midnight Ride of Paul Revere' into 'Hickory, Dickory Dock.'" She passed out copies of the three verses, the entire last one reading: "Hickory, Dickory, Dock/
The mouse roves with the wind/The clock strikes ten/Hickory, Dickory, Dock."

"Does it follow Longfellow's timeline exactly?" asked the LT.

"No, I can't discern any rational order. I suppose I'm the mouse? I'm stymied because my case is done—or at least out of my hands, in the court's. But the sender has to be a re-enactor, so apparently there's more," Mac said.

"What's that mean—'roves with the wind'?" Fields asked. "That doesn't sound like a warning. Taken together, they do, but about what? Emma's been rescued and is in custody, so the rhymes must refer to her mother's homicide."

"Or Dr. Davies's," Savage remarked. That arrested everyone's attention. "Like Gwen said, she's lost her father and boyfriend. Could that be a woman's voice disguised on the phone message?"

"Definitely. I haven't been able to determine gender." Huddleston pushed his wire-rims up the bridge of his nose with his pinky. "Hadn't considered Savage's angle, but he's right."

"No, can't see Susan Davies doing this." Mac shook her head.

"What about the daughter? She's feisty enough," Savage said.

"Snow, did you pry anything useful out of Samuel Gray?" asked Chief March, combing his hair with the eraser end of his pencil, and then dropped it absently on the conference table. He swallowed cold coffee, made a face and sat it down.

"Only that he was having an affair with Margie Hawthorne, which we surmised. Lab hasn't returned his DNA results, but my money's on him. If he did her at the cemetery, he's guilty of more than adultery. He either knows about, participated in, or witnessed her murder. Maybe Margie found out about his extracurricular activities. Booked him on the porno charge. I'm still working on him. Agent Howard will try the others in federal court."

Fields scanned his copy. "But Mac accompanied Snow and the others to Valley Forge, so perhaps the killer assumes she's involved with the homicide case, too—as you are. It definitely connects to the reenactors, but I don't think we interviewed anyone acting as Paul Revere."

"Because the Battle of Monmouth is much later—July 1778," Snow said. "I just wanted to apprise you of this development, assign Huddleston to track the calls and send the note to the lab for prints. Jack Hawthorne portrays Paul Revere. There's another possibility."

"Don't keep us in suspense," Savage deadpanned.

"Suppose we don't have all the porn purveyors?" Snow suggested. "One of these men could be covering for someone higher up the food chain."

"Distinct possibility," said March, "But unless you have proof, not much we can do at this juncture. Did you and Agent Howard pursue that line of questioning with the other men?"

"No, but we will. If we'd arrested all of them, Mac wouldn't be getting these warnings." He turned to his wife. "I'd like Shadow to stick by you for the next few weeks—wherever you go."

"Oh, sure." she smiled. "I thought you were going to say—"

"And I've assigned Savage to your detail," he said firmly. The smile died, but she kept silent at the briefing.

"Then we're actually no closer to closing the homicide case?" asked the Chief. "How can there be so many involved and so little evidence that we can't arrest the killer? Or even find one to charge?"

"You just answered your own question, Chief," Savage said.

"How so? Spell it out for us less informed peons," March replied testily. He tapped his pencil impatiently against the tabletop.

"Because with so many suspects, until we comb through all the evidence and interviews, including what's filtered through the FBI, track down all the clues, corral all the perps or get someone to roll over, we are stuck."

"Snow, are you planning a trip?" asked March. "Or shall I assign one?"

"Chief, we're leaning hard on Gray. He admits to an affair but nothing else. Hasn't even admitted yet that he's a judge. I'll question him while Savage and Mac cover the teen's trial, and Huddleston tracks the nursery rhymes.

The Musketeers will be testifying, so they stay. Dr. Chen can track the lab results. Have I missed something?" The lead detective wondered.

"And you're convinced the husband's not a party to this?" March looked to the Vic's partner first and last.

"He has an ironclad alibi with Franklin, Washington and von Steuben but we can look at him again, if you want to expend the resources."

"Check again and submit a timeline that others can verify. Just report back when you're done. Everyone else, work your assignments. Mac, submit a K-9 training summary ASAP. McCoy, Savage, and Fields, review the interviews. Go over everything again when you're not in court. Better yet, rotate the court coverage. I'll have Storm blog the police reports. Otherwise, hunker down and close this case. Dismissed."

Mac and the men left for their offices.

"Come on, girl, need a potty break?" Pacing the perimeter of her handler's office, Shadow trotted willingly outside to find some greenery. The iPhone trilled. "McCoy."

"Lafayette here. If you want to continue our conversation, I'll be at the sutler's in Gettysburg. I can meet you for a late lunch at the diner on Route 30 south of town. Come alone or I'll be gone. And no recordings, what I have to say is FYI only."

Mac consulted her watch, swinging toward her car instead. "I need a half hour to get there." She didn't mention bringing Shadow, but she could stay in the car. On the way, she called her Dad to let him know she'd be in Gettysburg, omitting details. "Oh, will you let Chris know? He's in interrogation at the moment, so . . ."

"Sure thing. See you in a few hours."

Stopping at the sutler's on Steinwehr Avenue to check du Bourbon's story, she learned nothing valuable; the clerk couldn't recall a customer that she described. "Speaks with an accent? He's French." The clerk shook her head at the photo taken at the funeral and moved on to the next customer.

"Stay. I'll be back." Erin handed her dog a rawhide chewy in the back seat, unbuckled her restraint and scurried into the diner. Du Bourbon sat at the booth by the door, stirring coffee. He looked up as the bell sounded, finger-combed his dirty blond hair off his forehead, motioning her to sit opposite him. Mac slid into the booth, her slacks crackling with static. She ordered decaf mocha and waited for him to speak.

"How's your investigation going?" he asked nonchalantly.

"Slowly, though I can't discuss specifics. We need to sift through a lot of information and interviews. What did you want to tell me?" The waitress brought coffee, laying a packet of chocolate mix beside the cup. Mac sprinkled in a third of it, then sipped, testing the mixture.

He smiled enigmatically. "I'll rather show you. Follow me."

Dropping a five on the table, he stood abruptly and walked out.

Nonplussed, Mac gulped her coffee and followed. Rounding the corner, she caught du Bourbon climbing into a late model Beamer with government plates. He pulled out of the parking lot, so she hopped in Silver and followed him south out of town where he peeled off the road after roughly three miles.

She pulled up along side his vehicle, climbed out. "Hey, wait up! What' so import—"

He turned on her—the royal mask of polite, debonair Lafayette gone, a gun pointed at her gut. "Shut that dog in the car. Leave your purse. Then drop your weapon slowly, curious little mouse. Didn't figure you'd come alone, but then I guess you didn't know."

"What's the problem?" Mac complied, bending down to lay her gun on the grass, while popping the trunk latch with her left hand. A path meandered through a copse, if she remembered rightly, that wound its way through the cemeteries along the ridge about fifty yards along. Except for birdsong, the land was eerily quiet—too early in the season for tours or tourists to be trekking through.

"Drop the act. You know too much as it is. Didn't it occur to you that someone might be trying to shield others higher up?" Du Bourbon asked.

"You're driving a government vehicle, which means you work for the government, maybe with the diplomatic corps. You don't live in Philly but D.C. Who's the higher up you're shielding? A judge?"

"Clever girl." He motioned her ahead with the gun barrel.

The sun brightened the grass, the leaves, the blossoms on trees and wildflowers sprinkled over the gently rolling acres. Weeds choked the long grass along the footpath. Vines wound around tree trunks; witch hazel and spindly plants struggled under the canopy for light.

How can one compact a life into a few minutes? Fear sharpened her senses, her mind trolling the possibilities. *Engage him in conversation.* "What's the purpose of the nursery-rhymes? Were they meant to be a warning?" Mac tried buying time. "Who's running out of time? Is your entire regiment involved? Are we missing a piece of the puzzle?"

"You're out of time. Let's go. Walk ahead." He jabbed the snub-nosed pistol into her back. They walked while he explained the need to be rid of her. "You're too close. I need to protect my position, our business. Reenacting is just a diversion, albeit a welcome one." After following the trail for ten minutes, he ordered, "Turn here." A copse of trees separated a Civil War cemetery from the hiking path.

Blood rushed, an ocean in her ears. Her hands chilled, turned clammy. Anger crept along for the ride, rising into her throat, surfacing as her eyes focused on a dirty spade propped against a pin oak, shading the spot where snow etched a ring around the tree. Beyond, aged concrete slabs tilted like rotten, crooked teeth marking soldiers' graves from a battle fought here 143 years ago.

Perspiration beetled down her face. "You're not involved in Emma's kidnapping and porn ring, are you? Trafficking in minors? Covering for Judge Gray?" They stopped three feet from the freshly turned earth, the gaping hole in the ground roughly five by four feet, and three feet deep.

"See? In a few days, you'll unearth it all." He laughed. "Pardon the pun!"

If she could reach her knife, she'd stop this business. Her fingers found her cell in her pocket; she pushed on, then the phone icon, and thumbed number one. The activity distracted her momentarily. Du Bourbon swiped at her arm, but she sidestepped, the barrel clipping her elbow. She turned sideways, rammed her right foot into his groin, the knife sliding into her hand. She slashed his gun hand, disarming him; blood gushed from the wound. The blade flashed against his palm, his wrists, blood blooming.

Du Bourbon stumbled backward into the freshly dug grave. "You vicious little beast!" Simultaneously, Shadow hurled across her field of vision, a blur of snarling fur, pinning the man to the grave. Her cell, lying trampled in the dirt, emitted faint 'Hellos." Shaking, Mac bent down to pick it up.

"Want to tell me what you're doing?" Snow's tight, angry voice demanded.

"Bringing in the nursery-rhyme criminal named du Bourbon for assaulting and threatening a police officer with a deadly weapon." She wiped her knife on the grass and sheathed it, restrained the bleeding man, and hauled him to his feet. Du Bourbon moaned the entire time, his blood dripping onto the dirt. "Shadow, guard." Trapping her cell between chin and shoulder, she tugged on gloves to collect and bag the man's pistol.

"Where's Shadow?" asked Snow.

"Standing on him."

A sigh crawled across the line. "Bring him in. We'll talk later."

"Back to the cars! Stop." From Silver's open trunk, Mac lugged out chains to shackle the prisoner's legs. "Good dog." Rewarded her with a treat for coming to her aid. Recovered her pistol, pushed him into the vehicle. Dialed Adams County police to collect her prisoner's Beamer.

"I'll bleed to death before we get there." Du Bourbon whined.

"Tough shit." Mac tossed a first aid kit into his lap. "Bind your wounds with gauze." She buzzed the ER to see if Janelle were on duty. "I'm bringing in an emergency. Knife wounds."

"We already have Gray in custody." Mac cuffed him to the hospital bed while her stepmother cleaned the wounds, patched him up, stitching his hands and arms. Bonded his wrists and covered them with butterfly bandages. "Surface wounds, so you'll live. Avoid using your hands for a few days." She wrapped each in sterile gauze, taping them in place while giving her stepdaughter a sidelong glance. "I have to report this."

"Yes, ma'am," Erin replied. "I do too."

"When was your last tetanus shot?" Janelle asked.

Du Bourbon shrugged indifferently. "Years ago."

"Roll up your sleeve." In an instant she'd flicked the hypo, swiped his arm with an alcohol wipe, then plunged in the dose.

At HQ, Mac lugged him in for processing. Officer Castle took the prisoner to interrogation after booking and fingerprinting him. He handed the card to Mac, who asked Sonja to run it through AFIS as Snow glowered in the hall doorway. "Savage can interview him. I have a feeling—"

"In my office now, McCoy." The lead detective wheeled and stormed into the tidy, airy end office. Fresh cold air flooded through the window, cracked open an inch. His desk had folders stacked neatly in black mesh organizers, pens jutting from a round container. A legal pad with notes sidled up to two open folders covering his desk. Hawthorne's homicide photos spilled across the top. On the left, a landline sat beside a five-by-seven of their wedding photo. On the back wall, framed photos displayed a commendation, the homicide squad at a local pub, and various plaques and certifications. Snow closed his door, waved his hand to the visitor's chair for Mac to be seated. She remained standing.

"Did you ignore a direct order *again*? I assigned Savage to you for a reason."

"No, du Bourdon called, asked me to meet—"

"Shut it! I don't give a damn if Christ called you from the clouds. You should have come into the station, informed me, located Reese and received permission first —if not from me, then the Chief. Sorry, this time I will write you up for insubordination."

"You don't understand. I—" Mac halted mid-sentence because Snow pushed into her space, in her face, a vein pulsing in his neck, yelling. But she refused to back up or back down, even though he was right.

"You needlessly put yourself in the line of fire again, hot dogging after an unknown without preparation, a partner or backup—heedless of your training, your experience and my direct orders. Then you offer excuses. You're off the case! You're suspended for a week. Only smart thing you did was taking Shadow with you. Now go home. ONE WEEK!" Pulses at his temple and neck throbbing, his face red and his lips a slash in his face, the man looked moments from exploding.

As Chief March stood silently in Snow's office doorway, Mac knew she'd crossed the line. "Sorry. Yes, sir!" She saluted. "Come, Shadow." Marched out. Climbed back in her vehicle, and anchored the dog's harness. She stopped by Wendy's for burgers, cokes and fries and drove home. "Let's just see how far throwing your weight around gets you, Mr. Senior Dick! Oh, if I were a man, you wouldn't upbraid and suspend me."

Shadow's sage brown eyes regarded her mournfully.

"I'm not talking to you, baby, but about that pig-headed patriarch I married. And I know he's upset because I could've been hurt, but I wasn't hot-dogging. I was following a lead, damn it, and collared the guy. And the man can get his own damn dinner!"

At home, she shared sandwiches and fries with her dad, who'd been minding Ian.

"Rugged afternoon catching villains?" asked Ethan, juggling the whining baby in his arms. "Had to give him some cereal with strained bananas."

"OK." Wide-eyed, Erin said as she took Ian. "How did you know?"

"Cause you look like someone dragged you through the briar patch. And Janelle called."

"Actually, I drove to Gettysburg. One of the reenactors called, and . . ."

Mac related a sanitized version of the day's events. "When I arrested and dragged the guy into HQ for questioning, Snow lambasts me for hot-dogging."

"Stop right there, lass. I'll just go let your critter out while you feed the bairn. I can't take sides, but I'm thankful that you are well enough to vent. It could have turned out differently. Besides, you didn't tell me the whole story, either." He patted her shoulder, poured her a glass of red wine, and turned toward the back door. "But I'll head home after I let Shadow back in. I don't want to referee when Chris gets here."

"I'm sorry. Neither do I, Dad; neither do I."

The door closed softly on Shadow and her dad.

She concentrated on nursing her son, forcing herself to relax as she sipped a little wine. Then picked up her iPhone to call Danelle.

Her husband thundered through the door a few hours later, after she'd put Ian in his cradle for the night. She performed her nightly ablutions without conscious thought, meeting his every word and motion with mute silence. They went to bed without conversing for the first time in their marriage. Instead, her weekend plans mentally drowned out his words.

25

The next morning, humming quietly, Mac changed and fed Ian. After Snow left for work, Mac packed Ian's diaper bag with clothes, diapers, toys and supplies, zipped it shut. Packed hers in an overnighter. Loaded Silver. Next, she measured dog food in a plastic container. Called her dad, asking him to dog sit if she brought her to Gettysburg. He reluctantly agreed. "Don't go haring off without a call to your husband. He'll worry. I don't think it's a good idea, but—"

"I'll take care of it, Dad. Thanks. See you in about half an hour."

After dropping Shadow at her parents' place, Mac motored south, veering off before the Beltway onto a suburban street lined with flowering cherry trees, the propagation of pink blossoms stunning. Danelle's corner townhouse, stone on the first story, vinyl siding on the second, faced Cherry Lane—of course. When she rolled into the drive, Danelle and Sydney rushed out, pretty and peppy as spring. Her friend handed Ian's bag to her daughter, and then popped the handle on Erin's wheelie. Mac eased a sleeping Ian from his safety harness in the back seat, shouldered him and followed her hostess inside a tastefully furnished foyer and living room, up the stairs and into a guest room where a crib stood waiting.

Downstairs, they hugged. "Trouble between you and Chris?" She held her palms up. "You needn't share details if you don't want to. Come out to the kitchen, I'll fix you a mocha and breakfast."

"Don't go to any trouble," Erin said. "I just needed to get away and simmer down. And yes, Snow wrote me up for insubordination."

"No offense, but I'm surprised this is the first time. Not to worry, I'm just reheating cinnamon-nut rolls from this divine bakery called A Bit of Heaven. Sydney, why don't you finish your picture book for preschool? Later we can show Aunt Erin and Baby Ian the back yard. If it's nice, we'll take a walk."

Erin sat in one of four chairs at a round, dark cherry pedestal table in the bump-out dining area with a bay window that overlooked the fenced-in back yard. A column of mature arborvitae blocked the view to the left. She observed Sydney, who was sitting at a child's wooden table tucked into the kitchen corner. It held cans of pastel Play Doh, a Lego tower, and a stuffed furry puppy. A packet of markers and crayons stood ready. Syd drew a round head and two ungainly ears on a sheet of paper. "Aunt Erin, why is Baby Ian still sleeping? It's time to get up."

"Because he's a baby and needs his sleep to grow."

Sydney considered her words. "When he wakes, can I draw him?"

"May I," Danelle corrected as she operated the cappuccino machine like a barista. It hissed and spit frothed milk. Then Danelle nuked the buns.

"*May* I draw the baby?" She held up her marker and twirled it in the air.

"Yes, but I don't know if he'll sit still like that puppy."

"Oh, I know that. He's real. But I'd like to try for my project." She jumped up and hurried to the counter. "I'll serve."

"Be careful, the rolls are hot," her mother cautioned.

"I know. I see steam." Sydney carried two plates to the table with studied care as her mother sat mugs of mocha on the table. Then the girl collected her own cinnamon roll and carried a cup of hot chocolate to her little table.

She took a bite, then a sip and turned to her drawing. "I need a napkin, please."

Erin handed her one from the table.

"Tank you," the child nodded, unfolded the square and spread it across her lap.

"So what happened? Something serious or you wouldn't be here." Danelle said.

"Let's say I acted without thinking and wound up in a potentially precarious situation." Erin was mindful of little pitcher's ears. "But after a brief altercation, I subdued my assailant and took him to the station. Then Chris reamed me out in his office for hot dogging and ignoring a direct order for Savage to babysit me."

"You're not a baby! I don't like orders, either," Sydney contributed as she drew the dog's body, an oblong an inch below its head. "They're not nice."

"Adults are talking, Syd. Does Mommy interrupt your playtime?"

"No, but I can hear you," she answered.

"Would you like to watch TV?" her mother asked.

Sydney popped up. "You'd let me? Yes, please. Does this mean I'm not going to pre-school? You're not going to work?"

"No, I'm working from home today; I need to print photos later for the ads. But no markers allowed in the living room. And finish your roll and hot chocolate first."

Danelle turned to Erin. "Bet it's hard to separate personal from professional when your boss is your husband. I'm not taking sides, but look at you—stitches, a broken finger and cracked tailbone from rescuing that kidnapped teen. Oh, yes, I read the news online. Seems that Michaels reporter has inside info." She nodded as she bit into the warm cinnamon. "Yum." Sipped her mocha daintily, like Sydney had. "Was Shadow with you?"

"Yes, she was shut in the car, but I unlatched the trunk; she crawled out and ran to the rescue, pinning him where he fell . . ." She canted her eyes sideways, but

Syd was ensconced on the sofa engaged in *Toy Story*. ". . . into a freshly-dug grave. Luckily, my stepfather had just given me a knife, which I keep in my boot." Erin then vented her grievance at being upbraided for action for which a man would be lauded.

"Admit it. You take more risks than usual, but you're right. Taking flak from your husband adds stress to the work. Whew! Listening to you, I'm glad I'm single. I can make nearly all my own decisions, but my job's not life-threatening either."

"O, come one. Even driving is a risk. Or walking alone in the city after dark. Or setting up a photo shoot by yourself in a strange place," argued Erin, as she drained her mug and sat it down.

"Except for driving, none of which I do," her friend reminded her.

"I know. And the worst part, Chris is right. I should have had a partner or called for backup. But might and right won't change my feelings."

"And he won't be pissed that you left for the weekend?"

"I imagine he will when he finds the note." Erin felt a twinge of remorse that she didn't tell him in person, but she'd been too angry to speak.

"He doesn't know where you are?" Danelle eyes widened. "Call him!"

"I said I was visiting you. That's true. Let me check on Ian."

Danelle stood. "I'll tidy up. If Ian's awake, we can take a walk after you're finished feeding him. We'll give you a tour. I'll dig Syd's stroller out of the hall closet. Let's go out for lunch, then work this afternoon." She whisked the dishes into the sink, rinsed and slotted them into the dishwasher.

At the top of the stairs, Mac heard the baby fussing. Followed by an angry yowl. "OK, Ian, you're in a strange place, but Mommy's here." She eased into a white rocker sitting on a cream area rug edged with ivy. The double bed sat off-center to accommodate the crib and a dresser. On the bed's opposite side, an antique hurricane lamp graced an end table. The en suite smelled like lavender with the cream and pale green shades carried throughout.

Just eighty miles southeast of Carlisle, Maryland's balmy air and gentle breeze heralded spring. Off the kitchen, French doors opened onto a screened-in porch with spicy purple lilacs on either side. Honeysuckle spilled over the fence that blocked the ravine. No weed dared appear on this immaculate carpet of green. The spacious yard boasted a swing set with a covered sandbox underneath the slide's platform.

They strolled down the street for several blocks, turned the corner and came upon a cluster of shops—including the Bit of Heaven Bakery, a gift shop, an art gallery, the Stitchery and Sundry with samples in the window, decorated for Easter. At the end, a deli held the corner spot. By that time, hunger gnawed.

Studying the chalkboard, Erin and Danelle ordered quiche; Sydney chose a child's chicken tenders plate with a strawberry shake; all had a side of dressed field greens. They settled in a window booth. Erin parked Ian's seat by the window and fed him strained apricots while they waited.

A waitress delivered their meals as Erin's cell trilled. "It's Chris. I better take it. Can you—"

Danelle made a shooing motion as she scooted over beside Ian and continued spooning in the fruit. "Umm, good."

Erin stepped out into warm sunshine.

Without waiting for a greeting, Chris said, "Couldn't bother to tell me? You left me a note and sneaked off? Guess what? I don't know Danelle's address. If you'd be so kind as to enlighten me—"

"Don't. I can't argue now. Please don't call or come to get me. I'll come home Sunday."

"That's it? You come and go as you please without so much as telling me? What kind of behavior is that for a married woman?"

"We're eating lunch. I can't talk now. I need some space. Besides, I'm suspended, so what's the difference?"

"Did you forget about Emma Hawthorne's trial? And taking Ian's a cheap shot. We've never been separated."

"Yes, you were, while tracking Sienna Greer last December. I said we'd talk Sunday."

"That was work. Oh, we'll do more than talk," he fumed.

"Goodbye, Chris." She ended the call and returned to the table. The waitress approached. "I kept your plate warm while you were out."

Surprised, Erin smiled. "Why, thank you." Danelle returned to her seat, wisely refraining from questions or comments. Sydney was spooning in her shake rather than using a straw, cooing to Ian across the table. He seemed utterly engrossed in that other little person.

"Here. He wants a taste." She picked up her mother's spoon and dipped some up, offered it to Erin.

"I'm not sure, but thanks for sharing." Erin took the spoon. He opened his mouth as the creamy concoction met his lips. At first he looked surprised, then he smiled and grunted—extending his arm toward Sydney, who obliging scooped out another spoonful.

"OK, just one more," Sydney said. "When Mommy works, we can have a tea party on the porch. Pretend, 'cause my tummy's full."

After the walk home, Sydney and Ian both napped. While Danelle worked, Erin pulled out her laptop to research the case. She emailed Sonja, requesting a background check on du Bourbon and wrote her arrest report. Scanned the news on Emma's trial. Finally, she called Agent Howard to inquire after Kevin Lowe's health. "Is he well enough to interview? He's the missing piece. I need to speak with him," explaining that she was in the area.

"What a delightful surprise. Know the FBI building?" Howard asked, but continued without waiting for her answer. "I'll escort you to our patient. He's conscious but smoke has damaged his throat, so he can only whisper. He's had skin grafting for his burns, but . . ." his voice trailed off. "Shall we say one o'clock?"

With the kids still napping, Erin popped her head into her friend's cozy office. "I need to interview a witness. Can you keep an ear out for the kids?"

Danelle hesitated while she finished scrolling through and scanning photos. She stopped, sighed and said. "Sure, if you'll watch them both when you return, so I can finish."

"Done. And thanks. This kid may break the case wide open. Lord knows I need some kind of leverage when I get home."

* * *

Surprised to find Kevin Lowe awake, propped up in a hospital bed, mired in an octopus of wires and monitors in the FBI's infirmary, McCoy watched a nurse applying fresh bandages to the burns on his face, arms and legs. She smiled in greeting.

Howard said, "No longer than fifteen minutes, or his doctor will skin our hides." But he smiled congenially as he left her to her task.

"I need to use my iPhone to record our interview," she explained as she reminded him that he was still under arrest for drug possession and intent to sell. She tapped the video mode and provided the required information. "We know that you were at the Davies' and the Old Carlisle Cemetery prior to Emma's kidnapping and her mother's demise. Can you describe the scene?" She handed him a glass of water so he could moisten his mouth and throat.

Slowly, painfully in his raspy whisper, he began. "Emma and mother argued. Doc and I tried to intervene, but Mrs. H went ballistic. Jabbing us with a fork. Tied her to the cannon. Cool down. Emma left with Doc. She thought he'd take her home." He stopped, sipped more of the cooling liquid, savoring its effect on his damaged mouth and throat.

"But Dr. Davies didn't take her home. Did you know that?"

He nodded. "Took her to his . . ." his voice trailed off.

"You have to answer verbally."

"Yes." Lowe looked uncomfortable or impatient. His eyes strayed to the ceiling.

"And?" Mac prompted, sensing he was debating with himself.

He glanced at her, then the cell phone and shook his head no.

"No, you didn't know or no, you refuse to say? Let me remind you that your cooperation may go a long way in helping your case, unless you killed Marjorie Hawthorne yourself and want homicide and accessory to kidnapping added to your charges."

"No, I didn't. Confusing. Mrs. H lost it; hit Emma. Em slapped back. Nose bled. Marched off with Doc. Felt but didn't see . . ." He paused for a breath. ". . . someone else watching or waiting. Maybe Gray in car . . ." His eyes slid left.

"Yes, we have Samuel Gray in custody. While that's possible, you're omitting something. Are the men covering up the porn ring, Kevin? We've arrested seventeen men who paid to see Emma disrobe. What else happened? Keeping secrets is dangerous at this juncture."

"Emma, Emma . . . Her mother didn't know." His eyes fluttered then shut.

"Know what?" McCoy asked.

A doctor entered the room. "I'm afraid that's all for today. You've tired the patient." He unlooped his stethoscope from around his neck, clamped the buds into his ears and listened to Lowe's chest.

"He's the Carlisle Police Department's prisoner," Mac said but complied nonetheless, pocketing her cell and gathering her purse. "His testimony is crucial to our case."

"Agent Howard informed me. But he's my patient. He's not going anywhere." The doc motioned her out.

"I'll be back." She cast one last look at the injured teen and wondered what thorny secret had such a hold on him that he would risk his life and future to hide. Her heels clicked loudly as she left the building. Disappointed she hadn't learned more, she mulled over the teen's words.

26

Steering into their driveway after collecting Shadow and eating lunch at the Ragged Edge with her Dad, trepidation crept into Erin's consciousness. She tapped the garage door opener, leashed the dog. The mudroom door flew open; Snow tore out and rounded the vehicle, removing a sleeping Ian from his car seat and carried him inside without a glance toward his wife.

She shrugged, closed the garage and let Shadow roam the backyard, patrolling the perimeter. The sunny day promised warmth later. She wound her hair up, anchoring it with a claw clip. Procrastinating. Breathed in the fresh air, as branches threw their hair forward, scattering the scent of blossoms. "Hmm," she said, despite feeling queasy. Erin called her dog and walked into a convocation. Her in-laws sat placidly on the living room sofa. Erin peeked into her and Chris's bedroom: Ian was still asleep. She eased the door shut.

"Sorry, I didn't know you were waiting—" she started, but Chris interrupted her.

"Mom and Dad are watching Ian for an hour or so while we go work out." He strolled over to her, gripped her arm, pulling her toward the mudroom.

She jerked away. "No, I don't feel like working out—"

He grabbed her again. "No is not an option. OK, we're sparring. I've signed out the CPD workout room. We both need it." He steered her out the back door and into the Explorer, his hand a vice at the back of her neck. Shoved her in the passenger's side, belted her in, rounded the SUV, climbed into the driver's seat. Erin was releasing her seatbelt to get out, so he cuffed her left wrist to his right, drove to work, practically hissing. "You sneak out of the house, take my son without so much as a by your leave and disappear for a girl's weekend when we have an open case? Leaving me a note? It's irresponsible and childish. You're a grown-ass woman! I wouldn't treat you that way."

"You most certainly did! Reprimanded me in front of the Chief, suspended me and dismissed me. Had I been a man, you would've given me a commendation. *I* needed a break from *you!*"

"Not gonna happen any time soon." He jingled the cuffs.

At CPD, he pulled her out of the vehicle and along to the side door, downstairs to the old gym, past the workout equipment shrouded in darkness, through a dingy hall and into the smaller room with padded walls and mats covering the floor.

"Shoes off! You know the rules," he ordered.

"I said I don't feel well."

"Tough shit. Limber up." He stretched and jogged in place.

Erin stayed glued to the spot. Light filtered through the basement window; dust motes spun in the musty air. The room smelled like rubber and sweat—a bit nauseating. Snow bent, removed her shoes, and straightened, tapped her face with his palm, a signal to begin. She backed away. He swung; she dodged. His arm came toward her; she batted it away, bounced up on the balls of her feet, dancing side to side. He kicked at her knee, but she'd already ducked between his legs, grabbing where it hurt most, clutching and squeezing hard. She heard him suck in his breath and drop to his knees, groaning. Up again, she kicked, but he grabbed her ankle, yanked her leg up. Erin landed on her hip, but rolled away while he had trouble getting up, still seething. Finally on his feet, his hand caught her throat, pressing on both carotids. "You fight dirty."

Light-headed, Erin felt his hand rip at her jeans; then the turkey special spewed up her throat, exploded from her mouth, splatting his face, arms and clothes. He dropped his arm and backed off. "Damn it, Erin! Damn you!"

"Serves you right. I said I didn't feel well." She headed toward the showers, Chris right behind her, peeling his sweats off as he went. Then he peeled off her clothes, pushed her into the first shower stall and flipped the lever full on. She gasped as cold water needled her, backing away—right into Chris.

"I'm really sorry! Didn't know you were sick. What's wrong?" he sounded contrite.

She shook her head, opened her mouth and rinsed it repeatedly until the sour vomit washed away. She reached for the soap dispenser, but Chris beat her to it, green liquid dropping into his hand. Trying to ignore his hands, she opened her palm, let the shower gel drop and scrubbed her face. Still angry, she ignored him, but her body wouldn't, as his hands soaped, cupped her curves. When he turned her to face him, her mouth parted as they fused. His hands drew her bottom closer. Warm water pelted them, glancing off shoulders, running in rivulets down bare bodies and pooling at the bottom, until the slow drain caught up.

He turned off the water. She pushed away, grabbed a towel. "I don't like you very much right now."

"Please don't do that again. I was sick with worry about you and Ian in D. C. traffic, knowing full well you were in shock from du Bourbon's assault. I'm sorry I sent you home. Dr. Drummer should have debriefed you first. But, Erin, you must follow orders. I need to know my men —and woman—will comply, focus on task and get results. The others rarely, well, except Savage, hare off to do as they please. If a lead arises, notify me, and I'll delegate who does what. It's my job as lead detective." Locking the gym door, Chris led Erin to the vehicle, handed her in, and folded himself into the driver's seat. Snapped his fingers and turned.

"Oh I just remembered. Franklin called several times. He insists that you stand in as Molly Pitcher for the Battle of Monmouth rehearsal, but I'll call him back and tell him you're sick—"

"When is this rehearsal?" Erin interrupted.

"Next Saturday—Bowman's Mill in Bucks County." He glanced over at her, then back to the road. He stopped at the red light at Fairview and R74 South.

"I should be OK by then; I'll do it." It would be a day away, a diversion from their argument and the case.

"How long have you felt ill?"

Erin shrugged. "Oh, I don't recall. A few days."

"If you're up to rehearsing as Molly Pitcher, we can all go. Mom and Dad would enjoy it, and they can watch Ian until you're done. I'll take the camcorder." His shoulders shrugged. "Are you sure? What's wrong?" he asked again.

"I don't know. A stomach bug, I guess. Maybe we'll be done with this eternal, infernal case by then. Did you wring anything out of du Bourbon?"

Back on equal footing discussing work, Chris smiled. "I did. He thinks he has diplomatic immunity, so admitted using a Philly condo to film soft porn flicks to distribute among 'like-minded, consenting adults.' He claimed, however, not to be involved with Emma's ordeal. I've got a warrant for the condo."

"Did you find the burner he used?"

"No, but his prints were on Samuel Gray's pad; he claims that could have happened anytime. From a legal standpoint, he's right."

Emptied, Erin felt better. She snorted. "Hah! He said I knew too much. What do I know? I just asked him the usual questions at Marjorie Hawthorne's funeral."

"What did he tell you?"

"That a funeral wasn't the time or place for an interrogation." She glanced out the window at all the green. "He'd call me later."

"What about when he accosted you?" He reached over, squeezed her hand in encouragement.

"Said nothing really helpful, implied he and maybe the others were protecting someone higher up."

"Like who? We have the legislators and Gray's a state Supreme Court judge. Who's higher than that?"

"I think he meant Gray. But du Bourbon, Franklin, Von Steuben, or Washington might be, but I hope not," she mused.

"You think they're all involved?" His eyes sought hers.

"No, but what if this is not about child porn but sex trafficking? Emma's fifteen but looks twenty with make-up. Did Marjorie allow her daughter to be kidnapped or did she die trying to prevent it? Was that why she was killed? Gray had images of Emma on his iPad but no young children. And du Bourbon claims that only consenting adults were involved. Is Jack Hawthorne's alibi airtight?"

Chris smiled. "No, it isn't, but Hawthorne claims when he returned home late, he and his son went to bed. He said he wouldn't leave Ash alone, and I buy that. Wilhelm has subpoenaed him to testify Tuesday or Wednesday. The defense has recalled you as well; you're up tomorrow.

"And our French diplomat no longer has immunity. His term has expired. He's been arrested, arraigned and trial date set for assault on a police officer with a deadly weapon, attempted homicide, and criminal conspiracy. A mitigating factor, however, his gun wasn't loaded when he accosted you."

"Well, I didn't know that." Mac felt tricked. "Will that matter?"

Her husband shrugged and tugged her into an embrace. "I'm so sorry—didn't know you were ill, but in the future, will you promise not to crush my nuts?"

27

In court, Mac felt she was sleepwalking through a
nebulous dream—reality edged in soft focus, her mind
fuzzy, slow to react. She answered Wilhelm's questions
robotically, reviewing facts, reiterating earlier testimony.
After stepping down, she roved to the nearest vacant
chair and sat down next to Jack Hawthorne. *Coffee,* she
thought, *I need caffeine.* Dr. Drummer and the defense
psychiatrist provided their assessment of Emma's mental
condition during her captivity. The courtroom stilled, the
gallery expectant. Pens and fingers stopped scratching
and tapping. All waited on the defense's next move.

"I call Mrs. June Browning to the stand," Wilhelm said.
Dressed in a navy pantsuit, Browning was sworn in,
stepped to the witness chair. Defense asked her
relationship to the defendant. Then, "How would you
describe your granddaughter?"

"Emma's a typical teen in some ways but unique in
others."

"Can you explain what you mean?"

Browning detailed the teen's traits and talents.
"Emma's more mature than many of her peers. She's
serious, studious and has nearly completed high school
requirements at fifteen." The woman summarized her
granddaughter's typical day, her interests, hobbies and
her part-time job at PetSmart. Her answers were clearly
expressed—knowledgeable without sounding rehearsed.
Yes, she knew Gwen Davis, Kevin Lowe and Wyatt Weber.
Yes, she was aware her daughter and Emma were
estranged. Finally finished with questioning, Wilhelm

said, "Witness dismissed." Prosecution had no questions for her.

"I call Emma Hawthorne to the stand." Murmurs of surprise simmered from the spectators. Papers rustled; reporters shifted—heads up. Jury members exchanged eye contact with one another.

The gavel slammed down. "Quiet in the court."

Quietly, the demure teenager rose from her chair, head and back erect. In a baby-blue sweater and matching, gauzy skirt and ballerina flats, her dark hair artfully mussed, she walked to the front, an elfin—sprung from Tolkien's Middle Earth. Sworn in, she took the witness chair.

"Emma, how old are you?" asked Wilhelm.

"Fifteen." Audible breath in-takes followed.

"Yet you're a junior at Carlisle High School? Can you explain why?"

"I was home-schooled until last year. My placement tests landed me in junior AP classes, senior English, and I take college courses online to fill my schedule."

"Tell us how you came to be at CHS," Wilhelm said. "Since your family doesn't live in Carlisle."

The dark hair shimmered as Emma shook her head. "My parents live in Lancaster. They're Revolutionary War reenactors. Dad portrays Will Hayes, mother, Molly Pitcher. But my grandmother lives here, so I came to stay with her last summer to attend public school."

"You've spent a month every summer with her?" asked Defense.

"Yes, since I was twelve, so I knew some kids, the area."

"And your parents permitted your move to Carlisle?"

Emma's round blue eyes sought her father's. "Reluctantly, yes."

"Explain." Wilhelm said.

"I convinced Dad. Mother was opposed."

"Why?"

"She wanted to stay as we were—reenacting, living in the eighteenth century. I'd had ten years of that. She insisted that I major in American history and eventually take her place with the regiment."

"But you didn't want to?" Wilhelm probed.

Emma turned her eyes to the jury. "I want to be a normal teenager. To go to the mall, buy jeans and tops. Go to public school. Have a cell phone. Watch TV or go to a movie. Live in *this* century. Dad and Nana made all that possible." She smiled at her grandmother, then her dad, who nodded encouragingly.

"The DA has mentioned and asked the psychologists about your art. What can you tell us about those paintings displayed in the art room at CHS?" Wilhelm asked.

Emma shrugged. "Art's my creative outlet. I don't think about 'themes'; I just sketch and paint. An idea germinates; then I go to the easel. A week later, I'm finished with that piece. If I'm not satisfied, I usually paint over it. Few ideas come from my art classes 'cause we have assignments. For me, creativity comes from the inside out, not outside in. But Ms. D encourages us, lets us work during our study halls. She entered the three displayed at CHS in various contests."

"The one with the African woman and wolf woven into a tree won a gold key." Wilhelm stated. The painting flashed on the screen, its sea-foam green and blue images muted by speckles of tan: the woman's head in profile and the wolf, part of the tree's foliage. Sponged leaves topped the twisted trunk. The fetus, head down in the tree's swollen base, barely fleshed in. "How would you interpret this painting?"

Emma frowned, chewed her lower lip. "I don't know. Life—the opposing urges we are born with. I see the wolf as the wild side—like the id—and the woman, mother of us all—the civilizing influence, akin to the superego. But others may see something entirely different." She shrugged. "The snake signifies sin in Eden, and the unborn child—ego—a symbol of each of us."

"And the moss that surrounds the tree?" asked Wilhelm.

"A soft landing. I wish every baby born had a soft landing and joyful journey, but that rarely happens . . ." Her eyes wandered to the gallery.

"What does the eye buried in branches communicate in this one?" Wilhelm thumbed the remote, displayed the next painting.

"Social constraint. Isolation. Stagnation. Rules and regulations, like tangled dams, jam us up, stymie our potential and paralyze us from meaningful action. I want to make my own choices. To do that, I must leave the nest."

"And you're planning on going to college?" asked Wilhelm.

"I want to major in art." Emma looked at her lawyer, then the jury.

Next, Wilhelm walked her through that brutal cemetery scene—glossing over the homicide—focusing on the kidnapping and the long week of incarceration. Defense displayed photo after photo, asking Emma to describe each; the teen's eyes filmed; her chin trembled. At the photo showing her exposed, bruised thighs, the teen broke down. "I'm s-s-sorry, so ashamed." She sobbed, her hands covering her face, tears leaking through her thin fingers.

"You have nothing to be ashamed of; you were victimized!" claimed Defense.

Restless reporters shifted; jurors looked to the judge to stop this traumatic line of questioning.

"Do you wish to take a short recess?" Judge Acorn asked the witness gently, but Emma shook her head no. Pulled a tissue from her pocket, wiped her eyes, sat up and took a deep, cleansing breath—shuddering. "I want to get this over with, your honor." She nodded stoically for defense counsel to continue.

"Defense may resume." The judge nodded. "When you've concluded your questions for this witness, we'll recess an hour and a half for lunch. I'll ask the reporters to leave the courtroom now." She turned to the jury. "You are under a gag order. Keep mum on the sensitive testimony you are about to hear." The jurors waited until the grumbling Fourth Estate exited.

Wilhelm covered the late Dr. Davies's advances, the intervals of total darkness during her kidnapper's absence, her injuries, his drugging her, keeping her cuffed to the bed, and filming her disrobing. She asked the teen to describe the deceased's actions, including details about his assaults. She queried the teen about the location of her cell phone, her purse, the house in which she was kept, and finally, her rescue. "Did he make any attempt to disguise himself?"

Hawthorne shook her head. "He uncuffed me to take a ride to his cabin in the Poconos." Her right hand waved vaguely out. The implication rode on the silence.

"Implying . . . ?" asked Wilhelm.

"Objection," the DA said. "Leading the witness."

"Rephrase," the judge told Wilhelm.

"Did he say anything else?"

"No, the cops' arrival interrupted him. The door crashed open, a body thudding down the steps. Another stumbled down."

"What happened then?"

"I'd seen a club on that side of the basement in a golf bag. I groped for it, grabbed it and swung at the doctor because I thought he'd kicked Detective McCoy down the steps. I heard her cry out. I was trying to distract him, save her in case she was injured."

"Not to get revenge?" Wilhelm whirled around and approached the stand.

"No. No. I wasn't even thinking—just reacting," claimed Emma.

"The witness may step down. The defense rests."

The judge smacked the gavel. "Court adjourned until two p.m." Some jurors left the room dabbing their eyes with tissues. Officers materialized to spirit Emma out the side door.

Mac felt released from a murky current, turned to say a word to Jack Hawthorne, but he and June Browning had hurried from the room. So she took the elevator to the ground floor, slipping out the back door, where Dr. Drummer was waiting for her.

"Is now a good time to talk? I can take you to lunch." He smiled and waited patiently, buttoning his wool coat over his navy suit, white shirt and maroon-striped tie. Adjusted his glasses. His hair reminded her of dusky brown autumn leaves, his eyes pale water.

"I guess." She tied a silk scarf over her auburn curls and donned sunglasses. Walked with him.

"Will the Gingerbread Man suffice? We can walk." He turned to the alley that led along the dogleg to the restaurant, up the stairs and into a booth at the back. A waitress dropped off menus and water.

"Be back in a jiff." She scooted off.

The psychologist scanned the menu for a moment. "Ready to order?"

"I usually get the spinach salad," Erin said half-heartedly, wondering if she had the energy to pick over the greens and cut off the stems.

"I'll treat. Order whatever you wish. You need protein." He waited until the frowzy-haired waitress reappeared and took their order of Ruebens and slaw. The bell over the door jangled as others entered. "How are you feeling after *your* ordeal?"

"Do you mean court?" she asked, but then waved the comment off. "I know what you meant. Du Bourbon's attack?" She shrugged. "Our conversation is confidential, yes?"

"Definitely, unless you are about to report a crime." He laughed. "I know he's in custody. We can go to my office if you'd feel more comfortable there."

She shook her head. "'Snot what I meant. OK, yes, I was frightened. You know how the senses sharpen when you're in danger?" He nodded. "Hyper-alert, my heart drumming in my ears, I was sure that I would die, my limbs felt leaden, my movements slow motion. Did you read my report?"

Dr. Drummer nodded. "But I want to hear it from you."

"Yes, well. The mind plays many tricks—accept, evade, postpone—fight or flight being most dominant. I mentally pursued all avenues, discounting each because of the pistol in my back until I saw the fresh grave. Anger kicked in. First, I kicked him in the groin then slashed him with a knife stashed in my boot, disarmed him, and then took him to the Gettysburg ER. Long story short, I arrested and hauled him to CPD."

The waitress brought their platters, refreshed their waters.

"Would you like something stronger to drink?" he asked. "Just one."

The waitress waited for Erin to decide. "OK, a glass of Zinfandel, please."

"Make that two." He waited a beat, then nodded for Mac to continue.

"Thing about it is, I was seething with anger at Snow because he wrote me up for insubordination and suspended me for a week. I took off for the weekend to visit my college roommate, who has recently returned to the states." She paused to bite into her sandwich, which was oozing Swiss cheese and dripping sauerkraut. "Hmm, that's tasty. I'm still angry at the double standard. Had a male detective hauled in an assault suspect, he'd have been commended."

"Well, there is one gigantic difference: you're married to Detective Snow. I'm sure he was worried about your taking risks. It's natural for him to feel protective—" Dr. Drummer began.

Mac interrupted. "See, typical male reaction!"

"You will concede it's an important point to consider," the psychologist said gently. "Given the seriousness of the incident and the fact that you have an infant at home."

"OK, but it doesn't change my feelings. I'm still pissed."

"Can you change him?" he asked quietly, his fingers steepled over his platter, elbows on the table.

"Seriously doubt it." Finally, Mac smiled ruefully. "But I can't help my feelings, either."

"Your feelings are justified, but you must change your reaction to your superior if you continue to work together. Can you compartmentalize? He's your boss at work, husband at home. How did he react when you arrived home after your getaway weekend?" He bit into the second half of his sandwich.

"I don't care to go into it. And it's hard to separate the two, though I should have called for back up. I'm suspended anyway." She shrugged as she finished, wiping her hands on the napkin and sipped her wine.

"Was he violent?" the psychologist asked.

Mac made eye contact. "He insisted we go to the gym to spar." She shrugged. "I didn't feel like it. I was tired, had an upset stomach, partly because I felt guilty. Pressured to do something I didn't feel like doing. Nerves on edge. Then pissed because my in-laws were waiting to —interrogate me, like an inquisition. Of course, they sided with their son. I could see it in their eyes."

"And . . ."

"After we arrived at the gym, we started sparring. I threw up on him!" she laughed. "That broke the tension."

Dr. Drummer smiled wryly. "Drop by to see me when you return to work, say Monday at nine?"

"Why?" Mac stiffened, ready for criticism.

"Let's see how you feel then. You were assaulted—a traumatic incident, then retaliated and was later reprimanded for doing your job." He jotted a note to talk to Detective Snow. "I'll also speak privately with Detective Snow as well."

Her phone buzzed in her purse. "Excuse me, I must take this. Thanks for lunch." She stood. "And for listening. I'll try to follow your advice."

"That's why I'm here." Dr. Drummer laid a twenty on the bill, anchored both with the saltshaker, rose from the booth and escorted Erin out into a gusty April wind. He strode back toward the courthouse, ducking his head against the wind.

28

"Hello? McCoy." Mac looped her purse strap over her shoulder.

"March here. Are you finished at the courthouse?" asked the Chief.

"We're on lunch recess. Why, need me at HQ?" she asked.

"Have you finished testifying?" he repeated.

"Yes, sir. The defense rested. Unless the DA has news up his sleeve, the jury may deliberate this afternoon. Snow suspended me for a week, remember?"

"We have a situation, and Dr. Drummer's not here either. Your prisoner du Bourbon just attempted suicide. He's at the ER now with Savage as an escort."

"What would you like me to do?" In light of the circumstances, Mac wasn't sure her presence was needed or whether proximity to her assailant was necessary or wise.

"Savage just called. Seems the man will only talk to you. Take the doc with you. Once you're done, feel free to go home for the day. Whatever he says, get it on tape, McCoy."

"Should we cave in to his wishes?" she asked. "And what if he lawyers up?"

"Then he does, but we'll have made the effort. I can't send Snow. He's grilling Hawthorne. May take awhile. And keep it on the QT—no reporters. He's still under arrest."

"How did he attempt suicide? Was he on a watch?" McCoy wanted more information.

"Opening the wrist wounds you gave him. Don't know the details. That's what I expect you to get. File your report today. Over."

She dialed Dr. Drummer, filled him in. "Can you meet me at the ER? Then I need to go home after we talk to du Bourbon."

At the ER, Mac flashed her shield; a receptionist buzzed her through the doors ahead of the CPD psychologist, who'd taken off his coat, tie and sport coat. Rolled up his shirtsleeves. Savage leaned against the wall outside the room, nodded as they entered.

"We're here to see Jean du Bourbon," Mac said.

Wordlessly, an attendant escorted them to the patient, who lay on the bed, tethered to monitors. Eyes closed against the fluorescent's glare, his palms and wrists were bandaged, an ankle restrained to the hospital bed. Languidly, he squinted at the visitors. Dr. Drummer doused the lights.

"Thanks. No shrinks please. I want to talk to Mac alone."

"Then no suicides, please. My presence is required now that you're in CPD custody. Prosecution has ordered a full psychological evaluation, as will the defense before your trial."

Du Bourbon chewed on his lower lip, considering. "Then what if I request a judge?"

Dr. Drummer said, "Same conditions. In order to make an informed decision about how to proceed, the court needs as much information about you as possible, including your mental state before and while committing the crime."

Du Bourbon nodded, his complexion pale. "All right. I need to consult with my lawyer, but what if I plea bargain?"

Mac answered, "What do you have to trade?"

The man's eyes leveled at hers. "My gun wasn't loaded."

Mac shook her head. "I've been informed, though I didn't know that at the time. Sorry, not enough. Did you plan to beat me to death or just bury me alive?"

"Don't be ridiculous. You're stronger than I am." He'd lost weight while in custody. Lean and trim before, he looked almost cadaverous, his dirty blonde hair tied back in a rat's tail. Without his Colonial splendor, he looked unassuming. Gone were the impeccable dress and manners, the aristocratic affect. "I have more information. And I'm sorry my foolish attempt to silence you was so juvenile."

"Yes, you should have thought of something more sophisticated," Mac quipped, finally easing onto the one visitor's chair.

"That's not funny, detective. It's not in my nature to be violent." He looked at Dr. Drummer with an air of aloofness, his aquiline nose lifting, thinning. "If you'll excuse us, please."

"Only if you agree to talk with me afterwards." Dr. Drummer pushed his glasses up the bridge of his nose, crossed his arms. Though similar in age, the psychologist's sinewy limbs, taut from cycling, displayed strength and health that contrasted sharply with the prisoner's.

Finally, du Bourbon nodded, and the doc backed out to confer with Savage. Mac waited patiently, hooked her purse on the chair back, slipped her recorder out, and thumbed the power button.

"There's a conspiracy," Du Bourbon said quietly.

"Of course there is, Fox Mulder."

The patient sighed. "Will you take this seriously?"

"What, the entire regiment's covering up for the pedophiles or sex traffickers in their midst?" she asked.

He studied her, his head cocked as if deliberating with himself. "I'm truly sorry, but I'm in deadly earnest."

Mac shook her head again. "No. You're the one who's in serious trouble for assaulting an officer of the law and making terroristic threats. Hasn't anyone informed you of the charges leveled against you: a string of felonies that could net you thirty years."

"Yes and no. I wasn't paying that much attention. I'm more afraid of going to jail. They would find a way to silence me permanently." He shuddered. "Samuel Gray headed the trafficking triumvirate with Dr. Davies and an unnamed other. The Regiment's not really involved, but perhaps Molly, Marjorie rather, found out and attempted to intervene, but that's conjecture on my part. Gray threatened me with exposure because I wouldn't be a party to his paltry criminal avocation. They keep girls in a condo in Philly on South Street behind bars—most are between eighteen and twenty. Some are straight off the boat.

"So I devised the nursery rhymes to warn you away. The men think they'll receive suspended sentences for a first offense. Set bail and be free." He waved his hand to dismiss the claim. "I don't know. I'm not a lawyer. Gray said if I didn't silence you, he'd see that we were both eliminated."

"Why me? The entire CPD squad has seen Emma's video, the list of names. That's how we obtained arrest warrants for them." Mac wasn't buying the man's story. "If what you say is true, I need specifics."

"I don't know specifics! Didn't you hear me say I wasn't part of his inner circle? He's blackmailing me. Who knows what else he's planning?"

She thumbed the recorder off. "What, because you're gay?" Mac asked quietly.

"Ah, you know. See? You are dangerous." He shut his eyes, pinched the bridge of his nose, and sighed deeply. "Such a tangled web."

Mac thumbed the record button. "Only to criminals. For them, 'No light, but rather darkness visible.' For us, the night is darkest before the dawn. So can you tell me the particulars?"

"Look. You want me to wear a wire? Tell me what you know; I can try to find out the rest if you put me with the others."

"I can't give you that information. Besides, you'd be stripped searched. The guards or other prisoners would discover the wire and shank you in your sleep. You're actually not safe anywhere—even here, unless we put an officer on the door 24/7."

"What can we do?" He twisted his fingers nervously.

"We?" McCoy asked.

"I said I'm willing to help in exchange for leniency before the court."

"You have any proof to support your claims?" Mac inquired.

He leaned back against the pillows, his face bleached ghastly pale. "I was there once. I can describe the townhouse; limestone, circa 1800's, two-story with black shutters, wrought iron fence surrounds the property with bars on the doors and windows at ground level. There's a dry cleaner establishment on the corner of the block, a deli opposite that."

"Do you have a photo?" Mac sat forward, suddenly alert.

He nodded. "On my cell, at night, but the cops confiscated it."

"House number visible?"

"No. The gate blocks it. Two spindly trees block visibility from the ground-floor windows. And the girls have names like Kitty, Ariel, and Sojourn. Not their given names, but one told me her real name—Cassidy Branch. Whispered in my ear that her grandparents who reared her were fans of Butch and Sundance. Does any of this qualify as help?

"Oh, Davies rotated guards, but usually two were on duty at a time—to cover front and back doors. That's all I know."

"If we put a sketch artist with you, can you describe the guards?"

He nodded affirmatively. "Can I get protection? Leniency?"

Mac stopped the recorder. "Yes, if this information leads us to the house and connects to our offenders. I'll get on this, but you need to drop out of sight and—."

"Prison's out of sight."

"No, it isn't. Let me see if I can obtain you CI status, then we'll change your looks. Start eating; pack on at least fifteen pounds. Change your hair color and style. You'll withdraw from the Regiment, of course. Do you have a condo in Philly? Tell me it's not the same one."

"No, mine's just outside of D.C." He watched her closely.

"Hmmm. Let me see what I can do." She stood just as a pregnant Physician's Assistant walked through the door, carrying a tray of gauze bandages and tape. Dr. Drummer followed.

"I'm here to change your bandages." She sat a small paper cup down containing two pills. Dr Drummer picked it up and inspected the pills.

"Excuse me?" the PA said.

"What are these?" the psychologist asked.

"And who are you?" she returned, her back rigid, as she squared off to face Dr. Drummer.

"The Carlisle Police Department psychologist, Dr. Gerard Drummer. The patient is our prisoner. Nothing passes through his system without the express permission of the CPD and his primary caregiver." He dumped the pills into his hand, peering at the markings.

Mac stood aside, observing. Savage stepped into the room to lend support.

Color crept of the woman's neck. "Let me get the doctor. You can address this issue with him. I wash my hands of this patient."

"Look, I have to run, see if the Chief will OK my request. In the meantime, we need to move him to the maternity ward." She described her plan to disguise the prisoner until she worked something out. "A pillow and wig should do the trick. Pull up the covers. Hide him behind the privacy screen. Can you guys handle this? I need to get back to HQ."

"Sure thing, sugar," Savage said.

The psychologist's eyes widened but only nodded. "I need to speak to him first."

She turned to du Bourbon. "I'll get back to you as soon as I find out anything." Whipping around the corner without waiting for an answer, she was buzzed into the lobby. Mac marched out of the medical center, sprinted to Silver to get du Bourbon's cell phone.

29

Back at HQ, Mac signed the cell out of Evidence, donned latex and scrolled through the photos. Sure enough, though dark, the detail was clear enough and exactly as the man described. She dropped it at Huddleston's desk to lighten, brighten and print. "We need a clear copy of this house on South Street in Philly. Please give it to Snow when you're done."

The IT guy started wiggling in his chair, index fingers dancing. "The hippest street in town," jiggling to the tune threading through his head. "Yes, I'm fine, thank you, detective. And how are you this glorious spring day? Not that I can enjoy it, mind you, chained to this computer." He tapped his 'IN' box. "I live to serve, so I'll get to it today, but I need to finish this for court."

"Emma's trial?" Mac asked, leaning over his shoulder.

"Yes, other videos on Gray's iPad. Look what else I found." He handed her Gray's court schedule. "He's referred over a hundred juvies to one detention center before he was elevated to the state Supreme Court."

"How many? Females? Are there other girls on his iPad? Do the vids show their faces? So you think he's a dirty judge, too?"

"Several. Yes, similar to Emma's. Yes, he's dirty. All those cases have to be reexamined, maybe overturned. So scat. I need to work!"

"Can you print stills of the girls' faces? We need to ID them, send them to the FBI. They could be illegals or minors imprisoned at that Philly townhouse. If the site pans out, it may boost our Hawthorne case."

Huddleston nodded, waved her away. "Check with me tomorrow about this time, provided I'm not in court all day."

"Thanks, Jay." She gave his back a quick pat, then left to find Chief March or her husband.

Chris leaned against the doorjamb of his office. "What's up?" He backed in, pulled her into the room and sat down.

Mac filled him in on her plans to hide du Bourbon until his trial, his offer to plea bargain and turn into a Confidential Informant. "With his testimony, we can send the rest of the sex traffickers to jail. And Huddleston just gave me a record of Judge Gray's former juvie cases. Seems he's taken kickbacks to send them all to one site."

He frowned, considering her words, accepting the papers.

"Du Bourbon captured a photo of a Philly condo where the ring operates; he claims other girls are kept there. Jay's printing it and their photos this afternoon. You can search the house or call the FBI, interview then release the girls, and wrap it up tomorrow."

"And what will you be doing?" He leaned forward, chin propped on his thumb and index finger, elbows planted on his desk. Deep amber eyes absorbed in his wife—the dance of cinnamon freckles across her forehead, russet lashes, jade eyes, the swirls of auburn curls and that wide, soft mouth, those sensuous lips. Angry stitches could not diminish her beauty.

"I'm suspended—remember? I'll attend Emma's trial. I'll bet the jury deliberates no more than three hours. Then Saturday, I'm going to man a cannon at the Battle of Monmouth rehearsal. But first, I have to get the Chief's permission to protect du Bourbon from the porn ring pact, or he's a dead man. He claims Gray sicced him on me, though why is still a mystery. Du Bourbon's willing to be a witness for the prosecution." She smiled. "I've always wanted to say that." She leaned down and whispered where they were hiding him.

Snow returned the smile. "It's a good plan, but how does it help solve our homicide?"

"Well, one of them likely killed Marjorie to silence her. Maybe *she* knew too much. We just need to find concrete proof besides Kevin Lowe's interview," Mac stated. Her husband's brows shot up.

"Howard let me interview him last weekend. Couldn't or wouldn't tell me much." She shrugged. Touched her throat. "Larynx is damaged, voice rusty. Told us nothing new; he's still withholding info. Interview's on my cell if you want to watch it."

"OK, later. Which reminds me, I need to call Impound for the lab report on the Vic's Camry." He stood, rounded his desk and planted a lingering kiss on his wife's lips. "Carry on, Molly Pitcher. I'll be there when we're done searching the townhouse. We'll plan the Saturday trip then. Maybe pack a picnic lunch?"

* * *

That morning, Chris left at six—in concert with the FBI—to search the Philly domicile. His parents arrived at the bungalow to watch Ian—fed, bathed and ready to play. Shadow had run through her obstacle course, discovering hidden contraband. Professor Snow promised to walk her later because the day dawned sunny, spilling light and good cheer.

Mac arrived at the Courthouse, head buzzing with plans to hide du Bourbon until Samuel Gray's trial, who'd been charged with one felony count of sex trafficking in minors, aiding and abetting a kidnapping, criminal conspiracy and blackmail. DA would add the new charges. Agent Howard would prosecute the others in federal court.

At the courthouse, she slipped quietly into an inconspicuous seat near the exit, a folded newspaper peeping out of her purse. Checked her iPhone while waiting. Curt Dash from Channel Twenty-one News and ABC News reporter Elena Michaels spilled through the courtroom doors, conversing. Other reporters entered and assumed their seats. Tanya Storm sat beside Mac. "Police blog/report," she commented, pulling out a tablet. Mac smiled and nodded but said nothing. Storm, still green but learning quickly, accepted any assignment thrown her way. Family members of the deceased, defendant and others filed past. Wilhelm entered with her defendant from the left Exit, the DA and ADA from the right.

The bailiff entered. "All rise." Then he announced the judge, who climbed the podium once more, her petite frame swallowed in black. The gavel cracked; eyes and attention focused front.

DA Collins remained standing. "Redirect. I'd like to call Kevin Lowe."

The courtroom erupted—an electric buzz circulated. The gavel pounded; the judge admonished the room for quiet. "ORDER! Next outburst, I'll clear the court."

"Objection! Oxymoron!" Wilhelm leaped to her feet. "Prosecution cannot cross a person who hasn't testified. We assumed he died in the hotel fire, your honor."

"District Attorney Collins, this is highly irregular at the eleventh hour." But Judge Acorn's curiosity was piqued.

"Yes, your honor. We beg the court's indulgence. He's been on the list from the beginning, but we only recently located him. He's been recuperating from severe injuries sustained in a fire." Then Collins smiled in jest. "And 'oxymoron' is not a legitimate objection."

Mac cut her eyes to Emma, who had frozen at his name, a sharp intake of breath her only sound.

"I'll allow the testimony." Acorn acquiesced.

"I must beg the court's indulgence to provide a context for this witness's testimony, as he witnessed Ms. Emma Hawthorne's kidnapping," the DA explained.

Kevin Lowe was wheeled into court, escorted by a suit to the witness chair but remained seated. One side of his face bore red burn scars; his right eye drooped. He wore casual, loose clothes, a mic pinned to his shirt collar. Once the teen was sworn in, Collins approached.

"For your testimony, have you been promised any compensation or payment for coming forth?" asked Collins.

"If you're offering. . . ." A raspy voice responded.

"Just answer the question please," the DA said curtly.

"No, sir." Spoken barely above a whisper.

"And the Carlisle Police Department arrested you for . . ."

"Possession with intent to sell marijuana, running from the scene of a crime and resisting arrest."

"Tell the court what happened to you at the hotel," Collins said.

"I was supposed to meet Mr. Gray to deliver an order. After I arrived, I don't remember anything after climbing the stairs. Next thing, I woke up in the hospital, burning —my mind blurred by an OD." He turned to the jury, his face contorted with the effort to speak clearly. "I don't do heroin."

"Who is Mr. Gray?" the DA probed.

"Samuel Gray's a state Supreme Court judge and a Revolutionary War re-enactor. He's Dr. Davies's partner and my boss. He was with Emma's mom that night too."

"Why were you at the Old Cemetery at South Bedford and East South Street in Carlisle that Friday, March twenty-first?"

"I took Emma," nodding toward the defendant's table, "to meet her mom, who was at Molly Pitcher's gravesite."

"What happened next?"

"They started arguing. Mrs. Hawthorne wanted to take Emma to Lancaster, but she refused to go." He stopped for water.

"Why?"

"Emma wanted to finish classes at CHS."

"So what did you do next?" asked Collins.

"Drove around the block. Parked in Cemetery Lane. Got out."

"Mother and daughter were involved in a physical altercation?"

"Mrs. Hawthorne slapped Emma's face; Emma slapped her back. The fight became a slugfest. Emma had a bloody nose. I tried to separate them. Then Dr. Davies emerged from the woods, trying to reason with Mrs. Hawthorne."

"Why was he there?"

"Doc offered to take Emma home." He stopped for another swallow of water. "Tied Mrs. Hawthorne to the cannon until she cooled down."

"Did Dr. Davies take Emma to Mrs. June Browning's domicile?" The DA paced back to the gallery, indicating the teen's grandmother.

"No, sir."

"Do you know where he took her?"

"No, sir."

"Do you know why the doctor kidnapped her?" asked Collins.

"I didn't know he did. But probably to teach her a lesson." Lowe took a minute to empty the water glass and clear his throat, hoarse from talking.

"To teach her what lesson?"

"To mind her elders."

"Did you return to the gravesite that night?" asked Collins.

"Objection! Relevance? How does this line of questioning relate to my client's subsequent kidnapping and incarceration?"

The Judge smiled tolerantly. "I'll allow the question."

"No, sir. I was told to deliver my stuff."

"By stuff you mean drugs?" asked the DA.

"Marijuana," Lowe admitted.

"Did you leave?"

"Yes."

"You had no fear for the safety of either woman?" Collins asked.

The witness hesitated, his eyes making contact with Emma, who sat statue-still during Lowe's entire testimony, leaning forward, eyes pools of concentration. A minute ticked by. "Emma . . ."

"Mr. Lowe? Should I repeat the question?"

The witness took a breath and looked at the District Attorney. "No, sir, not then."

"Did you realize that Davies and Gray were involved in child porn or minor trafficking?"

"I knew the doc liked Emma, heard rumors, but . . ." His words trailed away. "He also hated her mother."

"Why?" The DA probed.

Lowe shrugged. "A childhood thing. Doc—grabbed Emma, pulled her away."

"Did you see either Davies or Gray stab Marjorie Hawthorne?"

"No, sir." Lowe maintained eye contact with the DA.

"When did you realize these men were dangerous?"

"When someone tried to kill me." He dropped his head, spent.

"But the hotel fire was ruled an accident." Collins clarified for the record. "No further questions for this witness."

"I have one!" Wilhelm parked a pencil over her ear. "Did you report your observations to the police?"

"No, ma'am." His eyes fell to the floor.

Had Mac not been watching both witness and defendant, she would have missed the look that passed between them. "He's lying," she muttered to herself, mentally replaying the last few minutes of testimony. She missed Wilhelm's cross of Lowe, but his voice finally gave out, so Defense dismissed him. Mac barely attended the closing remarks and the instructions to the jury, as they filed into the sequestered antechamber.

She eased out of her seat. Called Chris. "Kevin Lowe just testified! His presence created quite a stir. What was McKenna's report on the Camry? Did the lab send anything back—like a DNA sample—on that hanky? I'm betting it's a match to Emma's. Something big happened between the defendant and Lowe just now. He lied about either leaving the scene or something that happened that night. I know it."

"I'll email the report to your laptop. Are you going home?"

"Yes, to feed Ian. I'll return for the verdict. Can you tell me if the report contains any evidence?"

"Matter of fact, my questing wife, the blood on the handkerchief belongs to Emma Hawthorne. The other sample is her mother's. Also blood of both on the scrap of cloth you think is part of the cape. But we already knew Emma was at the scene."

"What else did McKenna find?"

"The front right tire was punctured—three tiny holes. I'm sending it now. I got Savage on the other line. See you later. Bye, love."

Mac hustled back to the courtroom. "Hey, Tanya, would you give me a call if the jury returns with a verdict before I get back?" She jotted her cell numbers on the margin of the newspaper, gave it to the officer.

"Sure thing, Mac." Storm's thumbs kept moving.

Outside, Mac's senses attuned to Nature, she escaped into the vivid, vibrant April—trees pregnant with blossoms exuding sweet flowery scents, verdant grass and fresh air. For an hour, like a teen skipping school—she reveled in the joy of living. Happy with cocooning, nursing Ian and jogging with Shadow along the trail among the firs and newly leafed deciduous trees, Erin hummed all the way home.

30

"Storm never called me back," Erin explained over dinner. "So I assume the jury is still deliberating. That's surprising."

Chris scooped another bite of grilled chicken marinated in Italian dressing topped with parm. Erin had toasted walnuts, tossed them over the apple spinach salad and added dried cranberries. "Guess they're hashing or haranguing over the moral dilemma. Actually, a host of issues—her age, the victim turning on her assailant—even her mother's homicide layers the complexity."

His teeth crunched down—"A new kind of apple?"

"Honey Crisp. Yes, the debate over vigilantism goes back centuries like in *The Count of Monte Cristo*. We read it in tenth grade because one of the boys said he'd never read an entire book and never would. So the teacher challenged him with Dumas's adventure. We had intense discussions about the Count plotting revenge and meting out justice. And then watched the movie. However it's served, retribution satisfies." She spooned warm cereal mixed with stained applesauce into Ian. His mouth popped open for each bite. "Don't eat the spoon, baby. Wait, Ian, I'll give you more."

"Hearty appetite—Gotta like that." Chris smiled at his offspring.

"Just like his daddy," Erin grinned at her husband. When his bourbon eyes mellowed, facial lines smoothed out, and he stared into her eyes, she knew that look. She felt her body warming.

"What's for dessert?" Chris pushed his plate aside.

"Apple dumplings." Erin watched Chris's smile widen.

"My favorite!" He drew them out of the fridge, popped them into the microwave and squirted whipped cream on top. His fork cut into the pastry. "You cut the apples up. That's different."

"That's the way Dad makes them." She spooned the warm, gooey apple into her mouth—the sublime marriage of taste and textures, soft and flakey, warm apple spiced with cinnamon and cold whipped cream. "Yummo."

"Um, Um," Ian begged, thrashing his legs.

"OK, one itty, bitty taste of apple." She mashed it, and then shoveled that into her insatiable child's mouth. His little tongue flicked out, then tucked back in, testing the taste buds. His little face scrunched up, and he spit the bite out.

"Cinnamon a bit strong? Come on, then, let's wash it away with mommy's milk while Daddy does dishes." She picked him up, moseyed over to the rocker.

"And when Ian's done, Daddy's gonna do Mommy." Chris grinned and wagged his eyebrows, gathering plates and flatware. Sprayed the bits of food down the disposal and loaded the dishwasher. By the time he'd wiped the island, table and counters, lullabies floated out of their bedroom. The shower hummed, so he stripped to join his wife.

31

"**Has the jury** reached a verdict?" Judge Acorn queried the foreman.

"We have, your honor." A man like a garden gnome—white hair over his ears, a bulbous nose, and slightly stooped shoulders—stood and extended the paper to the bailiff, who carried it to the judge.

"Will the defendant please rise?" The judge requested.

Emma Hawthorne and defense council stood. She'd lost weight, wore a powder blue tunic over navy leggings. Her hair was limp and uneven; her face pale but prominent blue eyes stared forward. The teen's hands were clasped in front of her. Vulnerable and anxious, she bravely faced the jury.

"The jury finds you guilty of justifiable homicide. The court will consider the mitigating circumstances of your kidnapping, the physical and mental anguish suffered." The Judge thanked the jury for performing their civil duty and then instructed them on the sentencing rules. "Sentencing," checking her calendar, "will be tomorrow, ten a.m."

The courtroom erupted. Jack reached across the rail to hug his daughter. June Browning appeared nonplussed. "What does this mean?" Wilhelm conferred with father and grandmother in whispers while the media cut loose, filed out—beelined to their cameramen, reporting the sensational story.

Curt Dash, front and center on the courthouse steps scooped the verdict. "After ten hours—the jury finds Emma Hawthorne *guilty*, but 'justifiable homicide' signifies killing in self-defense. The mitigating circumstances—her abduction and imprisonment will translate into a lighter sentence. Kudos to Defense Counsel Denise Wilhelm for hammering home the terror this fifteen-year old endured at the hands of Dr. Donald Davies, who violated his Hippocratic oath."

Elena Michaels, flanked by Emma's family members, cornered Wilhelm in the vestibule, as spectators filed past. "Is this the verdict you expected? What's next for your client?"

"We would've preferred an acquittal, but the mitigating circumstances bode well in her favor. Beyond that, I will not speculate on the Court's sentence. We just have to wait." Wilhelm kept moving.

"So, you're convinced the girl is innocent?" the reporter asked.

Wilhelm gave Michaels a considered look. "Her *innocence* was stolen when she was kidnapped, imprisoned and violated; my client *is* the *victim*. Donald Davies is the guilty culprit in this case. The evidence is unequivocal."

Michaels asked. "Will Ms. Hawthorne hold a press conference?"

"I'll speak with my client and her guardians about her best interests. We hope she can finish high school. Thank you. That's all." She took her companions' elbows and directed them toward the elevator—away from the media massed outside.

Mac followed the trio. "Congratulations on your competent defense, Counselor. Mrs. Browning and Mr. Hawthorne, if I can be of further service, please do not hesitate to call. Please encourage Emma to continue counseling. And painting."

"We'll have to wait and see. And thank you, Detective McCoy for your kindness, for finding Emma. Now if you'll excuse us. It's been a long day," Jack said; creases across his forehead deepened.

He added, "You'll help Saturday with the rehearsal? We need you, as no volunteer for Molly Pitcher has stepped forward. And with the trial, we haven't had time to recruit." His palms turned out but he retracted his hands when Mac nodded.

"Of course, if you could just give me directions."

The elevator doors opened and swallowed them.

* * *

Next morning, cotton-candy clouds dotted a cerulean sky; Nature wore a riot of color: pink hyacinths, yellow daffodils and red tulips danced against the backdrop of spring green. Purple lilac buds sprouted. Sparrows, wrens, noisy blue jays and a pair of cardinals picked through winter's debris for string and sticks to build their nests.

In town, electric activity hummed: reporters, family members and spectators climbed the courthouse steps to hear the sentence. Seating was limited. Mac quaffed the last of her mocha before she crossed the threshold into Judge Acorn's domain, dropping into a vacant seat in the last aisle. The Hawthornes sat directly behind the defense table, the Davies women behind the DA's. Collins and Lawson, heads together, were conferring. Lowe's parents sat farther back.

Pale and ethereal, her ebony hair in feathery waves, Emma sat quietly in a heather blue knit dress. With hands clenched on the table before her and Wilhelm whispering a last word, they waited. Judge Acorn entered like a winged blackbird.

"All rise!"

"The court will come to order. Will the defendant please stand," the Judge said. "Yesterday, the jury delivered a guilty verdict of *justifiable homicide,* meaning the defendant acted in self-defense. Mitigating circumstances include her kidnapping and nearly a week incarcerated and assaulted by her kidnapper. The court has seen the evidence and has considered the long-term consequences of the trauma Emma Hawthorne endured, as well as the care she will need. In light of these circumstances, you will serve three years in juvenile detention, suspended." The gavel sounded. "However, you will be assigned a probation officer until your eighteenth birthday—May 30, 2011.

"You will continue seeing your psychologist and serve 300 hours of community service with a recognized charity or non-profit agency in Carlisle over and above the high school requirements. The adjudication includes your continued residence with Mrs. June Browning, your maternal grandmother, until sentence conditions are met. Therefore, Emma Hawthorne will now be released into Mrs. Browning's custody, where she shall remain until she enters college or her eighteenth birthday. Young lady, I do not want to see you in this courtroom again. Apply yourself to your studies and a career."

Down whacked the gavel.

The courtroom emptied, the stage dimmed. In direct reversal of the previous day, the counselors, a jubilant Wilhelm and dazed Emma, flanked by her father and grandmother, marched out to face the court of public opinion. A bouquet of microphones bloomed on a podium at the bottom of the courthouse steps. Wilhelm approached with the verve of vindication: "We want to thank Judge Acorn for her sagacity in considering Emma's act of self-defense in her judgment. Thanks, too, to the Carlisle Police Department, especially Detectives McCoy, Fields, Summers, Rivers and Mahoney for their swift response in rescuing my client and saving her life. And we'd like to extend our sincere condolences to the Davies family for their loss.

"The Prosecution," she nodded toward DA Collins, waiting his turn to speak, "did his duty, but this case begged for justice. My client has agreed to fifteen minutes of questions today, but she shall give no additional interviews. We request that the press honor the Hawthornes and Mrs. Browning's desire to return to their lives and routines without a media spotlight. Please ask your questions one at a time—without shouting at my client. Keep in mind, she is fifteen." She nodded, stepped aside as Emma approached the bank of mics, back straight, head up, hands palm down on the podium. She nodded. Questions rained:

"How do you feel about the verdict?" asked a voice from the crowd.

"I'm relieved that the jury felt my actions 'justified,' and the judge weighed the evidence. I'm thankful for the suspended sentence. The verdict is fair."

"Will you return to high school?"

"No, I'm enrolled in Cyber School now. I'll skip my senior year and apply to colleges or art school. And take online courses. I'll study and work hard," Emma pledged.

"Did you fear for your life in the Davies basement?"

"I did. I panicked and screamed for hours until I lost my voice but then realized no one could hear me. I didn't know where I was until the detectives rescued me. It's terrifying being chained to a bed in the dark. You lose all sense of time."

"Did your captor feed you? How often did he visit?"

"Yes, once a day—to both questions, but I was too scared to eat most of the time."

"Did you know your attacker? Was he an anesthesiologist at Carlisle Regional Medical Center?"

"Yes. Dr. Donald Davies, a friend's father. I'd been a guest at their house countless times at dinners, sleepovers, and pool parties. He was also the doctor for my family's reenactors' regiment for several years when I was a child." Buzzing and humming took wing.

She'd just given them an entire new angle to follow because the questions peppered faster then.

"Did he drug you to keep you subdued?"

"Yes."

"Did he give you any indication that he had designs or feelings for you?"

"I—uhm. He was cordial to all his daughter's friends. They socialize regularly. Since he had MS and wheelchair-bound, I didn't know he could walk."

"Did your parents know he was a pedophile? That he operated a porn site? Was there a conspiracy of silence?" asked Dash.

"One at a time, please!" Defense interjected.

"Why did you cut your hair?" Michaels lobbed her a softball.

"So I can't wear pigtails anymore."

"Why were you at the Old Carlisle Cemetery the night you were kidnapped?" A CNN reporter inquired.

"My mother wanted me to go home, but I wanted to finish my classes at CHS." Emma's soft voice quivered, but held her body stiff and still, except for her right foot— toe back, then ankle over.

"What happened then?" The CNN reporter had the follow-up.

"Do you know who killed your mother?" Another shot at her.

"Why did Kevin Lowe mention your name during his testimony?"

"What community service will you perform?"

"I don't know—" Emma turned uncertainly to her attorney.

Wilhelm stepped up to the mic. "That's enough, people. Let's not rehash her entire ordeal. This information was covered extensively during the trial. Go over the transcripts. Please do not contact my client or her family at their homes or places of business. Do not call or email. Thank you." She took Emma's elbow, deftly steered her back.

"Jack Hawthorne, will you answer questions? Will you sue for custody? As biological father, why don't you have custody? What effect has your daughter's ordeal—"

Leaning forward, Hawthorne said, "No comment." Following Wilhelm, the family members retraced their steps to the courthouse, nodding at DA Collins as they passed.

Collins held both palms out, and then formed a "T"— time out. "Barking out questions like this can intimidate most adults, so let's take a breath; one at a time! First I'd just like to say that the trial is over; the jury deliberated and returned a verdict, and the judge sentenced Ms. Hawthorne. The Prosecution is satisfied that the letter of the law has been met. Now, if you have questions . . ."

32

At the CPD briefing in Conference One, the Chief called the Homicide Squad to order. "The pastries are courtesy of the Carlisle Bakery. Grab one; be seated. I need reports from everyone. First, kudos to McCoy and the Musketeers on closing the Hawthorne Amber Alert case. Best outcome we could expect, given the circumstances. I expect reports on latest lab results.

"Second, Snow will update us on the Hawthorne homicide. Are we any closer to a resolution? Anything on the vehicle?" He waved a sheet of paper. "Is this requisition for a trip to Philly necessary?"

"If our CI claims pan out, yes sir." Snow nodded, ready to delineate Gray's illegal activities from drugs and porn to the felony criminal use of communications devices that could have a bearing on the Marjorie Hawthorne homicide.

March held up a palm. "Wait. Lady first. And third, Savage, what's the condition on the CI du Bourbon? Then LT Stuart has fresh assignments, one a shooting at five a.m."

Fields hurried in carrying a take-out coffee, sealed manila envelopes under his arm. "Sorry I'm late." His eyes lit up at the goodies. In one motion, he plopped down, plucked a couple of confections off the tray and dropped the lab reports, pushing one toward Mac, another to Snow. Elbowed a third to Savage.

Chief checked his watch. "Any time you're ready."

"I'll report," offered Mac, announcing the jury's verdict in the Davies homicide. Then she frowned at the lab report. "According to this, the scrap of cloth—part of a

Continental cape—contains blood specimens from Marjorie and Emma Hawthorne." She paged over. "The rust from the murder weapon transferred to the tire, so it was punctured, then used to stab Marjorie Hawthorne later. Also the dirt embedded on it is consistent with soil at the graveyard. Apparently she was weeding with it earlier."

"And a bloody thumb print was lifted from beneath the cannon at the Molly Pitcher gravesite," Snow added, his brows knitted in concentration.

"Did you ever find the cape?" Savage asked, toying with his coffee.

"No. But now I need a warrant for the Browning residence because I think it's there. First, I have to go home for Shadow."

"Probable cause?" asked March.

"Leaving the scene of a crime, perhaps murder." Mentally, Mac cast backward over the accumulated detritus of the combined cases. March nodded at Snow to continue.

"The Camry contained a Revolutionary War ledger with regiment names—real and portrayed, members' duties, notes, a map of the Monmouth Battle site. Hawthorne listed who was responsible for what and the cost of supplies, Von Steuben/Shultz kept a separate military roster and inventory of weapons. Prints from the paper include those belonging to Marjorie and Jack Hawthorne, Clark Winters/Washington, Ferris/Franklin and Andre/Samuel Gray. A bean pot, utensils, knitted scarf and the woman's purse containing a driver's license, wallet and an grocery card—to an Amish dry-goods store."

"Any evidence that may lead to a murder suspect?" The chief tried to act patient, but his thumb beat a tattoo on the table. He propped his chin on his palm, eyebrows raised.

"Well, the murder weapon stuck in her chest," Savage remarked. "But that had no prints. Killer wore gloves."

Chief shot his eyes askance across the table at the man but remained silent.

"The blood of the Vic and her daughter on the fork, piece of cape, tire and cannon point the finger, don't you think?" Mac asked.

Snow shook his head. "Without the rest of the cape, I doubt it."

"Well, the Lowe kid did say the women fought; Marjorie probably gave her daughter a bloody nose," suggested Mac.

"As the DNA samples on the handkerchief corroborate," Snow said.

"What about the father?" asked LT Stuart. "He has a good motive."

Snow shook his head. "No one puts him in Carlisle that Friday in March. I have a better case against Gray. His prints on the oil lamp and passenger's side of the car. We have the video on his iPad, his phone number—the bill for viewing the porn site—on Davies' computer. Plus his semen in the vic. The five girls in the Philly condo all positively ID'ed his photo when the FBI raided the place and took their statements. He, too, has a motive, means and opportunity: to shut his lover up if she learned of his seamy little avocation."

"Gray claims he left earlier," Mac added. "When Lowe testified, he looked right at the defendant and said, 'Emma,' but his sentence petered out. He perjured himself. I just can't pinpoint about what."

"Report only means Gray and Margie Hawthorne had sex, not that he killed her," Mahoney said. She picked a powdered sugar donut from the plate and stood. "More coffee, anyone? I'll make a fresh pot."

A number assented. Mahoney eased from Conference One for the break room, returned shortly with the carafe, pouring a second round.

"One case at a time, Snow," Les responded. "Let's leave Gray's case for next week. The daughter's kidnapping connects the Hawthorne and Davies homicides. Oh, how did the teen react to her sentence? Defiant or humble?" He glanced at Mac, knowing she'd testified and attended the trial nearly every day.

"She accepted it with equanimity. She will abide by the dictates of the Court. She and the Defense had a brief press conference. For a fifteen-year old, Emma comported herself in a mature manner. Obviously, the jury empathized with her but did not exonerate her. Seemed contrite."

"Good collar, by the way, Mac. Let's kick you up the ladder a notch. We'll get together next Saturday night to celebrate. Let's see . . ." March noted the information on pad by his cell phone. "Les, have Sonja reserve a room at Market Cross Pub from seven to ten. Fields, bring you camcorder."

Mac blushed at the compliment and promotion, as eyes turned to her. "Thank you, sir." She smiled at having her efforts finally acknowledged.

"Congratulations, partner. Hip, hip-popotamus!" Fields added, hoisting his cup to toast her.

Snow laid a hand on hers. "Good work, Mac."

"For she's a jolly good fella . . ." Savage sang, smiling crookedly, and saluted her with his mug. "Kudos, McCoy!" He said a shade too enthusiastically.

"Go ahead, get your search warrant. Take your K-9 officer, your partner and three officers, but tread carefully. What bothers me are the shades of grey, so don't make accusations that we can't prove. This case has enough tentacles to swamp the boat. Let's try to stay afloat. Anyone have anything significant to add?"

* * *

Half an hour later, the CPD converged on the Browning residence, served the warrant and executed the search. June planted herself on her living room sofa, arms crossed defiantly, her lips pursed. "You people are amazing; you change with the weather! Thought we were done with this!"

"No, sorry. We apologize for the inconvenience," Mac said, holding Shadow at her knee, "but it's necessary. Where's Emma?"

"She's with Wyatt. They went to the Gold Key presentation at the Forum and then out to dinner. Tomorrow, she reports to work at Pet Smart and later has an appointment with Mrs. Alwine and meets her probation officer." She shrugged.

"We'll be as circumspect as possible. Mrs. Browning, do you have an attic and basement?"

The woman nodded. "Attic, yes, but just a crawl space and cold cellar beneath the house. And a detached garage." She thumbed out back.

"We'll start upstairs. Shadow and I will take the teen's room." McCoy said. Fields, camcorder in hand, Savage, Mahoney and Officer Storm gloved up, fanned out, pulled open drawers, closets, slid hands around, behind and underneath furniture. Peered between and under mattresses, cubbyholes, alcoves and recesses. Moved furniture away from walls to examine backs.

In Emma's room, Shadow sniffed the scrap of patriot blue wool flannel; she obediently nosed the bed, closet, bookcases and desk. Mac opened and studied the contents of each item of furniture. She thumbed through the texts; a paperback copy of *One Flew over the Cuckoo's Nest* was splayed face down on the top. Glancing through, she noted the yellow highlights, but replaced it. She stood before the desk, contemplating the closed laptop. Sitting down, booting up the laptop, "It's not password protected!" Mac opened 'History,' found MapQuest directions to Niagara Falls. She frowned. A list of emails— one from Amazon: *Primal Fear* was added to her video list. *Is she planning to run?* "Guess we'll need to take this." Unplugged it, taped the cord to the top.

Methodically searching the chest of drawers, desk and closet, she found nothing incriminating. Tossed on the top shelf were an eighteenth-century skirt, muslin blouse and a fitted jacket. Ballerina flats, a pair of old Sketchers and red high heels were flung in the bottom of the closet. In one shoebox, Mac found a jumble of mementos—hair bands, an unfinished embroidery sampler, a pewter spoon, shoe buckle, tickets to various events and a hotel key card.

"What's more surprising is what's not here. Where are her powder-blue sweater, knit sweater dress, jeans and tees? Her new boots? Cell phone?" Concern germinated in her gut, taking root and spreading.

Mac lifted the window. Checked outside the dormer windows. Found a pack of cigs and lighter in a clear cosmetic case. Bagged that. Left the winter debris— withered leaves and maple seeds on the roof.

Shadow had reconnoitered the room, found nothing to bark about.

"Gotta hunch, girl. Let's get to the crawl space, see how that leak was fixed." Down the stairs, through the hall, into the kitchen, a partially finished rec room, two windows and an adjacent powder room faced the back. To the left, a door led to the crawl space. Erin shuddered, reminded of a similar door in a cabin at Michaux State Park. She took a breath, blew it out. Refreshed Shadow with the scent of cape scrap and opened the door.

The dog crawled straight to the pipe to the downstairs powder room. She crouched and woofed. "Good find, good girl." Mac gave her a treat. And unwound the blue flannel insulating the pipe with a dryer sheet clinging to it. It was damp near the middle, where someone had sealed the leak. She had what she'd come for and scooted back out, bagging cape and computer. Returning to check on her colleagues' progress, her steps led back to the living room. "June, are Emma's clothes in the wash or at the dry cleaners? None of the clothes she's worn recently are in her room. Does she have a suitcase?"

"Let me check the laundry." The trim woman led the way to the washer and dryer, examining both. Empty. "She does have a small wheelie. Should be standing on her closet floor."

"No, ma'am," Mac answered. "It's not. Do you know if she and Wyatt planned a trip to Niagara Falls?"

"Of course not. She knows the conditions of her probation. She has to stay here; Emma has appointments tomorrow. Oh, God! Has she run off? Why would she do such a stupid thing? Won't that get her in trouble?"

"Let's not panic. Call her cell, Jack, Wyatt's parents and anyone else who had contact with her, including Mrs. Alwine. If you cannot locate her, if she's not in the vicinity, I have to put out an APB on her. If she ran, that's a grave mistake. Tell her to come home immediately. I'll give you an hour. Call me the minute you reach her.

"Fields and Mahoney, stay for the duration; alert me if Emma can be located. Tanya, take the evidence to HQ, then drive to the Forum, see if Weber and Hawthorne are there. Savage, can you deliver the laptop to Huddleston to examine her computer?" She handed it to him.

"You can't take her laptop; how is Emma supposed to complete her assignments and email them to Cyber School?" complained Mrs. Browning.

"Afraid we can, ma'am, but that's the least of your worries at the moment. We'll return it. Please, locate your granddaughter." To her colleagues, Mac said, "I have to run home; report back to me within the hour. If it looks like she's running, put out an APB on her." Mac and Shadow stepped into the gloaming—twilight time—the dusky soft focus of possibilities, of decisions and indecisions—time to take the necessary steps, avoid any miscalculation. Close this case.

Tugging Savage along as she trod through the door and onto the covered porch, "See if you can get a chopper on stand-by. If so, call me. We may have to track her down. Can you get Wyatt's plates? May need to put a BOLO on his vehicle."

"Sure thing, sweetheart." Savage added, "Didn't know you cared, but I'm not your dog." He looked at her hand, which she dropped with exaggerated emphasis. "But, next time, thank me."

Mac had already cleared the steps and trotted to Silver before his sarcasm actually dawned on her. "Thank you." But the front door had closed.

33

At home, Chris stirred pasta into a bubbling saucepan while sautéing shrimp and scallops in a wine, butter and garlic sauce. Ian, content at the moment in his playpen, grabbed for stuffed animals and his musical cell phone. "How did your search go?"

Quickly, she let the dog out, scooped dog food from the bin, refreshed Shadow's water and whistled her back in. The dog skidded to her dish and wolfed down her dinner like it was her last meal. Erin shook her head, washed up and reached for Ian, but Chris lifted him up and out.

"Your tailbone," he reminded her.

"It's getting better." Erin settled on the rocker, took Ian; Chris returned to the stove, monitoring the seafood scampi. Added broccoli crowns to the steamer, set the timer. Emptied the pasta into a colander, tossed it back in the hot pot, and ladled the seafood over. Poured drinks. Set the table. Eased into the living room.

"I found the cape wrapped around a pipe that Emma used to stop a leak, sent it to the lab, but she's missing," Erin said.

"You're joking." Chris frowned. "Why would she hide evidence?"

"Wish I were. I don't know. Maybe she grabbed whatever was handy to stop the leak. Probably Googled DIY, caulked it, wrapped it and didn't have pipe insulation. The question is whether the act was intentional or incidental. She washed the cape, but Luminol will still light up blood spatter." She quickly summarized the search and June's explanation of

Emma's absence. "I found directions to Niagara Falls on her computer."

"Could be just a ruse. Why would she do something that brainless after remaining calm as frost during her trial? Sounds out of character to me. Maybe she went to see her Dad. Maybe she and Wyatt went out to celebrate."

"Yeah, maybe. Let's wait and see."

"Smart—giving her the opportunity to return on her own." He plucked Ian up to burp him. "Come on, let's eat. If you get the call, and depending on who calls with what intel, I'm going too." Slid Ian into his seat, buckled him in while Erin eased onto the kitchen chair.

"Had no idea I was hungry. This is delightful, Chris. The shrimp are perfect. And the steamed broccoli—it's so crisp and healthy. Your culinary skills continue to amaze and impress."

"Oh, darling, wait for dessert." His deep amber eyes sought hers as he held Ian while finishing his pasta. The baby grabbed at the strand of angel hair, but Chris turned his head, slurped it in. "Sorry, son, no garlic for you yet."

"What is it?" She felt her body relaxing. "You?"

He flicked his tongue out at her. "Tiramisu first, then me."

"We only have an hour," she warned. "No make that forty-five—"

He jumped up, pulled her against him. "Then we'll have the Tiramisu later."

"What about Ian?"

"He can watch." Chris pulled her into the bedroom. He laid the baby in his crib, switched the music on. "I mean to get under that hood and turn on your motor. Just let me find that ignition switch."

"I love it when you talk in metaphors." Erin watched him, backing towards the bed. "How do I start your engine?"

"You already have."

* * *

The landline shrilled. Chris strode to pick up before it woke Ian.

"Hello?" He listened to the Chief. Erin slipped into yoga pants and a jersey.

Mac's cell chimed. Quietly, she closed their bedroom door and picked it up, thumbing in her security code as the time flashed: nine. "Hello? McCoy."

"Detective, I'm calling to tell you Emma and Wyatt were in Lancaster. They're on their way back, but they can't make the trip in an hour. I also called Denise who said wait until tomorrow morning to question my granddaughter. She said please call her first. Thank you." The woman disconnected abruptly. Erin stared at the phone, then hit end and joined her husband in the living room.

Parked on the leather sofa, receiver to his ear, he nodded slightly. "Yes, sir. First thing in the morning." Frowning, he dropped the receiver onto its base. "What?" He questioned his wife's puzzled frown.

"That was June Browning. Wyatt and Emma were spending the night in Lancaster, apparently unaware of any wrongdoing. They're coming back; June called Emma's lawyer. I'll call Wilhelm to set an interview up for tomorrow morning. Who called?"

"The Chief. Said check with her shrink first before you question the Hawthorne teen about her mother's homicide. He wants us to proceed cautiously. The girl's been through a lot in the last three weeks."

She nodded. "Sure. OK. Just wondering if she'll stay put."

"Did the judge say she could not visit her family in Lancaster?"

"Not in so many words," Mac replied.

"Ah, so Emma has some wiggle room. Clarify that with Wilhelm tomorrow. I'll go with you." He absently rubbed the side of his nose. "Tomorrow's Friday. So. . . . that kicks any further action into next week."

"And Saturday, I'm playing Molly Pitcher. Everyone still going?"

"Of course. Wouldn't miss it. We'll pack up Ian's stuff tomorrow night."

34

They met downtown at Wilhelm's office on Pitt and Pomfret.

As Snow and Mac entered, the lawyer and her client were seated at an oval cherry table beside Vicky Alwine, the psychologist. Wilhelm gestured at a sideboard containing coffee, tea and an assortment of cookies. Once seated, Snow started the recorder, identifying those present and the particulars. He nodded at his wife to begin, then strolled over for coffee.

"First, everyone, thanks for meeting with us." The women nodded. To Emma, Mac asked, "How are you doing? Did you receive your Gold Key?"

Dressed in a teal cotton pullover and jeans, the teen seemed relaxed, scrunching her damp hair. "Yes, a picture of 'Lucy and the Wolf' will be published in local papers next week." A small smile curled her lips.

"We'd like to interview you about your mother's case," Snow said.

"I heard. Nana said you ordered me to return. I didn't know I had to stay in Carlisle. That I couldn't visit Dad." Emma's blue eyes shifted from one detective to the other.

"Just for the record," Wilhelm stated, "you don't."

"We'd like to focus on that Friday night in the Old Carlisle Graveyard. Who was present besides you and your mother?" Snow asked.

"Kevin Lowe and Dr. Davies. Samuel Gray had been there earlier, but I told him to leave. Didn't want him involved in the conversation."

"We know you and Marjorie Hawthorne were involved in an altercation about your returning home. Can you describe the scene?"

"Why are we rehashing information covered at Emma's trial?" Wilhelm pushed that white wavy streak off her forehead.

"It's necessary to establish an exact timeline of events and the participants' recollection of what happened regarding our homicide case." Snow spoke, his voice calm, reassuring, unhurried.

"Mother threw her cape at me, ordered me to cover up. Said I was indecent. Then slapped me when I refused to get in her car. My nose started bleeding. I slapped her back. She brandished a dirty cook fork in my face. Then Dr. Davies materializes, and a car door slams. Kevin returned. Mother turned on them, cursing them for interfering."

"Who did what exactly?" asked Snow.

"Kevin grabbed her arms; the doc pulled me away."

"Who tied her up?" asked Mac.

"They both did."

"Did either say anything?" Snow probed.

"'Calm down.' That pushes mother's buttons. She screamed at them.

I told her, "Be quiet! You'll wake the dead," Emma said.

"And what was Dr. Davies doing?" asked Snow.

"Holding me back. He offered to take me home. Doc ordered Kevin to deliver his stuff."

"It didn't occur to you to take the Camry?" asked Mac.

"I don't have a license. Besides, the tire was flat."

"Where was the fork during all this commotion?" Snow said casually.

Emma hesitated, looked at Wilhelm, who nodded.

"I'm not sure. I turned to say goodbye."

"Why 'goodbye'?" Mac said.

"I was leaving, walking toward Doc's Beamer." She shrugged, looked down. Alwine touched Emma's shoulder lightly. "You don't have to answer if the memory's traumatic." To the detectives, "We haven't broached this topic, so I'd suggest—"

"It's OK." Emma's eyes filmed; her chin trembled, but she shook her head. "Will I have to testify about this?"

"Yes," Snow and Mac said in unison.

The teen took a cleansing breath. "Doc's car was parked on the street. I climbed into his passenger's seat."

"Did he kill your mother?" asked Snow.

"He could've. Doc hated my mother since childhood because she made fun of him—'the geek creep,' she called him."

"You waited in the car? Why didn't you run?" Snow asked.

"Why? He *said* he'd take me home. How did I know he meant *his* mother's empty house?" Emma argued.

"You know, I've been pondering these cases for weeks and wondered what the trigger was. What would push you over the edge, from the anger into rage—" Anger flickered in Emma's eyes; her carotid pulsed.

"That's enough, Detective," Wilhelm interrupted. "You're antagonizing my client. We're done here."

"To kill. Remember, I've seen it before." She pulled the top sheet from the folder and turned the DNA results so Emma could see. "See, we found your *and* Marjorie's blood on her cape. See, the arterial spray on the cape means . . ." Mac laid the photo in front of the teen, so she could see how Luminol polka-dotted the front. "That Marjorie was stabbed first, then someone tried to make it look like a prank—or lied to fit your story."

"You and Kevin arrived at the cemetery first," Snow surmised. "We found cigarette butts with your DNA with a beeswax candle. Gray and your mother, approaching from the South Street Deli, didn't see you crouched inside the fence. The deli owner said, 'They were arguing.' What actually transpired that night? Did she find out about the porn site or sex trafficking?"

"My client declares her Fifth Amendment rights," Wilhelm stated.

"She's becoming overwrought." Alwine slipped a container of Lorazepam tablets from her purse, twisted the cap and motioned for Emma to take one, but the teen shoved her hand away, sending the pills flying, pinging onto the table and scattering across the floor.

"And wouldn't you want to kill your mother if she called you a worthless brat? If she said you weren't worth the gunpowder it'd take to blow your brains out? Not worth the salt in a slice of bread? Scarred you with hickory switches? Pushed you out of the house regularly? Slapped you for sighing? Sent you to bed without supper for talking back? Snapped your neck with a clothesline? Pulled your hair, put your hand to the fire if lessons weren't learned?" The teen panted, nearly hyperventilating, her face flushed and hands clenched. Alwine found a paper bag for the girl to breathe into. Then she pushed it away.

"So, yeah, I was pissed. She's a liar, hypocrite and a sadist. Making me trod the straight and narrow path while she's Hester Prynne. Then she improved at Reenactment camp; there were a hundred eyes and ears to eavesdrop, so she transformed into Molly Pitcher, the battle's heroine. Fooled everyone but me. I learned to steer clear of her and spent summers with Nana."

"That's quite enough." Wilhelm switched off the recorder. "Emma Hawthorne, I am advising you to remain silent." She stood, pulling Emma to her feet as well. Mac thumbed the recorder back on because she wanted the entire scenario spelled out.

Emma jerked her arm away. "NO! Don't touch me. Don't tell me what to do! Mother'd been brandishing that fork in my face, poking me in the chest, raving at my 'slutty' clothes. She ruined my new sweater mini. It was the last insult. I grabbed—"

"STOP!" Wilhelm turned the teen to face her. "Say another word and you'll need to find another lawyer." To the detectives, she repeated, "We're done here! You'll need to prove your case in court. My client will remain silent! Please leave my office!"

"And the Doc wrestled me—" The teen pantomimed.

"Not another word, Emma!" warned Wilhelm.

"What if the killer's dead?" Emma's inquired, ire dissipating like a withered balloon. She collapsed onto her seat. Alwine had been collecting the pills, one by one, returning them to the little amber cylinder.

"Good question, young lady. Is your question hypothetical or did you see it?" Look, we can conclude our interview here or arrest you and haul you into CPD Headquarters. Which do you prefer?" Snow asked.

The women returned to their seats.

"Did you witness the murder?" Mac asked.

Emma hung her head, lips clamped tightly, uncooperative.

"OK, when the doctor got in the car, how did he act?" Snow continued.

"Act?" She thought a moment, energy spent. "It was dark then, so I couldn't see his face, but his eyes glittered, so excited? See, I think he planned all along to kidnap and abuse me—just to get even with my mother."

"When did you realize his intentions?" asked Mac.

"By the time he pulled down that dark lane and stopped. He taped my mouth, and then bound my wrists. Let me out—darkness was visible. I wrenched backwards, tossed my cell over the fence. In the basement, he patted me down, searched for it, but I said I left it at the cemetery, so he cuffed me to the bed and left to hunt for it. You know the rest."

"Thank you all for your time and cooperation." Snow shut off the recorder, and they all stood. He rounded the table, cuffs in hand. "Emma Hawthorne, you are under arrest for matricide. You have the right to remain silent. . . ." He Mirandized the defendant.

The teen's mouth—a slash in a troubled face. "I have to go through all of this again?" She tried to wriggle free, but Snow and Mac each held an elbow firmly, walked her out to their vehicle and escorted her to CPD for processing. Hot pink blotches bloomed on her face. "Adults are liars! You pretended to be my friend, *Detective* McCoy—giving me advice and planning this all along? I'm calling my dad! You won't get away with this. Framing me for that bitch's death. She was no mother to me! I hate her! I hate you!

"I hope Dante's right! Hope you get the tenth circle in Hell with no hope of respite!"

EPILOGUE

Carrying a ramrod, Jack Hawthorne led the way across a meadow to a slight ridge topped with a stacked stone fence overrun with creepers, crumbing in places, notching 'Vs' where they could easily step through. Behind the stone, five cannons stood guard. Over the rise, a furrowed field with young cornrows marched across it. Hawthorne patted the cannon on the end. "This is ours. Let me show you how it works. See, you use the rod to ram the shot." He loaded the gunpowder, set the fuse and pulled her to the ground. "Cover your head!"

The cannon cracked, recoiled; the shot exploded from the barrel.

"Holy shit! That's really loud." She pushed herself up and dusted off her jeans, shaking as the adrenalin kicked in. She'd decided not to mention Emma's arrest unless he did.

"You do have period clothes? Spectators and the press will attend the rehearsal today for photos."

"In my car." Her eyes spotted several wooden buckets stacked against the tree trunks that formed a ragged line behind the fence.

"You need to put them on, get used to wearing them. At first, they'll hamper your movements because they're more cumbersome than what you're wearing. Just lift— well, you'll figure it out. See that next rise?" He pointed east. "Water's in the little valley—the head of the Delaware River; it's fresh. You'll haul it from there. I'll man the cannon for an hour until the redcoats are, say, fifteen yards away. I'll go down—"

"And I'll take over, loading and shooting this monster. It won't actually kill anyone?" Erin asked.

"Not as long as they stay out of range, but accidents can happen. Just be careful with the gunpowder. Move away from the cannon to check on me—I'll be on the ground here—and a shot will tear through your skirt. Don't worry but remember to spread your legs wide. Margie was never injured, and we depict the actual events all summer long."

Mac nodded nervously. "I know my line."

"Shout it out for all to hear. Then reload the cannon. Now practice."

Looking up at his black hair combed away from his face and clubbed at the nape, she noted concern or perhaps preoccupation in his cobalt eyes. He wore doublet, hose, and a blousy shirt with an open leather vest—looking his part.

"Don't worry, I can do this." She copied his actions, albeit slower.

"Faster. Keep working on it. Once you feel confident, lug a bucket to the creek, fill it and return. Give everyone along this row a drink with the tin ladle. Some guys carry their own cups; they'll dip those in. Bucket's too heavy and awkward to pour from. When I load the cannon, that's your cue to step to my side, so keep your eyes on me." His hands on her hips, he maneuvered her next to the cannon, a step beside him. "I'll take a drink, turn to reload—Bang! I'll go down." He pantomimed the actions. "You take over. Any questions?"

"No, it seems straightforward enough."

"OK. Let's run through the entire scenario a couple of times. Then I'll go get your clothes. Is your family here?"

Mac nodded. "My in-laws came to mind Ian. I planned to change in the vehicle. My stepmother's working; Dad's dog-sitting."

"No time. We're starting soon. I'll get them." Hawthorne canted his head toward the Regiment members taking their places, talking amongst themselves. Washington led his frisky horse, pawing the ground, to the middle of the meadow. He stopped as a scout in buckskin, a long rifle nestled across his body, asked him a question. In the distance, she saw dots of redcoats with white bands across their chests; the sun winked off bayonets protruding from the rifles. The man portraying General Charles Lee advanced on his mount.

Several yards away, von Steuben led thirty men behind the fence, his arm flanked left, giving directions. Across the meadow by the cornfield, a motley crew of militia, Scots in kilts and berets, and Continentals assembled, muskets ready. Fifty yards beyond, Tories milled around wagons loaded with boxes and barrels: folded canvas tents; tools, food, ammo and supplies. A donkey brayed. Major Andre, aka Samuel Gray and Lafayette/Jean du Bourbon were absent. Spectators and news media lined up behind soldiers at the fencerows, jockeying for good angles.

The daystar inched higher, bleaching the eastern sky. Drumsticks clicked against the rim, setting feet in rhythm. Time rolled backward. Molly grabbed the bucket handle, hiked to the next ridge, and padded down the slope—boots kicking pebbles into freefall, rippling as they smacked the river. No time to enjoy the stunning scenery. Ducked the bucket, capturing cold, clear water. "Oomph. Heavy." As she topped the ridge, Hawthorne stood before her—handing her an oversized tote.

"Change over there. We will discuss Emma's predicament when we've finished the skirmish. I've kept silent long enough." A screen of scrub bushes huddled around a trio of boulders. Hays took the bucket, turned his back, squared his broad shoulders and trod purposely toward the cannon.

"Do I really need two husbands?" Then Erin regretted her words, as Jack now had no wife and a daughter behind bars again. Behind the screen of rocks and greenery, Mac squirmed out of her jeans, pulled on slip, underskirt and gathered skirt. Peeled off her sweatshirt, donned a chemise, coarse white blouse, and a short patriot-blue fitted jacket. Imprisoned her unruly curls under a ruffled cap. Chris had scoffed when a re-enactor suggested she put a brown rinse on her hair.

She mumbled, "Can't even walk, let alone haul water." Bunching material in her hand, she hiked up her skirts and followed Hawthorne, thinking of the missing reenactors—one jailed, the other hiding; both facing trials and prison terms, unless the judge allowed du Bourbon CI status.

Noise climbed into the clearing, spreading: metal clashing, leather creaking and words clamoring for attention. Men were mounting breastworks in front of the cannons—eight-foot branches, four inches in diameter, sharpened at both ends. Birds rowed the current overhead; a lone hawk glided above the trees, hunting. Molly gasped as war commenced.

No time for stage fright, she again collected the bucket, trudged toward the river. Dipped in the unwieldy bucket. Climbed the ridge. Toted water to the men, extending the dipper time and again, the muscles in her arm pulling. Smoke curled in the air. Cannons retorted. Redcoats charged—the rearguard protecting the retreating British wagons. She made another trip for water. Ragged lines of Continentals and militia drove the redcoats back; the rebel lines broke. Men retreated. General Lee's men scattered to the tree line—

Washington galloped across the clearing, swearing, shouting at the men. "Form a fine. Advance! Damn it Lee, you bastard, you're a general! Act like one! Get your men to charge. Fight!" The man on the horse held the middle ground, ignoring the barrage of fire, holding his steed steady, reins tight. Lunging across to shout at the flank fronting the cornfields, gesturing madly, right arm pin wheeling, General Washington—furious and fierce—his face florid with exertion. He galloped back, shouting, "Lee, I'm relieving you of your command!"

To Lee's men, he yelled, "Follow me!" Slowly, the line reformed while their leader urged them on, redcoats advancing. *Clark Winters as Washington—a man for that season of rebellion and revolution, destined to form and guide a deeply divided populace toward union. Despite the opposition, critics, and an ambivalent Congress. A brilliant military strategist and valiant soldier, Washington struck an imposing figure then and now. And all who believed and followed, fighting for the ground they lived on, for the rights Americans were born with.*

"How to make a hundred soldiers look like 5,000! Come on, Molly!" Hawthorne snapped her out of reverie, bumping her shoulder with his. The cannon thundered; the ground shook. Redcoats advanced, bayonets fixed, the Continentals and militia's flanks swinging round towards them. Lee's men advanced behind General Washington. The Highlanders followed suit.

Molly stepped to Hays's side; his comrades stoked the cannons and fired—a show of force and might, smoke and heat. Suddenly, Jack crumpled and fell. Tremors rippled to her feet. Chaos! She shrieked but pried the ramrod from his hand, standing in his stead. Ram, load gunpowder, light fuse. POW! Again. A third time, her right arm tiring, aching. Shaking, *this too real to be fun.* And again. She smelled the powder burning—NO! Her skirt. Forgetting, she looked down at her smoldering skirt. "I—"

The bullet bored through epidermis, dermis, muscle, tissue and bone, crushing, burning a path through her body. Blood bloomed, soaking her skirt; Erin reached down to staunch the wound. *Too many layers!* Dizziness gripped her. Falling backward. Seconds strung out, suspending time. The men around her became blurs, sounds only distant echoes. Colors bled together. Images of Ian and Chris appeared, faded. Dickinson's words purled across her consciousness: 'Caissons rolling over her grave/the cornice in the ground.' *No, that's not right.*

Letting go of her wound, palms out, Erin tried to break her fall. Her hands slid out, ineffectual. Twisting to her side to protect her coccyx, jarring her elbow on impact, numbness crawling up her arm. The ground slammed her hip, back, shoulder and head. Edges dimmed as the light diminished. Darkness descended.

ACKNOWLEDGMENTS

I thank my readers for following my detectives as they solve the mysteries created by the human condition; I'm always amazed at criminals' audacity, their brazen acts that forever damage others' lives, their lies and attempts to hide or cover their tracks, the excuses they provide when caught. So the chase, the struggle, and the journey are as realistic as I can render them. Thanks to my editor Celeste, for the countless hours spent combing over my manuscript. To the Knorrs, I am indebted for their ideas, suggestions, trust, energy, patience and encouragement.

Thanks to those, including my sons Mike and Jarod, and their friends, especially, Jorie, who penned reviews, 'liked' my Carlisle Crime Cases Facebook page or mentioned my mysteries on theirs. Thanks, Alida Hodgson, for designing and providing my business cards. Thanks, Terry, for understanding, buying meals and watching our little alien, E.T.

Thanks to the enthusiastic people I meet at book signings for their kind words and encouragement, recognizing the work involved. I'm indebted to readers for asking so many interesting questions. Thanks for businesses like History on High and Jake at the Ragged Edge who lent their bricks and mortar during book signings. Thanks to those like Deb at the Mechanicsburg Mystery Bookshop for organizing conferences and advertising the Carlisle Crimes Cases. And to friends like Judy Martin and Sandy Kearns who lend their support, provide suggestions, kind affirmation and feedback.

Finally, thanks to my family, including cousins for everything, but especially listening as I worked, ironed out the kinks and revised. I extend my gratitude to all at the Bookery like Barb, Karen, Bill and Chuck who read, volunteer feedback and promote my books.

SOURCES

Bobrick, Benson. *Angel in the Whirlwind: The Triumph of the American Revolution.* Penguin Group. 1997.

Burgwyn, Diana. *The 1776 Guide for Pennsylvania.* Harper & Row. 1975.

Cantrell, Bridget, PhD and Chuck Dean. *Down Range: To Iraq and Back.* Seattle: Word Smith Publishing. 2005.

Fifth Pennsylvania Regiment. "Military Timeline." www.5thpa.org/military-timeline-

Karr-Morse, Robin and Meredith S. Wiley. *Ghosts from the Nursery: Tracing the Roots of Violence.* NY: The Atlantic Monthly Press. 1997.

"Mary Ludwig Hays McCauley." Bio. A & E Television Networks, 2014. Web. 29 June 2414.

"Molly Pitcher"

http://pabook.libraries.psu.edu/palitmap/bios/Pitcher_Molly
.

HAD A DYING FALL

Carlisle Crimes Case #4

A Christopher Snow and Erin McCoy Adventure

J. M. West

From *The Twelfth Night*

"If music be the food of love, play on,
Give me excess of it; that, surfeiting,
The appetite may sicken, and so die.
The strain again—it had a dying fall.
O, it came o'er my ear like the sweet sound
That breathes upon a bank of violets,
Stealing, and giving odour. Enough, no more,
Tis not so sweet now as it was before."
                              —*William Shakespeare*

A Complex Sentence

I am a sentence waiting,
You—the grammarian,
Anxious to diagram,
To see what part is missing.
You'll find I'm not so simple,
No subject without complement.
But parse my clauses as you may,
Diagram away; you'll find
The syntax fragmented—hidden
In the subordinate clause.
                              —*JM West*

PROLOGUE

Waving goodbye to her baby who was returning to college for a summer internship and marveling how composed and efficient Camie seemed, Kelly Sims took a deep breath and closed the front door. "You know, now the kids are grown, we should make an appointment with a lawyer about writing a will and—"

Denny stalked across the room, shoved his wife against the front door, held her there, left arm pressing on her windpipe. "I'll never leave a will, so some other man can enjoy what I've worked a lifetime to achieve. Or this." His right hand grabbed her crotch. "Understand?" His craggy, chiseled face inched closer to hers.

She broke eye contact, turned her head aside. "You're hurting me." She tried to gauge his moods, guarded her own anger toward her husband of twenty-five years—the man she'd vowed to love until death, the man she no longer knew or liked.

Fifteen years older, Dennis Sims retained the lean frame of his youth, though his silver hair, crow's feet and severe slashes from nose to mouth revealed his age. He owned the Warehouse on High Street housing Party Time with the Sport Hut behind. The other four rooms he rented. He and his men were renovating the upstairs into urban industrial suites. Yes, he'd worked long, hard hours. "And I don't need your aggravation just now; I've a lot to do, enough to worry about. On top of burying my father, helping my mother."

On tiptoes, knowing better than to push back, Kelly held her body rigid, head, back and palms flat against the front door. He planted his body against hers. "Understand?"

She nodded. Tried to understand. "Sorry. That's why I thought—"

"Well, don't. I'll do the thinking." He released her. "Now clean up the mess in the kitchen."

Kelly had fixed dinner at noon, packed the leftovers into a Styrofoam cooler for Camie, so she wouldn't have to cook after driving two hours to campus, unloading her gear and groceries and setting up her room in an apartment she'd share with two others. She sighed, waiting for Denny to move away from her, saunter to the garage for the mower, having brandished his power. Finally the motor spurted, started and the rider lumbered out—a bear out of hibernation. Mowing would take about an hour, including cleaning and parking it in the shed.

While scraping and rinsing dishes, Kelly planned. She and her younger sister Shannon had scheduled a lady's day out next week—a trip to New York to lunch at Junior's and see *The Jersey Boys*. She could empty the savings account, pack a wheelie and launch a new identity from there. She already had her vita and job recommendations in a folder, medical records in another.

Dennis and Kelly's Sims rift resurfaced when Drew left for college. Since Kelly worked in academia, she helped her son through the maze of college prep, admission procedures, essays and the like. In the end he elected to attend Dickinson because of the tuition remission. Yet he'd chafed under his father's strictness, transferring to Drexel his junior year.

Dennis ordered her "to quit coddling the kid," urging Drew to "cut the apron strings from your mother. Time to step up and be a man."

When Camie elected to go to Penn State, he'd lauded her choice. "At least one of our kids shows some backbone. No need to worry about her. She has enough chutzpah for both of them."

"They have different personalities and strengths. Both will be self-sufficient once they graduate—" she'd started to explain, when he'd slammed her against a wall the first time, his arm across her windpipe.

"Don't contradict me or act condescending," he warned. "Mrs. High and Mighty in your Ivory Tower. Well, climb off that high horse, join the rest of us."

"But why should I leave?" Kelly asked herself. "I can't leave my job and its benefits now. Besides, I make half of what Denny does. How could I afford this house?

"And where would the kids visit for holidays? With Camie at State College and Drew working in Philly, having recently become engaged, they'd have nowhere to come home to. No, leaving is not really an option. I'll just have to think of something else."

1

"Sorry about Mac," Savage said while he and former partner and lead Homicide Carlisle Police Detective Christopher Snow sped to a suspicious fire on South Street. The Explorer screeched to a halt in front of a two-story brick Colonial in time for the explosion. "We took up a collection for flowers—had them sent to your house for the family plot."

"Yes, thanks," He swallowed hard and nodded. "I can't talk about that right now. It's just too raw." He scrubbed his hands over his face and shook his head.

"Bet the gas grill blew," Snow muttered. Orange mushroomed from the back yard. The shed's roof splintered, pieces somersaulting skyward. Flames erupted, feeding on the fuel. Sparks like fireflies flew. Back smoke roiled. Requesting fire trucks, the men raced to the rear, waving back curious neighbors. "Stay back! Other explosions may follow."

Just as the words left Snow's mouth, a second eruption lit up the dawn. Wood and metal spewed from the flames, hot and dangerous. Sirens approached. Dressed in full gear, Fire Chief Lane Rusk jumped down from the cab; other firefighters hooked into the nearest hydrant, water spewed forth on grass and house while another hose sprayed white foam over the shed.

The detectives sprinted to the back door, pounding to raise someone. The house sat mute, windows shuttered and curtains drawn against the resurrecting light.

Reese flipped open his cell, called HQ to find out who owned the house.

"Court records list that domicile as belonging to a Dennis and Kelly Sims." Sonja Hamilton, always the first on the job, was CPD admin extraordinaire because she had her pulse on the department, its staff and personnel.

"We can't raise anybody here. Their shed just blew to smithereens, but nobody came from the house to investigate. Could be on vacation, but we should notify them." Savage said.

"I'll Google them." She hit the keys. "OK. Dennis Sims owns the Warehouse, Party Time and The Sport Hut. A work permit on record shows he's renovating apartments at the site. Wife Kelly works for Dickinson, Coordinator of High School Gifted Programs. The Sims have two grown kids, one male Drew, 25—resides in Media, PA; one female, 20, a senior at Penn State, main campus. Let me try Facebook."

The shed continued to burn combustibles. Debris spiraled up the heated waves, then rained down upon the lawn; paint cans exploded, spewing syrupy liquid like Jackson Pollock. Metal fragments flew. A riding mower husk remained, its seat smoldering.

"No mention of a vacation, no photos to suggest that. Oh, look, guess what? Her sister is Shannon Mahoney."

"No shit?" Reese reacted. "I've got her number. I'll call. Parents live in the area?"

"If so, no mention of them. I'll check Mahoney's file, get back to you." Her fingers tapped the keyboard.

"Thanks." He thumbed end, turned his head at the thunder of cycles. Two of the Musketeers drew to the curb in single file, Rivers first. Then Summers. Laying helmets on the seats, the men bounded upon the lawn to join Savage and Snow. "What gives?"

"Nobody's come out to inquire, watch or try to extinguish the fire. Do you know the residents?" Snow asked.

"Yeah, Shannon's sister's family. What's probable cause for entering?" asked Summers. His sandy brows shot up. "Why's Homicide here?"

"A neighbor called it in. We're on duty. Where's Shannon?" Snow motioned to the house on the right. Spectators gathered along the street, gaping at the fire. Fire trucks continued to pump retardant on the ruined remains of the shed.

"She's in New York City with her sister. Stay here. I'll see if anybody's home." Rivers jogged up to the front door, rang the bell. No one answered.

"We tried that already. When are they due home?" Savage asked.

"I dunno. I'll call." Summers pulled out his cell, thumbed a contact. "Hmmm. Shannon, need to give us a call. Your sister's shed just burned to the ground. CFD and CPD on the scene, dousing the flames, but nobody answers the door. Give me a call back. We'd like to talk to the homeowners. Neighbor called nine-one-one." He ended the call. "Voice mail. Sorry to hear about your wife, boss."

Snow nodded but seemed mesmerized by the fire, the flames dancing in his eyes. Liquid filmed them; he blinked hard. Behind him, Savage shook his head in warning. Gabriel nodded in understanding. Currently, too raw a wound to rake over.

"I can ride over to the Warehouse, see if Dennis Sims is working overtime on those apartments. He's trying to have them ready for the Fall semester. Exposed brick walls, pipes and wood beams, clean lines—really sharp." Rivers reported.

"Know him?" Snow pulled his attention from the fire to look at Rivers while Summers peered in windows, knocking to raise someone, sliding quickly to the next one and repeating his actions.

"Yeah. Six-two, silver hair, sixty, owns the Warehouse, Party Time and The Sports Hut, far as I know. Type A personality. Puts in ten-twelve hour workdays. Plays poker once a month, softball once a week; the couple entertains occasionally but mostly keep to themselves. Wife works full-time too; she's pretty serious, quiet—opposite of Shannon. Kids are grown. I'm sure you've seen him around town. Ever been to Party Time or the Sports Hut?"

Snow shook his head. "Can't say that I have. Ian keeps me busy now that his mother's—" His throat tightened at the mention of Erin. He cleared it, cupped his hands around his mouth. "Summers, come on. If no one's home, we'll have to notify them by phone. You and Rivers try to track down the husband. It's just strange."

Savage's cell pinged. "Savage. What'd you find out?"

"Parents—Gavin and Megan Mahoney, live in South Middletown Township. Three Hundred Front Street in Boiling Springs. That may be on the lake. Phone number—" Sonja rattled off a string of numbers. "Found no listing for another Sims. Anything else?"

"No thanks. I'll give them a call. See if they know where their children are. Thanks. Over, out." He tapped Snow's shoulder. "Let's go talk to the parents."

No one answered at 300 Front Street, so they moseyed around back, where the detectives found the couple on their back porch nursing their coffee. An outdoor furnace glowed with heat. The Children's Lake shimmered; a low, calming surrusus accompanied by an occasional splash of a duck dipping or paddling along and the loud chirrup of crickets. Morning sunlight played in the ripples, refracting and creating tiny rainbows.

Mr. Mahoney stood, shook their hands. The Mrs. nodded, waving them into chairs.

Snow briefed them on the burning shed, asked the owners' whereabouts. "I don't think Shannon mentioned taking a day off, but, well, I could've missed that conversation."

"Oh, lord, No! The house is OK, though?" Mrs. Mahoney asked.

Snow nodded. "Firefighters have it under control."

"Shannon and Kelly went to New York City yesterday for lunch and a play, shopping if they had time. Kelly's experiencing empty nest syndrome. Shannon wanted to treat her to a day in the city. You know, a lady's night out so to speak, a diversion. They planned to spend the night."

"What about Dennis Sims?" Savage asked.

"How about a drink?" Mr. Mahoney asked. He stood. "Fridge right inside the back door: soda. Coffee's still hot. Little early for beer." He chuckled.

"I'll take a Coke, if it's not too much trouble. Smoke in the lungs." Savage showed the soot on his hands, wiped his hand across his brow, smudged it across his forehead. Snow nodded too, and their host hobbled off to get the sodas.

"Don't really see Denny that much anymore. At his age, I'd think he'd be slowing down, but he keeps a half dozen projects going. Kelly's busy, too, with the Dickinson camp season just getting under way." Mrs. Mahoney explained.

"What does she do exactly?" Snow asked, lowering himself to a chair.

"Her department makes all the arrangements for summer sessions for advanced high school students: robotics, engineering, music, ballet and athletic camps. Hundreds of high schools students are involved, maybe a thousand. Kelly arranges the summer schedule, obtains the instructors and locates scholarships for students who can't afford the cost. That sort of thing."

"How long has she worked there in that capacity?"

"Why, must be goin' on twenty years?" She turned to her husband, who shrugged; a smile creased his weathered face.

He handed the detectives the sodas. "You'd know more than I would about such things. Yesterday, the girls were kids, you know? Now her kids are grown. So everything in the shed burned?" he inquired.

"Yes. Husband and wife get along?" Savage asked.

"About like most couples. Why all these questions about a shed fire?" asked Gavin. He extended his bare legs, crossed his feet, jingling the change in his shorts pocket. "I'm sure they have insurance."

"Routine." Snow and Savage answered together. Snow added, "Strange that no one came to the door, though."

"Not if they're not home," Megan said. She sipped coffee and finished her toast, wiped her hands on a damp paper towel, and dropped it into the fire. "But we'll call Kelly and Denny, let them know. My granddaughter left for a college internship last week. My grandson lives, works in Media. No use in calling them."

"Well, thanks for your time." Snow stood. "Let's call it a day." They climbed into the Explorer; he fired the ignition, pulled away from the curb. "I want to get home, play with Ian, at least, and then fix breakfast. I'm getting too old for all nighters."

"Buck up buddy, you're younger than me. You OK? Need any help?" Savage's coffee eyes ranged over his friend's haggard face, eyes red-rimmed and bruised with shadows. They could both use a shower and shave. "When did you last get any sleep?"

Snow cast his eyes sideways, turning onto East Springville, right on 74S, left on Shughart, Middlesex and then onto Lisburn, right into Savage's driveway. "It's tough, but my parents and Erin's Dad help with Ian. Thanks, but we'll manage. Let me know when you start tearing out your kitchen. I can help demo. Getting used to the new digs yet?"

Reese hopped out of the vehicle. He'd bought the house last month. "Settling in. I'm painting the bedrooms first. But when I get to that point, I'll give you a call. Got a lot to do before then. The Musketeers offered to help too. Thanks. Go'night, mate."

"See you tomorrow. We'll interview his parents first thing. Can you check with Sonja, see if Shannon's off tomorrow as well? I'd like to touch base with Rusk, too, see how that fire started. Need to catch a few z's first."

"There's just his mother, Marsha Sims. Dad's passed a few months ago. Switch it off, Chris. Go home, rock your baby." The lean veteran with taut shoulders and military bearing tugged his keys out of his Dockers, patrolled the perimeter before letting himself indoors.

At home, Chris found his mother in the kitchen, warming Ian's bottle. A custard cup held remnants of rice cereal mixed with strained applesauce. "Let me wash up. I'll give him his bottle." Chris offered. Scrubbing until the water ran clear, he dried hastily.

Erica Snow stopped, glanced at her youngest son with concern. He needed a haircut. Permanent parallel line furrowed his brows. He scooped up Ian from his little seat and tossed him gently. The baby laughed, showing dimpled cheeks.

"He just ate, Chris. Do you want breakfast? I fixed you a sandwich for lunch. There's salad in the fridge, too, for later."

Chris kissed his mother's forehead by way of greeting. Plucked the bottle from the water, tested it, tucked his son in the crook of his arm. Dropped in his wife's accustomed place in the living room rocker. "Thanks, mom. I'll eat later."

"The CPD sent flowers—a beautiful spray of baby pink roses. They're in the fridge. Do you want to take them—"

"Savage told me. Tomorrow, maybe." He hadn't meant to sound curt. "I'm tired, Mother. Thanks for helping. Can you come back around noon? I need a couple of hours sleep." He watched his son inhale milk. "Take it easy, baby. No need to be greedy." Ian's fingers grasped his father's pinky. Chris smiled wearily.

"Of course. And you're welcome. Really, Ian's a pleasure." Erica sighed, set the cup in the sink, ran water in it.

"A treasure. His coloring is so like his mother's," he added, looking at the baby's shiny auburn waves, bright blue eyes and dark lashes. The infant's eyes drooped; his father gently pulled the nipple out. "Looks like he's losing weight." He hefted him to his shoulder, rocking and patting.

"But he's built like you. Look at that barrel chest and long legs. Except those blue eyes are his alone," Erica added. "Maybe because he's growing. I'll check with his pediatrician if you like. He's been fussy lately but that's to be expected." She omitted the obvious: he misses his mother.

Her son's eyes filmed, and then closed, burning from the fire and loss. His throat ached, stomach yawned with hunger. He leaned his heavy head against the rocker. Erin's shooting at the Monmouth battle reenactment last month had aged him. Though thirty-six, he looked forty, the lines on his face more prominent.

"Give me a call when you have to report to work." Erica sighed again, turned to tidy the kitchen and then slipped out the mudroom door. She'd have time to change and launder her sheets, perhaps grab a bite of lunch before she and her husband trekked back down the driveway to the bungalow to watch their grandson. "Don't know how much longer Chris can burn the midnight oil."

www.ingramcontent.com/pod-product-compliance
Lightning Source LLC
Chambersburg PA
CBHW071802020726
47502CB00004B/984